Margaret

of the North

EJourney

Text and Art

DEDICATION

For anyone:

Who believes romance is essential to our humanity;
that we find it not only in longing aching gestures and smoldering
eyes;
that it, in fact, infuses everything which nourishes our souls—art,
music, books, even religion and philosophy;
and that letting go and making a mess of things can be exciting,
mysterious, adventurous; in other words, romantic.

Especially dedicated to:

My husband, a romantic old soul
My son, a caring young soul.

MARGARET OF THE NORTH: Contents

PREFACE

Doing art—whether it is painting or writing—commits the creator to a series of decisions. How big a canvas should I use? Or, should this story swirling in my head be a short story or an epic? How should I apply my brushstrokes—with a brush of a certain size or a palette knife? With what colors? Or, what kind of viewpoint would make my story more intriguing? And how should I express the themes of the story? On and on. Many times, we may not be conscious that as we create, we are making decisions or even problem-solving.

With Margaret of the North, I chose to write in a style as similar as I could get to that of 19th-century writers. I suppose I thought it would fit the story better. Besides, I wanted to see if I was up to the task. I had read enough Charles Dickens, Jane Austen, and the Bronte sisters that I thought I could pull it off. So, in fact, it was a dare I posed myself. I know this approach has its problems: It can seem antiquated. And I do use some words not too familiar to modern readers and are probably hardly ever used nowadays. Still, I had some trouble imagining the characters in my novel talking like my niece or my son and using currently popular forms of expression.

In this novel, I pay homage to Elizabeth Gaskell and other writers of her century. I was particularly conscious of trodding in their footsteps, most probably Jane Austen's, when I was writing the second to the last chapter. Some literary analysts believe that Austen may have influenced Gaskell. In her opening chapters of North and South, Gaskell depicts an Austenian novel of manners. I wanted to show my admiration and indebtedness to these authors, as well, by depicting some of the vagaries of courtship—a frequent theme in Austen—among young people of the period.

Everyone of us is the sum total of varied life histories that determine what we do or not do, what we love or hate. I don't think the decisions we make when we create can be judged as either right or wrong. We should expect, however, that the consequence may appeal to some and repulse others. Some may think my attempts successful and others, utter failure.

I. PROLOGUE

The train chugged out of the station in a shroud of grayish white smoke. As it gained speed and the smoke swirled up above, the May countryside slowly unveiled itself, vibrant with the young greens of fresh growth and luscious with a spectrum of yellows and reds on meadows glistening from the lingering moisture of winter. Margaret knew that it was not too long before this lush landscape, which she watched distractedly from her train window, would give way to more grayish white smoke, diffused but more pervasive, billowing not from the train but from ever-churning machines in cotton mills that meant life for the denizens of the modernizing city of Milton. At that dense city, as different as it could be from the hamlet she grew up in, a city of stale, particulate-laden air and of somber shades of gray—from its atmosphere to its buildings to the mood of its inhabitants— Margaret had chosen, on this fateful day and at the age of 22, to make her home. There, she would marry, raise a family, and fashion a future for herself that she hoped to look back on with some measure of fondness as well as gratitude.

She smiled at her reflection on the train window and gazed with not a small measure of amazement at the image behind hers, a bit blurrier but unmistakable—the strong profile, tan complexion, dark hair, and aquiline nose. John Thornton was deep in thought, an arm resting on her shoulders, his head slightly bowed, and a smile playing on his lips. Margaret studied his reflection for some moments, incredulous at how quickly her fate changed; how the aching emptiness of resigning herself to the loss of his regard was supplanted by a wondrous, unbelievable happiness at regaining it. What sweeter bliss was there than getting what one's heart desired—after that desire had seemed so impossible that, just a short hour ago, one dared not hope at all?

Margaret had made a choice, a clear and inevitable one, in her mind, that sprung not from thinking through her alternatives. Instead, she merely yielded to sentiments that refused to be tamed any longer and to happenstances so favorable that they renewed her belief in a divine hand. She hardly ever made momentous decisions impulsively or suddenly. Encouraged from childhood to be reflective by an intellectual clergyman father whose collection of books she could explore at will, in a small hamlet in the country free of distractions from too many competing pursuits and compelling company, she was inclined to brood and mull a long time over her choices. But in her mind, returning to live permanently in Milton was not a question of making the right or wrong choice. It was, simply, the most natural thing to do, after nearly two years of sorrow and mourning, to seize happiness when it was right there before her. This happy choice was taking Margaret back to Milton for the second time on this day.

Neither Margaret nor John noticed when the train slowed once again and stopped. The train inspector knocked on the door of their compartment and opened it. "Good afternoon, Mr. Thornton, madam. May I see your ticket ma'am?"

John and Margaret were startled to find themselves at another train stop, bustling with people getting off the train, rushing out of the station. Margaret, still distracted, straightened and glanced at the train inspector. He smiled apologetically. She absentmindedly reached into her bag and handed him a train ticket.

"This is for London, ma'am. You're on the train to Milton."

Before she could reply, John addressed the inspector with a smile. "Inspector, Miss Hale is my fiancée. I am taking her back home to Milton. We're getting married. Her ticket is for the opposite way but it costs the same, doesn't it? What's the harm? Are we not almost there?"

His tone was calm but firm, assured that he would not be contradicted. The train inspector nodded. "Yes, sir, Mr. Thornton. I suppose it will do. I am sorry Miss Hale. I was just doing my duty."

"It's quite all right, Inspector. I understand. In fact, I thank you for being so accommodating."

The inspector bowed, scanned the length of the train quickly, and stepped away. He blew his whistle and the train was soon speeding back to Milton.

Margaret smiled gratefully as John drew her closer. "I hope it will be all right meeting my mother again?"

"I did see her this morning," she replied. "At the mill."

"You went to Marlborough Mills?" He exclaimed, surprised and curious.

"Yes. How else would I find you so we could discuss business?" She answered, amused.

"Was Henry Lennox with you?"

"No, he went for some breakfast. We left London quite early." Margaret paused thoughtfully. "Your mother is a formidable woman, frank and sincere. I admire her for that. But I think she does not find it easy to like me."

"She will probably find fault in anyone I marry but particularly you, I'm afraid."

Margaret flashed him a worried look but said nothing. She was not surprised, aware that Mrs. Thornton thought her, a Southerner with strange ideas, unworthy of her son. She turned away, hiding the momentary apprehension in her eyes.

But John did catch it, as fleeting as it was. "You are unlike the other women my mother meets in Milton. She may find you more daunting to deal with. I suppose mothers are anxious about being replaced in the affections of their sons when they marry. Mine is no exception."

Margaret chose to remain silent. What could she say? She knew only too well how strongly attached Mrs. Thornton was to her son, how her life revolved around him and his work. Margaret suspected that Mrs. Thornton would be unhappier than most mothers at her son's marriage to any woman and most profoundly so if she was that woman.

Margaret stared at the now wilting yellow rose on her lap. Only moments before, she had been so happy, ecstatic almost, in a way she had never known. She was not willing, just then, for such an exquisite sensation to be disturbed by concerns about Mrs. Thornton's distress. Margaret turned her attention back to the scenery outside her window. The greenery was metamorphosing into the structures on the outlying areas of a big industrial city.

Earlier that morning, she had been in that city with Henry Lennox, her adviser on the handling of her newly acquired wealth. She convinced herself that they came on important matters of business—to present a proposition to John Thornton that would keep Marlborough Mills in operation. But he was nowhere in Milton. Even his mother did not know where he was.

Margaret left barely two hours after she had arrived, certain yet again—as she had been when she moved back to London a year ago—that she would never return to Milton. She left with a leaden heart, her spirits sinking to depths almost as low as when she lost her parents. It perplexed her, this profound disappointment, this unexpected feeling of dejection. Did she not convince herself before undertaking that journey to expect nothing? Not the success of the business proposition, much less the fulfillment of hopes she had kept buried in her heart. Hopes she could now admit she had kept alive. She thought herself prepared for Mr. Thornton's indifference, even rejection and yet, his mere absence plunged her into inexplicable gloom.

But fate, God, or luck intervened. At a train station midway to London, Margaret's future took a blissful turn. Now she was on her way back to Milton; this time, she was going to stay.

For those in the habit of brooding, the new and unexpected invites reflection. It is a way to relive an experience, to relish happy moments all over again and, consequently, convince themselves that what happened was indeed real. Both Margaret—resigned to the certainty of mere regrets—and John—anxious and restless in the uncertainty of how she would receive his proposal when he renewed it—felt compelled to replay in their minds the delicious unfolding of their happiness in all its freshness. Meeting, being reunited at a train station was so improbable that they would talk about it throughout their lives—every look, every expression, every utterance, the tentative first kiss, and the passionate ones that came after. They would tell their children and their grandchildren about the wonder, the unexpectedness of it all, the unlikely setting, the sequence of coincidental events. But at this time, dazed and bewilderingly happy, they affirmed—with each recollection of events of the past hour or two and the plethora of emotions they elicited—that they were indeed in this train, together, on their way back to Milton.

Margaret first came to Milton when her family had taken up residence there, for a relatively short 18 months. But what months they were! Packed with turmoil and sorrow, unknown to her, at 19, until then. Her father, in a matter of conscience, had given up his life in the clergy and decided it was in this rapidly growing city that he could find both meaning and gainful employment. Unhappily uprooted from a sheltered life in the idyllic south, Margaret found Milton strange, harsh, the lives of too many inhabitants attended by perpetual need and suffering; the baskets of food and the few coins she could offer too meager to ease the privation and despondency among the few she knew. Those months showed her how helpless she was in the face of pervasive poverty.

Those 18 months also claimed the lives of her parents and a friend she had made from among the workers. They marked the nearly simultaneous death of the parents of six children, one of them by suicide and the other by wasting away from grief. Amidst all these, she had fallen in love, though unknowingly at first. John Thornton had proposed to her, professing love so strong, so new in her limited experience that she could not comprehend it. In retrospect years later, she concluded that the proposal was also ill-timed, coming on the heels of the strikers' riot, her mother's illness, and his sister's irksome remark echoing his mother's scornful notion that Margaret had designs on John to elevate herself and her family from poverty. As yet naive about affairs of the heart, hurt and offended at such insinuations, Margaret dwelled upon her initial dislike of Mr. Thornton. Then, she fueled that dislike with contempt for the Thorntons' disapproving and uncompromising disdain for workers.

She bluntly rejected Mr. Thornton's proposal although she had begun to take an interest in him, as each contentious encounter revealed to her his real character. Ruled by her mind and unwitting of her heart, she did not recognize what that interest meant. Her love blossomed, guarded from her awareness, from people around her and, most of all, from Mr. Thornton. But such sentiments could not be repressed for too long. She realized soon enough that his good opinion mattered much to her, that she valued it even more than her brother's. By then, it was too late. He had already caught her at a flagrant lie: She told police she was not at the train station the night of an unfortunate accident that led to the death of a man. It was a lie that she assumed cost her the high regard he had for her.

When her father passed away, Margaret had no choice but to return to London. There, with no demands on her for help and compassion, she had time for reflection, for looking inward and searching her soul, for acquiring wisdom and growing. She found it sadly ironic that it was the loss of people who needed her that allowed her that indulgence, impossible in Milton. Gradually, inevitably, solitary reflection replaced months of grieving.

In the end, she had to accept that much of it was beyond her capability to change, particularly with regards to the passing of loved ones and others whose miseries began long before she knew them. For that, she could only grieve and let the course of healing take as much time as it needed.

Her heart was a slightly different matter. True, she gained a clearer understanding of her desires. But she also realized she was left with only regrets at losing the person who had become dearest to her and she could only resign herself to it. It was a disconcerting, sobering insight that taught her to be wary of her own arrogance and less complacent about assuming she knew herself well.

Not everything concluded sadly in Margaret's soul-searching. It led her, as well, to one of those life-changing epiphanies: She was of age and free to take control of her future. The prospect of having to secure employment—if she could not live on the small allowance she inherited—never intimidated her. In working, she believed she could find more satisfaction than she did, whiling away her hours in her cousin's endless dinner parties and card games, as pleasant as they were. Then, a considerable, unforeseen legacy from Mr. Bell made that epiphany more intoxicating.

Becoming a woman of means multiplied her choices. She could do exactly as she pleased. She could choose a life of independence, even solitude, or move to Spain to be near her brother and live ruled only by her conscience. Who knew, she thought with a mischievous smile, if in that more permissive country, she might meet some tall ardent Latin lover. She surmised that Henry Lennox, an old friend, was just waiting to renew his proposal. As fond as she had lately grown of him, she did not love him and could not persuade herself to marry merely for companionship or mutual benefit.

A few months into living within that new level of serenity and a mere couple days before her life took on its present turn, Margaret heard from Henry of the financial troubles at Marlborough Mills. That night, she paced her room, extremely restless, agonizing nearly half the night whether she must do something. Although the ease with which her fortune grew might have bothered her conscience enough to directly help the families of unemployed workers, she could admit to herself, at least, that it was Mr. Thornton's misfortune that she was most anxious to relieve. It seemed logical to her. An offer of a loan to keep his business going was the best way to help workers. That way, he could give them work. But she was sensitive of his pride, painfully aware that he could refuse to have any extensive dealings with her. So, she thought that Henry must explain the proposition so that it would neither offend nor make Mr. Thornton feel obliged to her.

In the morning, she had a long discussion with Henry on how she could help restore operation at Marlborough Mills, reminding him that she was its landlord and keeping it going was in her best interests. Henry needed no convincing. The investment was a wise move, certain to earn her a higher interest than the bank could give. He was confident the business could only succeed.

The following day, Margaret and Henry had taken an early train to Milton, arriving there late morning. Though Henry understood that they were there on business, Margaret also wished, secretly, for a proper moment when she could tell Mr. Thornton casually about a brother who came to Milton when her mother had been ill, his presence concealed because his life was in danger. She was certain that Mr. Thornton would judge her more charitably once he realized that, in lying to the police, he was protecting her brother. Regaining his good opinion was essential to her peace of mind. If she had hoped for anything more, she did not articulate it to herself.

Still, Margaret wondered whether—behind his inscrutable stare on the day they bade farewell, never to see each other again—there lurked a lingering regard for her that he could not conceal completely. In London, in the luxury of dull but carefree existence, solitude and reflection, the deep recesses of her heart nurtured a sliver of hope. Even as her mind accepted that regret was all that remained for her, she secretly wished to put a spark to that regard once again.

From the train station, Margaret visited the mill alone. Henry, in less than good humor, went to a hotel restaurant for a late breakfast. They agreed that, if she saw Mr. Thornton, she would arrange a business meeting for the afternoon. She was grateful for the solitary walk. It allowed her time to think and compose herself.

She walked around the mill lost in thought and deeply saddened. It was quiet and empty, more desolate than she remembered nearly two years ago when the machines stopped during the workers' strike. Cobwebs and dust were already taking over the place, untouched since the day the machines stopped permanently just a few days ago. How strange to see this mill, bustling with a life of its own when she last saw it, now so still. The stillness was unnatural, disturbing, and so different from the peaceful stillness that wrapped itself around her, sitting on the beach, staring out at a gently undulating ocean that soothed her spirit, bruised, restless, and numb from all that she had suffered and lost.

Absorbed in her reverie, Margaret was jolted by a familiar but distant voice, more disapproving than she could remember. She turned to find Mrs. Thornton glaring at her, chin held high and eyes narrowed. Mrs. Thornton spat out bitter words as she approached. Unfazed, Margaret answered in a manner calm and conciliatory, admitting she had been wrong about John. Then, in a hushed voice, she lamented the fate of the mill. Mrs. Thornton was mollified. Deeply worried and helpless, she confessed she had not seen John since the night before. Nobody knew where he was. He was nowhere in Milton. For the first time, Margaret saw a vulnerable side to the strong steely matriarch. She reached out but Mrs. Thornton turned away, shaking her head, too proud or too angry to receive kindness from someone she blamed no less bitterly than the rest of the world for her son's unhappiness.

Margaret walked back to the hotel lobby, acutely conscious of an aching disappointment at not seeing John Thornton. There, she told Henry, her voice steady and seemingly unconcerned, that Mr. Thornton was nowhere to be found. They had to return to London, having accomplished nothing. He merely nodded, silent and annoyed. They took the train back to London immediately after and did not talk much. He concentrated on the journal he was reading and she stared resolutely at the swiftly-changing landscape to mask her dejection. The silence between them was precisely what she needed to reclaim that state of resignation she thought she had already achieved these last few months.

When the southbound London train stopped for a few minutes to wait for and allow a train to Milton to pass, Margaret decided to get off. She needed a few moments of respite from Henry who had assumed an extraordinary interest in a Milton newspaper to disguise his irritation at having lost precious time on the trip. She had just descended when the northbound train pulled in, clanging, squealing, hissing smoke. She watched it slow down without much interest until a familiar face in one compartment made her heart leap and her eyes brighten.

John Thornton was lost in thought, deaf to the clattering and rattling of metal and heedless of the purposeful rushing of bodies on the platform. His compartment came to a halt directly across from where Margaret stood, mesmerized, unable to take her eyes off him. The sight of him jolted her spirits. She felt herself soaring out of the void she had been in since boarding the train back to London a mere two hours before. She embraced her sentiments, her secret wishes that she had had since leaving Milton a year ago. Her heart felt light, as if it had taken wings, broken free of many months of self-imposed shackles. The likelihood that Mr. Thornton no longer loved her did not occur to her, at that instant. When it did moments later, the excitement of seeing him again and the full acceptance of her own desires prevailed, suppressing the inevitable dejection of coldly facing reality. Insensible of the bustle around her, she approached his train, cheeks flushed, heart racing, willing him to look up, to see her standing on the platform.

Still deep in thought, unaware of her presence, John reached for the door. But he stopped, perhaps finally drawn by her intent gaze to raise his head slowly, deliberately. He was met with glistening eyes, a wistful half-smile on slightly parted lips and a face radiant with joy. For a moment or two, John stared without moving a muscle, a mixture of disbelief and hope in his eyes.

Then, he broke slowly into a smile and stepped off the train unhurriedly. He approached her, in what seemed like measured steps.

Margaret could not hide from him how she felt even if she wanted to. Her face was burning, her breathing coming almost in gasps from the pleasant agitation that threatened to burst out of her bosom as he came nearer. He did not take his eyes off her and the tender smile lingered in his eyes and on his lips. She wondered if he was relishing the truth she wore nakedly on her countenance.

Between looking straight at John and casting her eyes downward, Margaret muttered breathlessly that she was in Milton that morning. He responded with the wonderful, surprising confession that he had just been to Helstone, pulling out of the left pocket of his vest a yellow rose she recognized so well. She was trembling inside, unable to look at him when he handed it to her—an offering, bearer of the deep feelings he wore in his eyes and his smile. She looked up then but dropped her lids to veil her luminous eyes. He still loved her, she thought with incredulity.

She was confused, uncertain about what to do next. She found herself explaining the business proposition. But she doubted that he heard much of what she said. He gazed at her lovingly—with amused fascination, she thought—while she flustered, blushed and rushed, through the plan she had rehearsed in her mind. When, finally, his lips touched hers for the first time, it was as if a delicate wisp of down, warmed by his breath, alighted on her lips. She was amazed that this man, who could be fierce in his anger and cutting with his words when provoked, had such a gentle side to him. He kissed her again, a little more intently, and she had instinctively lifted her face up, parted her lips and returned each kiss, oblivious that they were on the platform of a very busy train station.

The announcement of the departure of the London train intruded into the world in which they were momentarily alone together. She sprung to her feet. Surprised, he followed her figure with his eyes as she hurried away from him and towards Henry Lennox. His spirits sank for a couple of very long minutes. But she had formed her resolve by then.

John scanned the passing landscape, growing grayer from smoke spewing out of factories farther into the city. Stone buildings were clustering closer. They were less than half an hour away from the Milton terminal. He smiled to himself. He was nearly home and, amazingly, Margaret was with him. Was it only the day before that Nicholas Higgins told him about her brother who visited in secret when Mrs. Hale was dying? Astute, sympathetic Higgins had seen through him and, in seeming innocence, let him know the very fact he needed to lift his spirits and lighten the burden of losing the mill.

In the stillness of his room that night, he mulled over a suspicion, obscure until then, that before Margaret left Milton, her regard for him had grown. Earlier in their acquaintance, she had never shrunk from his direct gaze, returning it casually, frankly when they talked; and unflinchingly, even defiantly, when she disagreed with him. But he began to see in her an uncharacteristic shyness, a habit of averting her eyes or lowering her head. He had attributed it to the shame she felt from having been caught at an indiscretion in a public place. He did not allow himself any further curiosity about it, his pride stung by rejection and his heart tormented by jealousy of a handsome, well-bred young gentleman who, he now knew, to be her brother. Freed of that jealousy, he began to wonder if Margaret's downcast eyes meant a new self-consciousness about her feelings for him. Regardless of how others, including him, might perceive her conduct, Margaret would never avert her eyes in shame if she knew that she had done nothing wrong. Incredulous but hopeful; he paced his room and tossed restlessly in bed. In the morning before anyone in the house was up, he quietly left and boarded a train south to Helstone. He was not certain exactly why, merely that he felt compelled to do so.

By mid-morning, he reached Helstone. As he had expected, it was tranquil, luxuriantly green and bathed in mellow sunlight, the sort that would have been swallowed in the dense, dingy atmosphere of Milton. He found the parish where Mr. Hale had preached and a large cottage nearby where the family must have lived. Along a particularly well-trodden path near the parish, he passed a hedgerow of fragrant yellow roses, unseen in the bleakness of Milton where it would have struggled to survive. He paused, prodded by an urge to pick a newly opened blossom, its fragrance not entirely new to him and reminiscent of a pleasing citrus. As he stared at it, an image of Margaret haunted him once more; this time, of Margaret in this unspoiled, lush and placid setting—her spirit intrepid, indomitable and yet, vulnerable, sensitive. He frowned in annoyance at himself: How could he have allowed hurt pride and jealousy to preclude that Margaret had a defensible reason to be with a young man at the train station late at night? Could his resentment forever deprive him of happiness with the one woman he ever loved? But he was not one who gave up easily. He only hoped he was not too late.

John resolved to visit Margaret on the pretext of discussing the fate of Marlborough Mills. It was true enough that he needed to talk to her about it but his real purpose was to ascertain if his suspicions were correct. He would approach her with more care, listen more attentively, show her in many little ways how much he loved her, how he regretted the arrogant manner in which he proposed to her the first time. He knew she had not married and, he hoped, she had not formed an engagement with Henry Lennox whose interest in her was obvious. This thought made him uneasy, impatient to go as soon as he could. But first, he must reassure his mother, tell her he was ready to face the challenge of starting all over again.

On the train halfway back to Milton, what had merely been hope turned to utter happiness, what John had wished for became reality. Margaret's love was already his. The audacity of her quick decision to turn around and return to Milton with him enthralled him. Only deeply felt sentiments could have prompted such an act. Any other woman, less true to her feelings and more concerned about malicious gossip ruining her reputation, would not have dared to undertake it. Once Margaret knew what she wanted or what was right, she acted upon it. She had done the same when she stood between him and a rioting crowd.

"She must have cared for me even then!" John thought recollecting Margaret's arms around his shoulders, protecting him from the rioters.

His eyes shining, he said earnestly. "Margaret, my love, you must know that I never stopped loving you regardless of what I had said to the contrary, not even after that night at the train station. I saw you with that dashing young man, so refined and handsome and I thought: 'Someone from her world, just the man she would love.' I was devastated with jealousy."

Margaret was flabbergasted. "Jealous of Frederick?"

She thought all along that she had lost his esteem because he had caught her at a lie. And yet, Mrs. Thornton had told her in no uncertain terms that being out, alone and surreptitiously, with a strange man, was considered improper. Mrs. Thornton's insinuations had offended her then but it never occurred to her to attribute jealousy to John, particularly after her rejection.

"Is that your brother's name, Frederick?"

"You knew about Frederick! But how and for how long? Did Mr. Bell tell you?"

"No, but he tried. It was Nicholas Higgins I must thank, just recently, really. When he told me, I felt relieved of this great burden of losing you, losing the mill. And I dared to hope again."

Margaret touched his cheeks tenderly, her eyes brimming with both renewed wonder at the way events had unfolded and gratitude for his having continued to love her despite all that had passed. She felt humbled by his constancy, his deep love and, in a tremulous voice, she said: "Don't you know that I have loved you for some time now?"

"Since before you left Milton?" He asked, with some consternation, regretting once again the months of separation that they could have been spared.

"Yes, I think so. I know so. But at the time, I was convinced you thought badly of me because I lied."

"No, not because you lied. It hurt that you could love another man but not me, and you loved him enough to protect him and lie for him. If I was not so jealous, I would have realized that you had a reason to hide the truth."

"I was sorely tempted to tell you but I thought Fred was still in the country."

"Did you not think I would keep your brother's presence a secret if you had confided in me?"

"I was in great fear for my brother's life and I already felt so indebted to you that I could not let you compromise your position any further on my account."

For an instant, her eyes fluttered at an uneasy recollection. She turned towards the window at the hypnotic blur of green trees speeding by. After a few moments, she spoke again, her eyes on the yellow rose on her lap, her attempt to sound casual betrayed by the slight quiver in her voice. "I knew by then how wrong I was about you, just when you declared I was merely a foolish passion that was over, that you were looking to the future." She paused, took in a long breath, and assumed a more collected manner. "With someone else, I imagined."

Margaret kept her eyes glued on the rose as he explained, a hint of amusement in his voice. "Perhaps, I did mean to forget you. Fanny contrived situations to bring Miss Latimer and me together, with my mother's blessings, no doubt. Miss Latimer seemed quite interested so I did turn my attention towards her. But, alone in my room at night or even in my office at the mill, it was always your face I saw. Miss Latimer is very pretty and very much the lady. She would make any other man happy."

He placed a hand under her chin and gently turned her face up but she kept her eyes hidden behind half-closed lids. "But, me? I was haunted by this vibrant young woman with the skin of ivory and large expressive blue eyes"—he peered closer into her eyes— "or are they green? I have never seen a pair that can turn fiery with anger but also serene and radiant with love. I am afraid I found every other young lady very dull."

She met his gaze then but the intensity of his flustered her and she had to lower hers. Her cheeks burned and her heart raced once again.

She was still struggling to master her fluttering heart when he continued, his ardent voice just above a whisper. "When I first saw you on the train platform this afternoon, you looked at me with eyes glowing with promise and such a bewitching half-smile on your lips"—he bent over and kissed her—"that I could hardly control myself from taking you in my arms and whisking you away with me right there and then."

Struggling for control of her own emotions was impossible for her then and, with eyes half-closed, she swayed against him and buried her face on his shoulder.

John murmured, his breath warm against her cheek: "When you left Milton, it became clearer to me that it was only your good opinion I really cared about and yours the only face I wanted to gaze into were I to wake up with someone in the morning."

Her cheeks blushed deeply. She suppressed a sob, threw her arms around his neck and snuggled her face against it, amazed by how agreeable it felt and she thought: "This is where I belong. I could stay like this a long time.

John laid his cheek on her hair and clasped her close. "If I had known then what I know now, do you think I would have let you go to London?"

Reluctant as Margaret was to leave that exquisite niche she just discovered in the hollow of his neck, she raised her head and gazed into his eyes for a long moment. Then, she said frankly but regrettably: "I would have gratefully accepted your proposal had you renewed it then and things had been different. But the truth is I was incapable of any feeling but grief when I left Milton."

The anguish Margaret suffered all those months past came flooding back, taking her by surprise. She thought that she had been mostly in control of it and had tucked it away where she could regard it with proper detachment. But face-to-face with John, the weariness and sorrow she felt was nearly as vivid as it had been when she bade him farewell nearly a year ago.

"I was drained, apathetic, my reserves of energy and compassion depleted. I needed time to mourn, to put into perspective all that I had been through, to recover my strength." The quiver in her voice grew as she spoke and she sucked her breath in a few times to hold back tears.

He held her closer. "Oh my love, I am so sorry that you had to endure such sorrow when you first came to Milton. But I would have patiently waited for as long as you needed to arrive at this moment."

She laid her face on his shoulder and clung to him once more, trying to suppress another sob, but he felt a few tears dampen his neck.

A few minutes later, she whispered tremulously: "Maybe, your mother is right. I do not deserve you but my heart is yours fully and for as long as I live."

"My mother thought me too good for you but I did not think I was good enough and yet, what does it matter? You are finally home, my love—with me." He lifted her face to kiss her.

II. UNEASY RAPPROCHEMENT

Mrs. Thornton was pacing restlessly in the drawing room. Once in a while, she walked towards the window and looked down at the empty courtyard. She had not seen her son for two days and she was getting increasingly worried. He had not left any note nor said anything that gave her some inkling of where he might have gone. When she last talked to him, her heart ached painfully at seeing how broken his spirits had seemed, how profound his misery. She raged at the injustice of a world that seemed to have punished him, he who was all that was good in a man. The loss of the mill weighed on him deeply, she was certain of that. But she was also sadly aware that, since Margaret Hale left Milton, he had become uncharacteristically somber, more withdrawn, less communicative. She suspected that, were it not for that unfortunate matter with Miss Hale, the loss of the mill would not have plunged him into such deep despair.

Mrs. Thornton had never liked Miss Hale and, when she rejected John, that relatively passive dislike had turned into active hatred. So when she saw her that morning at the Mill, her rage at the world found its outlet. She accused Miss Hale of coming back to mock John for the misfortune that had befallen him. But Miss Hale disarmed her with guileless candor, conceding that Mrs. Thornton was right that she did not know John when she rejected him. Then, with sorrow in her eyes and her voice, she lamented the fate of the unfortunate mill. Still, Miss Hale was the woman who dared reject her son, causing him deep unhappiness. How could she forgive her?

Mrs. Thornton was roused from her musings by the unexpected sound of a carriage. Rather odd, she thought, because since the mill closed, no vehicle or horses entered the courtyard anymore. She hurried towards the window, anxious and curious, and sighed with relief when John descended from the carriage. But chagrin immediately displaced her relief: John turned to offer his hand to a woman alighting from the carriage.

"Miss Hale!" Mrs. Thornton stepped back from the window in dismay. She grabbed the arms of the nearest chair and sat down.

Exceedingly agitated, she did not immediately notice Jane who had rushed in and now stood looming over her, announcing frantically. "Madam, the master is back and a young woman is with him, I think it is the daughter of that parson from the south who lived here a year ago, the lady who stood in front of the rioters."

"Yes, Jane," Mrs. Thornton replied, irritably. "Calm yourself and go prepare some tea. The master must be tired from his journey." She tried to assume as normal and commanding a tone as she could.

When Jane was gone, she wearily rose from the chair, picked up her needlework, and sat on the sofa that was her preferred spot in the drawing room.

Trembling with consternation and foreboding, Mrs. Thornton, absentmindedly jabbed stitches on the linen she had been working on the past two days. She knew what the presence of Margaret Hale meant and her whole being revolted against it. Her breast churned with confusing emotions. On the one hand, she could not let go of her hatred, hatred aggravated by the ease with which Margaret acquired wealth and property that John had worked hard for, much of his life. But her return did mean John's happiness and by their marriage, Margaret would be giving him ownership rights to the house and the mill. He could reopen the mill much sooner than anyone would have expected. Mrs. Thornton knew she ought to be glad. Instead, her breast fluttered with trepidation: She was about to be supplanted. And, by whom? A Southerner with airs! Now, she would have to live with her.

Mrs. Thornton clenched her jaw and scowled, listening for footsteps, her muscles tense and her body rigid in her efforts to appear as calm as possible. The footsteps came too soon and she compressed her lips until they nearly turned white.

"Good evening, mother," John greeted her in a gentle voice as they approached. "We've come home."

Mrs. Thornton stood up slowly, with as much dignity as she could muster, and turned towards them. She could not answer and merely stared. John had drawn Margaret close as if he was trying to protect her. Margaret glanced at her for an instant but directed her eyes back at John. They had both smiled at her, hesitantly, their eyes anxious, but as they gazed at each other, their faces shared the warm glow of a new and joyous attachment.

Mrs. Thornton shifted her eyes from one to the other and stopped at her son's face. She blinked, amazed at its tranquility amidst his happiness. She saw brilliance in his eyes just as she had ten years ago when he came home to announce that he had successfully negotiated to run his own mill. His bearing wore the same confident and expectant air but, this time, she saw a placidity she had never seen—a calm expression that relaxed his often-furrowed brow and deepened the smile that reached his eyes—instead of the defiantly triumphant countenance of one conscious about having overcome difficult obstacles. Mrs. Thornton smiled at her son, the worries that had weighed on her for some time gradually crumbling. She uttered a prayer and, despite herself, she felt grateful to Margaret.

But Mrs. Thornton was the sort who clung violently to her emotions, whether for love or hate. Her mind rather than her heart was grateful to Margaret and deep within, her repulsion to the reality confronting her hardened her hatred against this young woman who was about to become her son's wife. She kept her eyes on her son and studiously avoided Margaret.

"Mother, Margaret and I," John hesitated. He found it difficult to say to his mother what he knew was obvious to her already but which he could sense she was determinedly resisting. He was keenly aware that his mother disliked Margaret but he hoped that seeing him happy would temper her ill feelings.

The "Margaret and I" spoken by her son chafed at Mrs. Thornton, however, and she could no longer hold back. With anger barely suppressed, she turned to Margaret. "So, you've finally come to your senses, have you?"

"Mother........."

Margaret laid a lightly restraining hand on John's arm, walked slowly towards Mrs. Thornton and around the sofa. The two of them stood face-to-face. While boarding the carriage at the train station, the thought of meeting Mrs. Thornton again had suddenly oppressed Margaret. She sat restlessly in the carriage, wondering how she could clear the air with Mrs. Thornton. By the time they reached Marlborough Mills, she decided she must do so now, rather than later. Perhaps, she thought, it would avoid awkwardness and lessen the distress of living with someone who clearly did not like her. It was, in any case, her duty and not Mrs. Thornton's to take the initiative at greater civility in their relationship. She hoped that some ease, if not warmth, would come with time. But Margaret was more rational than experienced about emotions and she proceeded on that basis to explain herself to Mrs. Thornton.

"Mrs. Thornton, I am truly sorry for any pain I might have caused," Margaret began, her eyes pleading but unflinching, fixed on the older woman in an attitude that Mrs. Thornton remembered and regarded as proud and haughty. Thrusting her chin out, Mrs. Thornton stared back with disdainful skepticism at Margaret and said nothing.

Margaret, who had calmly responded to Mrs. Thornton's accusation earlier that morning, was now disconcerted, her confidence replaced by a vulnerability borne out of her fresh alliance with John. She continued with more formality in her tone and voice. "When I first came to Milton, I was rather unhappy, more so when I saw my mother in so much distress. I struggled a long time to learn and adapt to Milton, so strange and so different from anything I knew in the south."

Margaret paused and took a long deep breath. The conviction with which she had started this attempt at a rapprochement waned steadily at the older woman's withering indifference. She was beginning to doubt that she was getting through but, having already started, she knew she must finish. She resumed, her voice somewhat louder, as if with it, she could negate her growing sense that her efforts were futile. Ironically, this sense began to free her, allowed her to say what came to mind more spontaneously—about her parents, Bessie, the Boucher children.

Mrs. Thornton's impenetrable countenance showed a little crack at mention of the workers' plight and she pursed her lips contemptuously. Margaret was not surprised. She had once listened to Mrs. Thornton's views of the working class and knew that she believed workers were inferior to those who rose to be masters, that they got what they deserved and were not worthy of sympathy.

Margaret glanced at John, who had been watching her with some apprehension. "I have no reason or excuse that would satisfy you as to why I rejected John's proposal after the riot. We had a rather inauspicious beginning and we seemed to clash at every turn."

She faced Mrs. Thornton once again and a hint of defiance crept into her voice. "Later, I was appalled to find that my behavior during the riot was interpreted as something calculated to generate a proposal. It distressed me that anyone thought me capable of that."

The revelation made a visible impression on Mrs. Thornton, her gaze darting briefly towards her son before being fixed again, superciliously, on Margaret. Mrs. Thornton thought: "Pride, Margaret, pride is definitely one of your failings. You had rejected my son for that."

The pain and burden of explaining to the older woman had begun to wear on Margaret and, turning away, she stared pensively into space for a long moment. Her voice was sad when she resumed with an explanation she felt she must make although she knew Mrs. Thornton would regard it as a quaint southern affectation. "Were I aware, much less capable, in those unfortunate times, of an attachment, I am afraid my pride and confusing feelings would have prevented my accepting John or anybody else, in fact. I did not know what it was to have strong sentiments for someone who was neither my father nor my brother and I was certainly unprepared to marry."

She reached out to Mrs. Thornton whose cold, inscrutable façade had returned. Margaret, determined to appear undaunted, looked her straight in the eye. "I admit that it took me some time to understand John and recognize my own feelings for him and by then, I had neither hope nor right to expect that his attachment had endured. I know you do not think me worthy of him and I suppose you and I will often see things differently."

She took another deep breath and as she finished, the strain of the encounter finally brought a quiver in her voice. "If you are inclined to doubt all that I just told you, then please believe, at least, that I do love John very much and that is really the only reason I am here now."

21

Mrs. Thornton studied Margaret's countenance and, in her mind, begrudgingly admired her frankness. She was nonetheless not about to cede her upper hand and she retorted somewhat scornfully. "What of that man at the train station and your disgraceful behavior with him?"

John had listened intently to Margaret and only then began to comprehend what she had gone through. He saw her blink a few times to hold back tears that had begun to well up and he felt compelled to answer his mother, a little vehemently: "Mother, that was Margaret's brother, Frederick."

"Brother!" Mrs. Thornton exclaimed incredulously.

John, who had held back despite his growing exasperation at his mother's uncivil manner towards Margaret, tried to answer as calmly as he could.

But Mrs. Thornton seemed unconvinced. "Really?" She looked askance at Margaret whose imploring eyes glistened with the struggle to keep from crying. Mrs. Thornton relented a little and demanded of her son: "How long have you known about the existence of this brother?"

"Not as long as I would have wished. He lives in Spain and may never return to England. Still, I ask you not to say anything about him to anyone, least of all to Fanny."

Anxiously, he looked at Margaret. She had been trying to compose herself and attempted a half-smile. He resumed, his eyes still on her: "Sometimes secrecy is necessary but it can lead to misunderstandings that cannot be helped." John smiled reassuringly at her. "Fortunately, truth has a way of coming out."

As tenacious as Mrs. Thornton's dislikes were, her attachment to her son was stronger and she was anxious to maintain it. When she heard the irritation in his voice, she reluctantly accepted, at least in words, the truth that she could not wish away. She addressed Margaret without much warmth: "My son is attached to you, that is obvious enough. And you say you are to him as well."

She approached her son and touched his cheek affectionately. "I can accept any woman who makes you happy and if that happens to be Miss Hale, so be it." Then, with her usual proud demeanor, she started to turn around.

Margaret bit her upper lip to suppress an urge to let her tears ago. To be merely tolerated was not exactly the reception anyone wanted in joining the family of the man one was about to spend her life with. For a few seconds, she wished she had gone back to London but she thought of John, his eyes tender with concern throughout her ordeal of explaining to his mother, and she knew she was where she wanted to be. So, despite the coldness and lack of enthusiasm with which Mrs. Thornton received her, Margaret could not help placing her hand on Mrs. Thornton's arm and planting a kiss on her cheek.

Taken by surprise, Mrs. Thornton pressed Margaret's hand briefly but kindly. "I'll see what's happened to the tea. After that, I'll show you to your room so you can rest and freshen up before dinner. We always have it at eight."

Margaret, in fact, surprised herself with the gesture she made towards Mrs. Thornton who was clearly not comfortable with public display of affection especially coming from someone towards whom she was indifferent if not outright hostile. But Margaret acted spontaneously, compelled by her natural temperament to act as she felt, and by her southern graciousness and London gentility, to do so with a blend of sincerity and cultivated directness in her manner. Mrs. Thornton was disarmed and Margaret's own uneasiness was relieved, if only for the moment.

As soon as his mother left the room, John clasped Margaret in his arms, searching her countenance for residual signs of distress. A little more serene, she snuggled closer in his embrace and he was content to hold her close in silence, delighting in the warmth of her against him. A few minutes later, he whispered, pressing his lips against her forehead: "So you do love me."

"How can any girl resist you?" She answered with an attempt at lightness, her voice muffled against his chest.

Mrs. Thornton rustled back into the room noisily. "Tea is here." John let go of Margaret reluctantly, his hand lingering like a caress on her back as he led her to the sofa. Jane, who had walked behind Mrs. Thornton, laid the tea tray on the table, glancing surreptitiously at the couple.

Teatime passed with the three saying as little as they could. Although thirsty, Margaret had difficulty swallowing her tea. She was, thus, thankful for the dainty cups in which it was served— somewhat incongruous with the gray massive drawing room, she could not help thinking with some amusement—so that she could finish her tea without leaving any of it in her cup. She was as anxious not to offend as to mask her discomfort, so she took a small piece of cake and ate it slowly. Mrs. Thornton sat tall and upright, in an attitude Margaret remembered from the only other time she had tea with the older woman who had called upon them then in Crampton. Then as now, Mrs. Thornton had an air of dignity but not ease. She did not hide her feeling that she would much rather have been somewhere else than sitting there, having tea with them. Both times, Margaret was conscious of being under Mrs. Thornton's scrutiny but in Crampton, the idea amused her; now, it caused her discomfort. John was too famished to notice the unease between the two women he cared most about. He had not eaten since morning and the exhilarating end of this particular day gave him a voracious appetite. He drank a copious amount of tea with milk and ate a large piece of cake.

Before Mrs. Thornton could lead Margaret away to her room, John asked his mother in a low voice: "You did set her up in the large bedroom?"

"Of course. Everyone, including the servants, might as well begin to get used to that room being finally occupied."

The room into which Mrs. Thornton placed Margaret was spacious but sparer than the rest of the house. The walls were predominantly dark blue with fleur-de-lis gold motifs and the heavy curtains on the one huge window on the courtyard side were of an even darker shade of blue. A large canopied bed stood somewhat off center, its headboard against the wall perpendicular to the window. By its foot, was a large fireplace, in front of which were a table and two armchairs protected by the same netting that could be found everywhere in the house. A dresser with a matching chair against the same wall as the headboard and a writing table and chair on the opposite wall not far from the door completed the furnishings. The room imparted the same steeliness as the rest of the house but escaped the oppressiveness of its heavy alabaster decorations.

Though it was a relatively warm day, Margaret shivered a little. She resisted an urge to run out of the room in search of John, to seek warmth in his embrace once more and calm the unease that she felt about this house and his mother. Instead, she looked around the room for her valise and found it on the low table by the fireplace. It was easy to miss in the large room. She sat on an armchair, opened the valise and took out a shawl that she wrapped around herself, relaxing into its comforting warmth. Exhaustion now came upon her and she leaned back on the chair and closed her eyes, partly to prevent tears that began to moisten them. The incipient tears perplexed her. Despite the chill and vague apprehension she felt being in this house, she was aware that she was happy, that she reveled in knowing that she loved and was loved. But, it had been a long, rather eventful day. She had just been through a range of opposing emotional planes—from hope to regret and dejection, to hopeful incredulity and, finally, joy that nearly made her heart burst. Then, there was the distress at the impossibility of explaining herself to Mrs. Thornton.

With that one act of turning back and going home to Milton with John, Margaret had indeed followed her heart and charted a course for her future. What lay ahead of her was less predictable, perhaps less tranquil, but also more adventurous than if she had stayed among London relatives and friends who cared for her and with whom she was familiar.

She was certain that her cousin Edith would be shocked upon learning about her decision from Henry Lennox. He would walk into the Harley Street drawing room that evening to make his announcement, in the direct and impersonal manner he assumed as a lawyer.

Born into wealth and ensconced in luxury and fashionable society in London, Edith would fret, probably cry, in the arms of her handsome husband, Captain Lennox, Henry's younger brother. She would lament her cousin's action, aghast to imagine that Margaret, her companion and confidante of ten years, chose a filthy industrial place to find her happiness in. How could Margaret, beautiful, keen of mind, and now the heiress of a large fortune, marry a man in the trade? And how could Henry who Edith had marked for Margaret, share this news with equanimity?

Together from age nine, Edith and Margaret learned the arts and skills of accomplished young women, shared each other's tears and dreams, anticipated each other's desires and reactions, and thus, nurtured a mutual affection as close as two sisters could have. Edith would naturally expect a letter from Margaret.

Edith's mother, indulgent and generous Aunt Shaw, would be dismayed but would merely shrug her shoulders and remind herself that Margaret was, after all, of age, rich and, therefore, independent, free to do as she wished. She would recall meeting Mr. Thornton—a tall gentleman, handsome in a dark sort of way, with an air of quiet authority—who bade Margaret a solemn, even mournful, farewell when she left Milton. Mrs. Shaw attributed his lugubrious air, at the time, to mourning his friend and teacher, Mr. Hale. But Henry's news presented her with a new interpretation.

Mrs. Shaw and her daughter, both languid in temperament, knew enough of and accepted the independent streak in Margaret's generally good judgment. They would be inclined to believe— once the letter was read, the likely groom described to Edith, and the shock passed—that Margaret was in love. A defensible reason, they would agree, the only one that should compel anyone, in need of neither beauty nor fortune, to return to a place like Milton.

Margaret now openly acknowledged to herself that she came back to Milton that morning because of John. Intuitively, she knew that it was with him that life could be happy in a way she had never known and stimulating in challenges she would be facing for the first time. That Milton would be the place in which this future life would happen seemed inevitable. She could not imagine John in any other setting. Although her own preference would have been a town that also had the endearing attributes of Helstone, she no longer felt the attachment she once had to the hamlet where she grew up. Margaret slowly slid into much needed slumber, her thoughts dissolving into vague random dreams which were immediately forgotten when she awoke an hour later.

John had wanted to retreat to his room and be alone with his thoughts. But he knew he had to talk to his mother and ease her mind about questions that he sensed were distracting her usual demeanor. He did not know quite how to explain to her where he had gone and what happened during the fateful stop at the train station. He hesitated, for the first time, to give her even a glimpse into the deep love he had for Margaret and all the agony, hope, and bliss it occasioned. On the way home, relishing the wonder of having Margaret nestled in his arms, as if she had always belonged there, he had neither the time nor the inclination to rehearse what he should say to his mother.

Mrs. Thornton sat without a word, occasionally glancing at John, waiting for him to explain the events of the last two days. He began: "Mother I am sorry to have left without a note or a word. I know it must have worried you very much."

He paused and faltered a little. "I needed to be alone and away from here to think more clearly about what I must do next. I took the first train going south towards London." He stopped and looked away, unsure how to proceed.

Although taken aback, her curiosity was piqued "London! Did you go to see Margaret there? Was it about the mill or about her?"

"Well, in fact, I went to Helstone."

"To Helstone! Had she moved back to that place?"

Mrs. Thornton's voice had grown more agitated and John decided that straightforward was probably the best way to talk to her. But how could he explain the turmoil he had been through or the ensuing happiness that eventually overcame all the heartaches that came before?

"I went to Helstone because it seemed the farthest away in spirit from Milton as I could go."

"But I don't understand. Why did you want to get away from Milton? Your life has been here, your trials, your successes, those who have supported you." She stared at him, unable to hide the hurt in her eyes behind the skeptical tone of her voice.

He clearly saw her worry, sensed the impatience in her manner but he was reluctant to confront her reproach. He hurried on to describe what happened, concluding, "When I saw her again, I could no longer deny that to be with her was what I wanted most. I am not a great believer in fate but, perhaps today at that train station, it did favor me."

When John first confessed his sentiments for Margaret, Mrs. Thornton felt as if a dagger had been thrust into her chest. Now that she was certain of being displaced in the primacy of her son's affection to a woman she disliked, hearing him reaffirm that attachment pierced deep into her heart. Overwhelmed by what lay before her, she felt suddenly exhausted, her body and her spirit battered by days of worrying and coping with unexpected, unpleasant events. She could only respond with a noncommittal "Yes, well, that was quite a coincidence meeting at a train stop."

Then, not ready to accept the waning of her influence, she said: "I did see Margaret at the mill this morning. She must have thought a lot about what I had said to her because she admitted she was wrong about you."

If Mrs. Thornton had meant to remind his son of a mother's wisdom and constancy, her attempts seemed futile. John scowled, his eyes questioning her. Dismayed, she explained irritably: "Mrs. Hale asked me, before she died, to give counsel to her daughter when I judged her to be acting inappropriately. I talked to Margaret about rumors of her improprieties at the train station."

Suspicions of what exactly his mother said to Margaret vexed John vaguely but he thought it more important, at the moment, to restore the effortless familiarity of their past interactions. She looked pale and worn out and he did not believe anything more needed to be said about what happened that afternoon. He smiled warmly and said: "I understand. I am glad she was honest and frank with you."

With his change in tone, they both relaxed, almost regaining the intimacy they used to share. His eyes glowing with wonder and joy, John said: "Mother, I love Margaret very much. That she loves me as sincerely as I had wished for has made me happier than even I imagined."

"Then, that is all I could hope for. I knew you remained attached to her." Mrs. Thornton answered simply, unwilling or unable to reveal anymore of her apprehensions. She could not endure any more explanations and was merely desirous then to be alone for some respite. "I am happy that you are happy. You deserve to be after all you have been through."

She stood up wearily and gently laid a hand on his shoulder. "We've both had a long day and it's not over yet. You need to freshen up and I need to lie down and rest."

John was uncertain if his explanation allayed Mrs. Thornton's anxieties. She did not exactly seem satisfied with what he told her but he could do no more. What else was there to say? All his mother really needed to know was there for her to see. He knew that acceptance was going to be very difficult for her. So much had happened in recent weeks that exacted a heavy toll on both of them. For her, Margaret's return was, perhaps, devastating on top of the closing of the mill. But he had faith in his mother's resilience and strength and was certain that, eventually, she would adjust and be at peace with her changed world. In any case, he was, too full of Margaret and this unexpected state of joy and exhilaration to concern himself with his mother for too long.

Alone in his room, he marveled at how differently he felt and how his outlook and his future changed almost abruptly from early that morning. He had quit this room restless and despondent. While there was, in fact, much that could not be predicted about his future in cotton manufacturing, he was not truly deeply apprehensive about it. In fact, he felt a certain excitement at the challenges he would be facing with beginning anew, as late in life as it was. No, what had earlier disquieted him was not so much his rising again from his fall but the prospect of the rest of his life without Margaret. When his time and energy were devoted to saving the future of the mill, he had not much time to think of other things and Margaret intruded into his consciousness only in the hours before sleep could take over. When the mill closed down, she invaded his thoughts much more despite his belief that she could never be his.

This evening, Margaret was separated from him only by a couple of doors, probably resting, in the room intended to be his marriage chamber. Still in the throes of happiness so new and, only yesterday, so improbable, he felt he could not yet endure being away from its source for too long. He ached to be with her, to hold her, to kiss her warm, yielding lips once more. He stared at the door a long time, thinking how easy it would have been to open it and go to her. Instead, he walked restlessly back and forth until finally, he headed for the washbasin. Later, he changed his shirt, and went out for a short visit to the mill. Perhaps, Williams was still around.

Margaret was roused from her nap by a knock from one of the servants who came in to ignite the fireplace and light the lamps on the bedside and writing tables. Darkness had descended into the room. Glancing at a clock on the writing table, she found she had less than a half hour to freshen up for dinner—more than enough time. Without a complete change of clothes, her toilette was going to be simple and brief. She walked into the adjoining bathroom and splashed water on her face several times, welcoming its bracing coolness. Then, she patted her cheeks and pursed her lips enough to bring color back to her face. After rearranging the recalcitrant wisps of hair back into her chignon, she felt ready to face this new and, as yet, strange household.

She was walking towards the door when another knock hastened her steps but before she could reach it, the door opened. She brightened at the sight of John standing at the door, waiting to escort her down to the dining room. But instead of offering his arm, he came into the room and closed the door quietly behind him.

"I needed to reassure myself that you are indeed here with me," he said as he gathered her in his arms.

"I could hardly be anywhere else, could I?" Margaret smiled shyly up at him. "If someone from Milton had seen us at the train station, my already dubious reputation would finally be in tatters, ruined by gossip that would now have Miss Hale not just embracing but kissing no less than Mr. Thornton and in broad daylight, at that."

"Quite so," he replied with an amused laugh. "And the perfectly honorable Mr. Thornton could not do otherwise but marry Miss Hale to save her reputation. What they would never guess is how he would have gone to the other side of the world to bring her back home with him once he knew that she loved him."

He bent over to kiss her, his lips lingering on hers, luscious, and responsive. He tore himself away reluctantly and taking her hand in his, led her towards the door. "Mother is fanatical about punctuality at Sunday dinners."

Dinner was livelier than tea, sustained by conversation, mostly between John and Margaret, about impersonal topics.

Before coffee or tea was served, Margaret excused herself. "Do you mind if I leave you now? My aunt and Edith must not be kept waiting for an explanation of why I came back to Milton. I must write them tonight. My aunt especially needs to know right away that I am safe and if it is all right with you, I would like to send for Dixon to bring my belongings over from London and to continue to assist me here."

"Of course," Mother and son responded in unison.

John began to rise as Margaret stood but she smiled at him sweetly and said: "It's all right. I think I can find my way." She bowed towards Mrs. Thornton, said "Good Night!" and left.

John, amazed that he would be seeing her again the very next morning, watched Margaret moving towards the door. At the doorway, she stopped briefly to look back at him, her full lips barely curved into a smile. Mrs. Thornton watched the wordless exchange with narrowed eyes—her son, entranced, catching his breath, already in a world with Margaret that could never include her.

Margaret surmised that Henry Lennox did no more than announce to her London relatives that she had gone back to Milton with John Thornton. Deeply mindful of her obligation to fully explain her action, she sat down directly at the writing table. The first letter she wrote was to her aunt, relatively short and direct, containing an apology and reassurances that she was well, that her decision was well-considered, and that she was staying at the family home with Mrs. Thornton and a coterie of servants. She promised to write back immediately with news of when her marriage was to take place.

To her cousin Edith, Margaret wrote a long letter:

I do not doubt, my dear cousin, how surprise you must be that I have returned to Milton to marry John Thornton and I am equally sensible of your certain disappointment that Henry and I did not come together as you would have wished. I am heartily sorry for not having taken you in confidence before today but I was often bewildered, confused, sometimes rather distressed by so much that happened in Milton. I did not quite know how to tell you about John and how he proposed to me nearly two years ago when my parents were both still alive.

Margaret proceeded with particulars on what happened, before confessing:

I know well enough that I could have lost a chance at genuine happiness so I am deeply grateful that John remained constant in his feelings for me even through all the trying circumstances we have endured. And let me assure you since, indeed, I know my dear Edith will not be satisfied unless I say this: I love John very much and feel for him something Henry never stirred in me. There, I said it, certain that you will understand me, that when you meet John you will like him and support my choice. All is well that ends well—did we not learn that by heart all those many years ago? After all those past heartaches, I can hardly believe the blissful state I am now blessed with.

Margaret ended the letter with a plea.

Write me soon, please, Edith, for, like you, I need reassurance that you are not unduly worried about me.

Margaret wrote three more letters, a detailed one to her brother much like that to Edith, a short one to Mr. Bell who had written her only once, giving his address, and the last one to Dixon instructing her to come to Milton with such clothes and other possessions as Margaret specified. She finished her letters way past midnight and was too sleepy for all her usual bedtime rituals. She had considered borrowing a nightgown from Mrs. Thornton but by the end of the strained dinner, she decided her chemise would have to do until Dixon arrived. Exhausted and shivering in her chemise, she crawled under the covers and barely had a few moments of consciousness before she fell asleep, cradled within the warmth of the massive bed.

III. REKINDLING

The room was still quite dark when Margaret awakened. She could tell it was morning only from a sliver of light peeking through a gap between the curtains on the one window across some distance from her bed. When she returned to the bedroom the past night, she had not noticed that the curtains had been drawn. Now, she recalled that the room had been made rather cozy, with a crackling fire and lamps lighting the area around the bed, the darkness concealing much of the vast icy space. Her eyes darted around the room, searching for pale or bright colors that reflected light. But nearly everything was dark—furniture, walls, curtains, even the comforter that covered the white sheets on the bed. At night, the darkness did not bother her and it probably helped her sleep but, in the morning, she craved light for the clarity it brought—the world in all its beauty and its blight—and the inspiration that renewed hopes and fresh beginnings. In both London and Helstone, she had always left her drapes open.

She got up slowly and, in her bare feet, skipped on the cold floor towards the window to open the curtains to their full width. The gray spring fog diffused the light that came into the room and made it difficult to guess at the time. Spring in Helstone greeted her with luminous colors, bird song, and the heady perfume of roses growing around their house. During the first few weeks after she moved to Milton with her parents, her thoughts on waking up in the dreariness of a Milton morning were always of Helstone and how much she missed it. But in time, she forced herself to suppress those thoughts: They came too often with sadness at the passing of carefree halcyon days in the little village. This morning, her memories of Helstone did not come with sad regrets, only the detachment of objective observation. Somehow, it did not matter much anymore where she lived as long as it was with John.

She glanced at the clock on the writing table—past nine o'clock—and hurried to dress. She hated to be late for breakfast but she had stayed up late into the night to finish letters that needed to be posted right after breakfast. She wondered what Mrs. Thornton would say at her tardy appearance and she sighed. How long was she going to worry about what Mrs. Thornton thought of her or whether the older woman would ever warm up to her? Margaret shrugged: She would have enough time to worry about such things in the weeks to come.

While she was dressing, Margaret was interrupted by a knock. She opened the door to Jane who carried a large bouquet of red and yellow roses in one hand and a vase half-filled with water cradled to her bosom. "The master asked me to bring these to you, miss. I think he wanted to give them to you himself but he did not want to bother you if you were still in bed."

Margaret beamed and nearly snatched the flowers from the maid's hands, delighted at the surprise she brought her. Now, she had more light and cheeriness. With half-closed eyes, she kissed every flower and inhaled its fragrance deeply. Then, she stopped, suddenly, as she caught a glimpse of Jane staring at her with undue interest. It irritated her: Margaret knew that, after the riot, she had been the object of much gossip among these servants who saw her stand between Mr. Thornton and the rioters. She did not doubt that her unexpected arrival at the Thornton house occasioned even more talk.

"What a bother," she thought. "Don't they have anything better to talk about among themselves? But what could I do?" She shrugged her shoulders once more: Perhaps, gossip came with being John Thornton's fiancée, one of those things she must accustom herself to.

In the present instant, at least, she could deal with Jane. Margaret raised her head from the flowers, fixed her eyes on the maid, and with an engaging smile, said: "Thank you, Jane, please place the vase on that table over there." The flowers still in her hand, Margaret went to open the door and held it open, leaving Jane no choice but to hurry out of the room. Margaret placed the flowers in the vase and arranged them to her liking. Then, she headed for the dining room with a wry smile.

John and Mrs. Thornton were at breakfast when Margaret came into the dining room. John had been a little restless waiting for her, surreptitiously eyeing the door while giving his mother the impression of his full attention. He had been impatient through the night to see her again and he sprung up from his chair as soon as he saw her. Mrs. Thornton, momentarily startled, became aware only then of Margaret's presence. John walked around the table to pull a chair out for her and as she sat down, he caressed her back briefly. As light as it was, his hand sent a wave of warmth all over her and she looked up at him, smiling shyly. They exchanged a barely noticeable nod of unspoken intimacy, oblivious of his mother.

Mrs. Thornton watched the brief exchange, her lips compressed and her eyes clouded with a scowl. Her scrutiny and faintly masked disapproval was not lost on Margaret who felt suddenly ill at ease and hesitant. Forgetting that she had not greeted Mrs. Thornton, she turned her full attention to pouring tea in her cup and serving herself toast and butter.

John, still gripped by the unexpected wonder of Margaret's presence there having breakfast with him, hovered behind her chair and enticed her with other dishes. "How about some eggs or, perhaps, some fruit?"

With an uneasy glance at his mother, Margaret turned towards John to smile her refusal. He started to bend down to kiss her but Mrs. Thornton arrested his movement with an elaborate clearing of her throat. He straightened slowly, smiled with a little embarrassed scowl at his mother, and went back to his chair—but not before he had tenderly grazed his hand across the nape of Margaret's neck.

Mrs. Thornton's throat clearing reminded Margaret of her manners and she realized that she had neglected to give her a proper greeting. But it was too late to rectify her omission and all Margaret could manage then was a wan, reluctant, and apologetic smile.

Mrs. Thornton gave her a barely perceptible nod and said in a cold voice, "I will leave you two to finish your breakfast. I have things to attend to." She glanced at Margaret. "Breakfast is always ready by seven in the morning but it will wait for you if you are a late riser." She smirked as she turned to leave the room in a rustle of stiff fabric. Margaret bit her lip as she watched Mrs. Thornton walk briskly out of the room.

When they were alone, John reached across the table and grasped Margaret's hand in his. She turned towards him, her lips curved up at the corners to force a smile. John sensed her unease and stroked her hand as he spoke: "I hope it did not feel too strange sleeping in that room. Were you comfortable enough?"

This time, she smiled warmly at him. "I confess I found the room a little too grand but the low fire at the hearth made the room warmer and the bed covers were also nice and warm. Anyway, after writing many letters, I was quite tired and fell asleep right away."

"Did you finish all the letters you needed to write?"

"Yes," she blurted with a sigh of relief. "The letters to my aunt and Edith should arrive there tomorrow if I post them this morning. The one to Frederick will take about two weeks and I am not certain how long it takes for the mail to arrive in Argentina. I have heard only once from Mr. Bell and sadly, I don't know how he is but I must send him my good news anyway."

"I will walk with you to post your letters. We can go right after breakfast."

"You do not need to. I do remember the way to the post." She smiled, amusement in her eyes. "Besides I would like to go to Greens afterwards for some clothing."

"I can take you there later but we'll have to visit the parson first after we post your letters. We have to set a date, my love."

"Yes, of course." She replied, somewhat startled. She knew she was about to marry but it had not completely sunk in that it would happen sooner rather than later. The day before had been so dense with momentous events that she never thought of what needed to happen immediately as a consequence of her decisions. It was clear enough to her that, from that day on, her life would be in Milton. But it never occurred to her to consider the propriety of her actions—the social constraint which dictated that her wedding should take place as soon as it could be arranged.

She sipped her tea slowly and sadness overcame her at the thought that her brother, the only immediate family she had now, could not come to her wedding. With her father gone, she only had one sincere wish on her wedding day—that Frederick could give her away. But, of course, that could never be. Perhaps, she could persuade John to visit him and his wife in Cadiz sometime in the future. She was anxious for the two most important people in her life to meet, a wish that became more compelling with John's admission of jealousy. Knowing both of them, she was certain that they would like each other, once they got acquainted. For her part, she was eager to meet Dolores.

She had been silent a while and John surmised her mind was faraway. With a gentle squeeze on her hand, he interrupted her thoughts, and said, pressing her hand to his lips: "I would marry you today, if I could. I have waited for you a long time but I will defer to your wishes." Then, he added impishly: "Doesn't every young woman want to make the day she gives a solemn promise to love for always a day to remember?"

She smiled brightly and replied in the same vein. "That, I suppose is the conventional wisdom. But I used to think that, if that day ever came for me, all I would do was put on my best gown and walk through a lush arbor into my father's church, preferably on a beautiful morning in early summer with birds singing and roses of all colors perfuming the air."

"Did you doubt that day would come for you?"

"I had all those months of reflection after Papa died and I realized I was not prepared to marry just anyone. Edith was always inviting the captain's friends and his friends' friends." She stopped abruptly, lowered her eyes, and was silent for a moment. "With Mr. Bell's legacy, adventurous spinsterhood became an attractive possibility."

He asked, with a wicked smile: "Did I rescue you in time from those friends or deprive you of an adventure?"

She replied archly: "Would not a life with you be an exciting adventure?"

"Nothing but," he said, smiling. Then, he asked, a little worried: "Is marrying in Milton so bad?"

"No. Oh no! I did not mean to say that at all. I know I described Helstone but, seriously, aren't the vows we make what really matter? Still, I cannot deny that I would have wanted everyone I care about to have been there. But that is not possible, is it?" A lump caught in her throat and she smiled tremulously. "We will have a spring morning, anyway."

John could only stroke her hand sympathetically.

She turned pensive and said, in a sad voice. "I wish, at least, that Papa were here. How happy he would have been to see us together. He liked you very much and looked forward to your conversations. I am certain he was sorry that I did not accept your proposal. But my kind father rarely questioned my actions, never forced me into decisions I did not want to make."

"We were indeed very close friends and, perhaps, he does know wherever he may be that now, he is truly my father as well."

"It is futile to wish that I had known myself better when father was still alive or that I had been more mature because, in that case, he would have been more at peace knowing he was leaving me with you."

John pressed her hand to his lips again. "Your father was at peace when he passed away."

They sat quietly as she slowly sipped her tea. He waited for her to finish but he was getting impatient, eager to be alone with her, away from where they could hear his mother and the servants darting about busily with their daily morning tasks.

"Go fetch your letters. Let's get out of here. Too much is going on in here and I want you to myself for a while."

The way to the post from Marlborough Mills was familiar to Margaret although, in the past, she had often walked the opposite direction from the post to the mill. Outside the mill gates, the city buzzed, clacked, bustled, jostled in all the ways she remembered. She smiled up at John who tenderly squeezed the hand she had hooked around his arm. "Do you remember any of these, my love? It is noisier and dirtier than London but it is more vibrant."

"That, it is." She agreed with a smile, occasionally craning her neck to peek into store windows. "Not much has changed and yet everything seems different somehow."

"It will become much more familiar and I hope you will like it better this time despite its being so different from Helstone."

"I might have exaggerated the virtues of Helstone."

"Perhaps, you just have a different perspective now."

"Perhaps. I do miss the roses that grew wild around the Parsonage. Apropos of which, I wanted to thank you for the ones you sent me this morning."

"Did they please you?"

She smiled brightly at him. "They made such a difference in the bedroom, like a ray of blazing sunshine. They also gave out so much of the same fragrance that the roses at the Parsonage greeted me with every morning when I opened my window."

"I am happy that they give you such pleasure. I knew you would be up late today after everything that happened yesterday and all the letters that I am sure you stayed up throughout the night to write. I wanted this day, our first full day together, to start right for you."

"Well, it has. How could it not?" She gazed up at him, her eyes glowing. "But how did you get those roses? Where from? You could not have had time to get them yourself."

"You are right. I had no time but I do have my means. I went to the mill last night and sent William for the flowers early this morning. You remember him. He still comes to check around every morning and evening."

"I do, indeed. He is quite loyal to you."

"Yes," he replied simply. They walked some distance before he resumed: "There is much you have yet to learn about Milton that I am eager to show you."

She nodded and flashed him her most bewitching smile as she clutched his arm with both hands, conscious and amused that she was mimicking the gesture of possessiveness that Anne Latimer had made in front of the church on Fanny's wedding day. The smile he gave her back was different, however; it reached his eyes, infusing them with an inner glow that brightened his whole face. He lifted her hand to his lips before tucking it back around his arm. They gazed at each other, insensible of everything else around them, rapt up in a world of their own.

People on Milton's busy streets seldom failed to notice the tall lean figure of the well-respected manufacturer John Thornton as he hurried about his business. They impassively noted his presence and swiftly dismissed it as one of those usual occurrences that happened in the course of a day. But they were used to him passing briskly by, scowling and purposeful. It was certainly new and unusual to see him leisurely strolling along, gazing deeply into the eyes of a handsome young woman who most of them vaguely recognized but whose face they could not place. Thus, many of the storekeepers and other denizens of the city who saw them that morning were inevitably curious and, by noon, speculation about what it meant circulated in many parlors. By evening, these speculations were embellished with gossip from servants in the Thornton household. It was declared, to the dismay of many young women undeterred by his loss of fortune, that Mr. Thornton had finally chosen a woman to marry—a Miss Hale from the south who had indeed lived in Milton less than two years and then left to live with relatives in London when both her parents died. She was away for nearly a year and Mr. Thornton had then gone to London and brought Miss Hale back, after her year of mourning, so they could marry in Milton.

As it turned out, the parson counseled John and Margaret to set their wedding date for two weeks hence at the earliest. This was welcome news to Mrs. Thornton who wanted to invite important local business people and friends. One never knew when such a gesture might be useful to John when it came time for him to reorganize his business. She requested Margaret to write her aunt to tell her that she was willing to take care of inviting Milton guests and to organize a dinner after the ceremony if Mrs. Shaw and Edith attended to certain details such as flowers, decoration and whatever wine and meats they could bring from London. She knew exactly what to do while her aunt, being from London, would not have any idea how such things were done in Milton. Besides, only a year ago, she had managed the preparations for Fanny's wedding.

Margaret was about to protest that she would prefer a small intimate ceremony with only family. But she doubted that Mrs. Thornton could be talked out of inviting John's business associates and having a proper celebration. Margaret held her objections in check and, instead, thanked her for her kindness. With no time for written invitations, Mrs. Thornton kept John and Margaret busy visiting his business associates and extending invitations in person. She herself went to see quite a few people on the guest list.

Mrs. Thornton was glad to have preparations for the wedding to occupy her time and focus her day. She felt increasingly alone. Margaret, respecting the time in the morning that mother and son had alone together, naturally fell into the habit of coming down when John and Mrs. Thornton had been at breakfast for some time. Mrs. Thornton was grateful but also keenly aware how Margaret, without any effort, commanded her son's attention the moment she came into the room. While anyone else might only see him smile tenderly at Margaret, Mrs. Thornton could feel his excitement and see the fire behind the sparkle in his eyes. She knew her son quite well, knew that John was impatient for the wedding to take place. It had been two years since he first proposed to Margaret—too long for him who acted without hesitation or delay once he made up his mind or knew what he desired.

After dinner on Margaret's second evening in Milton, Mrs. Thornton pleaded fatigue and left the couple in the drawing room. She had had a tiring day of visits to friends and food purveyors and, in any case, she thought she ought to give the young couple the time to be alone together.

John was indeed impatient to be alone with Margaret and as soon as his mother left the room, he got up and pulled Margaret up from her chair and into his arms. "All day, today, I have wanted to hold you in my arms but someone else was always around."

She gazed up at him with glistening eyes. With a smile, she snuggled in his arms and laid her head on his shoulders but he tenderly lifted her face up to his. "And I have wanted to do this as well." He pressed his lips lightly on hers.

Holding Margaret in his arms at that moment and kissing her—after months of hopeless longing—had an intoxicating effect on John and he began kissing her more deeply. He felt her tremble and go limp in his arms. She did not draw back, but placed her arms around his neck as if to support her flaccid body, and she responded with an artless ardor that thrilled him, that surprised him. She seemed neither afraid nor shy of her feelings. He kissed her more passionately until, breathless and trembling, she pulled back.

Taking his face in both her hands, she cried in a low quivering voice: "John!" She stared into his smoldering eyes and pleaded: "Stop, please."

He stared back at her as he steadied himself to regain his self-control. "I'm sorry, I was carried away."

She placed her fingers gently on his lips. "No don't be. I am not. I need to become accustomed to this; that is all." She caught

41

her breath and resumed, still a little breathlessly: "I was surprised at how strong my own feelings were and how they seemed to just rush out of me."

"I understand. I did not mean to rush you into this," he replied in a voice still somewhat tremulous from the struggle to rein himself in.

He led her to the sofa and sat down next to her, enfolding her in his arms as she leaned back against him. "I had only intended to hold you like this. I wanted to hold you so many times today for so many reasons, sometimes merely because you are here."

With voice a little steadier but barely above a whisper, he continued. "This is all new to me, too, although not in the same way it is to you. Only two days ago, I would never have imagined us together like this. Much farther in my mind was the thought that you could express your feelings as strongly as you just did."

Margaret blushed, embarrassed and glad that John could not see her face. "Is that all right?"

"All right? Oh, my love!" He could say no more as he held her closer.

At length, she spoke again, somewhat shyly. "I really never knew what to expect, what it means to love, only that I am happier than I have ever been when I am with you. And being with you"— she paused, searching for words—"well, I am learning new things about myself." She turned towards him, laid her head on his shoulders, laced her arms around his neck and murmured, a hint of wonder in her voice: "And about you, too."

He did not answer, merely held her closer, content to take pleasure in the warmth of her cheeks against his neck.

At length, Margaret sat up again and faced John. She had been curious about his trip to Helstone since that day at the train station when he told her that he had just come from there. She wanted to ascertain—out of her own vanity, she admitted to herself—if he went mainly on her account but she was also genuinely interested to know how he found Helstone.

"Did you go to Helstone because you had business there?" Margaret knew that to be implausible but she thought it as good a way as any to start her inquiry.

"Well, it is not inconceivable that the south could be an untapped source for investors. But no, I had a more selfish reason for going. When I found out about your brother, I had this restless desire to do something. At the very least, I wanted to understand you better, to know what it was that made you who you are. You had seen my world but I had not really seen yours. Maybe, I thought Helstone would tell me more about you and that in being there, I would learn how to make you love me."

She smiled broadly but could not resist the temptation to tease him. "Did you think it very dull?"

"No, not at all. It was as I had expected—green and lush, fresh, mild, and sunny. I came across many grassy paths that seemed inviting, saw wild flowers to pluck and smell, and big shady trees to loll under." He paused, frowning. "I heard birds chirping all the time but I did not see too many people walking about."

She remarked with a laugh: "In other words, it was tranquil and dull."

"Well, perhaps," he conceded. "But it is a charming place and there is beauty in that tranquility that cannot but draw you in. I can see why you were so attached to it."

"And I still am although coming to Milton did change what I thought of Helstone. I was happy there, in a certain fashion, I suppose. But I have found happiness here as well, more deeply felt, certainly, more satisfying."

It was his turn to smile broadly, and to tease her. "Then you will stay?"

She nodded, smiled beguilingly, and answered flippantly: "Do I really have a choice after my shameless behavior at the train station?" Then, she continued more seriously. "Helstone is not a perfect place. I went back once after returning to London and realized that I could not go back to the way it was when I lived there. I clearly saw during that visit that the seductive simplicity of life in Helstone also has a downside. I found it a problem that so many people there think only in terms of black and white or are happy to be ignorant and to keep those around them so."

"Those are not light indictments. And was it really living in Milton that brought on this change in how you see Helstone?"

"Life here is harsher, more complicated and requires more out of you. But such is life, I suppose. If you can live here and thrive, would that not be a greater accomplishment than thriving in a place like Helstone? Would you not be stronger in spirit?"

"You do need to make many comprises to live here and that is a complicated matter. Dealing with workers' strikes proves that every time. But this city and all others like it also attract countless vultures and opportunists interested only in becoming rich and staying that way, no matter the costs. To them, life is also just black and white."

"I am aware that I should not think of this place as having the virtues Helstone does not. And Milton lacks the beauty and serenity that can soothe tired and wounded spirits."

He grinned, teasing her once more. "You have me."

"Yes. I have you." She smiled radiantly, her eyes misty and shining as she nestled back in his arms.

IV. REMEMBRANCES

John lay awake remembering that evening, a delicious tingle coursing through his whole being. He could still feel Margaret in his arms, her hands warm on his cheeks, her mouth velvety and moist against his, and he could hear her voice tremulous with emotion. Every moment they had been together only convinced him more of Margaret's feelings for him and of how her love was, indeed, thoroughly his. He had needed that reassurance after nearly two years of uncertainty and hopelessness. He caught his breath as he recollected how ardently she responded to his kisses, if only for a few moments. He knew she would love faithfully, tenderly, deeply but he never imagined her expressing her feelings passionately.

He paced his room as he had done only a few nights ago when he had been despondent. This evening, he was restless with anticipation. He and Margaret must visit Nicholas Higgins. He, at least, owed Higgins gratitude for helping break down the barriers he had imposed on himself that kept him away from Margaret.

John could only guess the extent of Margaret's acquaintance with Higgins. He knew of her friendship with Higgins's hapless older daughter which he understood had been close. He recalled the day he first proposed to Margaret and the sorrow he saw in her eyes when she told him her friend Bessy was dying. Bitterly stung only moments before by her disclosure that she never liked him, he was incapable of seeing, much less of sympathizing, with her grief. Instead, angry and hurt, he had insolently retorted that, of course, she blamed him as well for her friend's plight. And yet, even in his bitterness, he could not resent her, much less hate her.

He thought her rejection should have cooled his passion but it had not. If anything, he came away from that encounter loving her more. Only later—after the many times he reflected on his unfortunate proposal—did he understand that she reacted precisely as her mind and heart dictated. He had expected her to accept and be grateful for his proposal. His mother had convinced him of it after Margaret intervened to protect him from the rioters. Any young woman, revealing her feelings in that manner, knew she was risking her reputation; at the same time, she was probably calculating that the risk was worth the proposal that was certain to follow, if the man were honorable.

But Margaret was unlike most other young women. Her independence of mind demanded that she be regarded and accepted not on society's terms but on her own. She made it clear that her actions at the riot had been misconstrued: She would have done what she did for any man. Assumptions that her reputation needed rescuing and that she would accept a proposal just because it came from a rich man offended her deeply. Margaret, unswayed by society's notions of what is desirable or advantageous for young women, would marry only for love. How, then, could he help loving her?

John winced at recalling her assertion that she did not like him. Yet, now that the wondrous unfolding of a life with her lay before him, it was only natural that he would excuse her in his mind as he never before had done.

The three years since they first met had wrought changes in both of them, changes prompted by losses that, for Margaret, were unfortunate and permanent. He was luckier. For him, the biggest change, in fact, was her arrival into his life. Though she brought him torment at first, now that she was back in his life to stay, he tingled all over imagining the days to come and the moments of bliss that he had had a glimpse of that very evening. Those three years had not been for naught. To the contrary, they have assured sweeter, more precious moments together.

On her third day at the Thornton house, John asked Margaret when they were alone at breakfast whether she would like to visit Nicholas Higgins and his family in the Princeton district. Margaret readily agreed, eager to renew her friendship with Nicholas Higgins and his daughter Mary and anxious to know how the Boucher children were doing. After the children's parents died, she had taken greater pains to help them, bringing food and teaching them to read. It gratified her that six-year old Thomas had taken the lessons seriously, reading everything in sight and devoting hours to the books she gave him.

John and Margaret went in the afternoon on their way to the park. They brought a big basket of bread, cheese, meats and fruit for the children. Remembering the desolate poverty he had seen when he first visited Nicholas to offer him a job, John requested Williams to order loaves of bread and cheese for families of his former workers who lived in the area. Mrs. Thornton sneered at the gesture as her son's misguided generosity, without a doubt, influenced by Margaret. On being told about it, she gritted her teeth and walled away without a word. Margaret privately rejoiced at John's act of kindness. Her mother had many times been a recipient of it when he sent her baskets of the freshest fruit when she was ill.

The walk that John had taken through the district the day he offered Nicholas Higgins work had shown him something he had not dared look closely at before. He saw what Margaret saw—the hunger, the quiet despair written even on the faces of children who, at least, did not yet recoil from a little act of kindness nor withdraw, hopeless and resentful, as the adults had. He would always remember those faces, not only of children on the street but also of Boucher's children. He began to appreciate what he had initially thought of as Margaret's misplaced charity. Still, he disagreed with her reasoning. The charity was not a question of logic, as she claimed, but better yet, of humanity. Might she have appealed to logic because she thought he would not have responded to an argument for the necessity of being humane? Once again, he resolved to show her that his views about those less fortunate had indeed undergone, was still undergoing a change.

For a few moments, Nicholas stared speechless at John and Margaret, standing on his doorstep. His eyes grew bright and moist at seeing them—happier, more at peace than he had ever seen them and smiling warmly at him. Mary had stopped what she was doing when she heard the knock and ran towards the door when she saw Margaret almost colliding into her.

Margaret held out her arms to prevent Mary from falling before embracing her fondly. "You look well Mary."

Mary put her arms around Margaret and cried: "Oh, miss.........!" Mary, who had never been one for words, could not say anymore. She retreated, placing her hands on her face, ashamed of how she reacted.

"Miss Hale, you bring tears to my eyes!" Nicholas blurted out finally, a big grin lighting up his face. He glanced at John who smiled broadly back at him. "Come in, come in, master. Miss Hale, I knew you would never forget a friend." He swiftly swiped his eyes with the back of his hand.

Margaret reached out and grasped his hand with both of hers and held it for a long moment—a moment of memories rushing back to darken her eyes with sadness. "It has been sometime, has it not?"

"Yes, but not too long," he replied, too happy with the unexpected visit to see her sadness. He inclined his head slightly towards John, then handing Mary the basket he was carrying. "And I did not believe what master here said that we will never see you again."

John approached them with a wide grin and shook Nicholas's hand vigorously. His eyes brimmed with gratitude that Nicholas acknowledged wordlessly, nodding and grinning as widely.

"I am heartily glad that I was wrong," John said, glancing tenderly at Margaret.

Margaret turned to Nicholas. "How have you been Nicholas? How are the children?"

"We are doing as well as can be expected but I feel I am too old to deal with six young children."

"Can we help?"

"The mills did not want to hire me at first but Hamper reluctantly gave me work because they were short on men of my skills and orders were coming in that used to go to Marlborough Mills." He glanced at John before adding. "So I can put food on the table but it has not been easy with the little ones often missing and asking for their mother."

"I am so sorry." Margaret commiserated. "It is hard to lose parents, unspeakably so when children are this young."

"Yes but there is nothing anyone can do about it." He shrugged, uncomfortable about the attention on his troubles. In a lighter tone, he shifted the conversation. "You two are a sight for sore eyes."

John smiled gratefully at Nicholas once again. "I want you and Mary to come to our wedding. You helped make this all possible and we will forever remember it."

Nicholas frowned. "I am happy that I helped but how did I do that?"

"Do you recall the day the mill closed when you told me about Margaret's brother?"

"Why yes. I saw clearly how you felt about Miss Margaret but I could tell something was bothering you and making you miserable. I suspected it was all that malicious gossip about Miss Hale and that mysterious man."

"Well, that was it," John answered a little self-consciously. The direct rather simple manner with which Nicholas recalled that encounter and his astuteness at having seen through him at the time made John feel how foolish his jealousy had been. "And here we both are," he added, putting his arm around Margaret's shoulders and gazing at her for a long intimate moment.

Nicholas shifted his eyes from one to the other with a mixture of some discomfort at their frank display of affection and a feeling of satisfaction at his role in bringing the union of two people he liked and admired. "Miss Margaret never let on how she felt but it was clear to me that she admired you. Why, she sided with you many times, instead of me, about the strike!"

John threw Margaret a surprised glance. She laughed, a little embarrassed. "Oh, Nicholas! Nothing escaped you, it seems."

"It is not often I see two people who seemed made for each other but who could not come together even when they are miserable without the other. I thought I would help matters along." He grinned mischievously and with obvious self-satisfaction.

"You have been a real friend to both of us. Say you will come," Margaret implored.

Nicholas was a bit dismayed. He wanted to go but how could he? Margaret understood the many reasons he hesitated and thought that she had the solution to one. "You are about my father's size. I still have a few of his things and I am sure we will find one that is suitable and could be altered to fit. As for Mary, I have just the thing."

Mary had been preparing a pot of tea and she approached with two cups that she handed John and Margaret. "Will you sit Miss?" Mary asked pulling a chair closer to Margaret.

"Thank you, Mary. Will you come to Marlborough Mills? I want to give you a dress to wear to my wedding."

Mary smiled shyly and looked at her father. Nicholas still seemed hesitant and Margaret declared firmly: "We will not take no for an answer, Nicholas."

He regarded her for a minute or two, then looked at his daughter's hopeful eyes. He grinned mischievously. "How can anyone say "no" to Miss Margaret? We will come as friends happy to watch you two get united but I will admit I also want to provoke other mill owners."

John laughed. "Well, that would be nothing new, just another aggravation from the union firebrand. I'm afraid I might be gaining a troublesome reputation myself. I had apparently committed a transgression in their minds when we started the dining hall. I believe they thought I had betrayed them."

The hill park John and Margaret went to for a walk was not far from the Higgins home and was familiar to Margaret. She had frequented it when she lived in Crampton. As soon as they reached it, John said: "Tell me more about Frederick. Higgins could not tell me much about him. Where has he settled in Spain?"

"Cadiz, in the south. He's married now, has a good job, and appears to have settled there for good." She proceeded to relate the particulars of Frederick's joining the Navy, the alleged mutiny and the flight to Spain. "Henry—Mr. Lennox—started some legal process so Fred could at least visit England but, at the moment, it does not seem very hopeful. There is still a warrant and a reward out for the capture of the alleged mutineers and since Fred was branded their leader, he remains in the greatest danger. I'm afraid Fred may never set foot here again."

Margaret paused, her eyes pensive and sad. They walked in silence for some time. After a while, she said little more cheerfully: "Fred is quite happy in Spain, smitten with his beautiful Spanish wife, and is sounding more and more in his letters like a proud Spaniard. He's even converted to his wife's religion."

"That's wonderful!" John remarked brightly, wishing to lift Margaret out of her sadness and lingering concern for her brother. "That man who fell at the train station and died later, was he from Helstone?"

"He was from a small neighboring village where Dixon comes from."

"Did he recognize Frederick?"

"He must have. Fred was barely a young man when he left. I doubt he was ever acquainted with that man. Dixon knew him well, saw him grow up to be a troublesome drunk who would have done anything for money."

John nodded and said no more. They continued on their walk along a path Margaret had favored in previous walks, sometimes stopping to look down at the city, straining to see it through the haze. She called his attention to small patches of wildflowers that her eager eye was constantly searching for. They talked little, mostly about what they saw on their walk. As they returned to the city. John asked: "How about visiting your brother in Cadiz? I know it will make you happy to see him and I cannot wait to make his acquaintance."

"Is that possible? Can we really go just like that?" Margaret stopped, her eyes, lustrous and wide with joy and incredulity.

"Yes, of course." He smiled at her childlike delight. "I have a few business connections that would help with reservations and accommodations, even last-minute ones."

"When will we go? I must write Fred."

"We can spend one week in Paris on our honeymoon. From there, we go on a train to Marseilles and sail to Cadiz. Write him to expect us about a month from now. I am impatient to meet this dashing brother of yours."

"That soon? I can hardly believe it! I had dreamed of going since Edith told me that Mr. Bell had talked about taking me to Spain before he fell ill. I never ever imagined that it is you I will be going with."

John scowled, flabbergasted. "Mr. Bell!" He had liked the old academic before he met Margaret but afterwards, his habit of provoking discord proved rather irksome. John suspected that he tried to stir Margaret away from him.

Margaret, somewhat perplexed by his reaction, looked at him quizzically. But John turned his face away and said: "It will do me good to get away from Milton for a while, particularly to a very different city. When I visited Helstone, I realized that a new place gives you a fresh perspective on things."

As they were nearing home, she said: "Will you allow me now to thank you for having prevented an inquest into the death of the man who accosted Fred at the train station?"

They were on the sidewalk of a busy commercial street but he stopped to plant a quick kiss on her lips and with a smile that lighted up his whole face, he replied: "You can thank me. All your life, if you wish. And, yes, I thought of you as I made inquiries and deliberated over the case."

While John and Margaret were at the Higgins home, Fanny visited her mother in a huff. "Is Miss Hale here? There is gossip all over town that John must now marry her. I told you she had designs on him all along."

"Fanny," her mother replied indulgently. "You know nothing. Your brother was bound in honor to make an offer to Miss Hale after the riot but she rejected him. Too proud, I imagine, and too much the southern lady to know her heart. But it seems that, despite everything, they have now reached an understanding."

"So, she is here! Where is she? What of that man at the train station? John should not feel obligated after she was seen with him."

"Gossip. We need not concern ourselves about it."

"Merely gossip! Are you saying there was no man? She was there at the station, she was seen."

"No, I did not say any of that." Mrs. Thornton was at a loss how to explain but she had made a promise to John not to say anything about Margaret's brother. She continued irritably. "How should I know? John assured me she was not involved with a man at the station and I believe him."

"Well, we know John never lies to you," Fanny smirked.

"Miss Hale would not have been my choice for your brother but I cannot deny that he is happy with her and something is different about him."

"Different? Is that in a good or bad way?"

Mrs. Thornton knotted her eyebrows, trying to hold on to a thought that still remained elusive. "I myself will reluctantly admit her return has done him a lot of good. He is relaxed, even looks years younger. For that, I can overlook anything."

"I cannot say that I am happy to have her for a sister. I shall never like her."

"I am sure that I will never understand her," Mrs. Thornton sighed.

"Well, one big problem at least is solved. Johnny's financial troubles are over and I need not pester Watson anymore about lending him some money."

"Miss Hale owns the mill and this house but the bank still has to be paid."

"Her inheritance should easily handle that, Watson told me. Did you know Mr. Bell invested a bundle on Watson's speculation and she is very rich?"

Mrs. Thornton, surprised, stared at her daughter. "No, I did not know that. John has said nothing about it. I knew she would live well from the inheritance she received from Mr. Bell. But rich? Are you sure Fanny?"

"Watson said Mr. Bell was a very shrewd investor, bought many shares that became part of the inheritance. He also said profit on the shares alone makes Miss Hale quite rich but she also owns other valuable properties. Perhaps, Johnny knew and proposed again for that reason. Just as well, I am sure. Anne Latimer would not have him after his financial collapse."

Mrs. Thornton glared irritably at her daughter. "Your brother did not have a financial collapse. He lost the mill and we would have had to give up this house but he had put aside enough for us to live on not only respectably but also comfortably. He would have regained what he lost and acquired another mill in due time, I am certain of it."

Fanny shrugged her shoulders, bored with talk of her brother's business affairs, and began to chatter about what most interested her. "Do you suppose Miss Hale will come to my house? She has recently lived in London so she can probably tell me about the latest fashion."

Mrs. Thornton's thoughts were engaged in something of greater consequence than Fanny's house. She was forming a resolve to be nicer to Margaret. She knew that a rich woman without much beauty would have attracted many men. If that woman was also beautiful—as Margaret was in an uncommonly appealing way—she would be a priceless catch. If on top of all that, she exuded the natural grace of good breeding which Mrs. Thornton begrudgingly conceded Margaret did, men from the best families, even those with titles, would be vying for her favor.

Yet, Margaret had chosen John over the many other men in London who probably swarmed around her after she came into a large fortune. Mrs. Thornton thought no other young man equal to her son so Margaret's choice did not surprise her; in fact, it showed her good judgment. She had to admit that Margaret must truly care for her son. Still, though it reassured her to have this further proof. Mrs. Thornton continued to have apprehensions about Margaret, a Southerner whose ideas and attitudes she distrusted. But out of a sense of fairness, she felt gratitude to Margaret for loving John and admiration for possessing the strong mind and will to go after what she desired rather than what she was merely offered.

"Did you know Margaret made a fortune from Watson's speculative venture?" Mrs. Thornton asked John at breakfast the next morning.

"No, mother, I did not. We have never talked about those things. I am marrying Margaret for no other reason than I love her. If she was Margaret Hale from Crampton, I would still marry her." John could not hide his irritation and before his mother could answer, he added: "By the way, I have invited Nicholas Higgins and his daughter to our wedding."

Mrs. Thornton started to protest but this time, she stopped herself, mollified by what she had lately learned about Margaret's wealth. She sighed as she realized that being agreeable to Margaret was not going to be easy.

V. READJUSTMENTS

Three days after Margaret posted her letters, Dixon arrived with most of her possessions. Among these were Mrs. Hale's bridal gown which she decided to wear on her wedding and an heirloom comb with which she intended to secure her veil in place. The comb first belonged to a grandmother several generations back. When a daughter was not born, it was passed on to the first-born son to be presented to his oldest daughter on her sixteenth birthday. On Edith's suggestion, Dixon bundled the gown with yards of white Spanish lace that Frederick gave his mother and his sister when he came to Milton. Edith knew Margaret's reason for wanting to wear items from her parents and thought she would agree that something from her brother would complete the sense of having her immediate family celebrating with her on that important day. Edith gave Dixon detailed instructions on fashioning the lace into a bridal veil and using some of it to let out the bridal gown for Margaret who was taller and shapelier than her mother.

As they were unpacking, Dixon said: "I cannot say I was surprised, Miss, about you and Mr. Thornton although everyone else at Harley Street was."

Margaret looked up from the trunk she was rummaging through and regarded Dixon with amused curiosity. "Oh? Why not? I never said anything to anyone about what passed between Mr. Thornton and me."

"No, Miss, but I always thought there was a spark in your eyes when he was around. Like that I saw in your mother when Mr. Hale was courting her," Dixon replied timidly, sensitive to signs that Margaret was annoyed or thought her impertinent for offering her opinion.

With Margaret about to become the mistress of her own household and wife of a man with some prominence in his trade, Dixon felt she had to show more deference if she wanted to remain the young Mrs. Thornton's personal maid. Mrs. Hale had always been kind, sweet-tempered, and receptive to her counsel through her silent suffering as the pastor's wife. But Margaret had always had an imperious streak which Dixon had smarted from when the child could not be persuaded to comply with what she was asked to do. As a young woman, Margaret kept her own counsel and Dixon stayed noncommittal, offering her opinions only in the rare instance when Mrs. Hale might object to Margaret's judgment.

When Margaret responded merely with an amused half-smile, Dixon added: "And Mr. Thornton was always staring at you in that intense way he has."

"When did you notice all this, Dixon?" Margaret's curiosity was turning into incredulity.

"I think since the evening Mr. Thornton came to tea and you worked so hard ironing curtains, Miss. I thought you wanted to make a good impression on him."

"That early? You must have known me then better than I knew myself," Margaret replied wryly.

Dixon regarded her for a long moment. Then, she smiled eloquently. "I was there when you were born and saw you grow up. I am familiar with your moods, the varied expressions in your eyes and your mouth, the spark in your eyes when something excited you or made you happy. I knew Mr. Lennox had feelings for you, too, but he never had you agitated the way Mr. Thornton did. No, unfortunately for him, that spark was never there."

Margaret smiled at Dixon with a wistful sadness. "Oh Dixon, how sweet you are! You are the only one with me now who has been around ever since I can remember."

With that simple declaration, they sat together in silence; bound by a past rich with shared meanings. Margaret thought it was something to be grateful for that she had someone so intimately acquainted with her history that explanations between them became unnecessary. It did not matter that Dixon was not of her flesh and blood.

Some minutes later, Margaret reached out and touched Dixon's hand. "We have quite a bit more to go through in those trunks, I'm afraid."

When they had finished unpacking, Margaret placed a hand on Dixon's arm. "Please sit down, Dixon. There is something I would like to talk to you about."

Dixon sat down, apprehensive at the gravity in Margaret's voice. She dared not speak and waited for what Margaret had to say.

"Dixon, I am aware that you never really liked Milton. I would not want to force you to stay with me if you think you will be unhappy here. Would you rather return to Helstone and be with your family? Or perhaps since you seemed to like London, Edith or my aunt might find a place for you in their household. In either case, I am now quite capable of providing a lifelong allowance that would make you quite comfortable and free from anybody else's charity. You could choose not to work for anyone anymore."

Dixon was dumbfounded and with a quivering voice, she asked: "Would you prefer that I go, Miss?"

"Were I the one who decides, I would say no, Dixon. Until you arrived, I felt as if John was the only one who wanted me here and it was only with him that I really relax. So, I very much appreciate your familiar presence. But you served my parents most of your adult life and since I have the means, you are free to take advantage of it to live your life as you choose. If you should wish to leave Milton where most of your memories were sad, I can understand and respect that."

Dixon bowed her head to hide the tears welling up in her eyes. She could not speak until a few minutes later when she had composed herself and could answer in a low, solemn voice: "I would rather stay with you Miss. Most of the life I have known is with the Hales and, truth be told, it is not so bad in Milton, with you here. And I do like Mr. Thornton who had been most kind to my poor mistress, your mother." She paused, hesitating. "But I confess this house gives me the chills. It is so stony and big. I cannot imagine you in it." Then, she smiled. "So, you see, you need me here."

"Are you sure this is what you want? I assure you, you will have more than enough to live on." With a teasing smile, Margaret added: "And you would no longer need to wake up too early in the morning and cater to someone else's needs and whims. You can do what you want any time you want."

"I know no other life, Miss. What will I do back in Helstone with my grasping relatives? You mean more to me than any of them."

Margaret regarded Dixon with glistening eyes. "Thank you. I am grateful and actually rather relieved to have you stay. We shall endure this place together and, with time, I hope that we both become less intimidated with it and learn to be content. But I want you to know that if you ever decide to be released from doing service, tell me so as my offer of an allowance is a permanent one and you shall have it, in any case, as soon as Henry sends me the legal papers. It is an amount on top of whatever wages you earn from continuing to work."

Margaret could now make her room a little more her own by filling it with her personal possessions—the books she treasured, some linens her mother had embroidered and a few other treasured family heirlooms. Dixon helped her arrange them in the room in a manner as similar as was possible to what they had been accustomed in Helstone. They piled often-read books on the writing desk, adorned the mantelpiece with a couple of antique chests and candelabras, draped her mother's linens on the back of chairs, and placed vases for flowers on tables. With these familiar items from her past and curtains now permanently drawn to the sides so that light streamed in through much of the day, the room felt less forbidding and asserted the presence of a vibrant occupant who lived day-to-day with things that she needed or that amused her. These small changes made the strangeness of her new home a little more bearable and, in her room at least, Margaret could do as she pleased in more familiar comfort.

Dixon immediately began working on alterations to the bridal dress, worn for the first time by the young Miss Beresford when she married the handsome and educated but penniless Mr. Hale. Mrs. Lennox's instructions had been very specific and because Dixon needed to lay the dress out on a large surface and occasionally check how well it fitted, Margaret decided it best for Dixon to work in her bedroom. There, she could also help with the sewing.

Altering the bridal gown gave Dixon time to adjust slowly to this new household which she found stranger than Margaret did. While catering only to her mistress's needs, she could observe the workings of the household and find some way of becoming a part of it with the least pain and aggravation. Mrs. Thornton was as different as fire and water from the kind and refined Mrs. Hale who spoke gently and often left many decisions about housekeeping to her. The formidable Mrs. Thornton held full control of her household and the servants were all careful not to incur her displeasure. They allowed, however, that she was always fair, never took anyone to task unless they were really amiss in their duties, and was known to have been generous when one of them was in serious need. She ran a tight, tidy household that tolerated neither a speck of dust nor tardy dinners. Dixon, still afflicted with the snobbishness of one who thought herself a lady's maid, doubted her capacity to fit well into a household she thought was run without grace, natural ease, or unstudied refinement.

Dixon could not imagine Margaret as the mistress of this big house, assuming its management in a cold, efficient manner. In her mind, her young mistress was as unlike the massive grey surroundings as one could be and would reject the formality and regimentation its current mistress imposed. "Well, it is Mrs. Margaret I serve and I would do it the best way I know how!"

John began to spend a little more time planning and working on reopening the mill. He resumed going to the club where he and his colleagues in the cotton manufacturing business met to socialize and hold meetings, discuss business, and resolve their common problems. At the first such meeting he attended since Marlborough Mills closed down, he announced he was getting married on the Sunday after the coming one.

"I know this marriage is news to you and this invitation is rather sudden and informal and not the usual way these things are done but we do not have the luxury for formalities. So please forgive me and tell me at the meeting next week if you can come. This invitation is for all of you and your wives, of course."

The news was naturally a surprise to his colleagues but not for too long. Many of them had guessed that the elusive Mr. Thornton might finally marry to recoup his financial losses and someone asked: "Is it the Latimer girl?" All his colleagues knew he had escorted Miss Latimer a few times and her inheritance was rumored to be rather sizable. She was thus the perfect answer out of his financial predicament. That she was also very pretty and the product of a finishing school might have been too tempting even for Mr. Thornton to resist. Most of them had not heard the more recent gossip about him escorting a relatively unknown young woman who was not from Milton and who was, in fact, staying in his house.

Before John could reply, Hamper volunteered: "I think it must be that parson's daughter, that handsome young woman from the south, Miss Hale."

Exclamations of disbelief greeted this declaration. Them remembered Miss Hale as the young woman who, at the Thornton's last dinner party, spoke with self-assurance about her sympathies for workers. At first, they thought her beautiful with the natural grace of a lady but the radical views she frankly asserted turned them off. Her charms were forgotten and she became just someone poor who was too independent-minded for her own good. Everyone, therefore, thought that if Hamper was right, then John Thornton had to be out of his mind, marrying imprudently for a more uncertain future.

Although John was annoyed that Hamper preempted his response, he continued as if he had not been interrupted: "I know you're all quite curious who I have been lucky enough to persuade to be my wife. You have all met her—Margaret Hale."

Hamper smiled triumphantly and was the first to congratulate John. The others stared at him, then at one another but quickly recovered from the surprise and followed Hamper in expressing their congratulations, most of which John knew were insincere. They were dubious about his choice and were convinced that, finally, John Thornton had made a serious mistake and proved that a paragon of a businessman could sometimes be stupid.

John could not control the urge to continue the provocation of his colleagues. "I am sorry but I must leave now. Margaret is at home with my mother and I promised to accompany her on her daily walk."

He could hear the buzz of sneering comments and speculations as he was walking out of the room. He could almost hear the gossip that would ensue when these men went home to tell their wives about foolish John Thornton. It did not matter to him.

In fact, he was realizing that he had begun to look at many things in a different way ever since Mr. Hale introduced his daughter Margaret.

At home, John found his mother, embroidering with Jane in the drawing room.

"Where is Margaret, Mother?"

"How should I know? I have not seen much of her since that servant of hers arrived. She seems to be spending a lot of time with Dixon in her room."

John replied evenly: "They were unpacking this morning. They must still be arranging Margaret's belongings." He hurried out of the room.

In the bedroom, Dixon and Margaret were quietly working on the wedding dress; Dixon was adjusting the hem and Margaret sewing one on the lace that was to be her bridal veil. Dixon was about to rise when she heard the knock on the door when Margaret stopped her.

"It's all right, Dixon, continue your sewing. It's John. We're going out for a walk." Margaret rose to open the door but John had already opened it and entered.

John immediately noticed the changes that Margaret had made in the room. With small touches, Margaret breathed life into what was, before, a cold large space and arranged it to her tastes for both gracious living and reflective pursuits just as the Hales had done in Crampton.

Dixon, sat on a chair by the bed, working on what John assumed was Margaret's bridal gown. She abruptly stood up when he came in. "Good afternoon, master."

"Good afternoon, Dixon. Please continue what you are doing. I hope you won't mind that I am taking your helper away for a little while." He turned towards Margaret who was carefully folding the lace she was working on.

She smiled brightly at him as she approached. "I am ready." She picked up a shawl hanging on the back of an armchair and draped it on her shoulders.

John stood by the writing table as he waited for her and, unable to resist his curiosity, he briefly opened a small chest on top of the table. He was not surprised that his quick perusal told him it was full of notes in other languages as well as English written in a feminine hand.

Margaret reached his side as he was closing the lid on the chest. She passed her fingers over it with obvious nostalgic affection. "It belonged to my mother, a family heirloom that was one of the few things saved from the pawn shop when her parents lost what little fortune they had. The piece is of Chinese origin, more than 200 years old and the design is a cloisonné."

"It is beautiful!" John was astonished at how like a caress her touch was on the chest. She clearly treasured it. If it had belonged to his mother, it would be untouched, displayed under one of her glass domes. John traced the path of Margaret's fingers over the chest with his own.

"It had always belonged to the youngest daughter in the family and was used as a jewelry box, if you had jewelry, of course. Mama kept the letters from her courtship in it."

He led her out of the room and closed the door behind him noiselessly. He pulled her close and planted a quick kiss on her lips. "They did not look like love letters to me."

"No. Except for one, my father burned those before he left for Oxford and that letter was buried with him. I'm afraid the chest now contains something mundane in comparison, notes on my reading or passages translated into French or Italian."

It was nearly evening when they returned. In the drawing room, they found Mrs. Thornton still busy embroidering linens. Jane was there, too, helping her.

Margaret picked up one that was finished. "What exquisite work. My hands have never been steady enough for such beautiful flourish."

She regarded Mrs. Thornton curiously and thought that she would never have suspected this stern woman, whose somber tastes in adorning her home were in keeping with her image, to have chosen such delicate and intricate motifs and do such fine embroidery.

She looked at what Mrs. Thornton was working on but shifted her attention abruptly to the pile on Jane's lap. She saw then that the maid had been very carefully cutting out the letter "H" from the initials "H.T." on every napkin and Mrs. Thornton had been replacing it with "M."

Margaret was appalled and she protested with a vehemence that surprised the other three. "Oh, no! Please. You do not need to change the initials on these linens. It's a shame to destroy the beautiful work you have already done. I do not need to have my initials on them."

Mrs. Thornton replied, annoyed. "Of course, you do, as mistress of the house. Perhaps, you would rather replace them with new ones. These are perfectly fine, made of the best material you can find."

"No! What I meant was there is no need for new linens nor for changing these to my initials."

Mrs. Thornton continued a little more kindly: "Well we have started and some, you can see, are already finished."

"Yes, of course, but perhaps you can leave the others alone as they are."

"I never do anything halfway, Miss Hale." Mrs. Thornton retorted superciliously.

"No, of course not. Still, you have been mistress of this household for a long time and your monogrammed linens would be like a wonderful legacy to us." Margaret tried once more, helplessly.

"As you wish," Mrs. Thornton replied coldly. She put down the piece she had been working on and rose as majestically as she could. "Anyway, I am tired and would like to rest before dinner." Turning to Jane, she motioned for the work to be taken away and left the room.

Margaret, dismayed, turned to John. He had been silent, judging it best not to interfere. He knew there would be more such confrontations in the future. She said a little mournfully: "I'm afraid I did not handle that well."

John took both her hands in his. "You held your own. She is not used to that."

"I could not quite tell her that I do not define my status as your wife with monogrammed linens. I think it would have caused offense that was not intended."

He pressed one hand and then the other to his lips. "It might have. Anyway, it will naturally take time to get used to each other and compromises are probably inevitable."

"I know that. But I do believe that she is irreplaceable as mistress of this house. I could never run it as she does."

"No, perhaps not. In any case, I believe my mother is aware that, as my wife, your decisions in this household will take precedence over anyone else's including hers. For her, that idea will take getting used to."

"But I don't want her to feel she has been displaced."

John, feeling her distress, gathered her in his arms. "Sadly, that may be unavoidable. I wish I could tell you what to do, but I am as much at a loss as you are."

In her room that night, Margaret sat staring at the fire, chafing at Mrs. Thornton's indifference and occasional hostility. She realized, painfully, that in marrying John, she was exchanging a day-to-day life of habitual ease and the implicit regard of relatives for one of cold civility in what was to be her permanent home.

Margaret did not doubt that life with John would be full enough to compensate for the discomfort of living with his mother. Still, her apprehensions refused to be quelled. She closed her eyes tight to hold back tears and bit her upper lip until it hurt. She thought herself at peace, reconciled with the passing of so many close to her. But this evening, grief had blindsided her again. Was it because Milton still sometimes seemed strange and her future life there held many unknowns? Did Mrs. Thornton's chilliness make her long for what she could not have—the immediate presence of her understanding father, the loving reassurance of her mother or even the cool rationality of Mr. Bell? She knew only this: She felt acutely alone, lost in the wide dark space of the bedroom.

She was barely nine the first time she felt this lost. She had cried herself to sleep then. But it did not take long for her to find solace in the affectionate nature of her aunt so like her mother in many ways, in the sympathy and patience of the wise governess who let her cry but stayed close by until she fell asleep, and in Edith's offering of toys, bonbons and frequent hugs. There was no one now wiser or affectionate to give her counsel or support.

There was only Dixon. Loyal, reliable Dixon—who could be trusted with the deepest secrets—had grown as solicitous and protective of her as she had been of Mrs. Hale. Dixon had shifted her full allegiance to her. A week away from being mistress of her own household, Margaret wondered how much she, herself, could open up to someone society considered below her station but who she had come to regard with affection?

VI. RAPPORT AND ROMANCE

Margaret's London relations descended on the Thorntons in the afternoon two days before the wedding. Mrs. Thornton heard the carriage enter the courtyard and watched from the window as the party descended. John and Margaret, unaware that they intended to arrive that day, were out for a walk so Mrs. Thornton was alone to receive them. She was acquainted only with Mrs. Shaw, who she first met on the day Margaret said her "goodbyes" after her father died. The London party was shown to the drawing room and Mrs. Shaw accordingly introduced everyone.

"My daughter Edith—she and Margaret grew up together and are like sisters."

Edith gave Mrs. Thornton a slight bow and a polite smile which the latter responded to in a similar fashion, quickly summing Edith up and dismissing any further interest in her—classic English beauty, refined like Margaret, but spoiled and used to having her way.

"Her husband, Captain Lennox. He will stand in for Frederick. You must know about Margaret's older brother who, unfortunately, cannot come or he would have given Margaret away."

Mrs. Thornton bowed again and smiled. She thought the captain handsomer than any man ought to be, with the air of indolence and indulgence typical of a London gentleman, a perfect match for his wife and, like her, was not an object of further interest to Mrs. Thornton.

"And this is Mr. Henry Lennox, the Captain's older brother, practically part of the family. We welcome him nearly everyday for breakfast or dinner at our home in London. He has been a friend to my girls for many years, but particularly to Margaret. He is a lawyer and since Margaret inherited Mr. Bell's fortune, he has also been her legal adviser and financial consultant."

Mrs. Thornton acknowledged Henry in much the same manner but regarded him curiously. She saw intelligence, cunning and ambition in his alert eyes and wondered why he had not sought Margaret for himself. Then, she thought that perhaps he did but her acute maternal bias could not imagine Margaret preferring him over John.

In fact, Henry thought it in his best interest to bury his disappointment and regret at losing Margaret and, instead, preserve the friendship and business relationship he had with her. A practical and unsentimental man, he did not suffer that loss quite as deeply nor as lengthily as John Thornton did when Margaret had rejected his proposal. So, when offered an invitation to the wedding, Henry accepted with only a few moments hesitation. He decided it wiser to make an effort to befriend Mr. Thornton, maybe even persuade him to be a client. From what he knew of Mr. Thornton, Henry was unwilling to risk resenting him or, worse, making him an enemy.

Mrs. Shaw named the two other women with them—her personal maid Anne, a spinster way past forty, modestly dressed, ladylike and very dignified; and Rose, genial nursemaid to Edith's son, not much above thirty, plump, her smile perpetually turning up the corners of her mouth.

Mrs. Thornton was uncomfortable during the meeting, uncertain about how to deal with Londoners with fashionable airs she privately scoffed at. She assumed a more formal manner than usual, distancing her young guests who, after being introduced to her, returned the compliment of her indifference by finding nothing more to say to her for the rest of the visit. Despite her aloofness, Mrs. Thornton was observant of proper decorum and desirous to show that northern hospitality was at least equal to that in London society. In as gracious a manner as she could manage, she offered to put the party up at her house.

"We have room for all of you." She proclaimed by way of concluding her offer, her eyes sweeping across all her guests including the two maids.

Mrs. Shaw politely declined. "How very kind of you but we have already reserved rooms at one of the hotels."

Mrs. Thornton needed no further excuse and did not press the offer, actually quite relieved that her visitors declined. Underneath her graciousness, she was uneasy about hardly knowing anything of courtesies accepted in London. She and her servants would have been constantly anxious attending to the London party. But Mrs. Thornton had a natural sense of what she owed her guests, wherever they were from, and that sense required further satisfaction. "Can I at least offer you some tea?"

Mrs. Shaw gently but firmly declined again. "How very nice but thank you. Since we are engaged here for dinner tomorrow and very tired from the ride, we should go to our hotel and rest. There is so much to do tomorrow."

Edith added: "Sholto is getting restless. I must spend time with him. He will be with the nursemaid and I won't see much of him during our stay here."

"Yes, there is the baby," Mrs. Shaw reiterated, then beckoned Anne to approach. "But I did want to offer help to you through my maid, Anne. She has been with me a long time and very ably managed Edith's wedding. She would be of valuable help to Margaret as she gets dressed on her wedding day."

Mrs. Thornton stared at Mrs. Shaw, uncertain whether to be thankful or offended.

Mrs. Shaw saw her hesitation. "Mrs. Thornton, Margaret is like a daughter to me. With her mother gone, we should have taken on the entire preparation for her wedding but because she preferred to have it here, we had to impose on your kindness instead. So please allow me to offer as much help as I can now. It would lessen my guilty conscience about not having done enough."

Mrs. Thornton listened patiently, still unconvinced. "Dixon would probably be thankful for her help."

"Indeed! They know each other and have worked together."

"Leave her here then. We should easily find some room for her in the maids' quarters."

Offering Anne to assist in wedding preparations was not the only reason the London party made Marlborough Mills their first stop. During their visit, their footman directed the unloading from the carriage of boxes of wine, meats, and cheeses for the wedding dinner and an even greater number of boxes carefully packed with roses, ribbons, and garlands of leaves with which to decorate the church, the dining table, and the carriage that would take Margaret to church.

Edith had insisted on the decorations through her mother's lame protests and her husband's breezy ridicule of feminine frivolities. Edith wanted to surprise her cousin with a touch that she knew would delight her. Margaret had been tireless in the preparations for Edith's wedding, had protected her zealously from unwanted social intrusions that came inevitably when her marriage was announced, and Edith wanted to reciprocate. Besides, Edith thought, Milton sounded so grim that it needed something bright and "a la mode" from the southern region.

The day before the wedding was frantic with preparations. Edith was at the church directing and occasionally helping Rose and two of the Thornton maids put up decorations. She had also dragged along Captain Lennox who protested the indignity to his manhood of draping ribbons on church pews but his wife prevailed with gentle threats and pleas of how they needed a man to do a very few difficult tasks. The Thornton household was busy cooking, polishing silver, cleaning and putting the house in order to Mrs. Thornton's spotless specifications. Margaret was spared from the frenzy and joined Mrs. Shaw at the hotel for a relatively restful day playing with Sholto.

In the evening, they all gathered for dinner at the Thornton house. Margaret was reunited with her cousin for the first time since she left London. They sat together in a quiet corner of the room for the first quarter hour of the evening, sharing news and exchanging other confidences, most of which were about the same things Margaret had already told Edith in her letters.

As the night wore on, Edith kept a discreet eye on Margaret, anxious to reassure herself that her cousin was happy. John Thornton was rather handsome, she thought, although a bit formidable in his intensity. Still, she suspected he was probably a better match for Margaret's intrepid disposition than Henry who, though witty and sophisticated, was probably too dispassionate and—Edith searched for the right word—lawyerly. She was also pleased that John seemed to take an extra effort to seek her out and talk to her.

Margaret had earlier given John a brief account of her London relatives so he knew Edith and Margaret had spent much of their youth together and were as close as sisters could be. Margaret also told him that Edith was marvelously proficient at the piano and one way to win her favor was to ask her to play. John thought it a great idea that would add an entertaining element that past Thornton parties never had.

He approached Edith with a warm smile and she, who learned from Margaret's letters about Milton civilities not usually observed in London, grasped the hand he extended to her. "I can see Margaret told you about our quaint practices here," he said.

"Yes, we grew up together and are quite each other's confidante." Edith looked across the room at Margaret, who was in conversation with her mother, before adding: "Yet, we are not really very much alike. She was always the independent one who had a mind of her own and I was the one who took to heart all that we were taught."

"I gathered as much. She said you are uncommonly accomplished at the piano. Our instrument here may not be as good as yours in London but I think it would please everyone if you would play for us after dinner."

She acquiesced with a slight graceful bow of her head, a gesture John had also seen in Margaret. "Margaret flatters me too much but yes, certainly, I shall be happy to." Then, she asked, looking towards her cousin: "Do you know that she could play fairly well if she practiced?"

John was pleasantly surprised. "No, I thought she did not play at all."

"Well, it is true, she never applied herself to it as I did when we were children and without a piano when she first came to Milton, she probably could not practice. She always preferred books and drawing to piano and dancing lessons. But Margaret has a sensitive ear and just before she came back here, she started practicing a little again and we played a few airs together."

"Then, perhaps, we could prevail on you both for some duets." John replied, gazing at Margaret who sat with her back to him. She turned and, for a long tender, passionate moment, they seemed oblivious of everyone around them.

Edith looked away, uncomfortable at intruding into this very private exchange between two lovers. She saw a Margaret she never knew, one apparently capable of intense feelings and, in

Edith's romantic imagination, probably even of irrational passion. She knew Margaret to be strong-willed, possessed of a lively intellect, the level-headed one who thought for herself and, when they were growing up, for Edith as well. Edith did not care to be bothered to think matters through while Margaret relied on her cousin's superior social skills and sense of style. It was reciprocity that suited the cousin's different temperaments.

It was a different Margaret Edith saw that evening and it thrilled her to imagine her clever cousin vulnerable to the fluttering of the heart and the trembling of limbs in the presence of the man she loved. Edith was sorry for Henry but her conviction grew that he would not have been equal to her cousin's passionate nature. Edith who married her young and handsome captain for love, thought that Margaret, clearly in love, was more like her than she had imagined. That night, she accepted her cousin's choice without question.

John was, himself, a bit vigilant, but of Henry Lennox. He wondered why Henry was at this family gathering because as Captain Lennox's brother, Henry was, at most, a friend and not a relation to Margaret. But he also knew that Mrs. Shaw would be too conscious of decorum to exclude him and leave him at the hotel by himself that evening. In any case, John saw nothing that concerned him; while Henry Lennox did look a lot at Margaret, she was equally gracious to everyone.

Sadly, John also noted that Margaret seemed more at ease and self-possessed in the presence of her London relations and friends. Regrettably, the past few days had hardly warmed his mother's manner towards Margaret who, in turn, was wary and hesitant in Mrs. Thornton's presence. For the first time, John confronted the difficulties occasioned by living with two strong-willed women. Although he could never imagine shirking his obligations to his mother, he never doubted that his wife would always come first. He was aware, for instance, that although she had not spoken of it yet, Margaret would want a house of their own, away from the noise and constant activity of Marlborough Mills. If so, he would find her one.

Fanny and her husband were at the dinner as members of the Thornton family and their presence lessened Mrs. Thornton's discomfort somewhat. Entertaining Londoners, whose ways she was unfamiliar with and felt some disdain for, taxed her equanimity too much and she welcomed having others take over the task of amusing her guests.

Watson was only too willing to engage the men in discussions about money and investments. In contrast, Fanny was content to closely observe Edith, her demeanor and dress, assuming them to represent the currently fashionable. But her attention was also often directed at John and Margaret, searching for signs to justify her unwavering notion that Margaret had designs on her brother all along. She and Margaret had scarcely said a word to each other and neither of them took any extra effort to advance towards a more sisterly relationship.

Fanny seemed obsessed with believing her brother was marrying Margaret because his choices had narrowed with his financial collapse. But she could not ignore what she saw in how John regarded Margaret—his eyes constantly seeking hers from everywhere across the room, following her figure as she moved among the guests, and when they were together, gazing at her in that intent way he had that Fanny always found mysterious. Fanny could never recall during their courtship and engagement when Watson looked at her the way her brother did Margaret although Watson doted on her and treated her with indulgence. She reluctantly felt envy for this woman who would soon become her sister and, several times that evening, she had to reassure herself that the relationship she had with Watson was exactly what she preferred.

When the group was seated in the drawing room for after-dinner drinks, John reminded Edith of her promise to entertain them with some music. He was also rather curious to hear Margaret play. She had never touched the piano in the Thornton house.

Edith approached Margaret. "I will play if Margaret will play a few pieces with me as we did often when we were growing up."

Margaret protested, shaking her head vigorously: "But I am out of practice." She refused to get up but Edith grasped her hands and tried to pull her up from her chair. Margaret laughed, continuing to protest in a self-mocking tone. "You play so well and have always done so since we were children that I am loath for everyone here to see how badly I play compared with you."

"But Margaret, have you forgotten how much we enjoyed playing together? It did not seem to bother you then how well or badly you played."

"I was a child and we had no audience then except our poor teacher and my kind aunt."

Edith was insistent. "We could do that short Mozart rondo we were practicing just before you came back to Milton." She looked at John. "Mr. Thornton did no know you could play the piano."

Margaret smiled at John and shrugged her shoulders. Then, she stood up. "All right, I will do this short rondo with Edith if she promises to play more. I am sure you will forget my fumbling when you hear her."

Edith and Margaret sat at the piano side by side. After a few practice notes, they paused a little and then played a lively piece that had them crossing over each other's hands to strike the piano keys. The piece brought back the delight the cousins always had playing together. Forgetting they had an audience, they launched into another rondo immediately after the first one, with Edith playing the high notes and Margaret the lower. During an instantaneous pause in the middle of the piece, the two exchanged places in a swift move that punctuated the music with the swishing sound of colliding skirts, almost knocking down the piano seat and inducing suppressed laughter in the two performers. They had started this maneuver as a game when they were children and never tired of doing it to amuse themselves when piano practice became boring, which it always did for Margaret. They continued the piece, this time with Margaret doing the high notes.

John watched and listened with great interest, as diverted as the rest of the group at the cousins' childlike ebullience. They sounded good together and even to his untrained ears, he could tell how well synchronized they were despite the differences in their skills. Edith was, without question, the more skillful of the two, playing smoothly and confidently. Also obvious to him was the relaxed camaraderie between them. Although he saw for himself the many ways in which the cousins were indeed different, he also saw that they developed complimentary dispositions, no doubt borne of necessity and long association, facilitated in the beginning by a child's desire to be agreeable. The lively music and the infectious exuberance with which the young women played together could not fail to lighten the mood of the group. When the two finished and got up for an elaborate but mock curtsy, their enthusiastic audience clapped for some minutes.

Margaret turned to Edith and gestured for her to resume her seat at the piano. "Now, you will hear something that will surely give you pleasure."

Edith played a few piano sonatas she knew by heart, from a repertoire she put together to entertain or divert herself. She combined her skill with a real feel for her music that came across clearly and infected her audience with whatever mood or sentiment infused a piece. Margaret knew that the piano was Edith's one true passion which she considered hers and hers alone. Edith had devoted the greater part of her day mastering it when they were children and continued to do so until just before she married. It was her antidote to boredom, the balm to her little frustrations and the diversion that made her forget anything annoying or bothersome. She concluded her performance with an airy and melodic morsel that continued to resonate in the minds of her listeners as the evening ended most pleasantly for everyone.

Mrs. Thornton who had never before understood the necessity of spending time on what she considered frivolities, was almost ready to concede that, perhaps, music did serve a purpose. Fanny was the only one she had listened to in the past and, to her, that required her maternal indulgence to endure. She ruefully realized her daughter did not have anywhere near the skill Edith had nor even the expressiveness of Margaret who, were she to practice more, would surely play much better than Fanny.

Fanny could not deny Edith's superior musical skills. Unfortunate in having been born without an ear for music and short on general cleverness, she was also never exposed to the sort of serious instruction and guidance that Mrs. Shaw bought for her daughter and niece. Fanny thought herself accomplished and her model for a superior player and lady had been Ann Latimer for the simple reason that Miss Latimer was the sole heiress to her father's fortune and she had gone to finishing school. And yet, through some instinct primal to all humans rather than real knowledge, Fanny could sense that Edith sounded several cuts above Miss Latimer's playing. Even Margaret, who might have been rusty with her technique, had played with more feeling for the music than her idol. She was almost regretful that she had once derided Margaret to her brother's face for not knowing how to play the piano.

Fanny began to think that, perhaps, she had not been thoroughly acquainted with Margaret and how well connected she was. She had learned for the first time that evening that Margaret had lived among the wealthy families of London for most of the ten years before her move to Milton. In Fanny's reckoning, that counted for much. Was she not passing a very agreeable evening quite unlike any she had ever had in this house or any other house in Milton? The pursuit of diversions that she was convinced occurred in wealthy London households. She thought, as she sat in the carriage taking them back to their home, that there was much to be gained from being more pleasant and attentive to Margaret from now on.

Later that night, as John kissed Margaret goodnight in front of her bedroom door, he said: "Will you never cease to amaze me? What else do you have up your sleeves that I should know about?"

She whispered saucily against his neck as he held her close. "You will just have to keep me around to find out, wouldn't you?"

The wedding took place on what passed for a beautiful early Sunday afternoon in Milton—when a late spring sun barely peaked out of the miasma of clouds, smoke and still stale air heavy with particulates from the mills. Still, the new leaves and buds on trees and grasses were vivid with color, not yet weighed down or discolored by the heavy smoke nor withering from want of sunshine.

Inside the church, a profusion of red and yellow roses— pinned on the pews and on green garlands adorning the walls— forced the look and smell of country spring into its somber and chilly interior. Margaret recognized her cousin's hand in the arrangement and the abundance of roses very similar to those that grew around the Helstone parsonage. She gave Edith, who was attending her, a bright and grateful smile as Captain Lennox led her towards the altar. There, John waited for her, handsome and distinguished—Margaret thought with some fluttering in her heart—in his dark coattails and light shirt and cravat.

John felt his pulse quicken at seeing her, a beguiling smile on her lips and, it seemed to him, anticipation in her shining eyes. She was resplendent in the simple white wedding gown first worn by her mother and the delicate Spanish lace from her brother draped simply on her luxurious hair, held in place with a pearl comb, a Hale heirloom. John took Margaret's hand from Captain Lennox and whispered: "Ah, my love, you take my breath away."

None of the guests considered the whole wedding celebration particularly memorable. But many women were impressed with the roses strewn all over the church, a display rarely seen in Milton and one a few of them would later try to mimic. More of the same roses graced vases on the dining table and other surfaces in the drawing room at the house, their pure vibrant colors even more vivid against the nearly unrelieved expanse of dark tones, flooding the room with the ambiance of a sunny spring afternoon. The men, mostly John's business colleagues, relished the sumptuous feast, particularly the wines, and thought that Mrs. Thornton outdid herself for her son's wedding. But with her usual frankness, she quickly disabused them of their mistaken assumption and told them that what they enjoyed the most, the wines and meats, were brought over from London by Margaret's aunt and cousin.

Many had earlier noticed these women, very elegantly dressed in rich finery. They were particularly struck by the beautiful young woman escorted by a tall handsome young man, who was obviously her husband. Before long, word was passed around among their wives that Miss Hale and her cousin were raised together in London. With such relations and such a background, most of John's business associates began to wonder if they had been wrong about Miss Hale. One of them, echoing what they thought, remarked to Mr. Hamper who was sitting next to him at the dining table. "You know Thornton better than any of us so, perhaps, you can tell us. Had Miss Hale been left with some money? If so, Thornton had not married as foolishly as we thought."

"You thought," Mr. Hamper corrected him. "I never thought. He is in love, all right."

Mr. Hamper watched John Thornton lead his new wife to greet the guests, an arm possessively around her. He recalled when he first saw Miss Hale at the last dinner Mrs. Thornton gave two years ago. He asked Mr. Thornton who she was, intending to seek an introduction. But when Thornton saw her, he walked away and left him behind to welcome her.

Mr. Hamper continued: "I suspect his attachment to Miss Hale dates back at least to that last dinner party Mrs. Thornton gave."

"You mean when Miss Hale defended Higgins? But that is not possible! Thornton seemed so consternated by her and pointedly ignored her through dinner."

"He did. But you can see he is quite enchanted with her. To be sure, she is beautiful and at least as fine as her London cousin but who would have thought Thornton would choose this outspoken belle from the south? I wager that she will test his fortitude. As it is, she has already made her mark on him. I miss that scowl, don't you?"

"Yes, but, perhaps, her father was not as poor as we thought and she did inherit some money."

"That, I do not know. I have heard some rumors that she might have had a legacy from Mr. Bell which included Marlborough Mills. But look—would you have predicted Thornton could be so smitten? He did not seem the type."

"No," the colleague replied and said no more, convinced nevertheless that he and his other associates were right that money was involved.

Nicholas Higgins and his daughter Mary were in church for the marriage ceremony and both John and Margaret made certain that they felt welcome. Nicholas suffered considerable discomfort at first about going to the Thornton house for the dinner reception. He was conscious that his demeanor and his unease in this crowd made him stand out, despite the unaccustomed suit he wore that could make him pass for one of the manufacturers. When they walked out of the church, the bride and groom had pointedly sought them out, a gesture that was not lost on the other guests. John shook his hand vigorously and Margaret embraced Mary and kissed her on the cheek. Higgins felt that after that greeting, he had no choice but to attend the dinner reception. There, John and Margaret sat talking with him and Mary for some time before taking their places at the head of the table. He found the dinner as painful as he thought he would but, conscious of his role in the couple's present happiness, he felt great satisfaction as he watched them mingle among the other guests.

Mrs. Thornton would always recall that Sunday as the day she lost her son to the new woman in his life. She was grateful that he glowed happily, appeared confident and in control of his destiny. But her own important role in his life had ended, curtailed by someone she doubted she would ever like. She smiled graciously at the guests but she was very subdued, weighed down by weariness, and she hardly talked to anyone, hardly left her chair. Her son was too rapt up in his new wife to notice her. But she watched their every move—gazing deeply into each other's eyes, huddling their heads together when they talked, whispering into each other's ear—and, all that time, they seemed oblivious to the crowd. John kept to his wife's side, leading her around, an arm around her shoulders or a hand on her back. Once in a while, he stopped to kiss her. Mrs. Thornton saw all this and was aggrieved. She was not prepared to accept Margaret. She had believed it was because Margaret did many things she found exasperating. But that night, she admitted to herself she resented Margaret because she had taken from her what was most precious to her.

To John and Margaret, the gathering after the church ceremony was a haze. Radiant as Margaret might have appeared on the surface, her spirit flagged and she was nearly exhausted, barely able to conceal from John her wish that the guests would soon leave. The wedding celebration was larger and more elaborate than she had wanted and it lasted longer than she envisioned. John hardly left her side, whispering tender words into her ear, occasionally caressing her back or the nape of her neck as he led her around and introduced her to business associates and their wives. At a lull in the introductions and bland niceties, he pulled her close to him and planted a lingering kiss on her lips, whispering: "Just a little while longer, my love." Margaret briefly leaned against him, squeezing his hand lovingly.

Most of the guests did finally leave and only the family remained for a night cap. The London party was returning to their hotel and Mrs. Thornton was leaving with the Watsons to stay with them for a few months. John did not wait for them to finish their drinks. "Margaret is tired and we must say "Good Night" to you all now."

Edith approached Margaret and as the cousins embraced and kissed each other, she said sympathetically: "You do look exhausted, my dear. We will see you both in London in two days. We leave early tomorrow." Then, she whispered something to Margaret who seemed amused and whispered back to her. The cousins parted from one another in subdued laughter.

John and Margaret ascended the stairs to their bedroom. Dixon was waiting for them in the hallway. "I've come to help the mistress out of her gown, master."

All right, Dixon, I shall be in my study." He kissed Margaret and whispered: "I will see you soon, my love."

Later in his study, he heard Dixon open the door and leave it ajar. She left without speaking.

VII. ROMANCE AND RAPTURE

John tapped the door to the bedroom lightly a couple of times. He did not wait for a response but he wanted Margaret to know he was coming. He had waited in his study with an anticipation that peaked as he opened the door with trembling hands and walked with measured steps towards where she sat. The room was illumined by only two gas lamps, one of which was in front of the dresser and the other, on a nightstand on the other side of the bed. The light rendered into view only the areas around the bed and the dresser, and merely hinted at the huge space within. John smiled to himself, somewhat amused at the arrangement. It appeared, to him, rather like a stage set where everything was thrown into darkness except for the scene before them that the audience was compelled to focus on. He thought that Dixon need not have bothered; his mind and all his senses had already been engaged all day in imagining his first night with Margaret.

She sat facing the dresser, calmly brushing her long hair down her shoulders, the light casting a glow over her that brought out gold highlights in her dark hair and a faint flush on her ivory skin. The room was warm enough that she wore only a light lacy robe on top of a silk nightgown. Stripped of layers of clothing and her hair unleashed from clips and pins, John thought she looked very young and fragile—quite unlike the young woman with flashing eyes who chastised him for beating a worker; or the alluring lady in an elegantly simple gown who finally captivated him, only to cause him chagrin for openly challenging his beliefs in front of his guests at dinner.

Under half-closed lids, Margaret had followed his figure on the mirror as he approached and stopped so close behind her that she could almost feel the heaving of his chest with every breath he took. She smiled at his reflection but the smile was fleeting and her eyes were shifted quickly away when they met his. She did not speak and continued brushing her hair.

John stood still a few seconds, rested his hands lightly on her shoulders. He gazed at her reflection with eyes dark and intense beneath his brow, overcome with feelings so strong that they made him tremble and hesitant to speak for some time. Margaret went on brushing her hair, occasionally stealing glances at him. Mostly, she stared, as if riveted, at the objects on the dresser but, in fact, she was attempting with little success to still her confusion. She wondered how long he was going to look at her in that way. The flush on her cheeks deepened and she breathed through barely parted lips. She was somewhat startled when she finally heard him speak, his voice tremulous with emotion. "You are really here, Margaret. My love, my life, my wife."

He bent over and pressed his lips on her shoulder. Then he straightened slowly and his eyes wandered around the room, catching bits of color and shapes gleaming in the dark. After a minute or two, he resumed, his voice a little steadier: "The night before I went to Helstone, I never imagined you here. I came into this room. It seemed so empty and forlorn, all the more so because it was so large and so cold and it made me sad that it would never be used. Not for what it had been intended. Not even as a room for guests."

He was silent again for a long moment, smiling at her tremulously. She wondered if she should say something but she was at a loss for words. All she could do was hold the brush firmly in her hand so she could busy herself with the only activity that steadied her fluttering breast. She was almost relieved to hear him speak again. "How different it feels in here now. Your presence alone has given it such warmth but the small touches you have scattered in the room have made it inviting. It is......"—he paused, glancing at her and searching for words—".....intimate, enticing, a sanctuary."

Without raising her face from its semi-bowed attitude, her shy eyes, luminous and large, met his in the mirror once more. She remained silent and she cast her eyes down again, flustered. She continued to glance at him sideways every once in a while, her mouth curved up beguilingly at the edges and the lower lip thrust into a sensuous pout. Through all this, she did not stop brushing her hair. He stood behind her for some time, delighting in her nearness, her unusual beauty so irresistible to him, and the droll and lively intelligence that enlivened those large blue eyes even in her agitation at being admired so ardently. Entranced by the deliberate and rhythmic motions of her arms and the repetitive passes of the brush over her luxurious hair, he picked up a handful of her locks and, with his thumb, caressed it, the back of his hand grazing the bare flesh on the nape of her neck.

Margaret stopped brushing and laid her hands on her lap. She met his blazing gaze on the mirror, the pupils in her eyes rounder and darker blue as they glowed from within, her lips slightly parted, her breath gushing through in a steady pant. John took the brush from her hand and realized then that she was trembling. He took a step closer and laid the brush on the dresser. Grasping her arms, he slowly turned her until they were face-to-face.

He lifted her face up to his, his eyes held hers so steadfastly that she could not look away. "My love," he whispered.

He grasped her shoulders, raised her from the chair, and pulled her close to him. He kissed her parted lips and then his mouth brushed lightly against her chin and down her throat where he took little nibbles of her smooth ivory flesh. On the day they were introduced to each other in her father's study, he could hardly take his eyes off her. As his eyes wandered from her face to her throat, he had wondered what it was like to kiss that defiant mouth, to bury his face against that neck and feel its pulsating warmth. Now, he could do as he desired and it thrilled him more than he had imagined. When Margaret arched her head back and rubbed her cheek against his, his mounting passion became harder to restrain.

He slipped the robe off her shoulders and down her arms. Her body, supple and pliant under her nightgown, melted into his arms. His lips roamed over every inch of her face until they found her mouth. She received his kisses, tentatively in the beginning but as his kisses became more insistent, she wound her arms around his neck and clung to him, returning his kisses with an increasing ardor that fueled his even more. There was, for John, such exquisite wonder in this moment of passionate surrender, a moment that only a couple of weeks ago, he had despaired would ever happen. He scooped Margaret up in his arms and carried her to the bed. She nuzzled her head against his neck and the breath from her slightly open mouth tingled his skin with moist pleasurable warmth. He felt her tremble once more.

He was, himself, trembling as he laid her down on the bed, but he moved deliberately, taking his time. He had waited so long and he wanted this night to last. At the train station, when he first kissed her, Margaret had responded with an eagerness that amazed him, that held promise for what it would be like for her to return his feelings. Now, in this room when it seemed they were all alone in the world, he made love to her, tenderly and unhurriedly at first, attuned to her responses and guided by them. She yielded to his every move, shyly in the beginning, her eyes closed. But her whole being was drawn into the sensations of those moments, meshing with his, her excitement rising along with his. As his caresses and kisses grew more intense, he felt her sweetly straining against him and responding with a passion that, because he had not anticipated it, surprised him, but only for an ephemeral moment. Then it incited him to heights of pleasure heretofore unknown, unimagined, and now unleashed in wondrous waves. Much later as he fell asleep, recollecting the past hour with some residual exhilaration, he knew he would never forget it.

When, finally, John pulled the sheets over their bodies, Margaret buried her face, flushed and moist, on his shoulders. Shy once again, she concealed from him her eyes, brilliant with lingering excitement. Everything that just happened was all so new to her and she wanted time to comprehend it. She had had no inkling how she would respond and she had felt anxious at her inexperience. But alone with John in their bedroom, she found herself reacting spontaneously and artlessly. She had been exhausted by all the goings-on of the day. By the time she sat in front of the dresser that evening, she felt herself wilting, uncertain of how she would hold up but when she heard the tap on the door, she sat up, a certain agitation infusing her with a second wind. When John came in, she felt confused, anxious, and yet expectant; she could no longer think, she could only feel. She allowed her mind to submit to her feelings, to her instinct and her impulses, to whatever her body willed her to do.

Margaret dreamily nudged closer to John as she drifted off to sleep, marveling once more at how tender he could be. This husband of hers was as intense in love as in anger, at least when provoked by the threat of danger, as he had been by a worker he caught smoking inside the mill. How remote that seemed to her now, how like an alien dream.   As sleep finally arrested consciousness, Margaret was still in the middle of an increasingly foggy reverie about her tender, intense, complicated husband.

John lay awake a little longer, stroking her hair, relishing the memory, the wonder of how naturally she responded to him. He turned toward her sleeping face and kissed her closed eyelids and slightly parted lips.

Although aware that she was asleep, he whispered: "Good night, my sweet temptress, my Margaret."

He reached over to turn off the lamp.

The next day, they awakened to a spring morning of characteristically hazy sunshine. Except for Dixon and two maids, nobody else was in the house. Mrs. Thornton was staying with Fanny while John and Margaret went on their honeymoon to the continent where they expected to stay for two months. They had no plans for the day but to rest from the hectic preparations and celebrations of previous days. This was the first day that they were practically alone and they intended to while away every moment of it together in aimless pursuits.

In two days, they would be in London on their way to Paris via Dover where they were boarding, first, a boat to Calais, France and, next, a train from Calais to Paris. Dixon was to accompany them to London and wait there until Margaret and John returned from Spain. From Paris where they were staying a week, they would head for Cadiz, taking a train to Marseilles and then a boat to the south of Spain. Frederick and his wife were expecting them in Cadiz in about three weeks. After a week in Cadiz, the two couples intended to travel together around Andalusia to enjoy Frederick and Dolores's favorite spots in the region. Frederick was anxious to show his sister what he found enchanting about Spain and was certain that she and her new husband would see his affection for his adopted country.

John awoke first and opened his eyes to an abundant mass of dark hair draped on his right arm and shoulder. Margaret had slept through most of the night in his arms, her arm draped on his chest. He smiled, saying to himself: "Margaret, my wife," as he kissed the top of her head and laid his cheek softly on it.

For a little while, he listened to her calm regular breathing, remembering its more frantic pace when he made love to her the past night. Then, he planted another kiss on top of her head and, imagining that her lips were thrust at him ready for his, he kissed them ever so lightly.

She began to stir. Just waking up, she opened her eyes slowly, slightly disoriented. She turned her head up to his and, her eyes still glazed from sleep, she was greeted by loving eyes and a voice just above a whisper. "Good Morning, Mrs. Thornton. Did you sleep well?" She blushed deeply, her eyes fluttering, and John knew that she was remembering the past night.

"Good Morning, Mr. Thornton. Yes. Indeed I did—well and long. I was exhausted," she replied, looking away and blushing some more. She saw the bright light outside the window and said, attempting some levity in her voice. "I must have slept so deeply that I think I did not dream at all. How late is it?"

He gently lifted her arm off his chest, sat up, and reached for a watch on a chain on the bedside table. "Five past nine. Should we ring for breakfast? We can be as lazy as we want today. We have the house to ourselves and no one is scurrying about."

"Yes, let's." Margaret acquiesced readily. She pulled the sheet to her chest, sat up, and asked: "Do you know where my nightgown is?"

John smiled, somewhat diverted by her attempts at modesty after her ardent response to his lovemaking the night before. He playfully tugged at the other end of the sheet to cover himself as he reached for her gown on the floor on his side of the bed. The sheet slipped off her hand when he bent over so she tugged back at it to pull it over her breasts. As he came back up, she pretended to glare at him, eyes flashing and pursed lips turned up at the corner.

Still holding on to the gown, he asked: "Shall I help you put it on?"

She regarded him for a long moment, her eyes half-closed and her chin turned up in the air. She crossed her arms in front of her and in as haughty a tone as she could muster, answered: "I suppose so although I am perfectly capable of dressing myself."

He hesitated and studied the impish look on her face. While it seemed that she was enjoying watching his hesitation, she also regarded him cautiously, waiting to see what her sauciness would lead to. He countered her manner with a scowl and held the gown out to her with both hands, amusement barely concealed in his eyes.

"Shall I come closer or will you?" The question was meant to provoke her.

She stared back at him in silence, lasting long enough, that he wondered if he should do something else. But then, she inched closer, stopped abruptly, and turned her back to him. He eyed the smooth ivory back and nape of the neck with pleasure, grinning to himself. Without hesitation, he tossed the gown back on the floor on his side of the bed, seized her by the waist, and pulled her closer. The sheet drifted of her breasts and down her lap but she made no move to pick it up again. He pressed his lips on the nape of her neck, then down her back.

"You realize this is a dangerous game you're playing?" He whispered hoarsely in her ear.

"How so?" She asked just as softly, refusing to grasp his meaning.

"You know this is a game of seduction?"

"No, I merely want to put on my gown so we can ring for breakfast." She countered coyly.

John grinned once again, intrigued and willing to play along although all he could think of was making love to her again. But he was hardly averse to their little game, curious about where else it might lead.

He raised his head and let her go. "All right, then. I will get your gown."

He reached down on the floor to retrieve her nightgown, straightened, gown in hand, and found himself face-to-face with her once again. "Come closer so I can help you into it."

She stared at him suspiciously this time but gingerly moved closer, her eyes focused on his face. She did not turn around but when she was near enough that she could have reached for her gown, he had swiftly thrown it back on the floor. Before she could react, he had clasped her close and laid her on the bed underneath him, caught between his arms. She had squealed as they both fell on the bed but she cupped her mouth to suppress the sound she made. She was still panting with subdued laughter when he bent over her shoulders, pressing warm eager lips there, then up her throat and her mouth, until her laughter quieted down and she returned his kisses. He whispered in her ears: "I warned you that this was a dangerous game."

She did not reply right away, then with her lips brushing his cheeks, she whispered. "What if nobody loses and we both win?"

He did not answer, apparently ignoring her question for the moment, as he continued kissing her. Once again, she yielded but with little of the shyness that she began their romp with the night before. She seemed more flirtatious, beguiling him by matching his kisses with soft nibbles on his face and neck. He groaned under his breath and murmured, his lips against hers: "But you win. You have me under your spell." He muttered between kisses that grew more passionate. "And, yet, I can keep playing this game with you."

It was late morning when, famished and flushed, they finally rang for breakfast. They were both dressed but still perched on the bed when a knock on the door announced the arrival of their delayed repast. Dixon, trailed by Jane, brought in a tray brightened by a small Chinese vase of fresh red and yellow roses left over from the wedding decorations and brimming with settings for a meal and servings for tea and toast. On Dixon's arm draped a table cloth that she laid on the table by the window before unloading the tray and setting the table.

Jane carried the tray with the sustenance John and Margaret could hardly wait to feast on, their appetites sharpened by both sweet and savory aromas from raspberry jam, ham, eggs, butter, and a bowl of mixed berries. Although smiling broadly, both Dixon and Jane only bowed their greetings and retreated stealthily from the room with empty trays, closing the door as noiselessly as they could behind them. John and Margaret looked at each other. She giggled and he grinned, diverted by the behavior of the two who just left. Margaret asked, still giggling. "Will we be in the next tittle-tattle when the maids of Milton get together?"

"You can bet on it. Jane wastes no time. I am sure she thinks it is a benefit we owe her for serving us." He answered laughing.

As she poured his tea, she remarked. "That is an interesting word, tittle-tattle. Quite modern, I think. I do not remember ever hearing anyone use it in Helstone nor in London."

He chuckled at her observation. "We invent a great many things here in the north."

After the late breakfast, they dressed more properly and went out for a very long walk. By midday, a light wind had blown away enough smoke and the world outside beckoned. It was too beautiful to waste indoors, within the grayness of the massive spaces in the house that clashed too jarringly with the ecstatic state they were in and were reluctant to relinquish. They were in no hurry to go anywhere or do anything but relish each other's presence, each other's thoughts as they talked, and the tingling warmth of each other's touch when they stopped to embrace and kiss.

With hardly anyone else around the park, they paused frequently, free in their expressions of affection. They meandered through the hilly paths overlooking the city and situated on its edge, seeking out sections that they had not explored before and lingering in many spots to admire the wild flowers that had begun to bloom. Apart from the pinks and greens on Margaret's shirt and shawl and the rosy undertone that exercise had infused on her cheeks, only the widely-scattered wildflowers imparted colors in the landscape, still somber in late May.

After bending over to inspect one of those flowers, Margaret remarked. "Cotton is not the only thing that Milton produces. Isn't it wonderful that even in this air and the want of sunshine, wild things do still grow bright and beautiful?"

John smiled, gazing at her. "Yes, bright and beautiful."

His eyes glowed with such ardor that she blushed and looked away. "I was talking about the wildflowers."

John laughed. "I know but can I not admire my wife as well? There was so much I wanted to say to you all these years I have loved you and I had never felt free to say them. Until now."

She did not answer and continued their slow progress towards another small patch of wildflowers. She stooped to pick a red poppy and offered it to him without a word.

He smiled as he took it from her and twirled the stem to inspect the flower closely. "Yes, I agree it is beautiful." He followed her along the path, relishing the sight of her lovely figure moving fluidly in front of him, his eyes glowing, a quiet happy smile on his lips. After a short distance, he caught up with her. "I never stopped to look at these things before. My days have been filled with machines and chemical dyes and keeping up with new inventions to make the mill more efficient and productive."

She detected a hint of regret in his voice and stared at him thoughtfully for a few seconds. "Yes. But are they not exciting? Inventions, I mean, new ways of doing things—those are all part of becoming modern, are they not? And you embrace them. There is something wonderful about that, I think."

He smiled warmly at her enthusiasm and approbation and answered, half-teasing and half-serious. "Yes and the things we cannot grow like this poppy, we can mimic or, perhaps, we might even invent something entirely new and strange at first but serves the same purpose."

She took the flower back from him, her lids half-closed, hiding the slight displeasure in her eyes. She retorted jauntily. "How could any invention of man create a flower as fresh and delicate as this? And would that invention, if indeed it were possible, wilt as gracefully but sadly as this one?"

He frowned, somewhat perplexed by the change in her tone that he thought intimated at a rebuke for something he believed in. They walked in silence for some distance before he placed his arm around her waist and drew her closer. "You are quite right. The best things about life are still those that we have been blessed with since the beginning of man." He paused in his steps and pulled her against him. "A kiss, an embrace," he whispered as he pressed his lips on her forehead, the tip of her nose, and her lips.

They began their descent from the hill just as the dusky orange sun sank slowly in the smoky evening fog.

VIII. RAPTURE AND DISCOVERY

A couple of days later, John and Margaret reached Paris in early evening. The journey had been long and exhausting, the first leg from Dover being particularly rough, as the steamer to Calais rocked its hapless passengers violently and nearly incessantly for about two hours. Dazed, lethargic and too queasy to ingest even a mouthful of food or drink, they boarded the train to Paris shortly thereafter, almost grateful for a long ride that gave them time to recover. Margaret, who had never travelled on a boat, looked very pale and barely able to hold herself up. She fell asleep in John's arms within minutes of the train leaving the station and woke up a couple of hours later, revived and famished for some nourishment.

The rest of the train trip to Paris was uneventful but long. By the time they descended at the train station in Paris, they were listless and weary until, ensconced alone inside the carriage taking them from the train station to their hotel, the exhilaration of finally arriving at their destination infused them with renewed energy. Before long, as they surveyed the city from their carriage, what they saw astounded them. They gawked, dumbfounded but with great interest, at the spectacle of a city undergoing massive renovation. Debris from the demolition of old structures lay next to new construction, vast areas were being cleared apparently for gardens and parks, and new gaslights illuminated more and more streets as they approached the heart of the city where their hotel was located. Most impressive to them, however, was the widening and extending of roads within the city and the new residential and commercial buildings that were springing up on both sides of stretches where wide boulevards had been completed. They were to learn later that the construction of these boulevards was quite extensive and that whole neighborhoods were being razed to the ground to make way for them.

"I have never seen such concentrated reconstruction of a major city." John said as they surveyed the chaos that awed them into silence.

"Why do you suppose they are making streets so wide?"

"To improve circulation within the city, I assume. This rebuilding is exciting but it must have meant quite an upheaval for many Parisians. It is controlled chaos, in any case."

"Perhaps, it is exciting but what happened to what was here before? They must have torn down a lot of old buildings. I read about the narrow curving streets of Paris, teeming with life and people, about neighborhood cafes where they met and talked. It sounded so vibrant, a place where lives touched and crossed paths everyday. Why, much of it might be gone!" Margaret felt increasingly sad as she spoke.

"That may very well be but after this is all done, I will wager on Paris developing into one of the most, if not the most, modern and vital city for some time to come."

"But what do you think became of the residents of those old narrow streets, displaced from a way of life they were accustomed to? And what of the old buildings that were on those streets?" Margaret persisted, her voice subdued with sadness.

"I don't know. Perhaps, we can find out at the hotel."

John had arranged for a hotel conveniently situated on rue de Rivoli, in a prosperous commercial district, a short walk not only to the river but also to some of the city's major monuments, the Musée du Louvre and two well-known Gothic churches, the cathedral of Notre Dame, and the Sainte Chappelle, famed for its colorful glass windows. The concierge also bragged about the new gaslights recently installed in the area and how beautiful the city was at night when those lights were turned on. On this, their very first visit, such inducements were too strong to resist and as they finished a light supper at their hotel, Margaret declared. "I would like to go for a walk tonight."

"Are you sure? Are you not tired? We have had a long day of traveling from London."

"The night air will revive me. My father had a friend, a Frenchman he met at Oxford, who talked in much detail about the area around the river, the two tiny islands, and the Cathedrale de Notre Dame on one of them, on the Ile de la Cité. He said this section of Paris was vibrant and fascinating for both its people and architecture. I am rather eager to see how much I could recognize from what he had described."

He studied her countenance, eyes bright and lips slightly parted from anticipation, and he could not but acquiesce. "Well, in that case, we should ask the concierge the best way to the river."

They proceeded on a path towards the Seine, the river that divided the city into the Rive Droite where their hotel was located and the Rive Gauche on the opposite side. They went along its banks, then up one of its bridges, towards the Ile and the cathedral, its two towers still visible in the evening and rising majestically from the distance, dominating the landscape of the city. They were informed by the hotel concierge that in Paris, finding their way out of any neighborhood was never a problem, that whenever they thought they were lost, all they needed to do was look up, take a direction towards the cathedral and, from there, trace their way back to the hotel.

The lights delighted Margaret. They drew people out to stroll in places that they might otherwise have feared too dangerous to venture into at night. Evening strollers like them, who walked towards the Seine, found their reward on its gently rippling surface which offered up the city in enchanting images, golden reflections that, in the darkness, would have been swallowed in the water's depth. John and Margaret joined other strollers as they paused, entranced by the city's ever varied images skimming the river's glassy surface—first, while they stood for some minutes on one of the bridges that crossed the river and several times later, while they ambled along the riverbank. Once in a while, they looked up from the dancing reflections to the matching structures, standing solid and immovable. But even on this walk, the tentacle of reconstruction wound its way, by the tip of the Ile de la Cité on the Rive Gauche where a medieval building was undergoing major work.

At their leisurely pace, they arrived nearly an hour later at the cathedral, its soot-smudged exterior magnificent even in the evening darkness. They stood for some minutes peering in the dark at the two towers, the circular relief between them, the statues that went across in a row on the whole façade and those surrounding the portals. Small spots of light peeking out through the open doors beckoned them in. Illuminated only by a few candles at the main altar and with fewer still scattered along the side altars, the light inside was hardly stronger than outside but it was enough for them to see the choir, the marble statue of Mary in the altar behind it and the massive striated columns that supported a nave rising to an impressive height. "Easily 30 meters or more," he whispered in her ear.

To their surprise and delight, the large circular rose window at clerestory height—its stained glass discernible from the natural light that bathed it from above—stood out even more in the relative darkness of the interior. Except for a couple in working class garb sitting on the pews, the church was nearly deserted, services having probably concluded some time before. John and Margaret decided to return the next day to see the centuries-old cathedral in its full grandeur.

They walked a little more briskly back to their hotel, charmed by their first night in Paris, grateful and in wonder once again that it was with each other that they were discovering the city. Paris, magical and even mysterious at night, seemed made for those like them, in the throes of mutual enchantment, their shared happiness expanding simple pleasures into grand adventures. Nearly every night of their stay, usually after dinner at a restaurant, they ended their day with a walk along the river bank and up its bridges just before they returned to the hotel.

Subsequent to their first enchanting night, they saw the city change face many times during the day, its surprises—not always pleasant—waiting in the most unexpected places. They returned the following day to Notre Dame and in the clarity and honesty of light that day brought, they saw more evidence of reconstruction. A spire was slowly rising at the crossing on the roof of the cathedral. Also evident were vestiges of stone foundations immediately surrounding the cathedral, suggesting the recent demolition of buildings that had apparently existed only a few short paces away. It was obvious that this flurry of activity was part of the whole plan to modernize the city, an extensive plan that seemed not to have reached, at least so far, all the labyrinthine neighborhoods of "Old Paris" that Margaret had heard about, the maze of streets teeming with life. They were still there on the Ile de la Cité around the cathedral.

But the reality—what she saw on those narrow streets—did not charm her in the way she had anticipated. Instead, she was struck by how her impressions of these Parisian streets paralleled those she had when she first arrived in Milton, searching for a home to lease. These streets were cramped with people and animals and a stench hung in the air, a stench that inhabitants of the street had probably become used to. The life of the working class who packed the houses on these narrow winding streets was in plain view for any passerby—in the bustle that occupied people, the wares displayed or sold on street stalls and, often, also made in open workshops visible from the streets, the laundry hanging out of windows, the debris occasionally thrown out on the streets, the lively concatenation of voices and sounds.

John and Margaret left the Ile, subdued in mood, sobered by what they witnessed. Margaret wondered sadly if there was as much despair in these Parisian hovels as there was in Milton. Abundance hand in hand with deprivation: Was that the fate bought with modernizing cities? They headed towards the Louvre and into the museum to soothe their spirits with pictures and sculptures for a few tranquil hours. Later, they walked to the Champs Elysées and their first café in Paris. Margaret had summoned, from deep in her memory, the fascinating stories about cafés she had heard from her father's French friend and she asked the hotel concierge, upon return from their walk on the first night, to recommend one they should go to. The concierge directed them to this café.

A couple of days or so into their visit, they noticed that Parisians made a pastime of going on promenade on early evenings and weekends. Couples and families went on leisurely walks by the riverbanks, along the sweeping boulevards, on the parks and gardens still sprouting around the city, on the quays lined by numerous stalls where they could browse through the offerings of *bouquinistes* (booksellers). Exercise was not necessarily the principal reason for this promenade. The primary attraction seemed to be more of a social nature, of being seen and discreetly scrutinizing those strollers they passed on their path, of running into and meeting friends, and engaging them in tête-à-tête that, for many, invariably continued in a café. John and Margaret joined in one day on such a promenade, going up rue de Rivoli to a public section of the garden of the royal residential palace, the Tuilleries, and up the Champs Elysées where they concluded their walk at another café.

As bracing as the promenade was, they found the cafés more intriguing, an ideal setting where visitors could idle over coffee or drinks among the French and observe them play out what being a Parisian meant. John and Margaret embarked on an exploration of the many cafés where Parisians crowded to talk and debate and, in some, even to be entertained by performers singing local airs and operatic arias. The first one they went to, on the concierge's suggestion, attracted the bourgeoisie and upper classes and proved in the end to be the dullest. The café was lively enough and had on an air of sophistication that it drew from its clientele of fashionable ladies and well-dressed gentlemen, who nursed glasses of wine and chatted endlessly. But its atmosphere was subdued compared to what John and Margaret saw in cafés they later happened upon on their own. Cafés were scattered throughout the city and it was easy enough finding at least two a day to fit in between sightseeing and where they could while away a couple of hours or so.

After they had gone to a few, John and Margaret realized they were particularly attracted to cafés animated by spirited discussions and they went to as many of those as they could manage in their stay. The Rive Gauche nurtured many such cafés, the haunt of swarms of artists, philosophers, and writers, mostly men, who talked and argued, sometimes across tables. On this side of the river were also located many universities, their students frequently housed nearby. These young men crammed the cafés with the *flaneurs*, the *philosophes*, and the *artistes*—inimitable observers and interpreters of the life around them. They all gathered for hours talking, arguing, reading, writing, sketching. Every café had its devotees,—individuals of similar persuasions, whether friends or strangers, who often inhabited the same tables at certain hours.

The animated interchanges—talks, debates, discourses—could not escape the avid curiosity of someone new to the culture of the Parisian café, fascinated by the world around them, and had enough facility with French as Margaret did. She listened in when she could and translated what she heard and understood to John. The topics across cafés were varied, ranging from art to politics to scientific inventions and discoveries but everywhere, people talked about the new social order that would derive from the massive reconstruction of Paris.

The cafés existed primarily to serve libations, often coffee, and sometimes wine or beer, but habitués who came nearly daily mostly sought the social interactions that invariably took place. Not everyone ordered a brew or a potion, and more than once, John and Margaret saw different groups of young men—evidently students who wore their shabby outfit like a badge—share single glasses of beer which they passed around not too discreetly while engrossed in earnest conversations. The practice was not unknown to servers and proprietors who apparently tolerated them.

At one of these cafés, Margaret heard a group talking about an art show where a painting was creating some scandal among both the public and the critics. Margaret was fascinated by the fervid arguments occasioned by the show and shortly thereafter, dragged John to it. The picture causing the uproar was of a nude woman on a picnic with two well-dressed gentlemen and it was attracting people who did not usually go to art shows. Shortly thereafter, Margaret cajoled him into going to other exhibits they found advertised in colorful posters plastered on café walls and in the local journals that the hotel provided its guests. He went along, initially a little hesitant, but he was intrigued by his wife's absorption in the pictures and delighted at the wide range of reactions they drew out of her. She stood in front of some a long time, peering at them closely, sometimes beaming with delight and at other times grimacing and scowling.

Their forays into cafés and art galleries took them to different neighborhoods. Margaret was relieved to learn on these excursions that although the full-scale renovation called for the destruction of numerous medieval buildings, it had so far spared many venerated old structures. Some in bad disrepair were actually being restored, including the Conciergerie, the historic medieval building they saw on their first night. The Rive Gauche was John's preferred place to search for a café to experience the exhilarating pulse of the city while leisurely sipping a drink. It was in that area at a café on the Boulevard St. Michel that they spent their last afternoon in Paris.

They sat close together, saying nothing and holding hands, each nursing a cup of coffee for a couple of hours, already feeling nostalgic for this, their first trip to Paris. It was a sojourn permanently etched in their memories with experiences they delighted in as well as the few that brought sadness and even some sorrow. They also knew, without uttering a word, that they would return. They did not expect the subsequent visits to be as magical as their first but happy remembrances alone were worth coming back to and reliving.

Of all that Paris offered them on this trip, John and Margaret were most struck by the lively interest in ideas that possessed café habitués and the zeal with which they defended their unique viewpoints. For Margaret, who had lived with books and had listened in on discussions among her father and his friends, such fascination was not unusual and she reveled in it. But John was astounded, thrown a bit off balance. Such fervent interest in ideas was an indulgence he had to forego, a luxury he could not afford in his pursuit of success in commerce. He did not really have much of a choice when, barely a young man, he had to work to support his mother and sister. Later, it was his single-minded quest for commercial success that rendered anything that had nothing to do with his business remote and unimportant. Here, in these cafés, however, he saw how much the French cared about arts, politics, and the social order, investing much energy and time thinking and talking about them, as much, perhaps, as he did in the manufacture of cotton. He saw all these and he envied the French. He envied, as well, their spontaneity, the naturalness with which they hugged and kissed on both cheeks not only when they greeted one another but, often, also when they parted, even after heated arguments. What strange concerns, obsessions and customs these were to someone like him bred on English reserve, particularly one imbued with Darkshire somberness. What a world away from the incessantly whirring, clanging machines and the swirling cloud of white cotton and, yet, it did not seem to matter, it did not bring on the trepidation he usually felt at being away more than a day from the work and the setting that had defined his life.

Through all those varied stimulating days of moving among Parisians, John was astonished to find that Margaret spoke rather good French, with little of the English accent he could detect among the young women in Milton for whom speaking French was a mark of the fashionable and accomplished. One night, after an exhausting day of monuments and galleries, they had dinner at the hotel, took a short walk, and retired to their room earlier than previous days. Margaret, who was particularly tired, sat in bed reading a French journal she had picked up in the lobby.

John sat on the other side of the bed and remarked: "You and Edith must have had a truly good teacher who taught you French. You speak it so fluently."

"I told you earlier that Papa had a Frenchman friend. Actually I first learned French from him when I was a child and before I was sent to London. My father met him in Oxford where he had studied English literature. He came back to England years later, when I was six or seven, to do translations and write a book. Papa invited him to stay with us and for two years, he lived with us. He said I was at the best age to learn a new language and talked to me only in French. When he returned to France, he wrote me and sent me books, all in French, of course. He entertained us with wonderful descriptions of paintings and drawings, even in his letters that he sent me until he died. I think he nurtured my interest in art." Her voice quivered a little and she looked away, her eyes sad and thoughtful.

John was surprised by the gravity in her voice and the melancholy that briefly crossed her brow. "How upsetting, I am sure, for an impressionable and sensitive young girl to lose an admired and trusted friend but you must have good memories of him."

He took the journal lying on her lap and placed it on the table. He inched closer to her, put an arm around her shoulder, and pressed his lips on her temple. She leaned on his shoulder and was silent for a little while.

She sighed a few times and in a sad voice, she reminisced. "I was 13 and living with my aunt and Edith when he passed away. Not really a child anymore but not quite a young woman either. And yes, I do have good memories but I have not thought about him in a long time. To my admiring childish eyes, he was the handsomest creature I had ever seen, with dark wavy hair, dark piercing eyes and a deep musical voice. I fancied myself infatuated with him by the time he returned to France. I was eight and fantasized he would come back in ten years to marry me. But he died young, in his thirties, I believe." She paused, her eyes poignant with memories of a young girl's awakening passions. John listened in uneasy silence, unwittingly stung with a pang of jealousy that he knew was irrational.

"I showed him my drawings and he said that I had an artist's eye, that he could tell from the way I chose colors and drew a line. His remark made me so happy and proud for days. Later, I began to doubt what he told me because I struggled at my drawing lessons with our London governess. I did find sketching with charcoal and colored chalks quite absorbing but I probably believed those chalks had a certain magic because they were his gift to me, sent over from Paris. In Helstone, I used to take my basket of art materials when I went out for walks so I could draw or do watercolors when I saw some interesting views and objects. As I grew older, other interests beckoned and, in London, Edith also drew me into grown-up feminine pursuits that occupied more of my time. Since leaving Helstone, I have had neither time nor inclination to paint."

She sat up and turned to face him, her pensive eyes had brightened somewhat. "But, you know, these last few days of going to all these art shows have reawakened my interest. The arts seem to be such a serious preoccupation with the French. They flock to shows in big crowds, write about them and debate endlessly."

He smiled, glad for the change in her mood and in her shift from the past to the present. "I do not know how much art one can find in Milton. We certainly do not have interesting subjects for it, unlike Helstone with its lush landscapes."

"No, but it's not only landscapes that interest artists. Remember the paintings and drawings of workers and farmers that we saw done by artists like Daumier and Millet and, of course, that one by Manet that everyone is talking about?"

He shook his head, smiling at her enthusiasm. "I do not remember any artists, much less tell one from another."

She pursed her lips and glared at him in mock annoyance. "I thought you were getting as much pleasure as I was from those pictures."

"I did find the pictures quite interesting, particularly that picnic painting but my pleasure came more from watching you and the many varied expressions on your face as you looked at them." He lifted her face up to his and planted a light kiss on her lips. "I keep learning new things about you that I sometimes wonder how much I really know of the woman I married."

"Oh? I am still me. Anyway, it is a bit too late to change your mind now, isn't it?"

"You are right, of course," he replied, grinning.

He held her closer and she laid her head on his shoulder. After some minutes of silence, he said softly. "If you would like to draw and paint again, then you should do so. Perhaps, we can set up a place for you to paint in and that way, you will have no excuse not to."

"I would like all that, but all in good time. I think I have many things to learn and adjust to as your wife and, for now, those will occupy much of my time."

He smiled, conjuring up a very pleasing image of her as mistress of his household.

"I will confess, though, that I much prefer sketching to needlework. Do you suppose people would think painting an inappropriate occupation for a master's wife?" She lifted her head and faced him. She paused, searching her memory for the proper expression and, in a quivering high-pitched voice, imitated a woman gossiping with another. "Did you see Thornton's wife? Her face is smudged and her apron is stained with paints. Scandalous! Can she not embroider or play piano instead?"

She giggled self-consciously at her bad mimicry and he laughed at both her unsuccessful attempt and her embarrassment. "It seems acting is not something you will attempt," he said.

"No," she answered, bowing her head and pouting in mock shame.

He was entranced by her flirtatiousness, and amused at himself for being so. She did learn feminine wiles, after all, and could use them when she wanted to. He had never seen her wield them until after they became engaged, certainly not when they were newly acquainted nor thereafter when everything seemed hopeless between them. Her artlessness was one reason he fell for her and yet, now, he tingled and willingly succumbed to all the flirtatious, seductive gestures she directed at him. If she so chose, he could be putty in her hands, he who prided his will, strength of mind, and imperviousness to influence especially of the feminine kind. She had thoroughly penetrated that special spot in his heart and he felt himself vulnerable to all the joy and pain she was capable of giving him. Still, he thought, the greatest pain he could imagine would come from losing her, now that he knew the bliss of living in their love for each other.

He was about to clasp her closer again when she raised her head and said coyly: "I'm glad you did not marry me for my reputation because, with all the gossip I seem to inspire, it is probably in tatters by now."

"But, of course, I did," he replied, chuckling. "When I met you I realized I wanted someone unlike the ladies I was acquainted with in Milton, a lady with an uncommon beauty but also a mind of her own that sometimes brought her a bit of trouble. Was that too much to ask?" He reconsidered what he just said and asked, raising a dark eyebrow mischievously. "Are there many like you in London?"

Margaret glared at him and thrust her lower lip, pretending displeasure. She retorted with a haughty lift to her chin: "What if there are? You have been spoken for and you can never go back to the way things were."

He appeared hesitant for a second but she broke into a bewitching smile, wound her arms around his neck, pulled his head down, and kissed him. "But bless your heart for being constant through my inexperience and confusion."

He smiled and said nothing but he lifted her face and kissed her.

She leaned against him and spoke again, slowly. "You asked me once if Henry Lennox had ever proposed to me and I did not answer. I was grateful then that you did not press the matter. I felt remorseful about Henry because I believe I hurt him twice. Years earlier, before we left Helstone, he did propose. I think he misunderstood a remark I made at Edith's wedding."

"You rejected him then? I am glad to know I was in good company."

She gave him that half smile. "In London, after my parents died, I believe he was waiting to renew his proposal. I like Henry. I have known him for a long time and I feel at ease in his presence. He is clever and sophisticated and with his ambition, he will go far."

She looked down, thoughtful, before continuing. "But Henry did not make me feel the thrill, the fluttering in my breast that I did, even at such a naive age, with my young Frenchman."

Again, that pang of jealousy hit John and, for a moment, he compressed his lips and scowled but he was smiling once again when Margaret said, her eyes fixed on his earnestly: "It was not until I met you that I felt that way again."

"Yes?" John's face lighted up.

"It did take me some time to see it. After our early encounters, I convinced myself that I did not like you but, later, when I finally admitted it to myself, I realized I had been attracted to you long before I saw it. Anyway, it was the sort of attraction I could not deny for too long. It was certainly no longer just a child's fascination."

John's whole being was suffused with a pleasurable warmth but he remained silent, his jealousy flung aside as silly. He hoped she would say more.

She went on, her eyes cast down once again. "I think I have changed since I met you particularly these last few weeks that we have been together. You have awakened so much in me, stirred up memories and feelings that were dormant all these years. I had actually buried those memories of Monsieur Fleury rather deeply, maybe because he was the first loss I suffered of people I cared about and I was then so young."

She raised her face, looked deeply into his eyes again. "With you, I learned what love is. Do you know that you actually began to interest me not too long after we met."

"At my mother's last dinner party?"

"Yes, certainly," she replied in a saucy tone. "But even before that, I thought the shadow your scowl cast on your eyes made you seem dark and mysterious. Dark and mysterious always arouses my desire to know more."

He laughed, a spontaneous merry laugh that had been relatively rare for him. "I knew that scowl would eventually attract the woman I would want to marry."

It delighted Margaret to see him in such mirth. He seemed more spirited and younger despite the deeper lines around his mouth and his eyes. Since the day they married, she found him evolving before her eyes in many wonderfully complex ways. For a few more moments, they smiled quietly, happily at each other. Then, she said: "But seriously, I thought we started out so far apart in our beliefs that it seemed impossible, in my mind, that I could ever like you. Later, after the riot, that was what I told myself. In any case, I would never marry just for money or to save my reputation."

"I don't blame you for rejecting me that first time. When I look back at my behavior then, I am heartily ashamed. I did expect you to accept me and was convinced that you could not do otherwise. I was arrogant—no, insolent—and did not really listen to what you had to say. I interrupted you several times, concerned only with what I thought and certain that my perceptions mattered more. But the irony was, hurt as I was by your rejection, you made me look more closely at you, at myself and I came away from that unfortunate meeting painfully aware that I loved you even more."

Margaret caressed his cheeks and pressed her lips to them, whispering in a tremulous voice. "And I love you even more each day. You make everyday something I eagerly look forward to." She settled her head against that comforting niche on his neck. "Believe me, that is quite a change, not just from the trying time when I first lived in Milton, but also from those safe, pleasant dull days in London. Thank you again for being so constant."

"Margaret, my love." He tilted her face up to his and kissed her. Then, he pulled her down on the bed on top of him. That night, he took his time making love to her, gazing into her eyes, whispering into her ears, caressing every part of her and relishing each touch. And, once again, he was thrilled at how ardently she responded to him.

IX. REUNION

Margaret and John arrived at the Port of the Bay of Cadiz on a blazingly bright day in mid-June when temperatures could easily exceed 30 degrees Centigrade. They stood on the top deck, watching the approaching city of Cadiz—a small peninsula jutting out like a tongue into the vast blue Atlantic Ocean and separated from the rest of Andalusia by the less imposing Bay of Cadiz. As the ship slowly entered the bay, John and Margaret waited among the dense crowd of passengers for the ship to come to a full stop and dock at the Port. Everyone listened intently for the announcement that they could disembark.

Margaret held on to her hat as the warm persistent sea breezes threatened to blow it away. She did not mind the breezes at all. They tempered the nearly unbearable heat that would, otherwise, have made her sweat profusely by now. Margaret wanted to present her best self or, failing that, at least to appear calm and collected. In fact, she was trembling a little, anxious to see and hold her brother close again and to make a good impression on his wife whose beauty and perfection she had heard so much about.

She had taken some care dressing up that morning and, the night before, she envisioned the meeting vividly in her mind and even planned how she should act. She looked up at John, standing by her side, and smiled a simultaneously anxious and joyous smile. He smiled warmly back at her and pulled her closer in a gesture of reassurance. She was shaking a little.

Margaret, surveyed the mostly dark-haired, colorfully-dressed crowd on the pier from her higher perch on the ship and saw her brother at once. His brown hair shone like bronze under the bright coastal sun and he stood at least half a head taller than most of the crowd waiting to welcome passengers from the ship. A petite woman with abundant curly dark brown hair that cascaded down her back clung on his arm. Margaret waved at Frederick and then turned to John. "Frederick. Do you recognize him?"

"Vaguely; I saw him only for an instant in a dark train station but, in this crowd, he looks unmistakably English and does stand out. That must be his wife."

"Yes. Dolores. Isn't she beautiful?"

He nodded with a smile and then he grasped her around the back of her waist and led her towards the ramp to join the other passengers who had begun to disembark.

With so many passengers on the ship waving at those on the platform, Frederick did not immediately see his sister but he did see John's tall dark figure looming a head above the largely Spanish crowd that slowly moved towards the ramp. He waved his hand frantically in their direction and Dolores, taking her cue from him, waved more daintily. Margaret kept her eyes on her brother as she took her turn down the ramp, impatient to reach him right away. She had forgotten all the preparation she had done in her mind for this meeting. John, behind her, held her arm in a steady grip, concerned that she was heedless of the danger of the steep ramp in her impatience to reach the platform.

As soon as Margaret stepped on the pier, Frederick ran toward her, oblivious that he was leaving his wife behind. He clasped his sister in a long tearful poignant embrace, kissing her repeatedly on both cheeks. They held on tightly to each other, bound by the remembered sorrow of the not-too-distant losses they suffered in common, but apart. For Frederick, the memories were laden with guilt that he was not there to share the pain, to comfort his younger sister, to assume the burden of unpleasant decisions that needed to be made; for Margaret, they unleashed the grief she had already bottled securely within her but which now once again flooded her whole being as violently as it had done when it was fresh. This time, however, there was an unburdening, a pouring out of her grief, of the desolation and the uncertainties that battered her spirit for too many months. She was shaking in his arms, her face wet with tears. He was not trembling any less than she was and his eyes were equally brimming with tears.

John stood nearby, watching and waiting, so drawn in by the emotional meeting playing out in front of him that he almost missed the faint "hello" coming from behind him. Before he could turn, Dolores was there, standing in front of him, smiling engagingly, and he heard her introduce herself in foreign-accented

English. In a spontaneous move that surprised John, she placed her arms around his shoulders in a brief but tight hug, and then she stood on her toes to offer her cheeks to him. Unused to such exuberance, he gave her a quick embarrassed buzz on one cheek and introduced himself.

Margaret and Frederick, eventually roused from their emotional reunion, turned simultaneously towards their spouses. Frederick, his eyes red and puffy, smiled tremulously at his wife and, looking contrite, whispered an apology into her ear. She kissed his tear-stained face. He placed an arm around her waist and, turning to John, he reached out to him with his other arm. John had been rooted in place, bewildered, hesitant, and watching his wife with concern.

He grasped the offered hand with both of his but in a quick gesture that he did not anticipate, Frederick clasped him in a tight embrace. "John, I feel as if I have known you for a long time from Margaret's letters. Welcome to our family! *Muy encantado*, as we say in Spanish. You have met my wife Dolores?"

John nodded and smiled warmly at both of them. "Yes, she has already taught me one of your charming customs."

Frederick turned to his sister who was finally regaining her composure, and presented his wife. Margaret, cognizant of Spanish customs from her brother's letters and already predisposed to like Dolores, embraced her for a long moment and kissed her on both cheeks.

"I feel that I know you quite well from Fred's letters. His letters are often short and to-the-point but he fills pages talking about you."

Dolores blushed and smiled with some embarrassment. "I hope I meet your expectations." Self-conscious about how her English sounded, she glanced at Frederick who nodded in approval.

"Dolores is unsure of her English but, in fact, she does quite well. Her English is better than my Spanish." He turned to John: "Margaret and my father were the ones good in languages."

Margaret smiled warmly at Dolores. "You are even more beautiful than I imagined from Frederick's description and you make English sound lovelier and more musical."

Frederick nodded gratefully at his sister for her reassuring words. Dolores had agonized for days, anxious for the approval of the sister-in-law she was meeting for the first time. Dolores, pleased at Margaret's remarks, hooked her arm around Margaret's and led the way. "Fred—he does not explain well. Like most men. He said, my sister, she is strong and her spirit, formidable." Dolores hesitated on the last word and glanced at Margaret for approval.

Margaret nodded with a smile and Dolores continued: "He made me anxious with his words. Now I see you. You are kind, sweet and you have the most beautiful large blue eyes I have ever seen, more beautiful than his."

"I can see we will get along well for we are both anxious to like each other." Margaret replied, smiling.

Frederick and John followed their wives and, as they walked behind, Frederick said, grinning widely: "You know we have seen each other before? At a train station at night, I believe, more than two years ago. I recognize you from that time, even hidden somewhat by the shadows. You have a rather memorable countenance although you look much younger under our Andalusian skies."

John grinned back at him, somewhat embarrassed, uncertain what had passed between brother and sister when they talked about him. But determined to be pleasant to Frederick to secretly atone for having been jealous of him for a long time before learning that he was Margaret's brother, John answered in a self-deprecating tone. "It must be that I appear less stern without a scowl. But then, you must understand, to me you were, at that time, a stranger embracing the woman who meant the world to me."

Frederick laughed and gave him another hug. "I like you already. I hope you were not left out of our family secret for too long."

John shrugged. "I would have liked to have known about it earlier but I am here now and that's all that matters, I believe."

John and Frederick got along almost as well as Margaret had hoped for. Frederick, having lived in Spain more than seven years, had adapted to the slower, informal pace of life and the warmer, more spontaneous demeanor of Southern Spain. He was as casual, open, and affectionate with John as he was with his sister. John initially felt uncomfortable with such informality and warmth. At home, Frederick and Dolores were even more demonstrative, touching, holding and kissing each other with a loving playfulness that John felt free to engage in with Margaret only in the privacy of their bedroom. But Frederick and Dolores acted so unreservedly towards each other, even in company with him and Margaret, that their natural ease began to have an effect on John.

The constant balmy heat was made for loose informal attire and Margaret was unprepared for it in her full skirts and long-sleeved blouses. She considered getting rid of her crinoline when she noticed that not all the women of Cadiz bothered with them. Before she could do so, however, Dolores insisted on giving her clothing more appropriate to the sultry climate. She said: "The skirt and your blouse, they are too hot for this weather, no? Also, your body, it is beautiful. You do not need the......" She groped for words as she gestured with her hands around her torso.

"Stays," Margaret said with an encouraging smile.

".........stays, yes. It is cooler without them, you think?"

"Yes, you are right. I am burning in these clothes." Margaret agreed with a laugh and accepted the offered garments gratefully.

That afternoon, Margaret emerged from her siesta wearing her new outfit, a relatively sheer short-sleeved deep rose blouse, a forest green flowing skirt that clung to her limbs when she moved, no stockings, and a pair of sandals open at the toes. John was a little taken aback. Up until that time, he had only seen his wife dressed formally in company and seeing her in scantier clothing outside their bedroom bothered him somewhat. And, yet, he thought she looked so beautiful in them and they showed her graceful figure to advantage.

Frederick, who was pouring drinks, saw the scowl that passed almost imperceptibly through John's brow. After serving everyone their drinks, Frederick sat down next to John. "Isn't my little sister beautiful? You know, when we were children, she hated wearing petticoats because she could not run fast enough to keep up with me. So, she would drag me to the fields away from Dixon's watchful eyes where she could take them off. Without them, she did sometimes outrun me, partly because of sheer determination, I think." He laughed a little as he finished with another recollection. "Unfortunately, after she was sent to London, she started acting more like a lady when she came home and she was not as much fun anymore."

John, replied without taking his eyes off of his wife. "She is indeed alluring. I suppose I always thought I was the only one privileged to see her dressed so.........casually."

Frederick chuckled. "You are on the Andalusian coast! We put on a public persona when we leave the house but in here, what you do is between only you and your conscience. You make your own rules. Most of the year, we cannot dress as you do in Britain. This climate encourages an informality that I find good for the spirit."

"But does not the Spanish temperament figure into it?"

"It must. It is spontaneous, less inhibited, well-suited to this particular area of Spain where nature is all around us and trade brings in such a diverse group of people. To live here, one cannot always insist on proper decorum and be resistant to change. Take me, for instance, I was bred to be a proper English gentleman and I believe I am now closer in disposition to a Spaniard. Their outlook on life has influenced mine entirely. It did take years, though."

"Meeting Dolores probably helped, too." John said, smiling.

"Yes, indeed." Frederick grinned with pleasure as they both looked in the direction where their wives stood in lively conversation.

John nodded with a smile, gazing at Margaret as she listened intently to Dolores explain something about some figurines on the mantelpiece. He observed with a mix of pride and concern: "Margaret might have adapted to this society with ease, particularly with you here."

Frederick shot him a curious glance and replied: "I did write her to come live with us after my father died but she was not ready for such a momentous change. I told her she could come any time but eventually, I think you two found each other. I cannot thank you enough for coming to visit. I despaired over not seeing my sister again and I have spent many sleepless nights wondering how she was and what would happen to her."

"I am glad she did not come here," John replied, hesitated a moment, and went on. "If she had done so, I would have invented some excuse to come for her after I found out who you actually were."

Frederick studied his countenance briefly and smiled. "I do believe you would have! You have been good for her. She has a radiance I have never seen before."

Luncheon, frequently a heavier repast than dinner, usually took two hours and was followed by siesta which occupied another two hours. During siesta hours, the sun was at its zenith in the summer and the local people tended to stay within the comfort of indoor spaces. Were Frederick not on vacation, he would have returned to his office after the siesta and worked from 4 p.m. to 8 p.m. in the evening. Margaret vaguely remembered siesta mentioned in one of her brother's letters and was not surprised at the practice but John, used to a schedule of continuous work during the day, found it perplexing. Frederick and Dolores were faithful to the custom, treated those hours of repose as a necessary indulgence that they spent in their bedroom, and left John and Margaret to entertain themselves.

John and Margaret found themselves, on their first two days in Cadiz, too languid from the luncheon and too uncomfortable in the heat to do anything but seek the coolest part of the house and laze around—talking or reading, with glasses of cold water and a fan. After a restless quarter of an hour in their bedroom, they settled on the verandah where ocean breezes blew enough of the heat away to make it quite tolerable. By their fifth day, Margaret started to dose off from reading her book. The verandah bed became too tempting to resist and she yielded to it.

As she was drifting off to sleep, she opened her eyes momentarily at the stirring next to her and saw that John had come to join her. The following days, John submitted willingly to the exigencies of the weather and adapted to the local custom right after lunch. Towards the end of their stay, he loosened up enough to banish his cravats and vests into their luggage, roll his shirtsleeves up to his elbows, and entice Margaret to the big verandah bed for an afternoon siesta.

On a particularly lazy afternoon, as they lay together, he said: "I could become used to this."

She sat up, suppressing a smile, and exclaimed, eyes wide with feigned disbelief: "What? And how could you survive a dull life of careless days of ease?"

He pulled her back so she lay on top of him. "How could you remember something I said so long ago? What if I would rather not be reminded of it?"

"Would you really not want to be reminded of that remark? Should it not flatter you instead that what you had to say made such an impression on me that I could remember it?"

"But it offended you at that time so I would rather that you had forgotten it."

"Well, you might think that but, in fact, what you told us shortly thereafter about what you had to do and endure after your father died rather impressed me. I was mortified and began to think I had been too harsh on you."

"A fine way you had of showing you were impressed by refusing to shake my hand!" He feigned offense by scowling at her and shaking his head.

"I really was ignorant of the practice at the time. Anyway, I could not admit then nor let anyone see that you had begun to interest me," she replied archly and kissed his mouth. Then, she lay back next to him, her head on his shoulder.

"That is not all, either. Do you recall when Mr. Bell asked you what you worked so hard for and when you intended to enjoy the fruits of your labor?"

John obviously remembered and did so with some pain. He groaned. "I was an ass because I was consumed by jealousy and still stung by your rejection. I told myself I should hate you or at least ignore you pointedly; instead, I could not get you out of my mind. And yet, you sat there looking serene and unconcerned. Mr. Bell must have thought me irrational and irritable."

"Well, yes, he did," she replied. "But I told him you were not your usual self that night, that something was troubling you."

He stared at her, his eyes wide and incredulous. "You knew that. You defended me!"

"I knew by then that I loved you just when I was convinced you no longer cared for me. How could I possibly reveal how I felt?"

"Did you think me uncaring because of my callous remark to you?"

She shrugged her shoulders and did not answer.

He clasped her close. "Oh, Margaret, my love! All I was waiting for was a look from you so I could show you how contrite I was."

She snuggled closer to him, still silent, thinking that all that mattered then was he had his warm, reassuring arms around her now.

After a long silence, John returned to the question of leisure. "Well, it is true. Leisure normally discomfited me. I had always been more at ease being busy, usually with work at and for the mill. I rarely did anything that was in service only of my mind or my knowledge until I started studying with your father. But this is a different place and, with you, certainly a different time. You have opened up my world and I can no longer imagine it without moments like this with you." He kissed her forehead and closed his eyes. On that verandah bed that afternoon, as he settled snugly next to Margaret, he smiled wryly at himself and thought: "Well, Mr. Bell, you won that argument."

In pleasing Margaret, John had to open himself up to experiences that were new and, sometimes, even strange to him. He initially saw some places and people through her eyes before he discovered something in them that he uniquely found intriguing or at least interesting. It had been so in Paris—at the museums and art galleries where his reactions were, at first, colored by hers; at the cafés and theater where she translated what she heard. Though this was her first Paris visit, she recognized many things from Monsieur Fleury's descriptions and the books he had sent her. Her delight and wonder soaking in the city, pointing to monuments and places she read or heard about was infectious, inevitably drawing him into her enthusiasm.

This trip that took them to new places and exposed them to people with different customs, idiosyncratic ways of thinking and of viewing the world had, indeed, been a journey. It had changed them both although it seemed to have affected him more than Margaret. Paris, in their brief sojourn, gave him a glimpse into a culture immersed in arts and pleasure and the pursuit of both. Yet, it was also deeply engaged in progress and ideas—was it not, after all, the land of Diderot and Voltaire—and was apparently on a well-planned path of modernization to better meet the needs of its inhabitants. It was a culture and a people equally at home with concerns of a nature he would consider serious and important as well as those he once relegated to mere "appearances" or even frivolities, nonessential to survival or comfort. He had to reconsider, to acknowledge that "appearances" and "careless ease" were created for a purpose, to nourish, perhaps, some higher human need.

Cadiz was a different experience. It had a careworn aspect about it, not surprising in possibly the oldest city in Europe. It did not have the frantic rush to modernity that pervaded Paris. Instead, underneath the constant buzz of commerce, it had the languid ambiance of an aging city, with its medieval churches and tree-covered plazas. The warm balmy climate encouraged living alfresco much of the day and public spaces—the open plazas, gardens, and beaches where breezes flowed freely and continuously—teemed with people, drawn out of the houses they inhabited on narrow winding streets.

It was, for John and Margaret, a carefree interlude—a time of playfulness, of kissing and caressing, of strolling on beaches under clear skies to the sonorous vocalizations of gulls and the soothing coolness of sea breezes. It was a time they would both often hark back to during cold wintry days in Milton, a sweet respite from events that came before and those that were still to come.

Margaret and John had originally planned to stay in Cadiz for only a week, after which Frederick and Dolores would take them to other towns and cities in the region. But before the week was over, everyone agreed they should postpone the visit to other places since they were all having a pleasant time together, getting better acquainted in Cadiz. The week stretched to two and John and Margaret only had time to see the cities Andalusia was well-known for.

The two couples went to Granada and Seville where they stayed a few days. Seen on the surface; Seville seemed much like a larger inland incarnation of Cadiz, with plazas and numerous churches, the most famous being its grand Gothic cathedral, the largest in existence. It had been built in the former site of a mosque whose tower, the Giralda, still stood. They also tried to see the Alcazar, the royal palace, but the royal family was there and it was closed to the public. In Granada, they visited the Alhambra, an enchanting Moorish palace on a hill up above the city, exotic in its intricate designs, its colorful tiles, and its fountains and pools. Margaret vaguely recollected hearing about the Alhambra and, going around its rooms a second time, she realized it was Fanny. She had to agree that the Alhambra was indeed a very special place.

The month with Frederick and Dolores passed too quickly for Margaret and Frederick whose parting was nearly as tearful as their reunion. They all vowed to meet again, anywhere else but England, of course. By the time, John and Margaret boarded the boat back to Marseilles, they agreed to meet Frederick and Dolores in Paris in two to three years.

X. CONCERNS

The passage back to England proved demanding for Margaret. She suffered bouts of dizziness and nausea from the constant swaying and occasional turbulence of the ship they took from Cadiz to Marseilles and, later, from the even more tempestuous passage on the ferry between Le Havre and Dover. By the time they reached England, she seemed in a stupor, her eyes glazed and her face drained of color and brightness. She leaned heavily on John as she walked down the ramp and once on the pier, she felt faint and enervated, her spirit sucked out of her. John was alarmed and insisted on spending the night at a hotel in Dover. There, he asked for a local doctor to see his wife. The doctor found nothing to be seriously concerned about and declared it a bad case of seasickness that should go away in a couple of days. In the meantime, he gave her a potion to control nausea and put her to sleep and prescribed very light bland meals for a day or two. Margaret slept peacefully through the night, woke up late the next day, and felt well enough to insist, despite John's hesitation, on resuming their journey back to Milton.

Before returning home, they stopped in London where Dixon waited at the Lennoxes with the remainder of Margaret's belongings not transported on Dixon's previous trip to Milton. They stayed one night during which Margaret rested further and was fussed over by Edith and Mrs. Shaw who, remarking on her looking ill, were informed of her troubles at sea. Even Edith's little boy was drawn into the effort, offering his aunt a small posy of flowers picked out of the vases all around the house and coming to see her several times during the day to embrace her and kiss her face all over.

John noted all the busy, affectionate gestures of concern over his wife with some amusement. His mother never fussed over him when he had been ill as a child and although she was more solicitous with Fanny, it was still in an efficient sort of way. John knew that what Margaret needed was rest and sleep and, indeed, that was what she preferred but she received the attention with gratitude, sensible of the fondness and caring behind all the pampering her aunt and cousin gave her. It did do her some good and by evening, she felt well enough to join them for dinner. John's anxieties were allayed for the time being and he turned his attention to becoming better acquainted with Mrs. Shaw, Edith, and Captain Lennox. Edith implored them to stay longer but despite her appeals, John and Margaret were impatient to be home and were back in Milton, with Dixon, on Sunday evening.

The morning after their return, John walked across the yard to the mill. There, he expected to find Williams who he intended to send on some errands in preparation for reopening the mill. After more than two months respite from the work that had been his life, he was eager to return to it. He knew that, this time, he was going to have to do many things differently to forestall or at least reduce the bitter effects of strikes, the last one of which brought about his recent failure. Since that bleak period when it became clear that he had to close the mill, he had spent endless hours mulling over what changes he would make if he could somehow restore its operation. He laid out alternative plans on paper that listed different possibilities for financing its restoration, among which was working for some other manufacturer until he could amass enough capital to resume the management of his own mill. None of those financing alternatives considered coming into wealth by marriage and, at that time, he had already resigned himself to approaching middle age alone as he struggled once more to build his business.

By law, the wealth that Margaret brought into the marriage was now also his to use as he pleased or saw fit and she made it very clear that she would not interfere in business matters. Still, he felt reluctant assuming control of that wealth and investing it freely in the mill. Perhaps, it was merely that he could not get accustomed to how easily his financial problems resolved themselves and that, despite his misgivings about starting all over again at so late an age, he had rather looked forward to the new challenges that were certain to come with a late restart. In marrying Margaret, he no longer needed to find employment with another mill. He could immediately start practices only recently put together, borne out of new perspectives he had gained through closer alliance with his workers. None of his colleagues would have allowed him free reign to try those practices at their mills.

How much Margaret changed his life! He leaned back, thinking about her. He would see her again at tea as he had promised her that morning. She told him she understood if he did not come, that she knew how much work he needed to do to reopen the mill. But John was still immersed in the pleasures of being with his new wife, still sometimes in awe that she had come back and that he could bask in her warmth, listen to her loving voice, touch her, caress her. Their first two months together had been blissful, full of wondrous moments he wanted to recapture as often as he could, for as long as possible. No matter what the future held, those moments were his to treasure forever.

They had never been apart for more than a few minutes at a time since their wedding and, alone in his office during a lull in his work, she took hold of his thoughts just as she had in what seemed like such a distant past when he believed he would never see her again. But the images of her he now conjured up had changed. They were no longer of Margaret, beautiful, bewitching, distant, unattainable. Now, they were mostly of her yielding deliciously, ardently to his lovemaking, of gazing at him tenderly, her full soft lips in a half-smile, before she swayed against him and settled contentedly in his arms.

It seemed that they grew closer every day but what was most wonderful to him had also been unexpected—something she taught him about women or at least, the particular type of woman that Margaret was. He had assumed, as many men did, that a woman's more delicate nature also made them more placid, more diffident, not so intense as men in their feelings and Margaret was, indeed, tender and sometimes, even shy. But he was amazed to discover that she could also be passionate, returning his ardor with almost equal intensity, and it thrilled him infinitely to be the object of such feelings.

Occupied as he had been with the mill before he met Margaret, John had never thought about what it meant to be married. He knew that there would be children to inherit his legacy, that his wife, not his mother, would run his household. Beyond that, he had no extraordinary expectations and, consequently, he never seriously contemplated marrying, much less, choosing a wife. Finding a woman to marry had not been, on the face of it, a problem because of all the many young women who would have welcomed a proposal from him. But not one of the women of his acquaintance could lure him into matrimony. He believed it was because the vision he had of marriage had not been appealing enough to tempt him to abandon the comfort and familiarity of his life with his mother and sister. Then, he met Margaret and she upset the equilibrium and complacency he had achieved.

He had been aware of a palpable stirring in his chest on that day they were introduced in her father's study. Her uncommon beauty attracted him first. It was not that she was the most beautiful woman he had ever met but hers was a different kind of beauty, one that compelled people to look longer or take at least a second glance or even a third one to ascertain what they found arresting in her face. He first noticed her large blue eyes, more limpid than he had ever seen, defined by thick lashes and well-arched eyebrows. What was more intriguing, however, was how expressive they were and how piercing her gaze was when she directed it at him that he could not tear his eyes off her and, yet, she also had a doe-eyed look about her that made him want to protect her. Her mouth was a little too wide, the lower lip a little too plump for classic beauty and too easily thrust into defiance. Yet, on that first meeting, he imagined kissing those lips and tingled at the thought of it.

Eventually, despite their vexing early encounters, his heart could not resist the depth and complexity promised in those lively eyes and intrepid mouth. By the time he was ready to propose, he had convinced himself that life with Margaret would be far from dull, perhaps, even occasionally unpredictable. Were he fortunate enough to persuade her to marry him, their union would not be the conventional sort he had seen among his business colleagues, the sort that had not attracted him enough to consider it.

He had been very worried about her during the return journey from Spain. Remembering her mother's illness, he hoped Margaret had not inherited the same constitution. No longer willing to conceive of life without her, he shuddered once again at the thought that he might have lost her to someone else. He tried to vanish those troubling thoughts with joyous recollections of their honeymoon in Paris and the trip to Spain. They were both enthralled with Paris and looked forward to returning there for a reunion with Frederick and Dolores. He liked Frederick very much, certainly because he had many of his sister's wonderful qualities, but John knew himself enough to suspect that he was determined to like Frederick to atone for the many months of unfounded resentment he harbored against him.

John was deep into his reverie, staring far away into space, a smile on his lips, when Williams returned from an errand John had sent him on. Embarrassed at intruding into his master's obviously pleasant thoughts, he mumbled a greeting and handed him a large envelope.

"Did you need me for anything more this morning, master? If not. I have an errand to run for myself."

"Can you come back late this afternoon, perhaps around three?"

"Yes, master."

As soon as Williams left, John opened the envelope and studied its contents. It was an accounting from the bank of the current status of the loan on the mill. He spent much of the morning perusing it and making notes, preparing for a noon meeting with his banker. He was poised to take the first step towards reviving the mill.

That afternoon, John joined Margaret for their first tea at home since their return. Dixon had prepared some special tea cakes and finger sandwiches and John could not help smiling at the spread before them. "This must be how it is done in fashionable circles in London. Dixon seems determined to elevate my tastes."

Margaret laughed. "Dixon takes great pleasure in food and will try different kinds of dishes. Generally, her cooking is quite good. But every once in a while, even an adventuresome eater might find it too exotic."

"Was tea at Harley Street always this elaborate?"

"Not really. Only on occasion and when certain friends of my aunt came. This is Dixon's way of welcoming us back. I wouldn't be surprised if she also prepares our favorite dishes for dinner."

John picked up a sandwich, ate it in two bites, and grinned. "Hmm. I can gobble these up." But he did not take another piece. Instead, he put his teacup down and regarded his wife thoughtfully.

Margaret arched an eyebrow at him when, after some minutes, he still had not spoken. Reluctant to intrude into his thoughts, she continued to sip her tea.

John stood up, picked up his chair and deposited it next to Margaret's. "Have I ever explained why I had to give up the mill?"

"No but I assumed it was because you could not pay the bank loan on account of the strike."

"The strike certainly made all the difference. It caused production delays, some orders could not be completed on schedule, and I did not receive payments when I expected them. But I cannot blame the strike solely for what happened. The market was on a downturn and some clients whose orders were filled could not pay what they owed me because they had difficulty selling their merchandise."

He paused, thoughtful again. "The bank loan is not a terribly huge amount and is actually the only outstanding debt on the mill. Workers were paid but I had borrowed money against the mill for new machinery and materials when orders doubled. I needed to pay the bank by a certain time but I couldn't without payments from my clients."

John compressed his lips and scowled. Margaret heard the regret and sadness in his voice. She wanted to say something to ease his guilt, if not his sadness, but she was afraid of sounding condescending and insensitive. Instead, she clasped his hand with both of hers. She knew that any other man would not have agonized over why he lost his fortune once married to a woman with a sizable inheritance; he would have merely considered himself lucky that his problem had been so conveniently solved.

"On that glorious day at the train station, you offered me a loan for a small interest so I could reopen the mill." The shadow on his brow lifted as he recalled that day and he smiled at her tenderly.

She smiled warmly back. "That money is now at your disposal to use as you see fit."

"That may be. But I prefer to still consider the money a loan to be paid with interest, out of mill profits. I don't know. Perhaps, my pride or my principles demand that I rise from this failure mostly on my own resources. But I also worry about the ups and downs in this business and am loath to place you and the children we will have through the hardships my mother suffered."

He paused, the burdens of the past etched once again on his brow. "For now, I only need a few hundred pounds to pay off the interest and a portion of the debt. The bank would restore the mill's credit which I would use to continue operating. I'm confident the mill will again be successful—I will do everything I can to make it so. I would, then, return the amount taken from your account and invest it in something relatively stable to serve as a hedge in the event of another collapse."

Margaret listened, touched by the nobility of his intent, and when he finished, she was speechless for a few moments. When she spoke, her voice was soft and her tone, almost humbled. "I came into this wealth reluctantly. Perhaps because it had been too easy to acquire, a big portion of it had not really meant that much. It is not that I was not grateful. I was very much aware of how fortunate I was. Mr. Bell's generous legacy alone gave me security as well as the luxury of living well. I could live as I wanted and my choices were multiplied. It was an incredible feeling, realizing that I only had my conscience to consult in deciding how to live my life."

She put her arms around him and he laid his face against her bosom, clasping her close. "But at that train station, I did not really make a choice. I merely went along with the inevitable, happy consequence of clearly knowing what I wanted. A life with you, whatever its ups and downs."

She was silent for a moment, her cheek resting gently on his head. "What I have is yours. I trust you completely to decide what to do with all that I have inherited including the money from Watson's speculative venture. I have learned a little about managing this wealth and know that it is wise to shelter some of it. But use part of it for projects you wanted to do to improve working conditions, whatever you see fit. I have all I want in my life with you."

She stroked his hair softly and he glanced up at her with smiling eyes, his countenance tranquil once more. He nestled his head more snugly against her chest, listening calmly to the regular beating of her heart. After some minutes, she spoke again. "There is only one matter I would like some say on. Your plans to do more for workers seem, to me, too worthwhile to delay. Workers are not much different from you or me, with the same basic rights, so we should give them their due when we can. There is still a considerable disposable amount in the inheritance even after the bank loan is paid so I see no reason to put off measures to improve their plight."

He did not disagree with her remark but its boldness startled him nonetheless. Having only begun, in the months since he had known Nicholas Higgins, to value an open honest relationship with his workers, he was dismayed to hear his wife stating, with certainty, notions still being formed in his mind. He looked up at her, the faint suggestion of a scowl coming back to cloud his eyes.

Margaret stared back, a momentary flash of defiance dilating her pupils. Were the differences in their views about workers going to become a matter of contention between them? She knew that, in the beginning, he had been of a similar mind as his mother. They assumed that people were dealt what they deserved and if they got the shorter end of the stick, it had been by their action or choice. Yet, he had reached out to Nicholas Higgins and talked about discovering much good in his character, much that he learned from their interactions and he wanted to pursue a similar approach with more workers.

Margaret had no desire for confrontation so early in their married life and she said in a conciliatory tone: "I know you have done more than anyone else about improving working conditions at the mill."

He acknowledged her remark with a nod but dropped his arms from around her waist and began to stand up. She stepped back to give him space but she could not help feeling letdown. He stood up and ran his hand tenderly down her back before he walked towards the fireplace. The caressing touch mollified her somewhat and she sat down on the chair he vacated, her gaze following his movement, waiting, wanting to be wooed back to those tender moments before she made her bold declaration.

John was as loath as Margaret to start any conflict between them but he was also cautious not to agree too readily until he was certain where he stood in his changing views about workers. He was aware that, in his plans, he was treading on unknown territory that could prove to be more complicated and, therefore, difficult to manage. After the recent problems with the mill, he was more anxious about maintaining control of his business. He was determined to be as frank as he could, however. "I admit that you and I disagreed in the past in our views pertaining to workers. I do have plans more in line with your thinking but I need to work them out further."

"I realize this is your province and have no intention of directly intruding in it. I was merely stating a principle that I myself would live by."

"I am not concerned about your intrusion. My mother went to the mill regularly and dealt with workers. I believe her visits allowed her to see things I could not and she made very helpful suggestions for running the mill."

"Yes but she knows the mill more than I ever could."

"You could learn." He approached her with a gentle conciliatory smile, grasped her hands and pulled her up from the chair and into his arms.

"Perhaps," she replied, gazing up at him and brushing the back of her hand against his cheek.

He enclosed the hand on his cheeks with his and pressed it to his lips. "Anyway, I do know your sentiments about workers and your generous heart that must do something to help those in need. You have a mind of your own which I respect and have no desire to suppress."

She did not reply but kissed the hand that held hers.

With soft smiling eyes, he murmured: "I must go. Williams is at the mill, waiting for instructions from me to run some errands. I will see you this evening, my love." He kissed her once more and left.

Mrs. Thornton would be back in two weeks from her long visit with Fanny. Margaret, thankful for this time alone with John, felt a touch of mortification in admitting her relief they had the house to themselves a while longer. She could not quite reconcile herself yet to the role of being in charge of a home that did not bear much relationship to who she was, set up and adorned in a manner quite opposite to her notion of a warm cozy home. But she must adjust to it. Still, she thought wryly, reaching some level of ease and familiarity with the household would probably be easier than courting Mrs. Thornton's good opinion.

Margaret suspected that Mrs. Thornton probably doubted just as much that they could ever be comfortable with each other. Their time together had so far been brief—not much chance yet to get to know one another intimately—but their differences might be too fundamental to overcome and neither of them was ever likely to change their beliefs. But her anxieties went beyond concerns about differences in how she and her mother-in-law saw the world and human nature. She could deal with those, despite the uneasiness they inevitably occasioned. It was the intricacies of emotions that perplexed her and she felt hopeless about influencing them, much less changing them in Mrs. Thornton whose dislike of her was all too obvious. Still, Margaret told herself that, having the advantage of being the primary object of John's affections, she had no cause to resent her mother-in-law, that doing so would make life in the Thornton household unbearable. It was her obligation, in any case, to nurture good relations with the mother of her husband.

But how could she court the good graces of the strong-minded Mrs. Thornton who was not only resolute in her beliefs but also zealous in her concerns? Those concerns gave direction to her life, consuming her energy, dictating her interests and inclinations, and structuring her time. Their principal object had been her son probably all those past thirty-some years—a rather long time in anybody's life—and in turn, she had been certain of having been first in his regard. John's marriage to Margaret had upset Mrs. Thornton's ordered complacent world, its main purpose taken away by a woman she did not think worthy, one who caused her son so much unhappiness, then returned to claim him. For all those, Margaret sadly acknowledged, Mrs. Thornton had reason enough to resent her.

Once in a while, Margaret found herself shuddering at what life with Mrs. Thornton held for her, fearful of her mother-in-law's unbending nature. Much more at ease with directness and pure sentiments, Mrs. Thornton either hated or loved, admired or felt contempt and she did all those intensely. She formed her opinions very quickly and found no reason to complicate her life by analyzing them. Such an approach to life had served her well within the realm of an extensive experience full of hard-fought triumphs she was justly proud of. Mrs. Thornton had no cause to regret anything she had done.

Margaret's sheltered life in both London and Helstone, with loved ones and friends of generous, easygoing temperaments, had not prepared her for someone like her Mrs. Thornton. Her limited experience allowed her only to try to be on some tolerable, if not pleasant, footing with her but she knew she must also accept the certainty of discord. Could she be blamed if, from time to time and for a few moments, she longed for the mellow, relatively carefree life she had at Harley Street? Those moments did not last, in any case, since she always reminded herself that it was with John that she was happiest and life would be most fulfilling. Had she not already convinced herself that she was prepared to endure the discomfort and irritations of living with Mrs. Thornton and to countenance the contempt each might feel about the other's views?

Mrs. Thornton's feelings about Margaret were about as complicated, suspicious and mocking of all that Margaret represented—her airs, graces, book knowledge, and other southern sensibilities—and jealous of the obvious changes she had wrought in John. Her son had confided much in her before he married. Mrs. Thornton disagreed, from the beginning, with his opinion of Margaret, believing her unworthy of him, but she knew she could not dissuade him from offering his hand, particularly after the riot. When Margaret rejected him, Mrs. Thornton breathed with relief, secretly rejoicing still being first in her son's affections. Ironically, what brought her relief caused her son much unhappiness. She blamed Margaret, her disdain for the young woman turning into hatred that she blurted out to her son. But she was taken aback; instead of hating Margaret as he ought to have, John confessed loving her even more. They never talked about Margaret again after that.

It suited Mrs. Thornton to dismiss all mention of Margaret until she found she had been too hasty to write her off. She was happy to see Margaret leave Milton, believing naively that London was far enough away that she could no longer disrupt their lives. But Margaret did return one day. Mrs. Thornton was aghast, forced to accept a reality she revolted against.

Mrs. Thornton had seen in Margaret a part of herself but knowing this did not predispose her to like Margaret. Instead, it disturbed her. Margaret, who did not shy away from letting others know what she thought and felt, was a formidable rival not only for her son's heart but also for his mind. Born with a good mind and guided in the improvement of it by a scholarly father and his friends, Mrs. Thornton had to admit that Margaret developed a mind keener and more receptive than she ever had, or even cared about. Margaret had ideas and sentiments she could never grasp, and it worried her that Margaret's sympathy for workers would undermine John's single-minded pursuit of his rightful place as a widely-respected manufacturer. Margaret had already influenced him. It was evident in his friendship with that man Higgins.

Still, Mrs. Thornton could not simply disregard Margaret. The wealth she brought into the marriage spared John the difficulties and anguish of having to start all over again. Then, there was the fact that Margaret did love John, had chosen him over others who might have courted her. But most of all, Mrs. Thornton could not deny that John was clearly happier since Margaret returned.

When the mill closed, he declared as he had many years ago: "It's just you and I again, mother." Those words, uttered for the first time so long ago, had carried a challenge, energizing and full of promise, propelling them both into a mission that—through hard work, sacrifice, and determination—brought success they had both been proud of. But those same words—uttered again when his business failed and in the midst of his certainty that he would never see Margaret again—conveyed a dispirited weariness, a quiet despair she had never seen in him. If seeing him happy now did not sufficiently calm Mrs. Thornton's unease about Margaret, it did mute any expression of disapproval she might have. By the time she returned to Milton, she resolved to be more agreeable to Margaret. And yet, in her heart, she doubted if she was capable of doing so.

XI. POSTERITY

The full force of summer hit Milton in the middle of August, bringing with it heat and still air, trapping smoky, heavy emissions from the cotton mills, and forcing most of the city's inhabitants to take refuge indoors unless they had business to do outside. Margaret was not one to be fazed by heat and sun. There had been more of those in the south although summer days were hardly ever as unbearable as they were in Milton. Cooling breezes and an abundance of sprawling shady trees always tempered the heat.

Margaret, determined not to let the weather disrupt her usual routines, went out for her daily walk. Walking was a habit she naturally grew into long ago in Helstone where everything outdoors beckoned her to explore and enjoy its delights. When she moved to Milton with her parents, walking in the parks granted her respite from their cramped quarters and the city's oppressive atmosphere. Later, when one sorrowful event after another struck, she sought relief, however temporary, from a brisk walk outdoors. It rejuvenated her exhausted spirits and gave her time for reflection. Walking became a necessity from which she was kept away only by dangerous snow, wind, and rain.

Margaret did think it wise to change her schedule this scorching summer. She usually went out early in the morning right after breakfast, before atmosphere and temperature were at their worst. After a particularly warm and muggy night during which she tossed and turned and slept fitfully, she and John arose earlier than usual. She was not her usual bright self in the morning. Her head throbbed, her stomach was a little unsettled, and her back muscles ached. She thought, at first, that she should forego her walk but she hoped some strong tea would cure those little ills from lack of sleep. In any case, she could change her mind if tea and scones did not help.

She could start on one of the many daily chores to keep the house as impeccable as it had been under Mrs. Thornton's supervision. These chores were more drudgery than pleasure but she was anxious not to give her mother-in-law something to criticize her for. As was her wont, she followed her chores with more agreeable occupation, reading, tending to pots of plants she started with Dixon, or if she had not yet done so, going for her daily walk. She kept her schedule flexible so she could take her walk in late afternoon if she was feeling better.

Margaret put the last pin on her hair as John, properly attired but without his jacket, indicated with a gesture that he was ready to take her down to breakfast. She began to rise but before she could straighten, a strange sensation gripped her of the room swaying, receding from her vision; of a wave of nausea seizing her stomach, quickly spreading to her chest; of her legs melting from under her as her body crumpled slowly to the floor. On her way down, her hand instinctively grabbed the back of her chair and held on to it with all the strength she had left. She was fading fast when steady arms enclosed her in a familiar embrace so safe and strong that she allowed herself to let go. John, a few paces away, had run to catch her. The alarm of only a week ago came rushing back, intensifying at the sight of her ashen face, the color drained from her lips and cheeks. She looked at him with dazed eyes, closed them, and collapsed like a rag doll in his arms.

"Margaret, my love," John cried, his voice fraught with fear. He picked her up, carried her to the bed and gently laid her down. He could barely control the shaking in his limbs and rang vigorously for Dixon to send someone straightaway for the doctor. Dixon came quickly, saw Margaret looking almost lifeless on the bed and, for an instant, was overcome by terror. She hurried to do as she was bid, swiftly but calmly.

Dixon had handled situations like this before, had learned critical signs to watch for. She doubted, upon recalling what she saw, that there was anything seriously wrong with her young mistress whose constitution she knew to be much sturdier than her mother. Despite the master's reaction, she had her own suspicions of the cause of Margaret's current affliction and the more she thought about it, the more convinced she was of them. In any case, the master would know soon enough.

John sat on the bed, caressing his wife's face gently. He fixed his eyes on her face, watchful for any signs of increasing distress. Her breathing was shallow and slow but regular. John called out: "My love, can you hear me?" She opened her eyes halfway, smiled faintly at him and opened her mouth to speak but no words came out. "Hush," he said in as soothing a tone as he could summon. "I'm here and Dr. Donaldson should be here very soon."

Dixon returned with a basin of cold water and compresses. "I will take care of her now, master. You might feel better waiting in your study. The doctor will be here any minute now. Williams went for him in a cab."

"No," John answered almost angrily but he stood up to give her room. "Do what you can but I will stay here with her," he continued a little more subdued as he pulled a chair by the bed and sat down on it.

Dixon smiled, actually relieved to have him stay. Mr. Hale was never able to endure his wife's illnesses and fainting spells and it gratified her to see Mr. Thornton so solicitous of his wife. She sat by the side of the bed and began applying cold compresses to Margaret's face. John held Margaret's hand, stroking it and, once in a while, pressing it to his lips. Soon, the color began to come back to her face and her faint breathing became stronger. She opened her eyes once or twice but closed them again as if the diffused light in the room blinded her.

Dr. Donaldson came shortly thereafter and glanced briefly at Margaret. "Williams told me she fainted. What was she doing when it happened?"

"We were about to go to breakfast and she was getting up from her chair."

Dr. Donaldson nodded. "So, she has not had anything to eat. How long have you been married?"

"About three months."

The doctor nodded again. "I would like to examine Mrs. Thornton in private. But please stay just outside the door, Dixon, in case I need your help."

John, worry plainly written on his face, hardly took his eyes off his wife and did not move from his chair. Dr. Donaldson stood next to him and took Margaret's pulse, smiling calmly at John. "Her color is back and I have not seen anything so far to alarm me so I am sure she will be all right. I will come directly to you after examining her."

He motioned with a hand towards the door and waited until John got up, reluctantly. John lingered for a moment, gazing at his wife, and then wordlessly walked toward his study. At the door, he paused to look back at her.

John sat in front of his desk, staring pensively into space. In the three short months that they had been married, Margaret had become the most important part of his life. Never had anyone caused him such consternation at her indifference, such agony at the thought that her affections belonged elsewhere—and yet—such pleasure at her expressive face and the gestures of her head, such tingling when he held her in his arms.

For her, he had acted in ways he never thought he would or could. Now that she was his wife, her hold over him was stronger than ever. Margaret brought pleasure to the commonplace and her zest for so much that her world could offer helped expand his interests, his perspective and his thinking. Her enthusiasm for art and music, her curiosity about new places and different cultures, her openness to new experiences had enticed him to venture into a world beyond the making and merchandising of cotton that had dominated most of his life.

John was even more fearful now of losing Margaret. He was intensely anxious about why she fainted but he could not, would not—even for a moment—confront the possibility that there was any actual threat of losing her. The notion of a future without her was totally inconceivable to him now. And yet, unlike Fanny's near-fainting spells, his wife's symptoms had been quite real and those that he just witnessed could no longer be attributed to seasickness. Her mother had died of some illness, the nature of which he was ignorant about.

John sprang up from his chair, trying to vanish those disturbing thoughts. He paced about the room in quick anxious strides. But physical exertion could not calm the turmoil in his mind and he picked up the volume of Plato that Margaret gave him when her father died, to seek some distraction there. He opened it at random and read as he walked back and forth but he could not make sense of the words even after reading them a second and third time. He put the book back on the desk and stared at the door that closed the bedroom off to his study. The doctor seemed to be taking an inordinately long time and he fought the urge to go storming back into the bedroom. In fact, it took less than half an hour before Dr. Donaldson knocked on the door and opened it without waiting for a response. He walked briskly towards John, grinning broadly, extending both hands to grasp one of John's. John let out one long breath of relief. His wife was going to be all right.

"Your wife, young Mrs. Thornton, is quite healthy and nothing is wrong with her that about eight months could not cure." Dr. Donaldson shook John's hand heartily and, seeing the puzzle still knitting his brow, he explained. "Nausea, lightheadedness, and fainting occasionally are not unusual in the first three, even four months. They tend to occur in the morning and the best preventive is a light breakfast in bed—tea, dry toast, and if she can tolerate it, some butter or jam."

John finally grasped what the doctor said and managed to grin back at him. "Thank you, doctor. That is good news." A fleeting frown crossed his brow. "But I had not anticipated having children right way."

"Well, man, what do you expect? Most young men like you rejoice at news like this. It reassures them that their legacy would continue. Anyway, you must pamper her." Dr. Donaldson laughed. "I suppose I need not tell you that. I will visit her next month, make sure everything is proceeding normally."

Once again, he shook John's hand and when it appeared the latter still seemed slightly dazed, the doctor hesitated to leave him "You know, I met your wife for the first time years ago—under sadder circumstances, as I recall. She and her father just came in from a party and hey were both surprised to see me there but she had been more alarmed than him. Later, when I returned to check on Mrs. Hale, her husband was out on one of his lectures and Miss Hale insisted on being completely informed about her mother, then in the last stages of her illness. I could see the deep anxiety on her face but she did not flinch at the bad news. I could sense her struggle to remain in control of her emotions. I wondered then who the lucky man would be who could win the heart of such a lovely, extraordinary young woman—self-possessed, perceptive for her age, for any age, but yet sensitive and so vulnerable that it made one want to protect her."

Dr. Donaldson paused, then said: "But I doubted that Miss Hale was the sort who would accept a man merely for the protection he could give her. No, she would cope on her own rather than give her heart away lightly." He paused again and with an impish smile, added: "That alone would attract any man who enjoys a challenge."

He peered closely at John who was staring at him with the faintest scowl over his now alert eyes. Amused and curious at his expression, Dr. Donaldson remarked: "I should have guessed it would have been you she fell for, Thornton, if she were to take fancy to any of us Milton men." Grinning broadly, he declared: "I have been in this profession long enough and I can pretty much tell how a couple feel about each other."

"Thank you again, Dr. Donaldson," John shook his hand again, more vigorously this time, a heartfelt smile brightening his eyes.

Dr. Donaldson nodded and took his leave with a parting advice: "She can do anything she wants to do and feels capable doing but she should be careful about those lightheaded spells in the next two, maybe three, months. They should pass."

Margaret was sitting up in bed when he came in. A faint blush had returned to her cheeks although dark shadows still circled her eyes. She reached her arms out as he sat down on the side of the bed and rested them on his shoulders, clasping her hands behind his neck. He gathered her in his arms, peered at her face, looked deep into her eyes that were very slowly regaining their brightness and clarity and said: "You gave me such a scare."

"But it is good news, is it not?" She replied, her eyes fixed on his.

He nodded and smiled but he did not answer.

"You're smiling but you don't seem too happy."

"I'm glad and greatly relieved that this affliction is of harmless consequence; indeed it is a happy one although"—he hesitated, gazing lovingly at her face—"truth be told, I wanted to have you all to myself a while longer, a year at least, anyway."

"Well, silly, what did you expect, making love to me as much as you have?" She laughed, kissed him lightly, and stroked his hair, pushing a stray lock off his forehead.

"Yes, silly me," he answered, burying his face on her neck, feeling the pulse beneath her soft warm flesh. It gratified and reassured him. His fear and apprehension had drained him and he rested his head briefly on her shoulder.

"Dixon is coming with breakfast, as the doctor ordered. How would you like to be found in such a compromising position?"

"I am making love to my wife in my own bedroom. She could have nothing to say about that."

"No, nothing. She's discreet and has grown quite protective of me. I was teasing." She pressed her cheek on the back of his bowed head and was silent for a while. Then, gently clasping his face, she raised it slowly to force him to look at her. "Don't you want to have children?"

"I do, of course, a couple of little Margarets and two sons perhaps."

She laughed. "That many?"

"Why not? It's just that—you and I alone together—I never imagined I could be this happy. I wanted it to last longer this way. I would have preferred to start a family, perhaps, two years from now."

"Sincerely? So would I but it seems we are being given one and I am actually happy about it. It is, after all, a new life you and I nurtured together."

He smiled. "Yes, I see, a new life affirming what you and I are to each other. I like that way of looking at it very much but I still wonder how a child will change our lives."

"Well, it will be different, I am sure. This gift, this new creation—yours and mine—" she paused to give themselves more time to relish the thought. "We must take responsibility for it, for quite a few years. But I hope we will always have a place like this of our own, a sanctuary of sorts, for just you and me."

"I would like that very much. You will be devoting much time to our child." He smiled and corrected himself: "Our children. But I want a time and place alone with you."

"Well, you will be out at the mill working much of the day and we will each have our own routines that would have to accommodate a child sooner than we expected. But evenings and early mornings will be ours alone in here as they have been the last few weeks."

"Has it only been that long?" He exclaimed rhetorically. "It's true I am eager to start work on reopening the mill."

"I know you are. It has been more than three months and you have probably never been away from it this long."

"True. And yet, I waited so long for you, for wonderful moments like these with you and I want to delay changing things as they are now."

"They will not change right away, not for seven or eight months, for me, anyway. You will probably open the mill before that."

"I am hoping around November, before the holidays."

"Is there much more to be done?"

"Yes but if I devote several hours everyday to all that must be done, I am confident I can do it. The debt to the bank has been settled and I am now working on rehiring workers and getting the machinery in good running order. Higgins will be coming any day now to help."

Margaret nodded but swayed towards him, feeling somewhat faint as fatigue and hunger returned. He looked at her pale face and gathered her in his arms, listening closely to her breathing, watching for signs that she might faint again. She leaned against him heavily and he could feel her bosom heaving against his chest, steadily, regularly, and in rhythm with his own breathing. He began to relax. Not long after, Dixon arrived, carrying a tray with breakfast for both of them. She seemed very pleased, her cheeks plumped up in a huge smile.

Later, somewhat revived but still weak, Margaret snuggled back into John's embrace. "The past months will always be a part of us even as we settle into a routine or go through other changes, don't you think?"

"Yes," he replied simply, his voice somewhat muffled against her hair.

"I am certain of it. I have left Helstone behind but I know it will forever be with me. It helped me endure the move to this city that was at first quite strange to me."

He raised his head, tilted hers to face him and, gazing into her eyes, asked softly, eagerly, needing reassurance she was happy. "Is Milton still so strange?"

"I have adapted to Milton."

Still anxious, he asked: "But are you happy here?"

"I have returned once to Helstone since I left it and I realized that, happy as I was there, I have changed and couldn't really go back." She gazed at him and stroked his cheeks lovingly. "Am I happy here? How could I not be when you are here? My life is with you now and it happens to be in Milton. This is where our first child will be born." With an arched eyebrow and eyes twinkling impishly at him, she ended "as will the other three who will follow."

John smiled tenderly back at her, grasped her hands, pressed each one to his cheeks and then to his lips.

Margaret asked: "Do you suppose the household has been told the good news?"

"Do you doubt it? Did you see the big smile on Dixon's face?"

Dixon told the household. A new addition to her mistress' family was an occasion to celebrate and, in her mind, celebrations were to be shared. A child had another special significance for her. It meant she and Margaret—still foreigners to some members of the household—were there to stay. Although her mistress never said anything, Dixon knew that Mrs. Thornton had not exactly given Margaret a warm welcome and had remained persistently cold—an attitude not lost on the servants and which rubbed off on a few of them, Jane, in particular. A child provided reassurance to Dixon of her place in the household.

Dixon promptly demonstrated her sense of an enduring, perhaps even elevated, status by taking over the kitchen and supervising the preparation of a dinner more elaborate than the servants were used to. Margaret's inheritance had an unexpectedly humbling effect on Dixon. In serving a mistress who actually owned much wealth and knowing that—with a generous pension accumulating and waiting for her—she, herself, no longer needed to struggle, Dixon began to realize it was of no great consequence how she was perceived by her peers. In this vein, she planned to produce a feast for every member of the household, masters as well as servants.

The servants grumbled at having to do things more elaborate than they were used to. Jane, who ordinarily supervised the cooking, did not mind. She never liked this part of her duties. The servants soon learned that Dixon was preparing her festive dishes for everyone. This was inducement enough. From then on, Dixon was in charge.

XII. PATTERNS

Some semblance of a routine slowly took hold once again of the day-to-day life at the Thornton household. Margaret's pregnancy inevitably changed some of the habits she and John had begun to fall into in the first three months of married life. Dixon understood Dr. Donaldson's advice on preventing Margaret's nausea and fainting as a sacred standing order. For a few more weeks at least, she was to bring her mistress a breakfast of tea and toast to their bedroom every morning.

The first two mornings, John kept Margaret company as she sipped her tea and nibbled on her toast. She offered him tea from her cup which he accepted without much hesitation. The next morning, after he went to have a full breakfast in the dining room, Margaret asked Dixon for another cup and more tea to be brought in on subsequent mornings. A few days later, John sighed, bemoaning that breakfast was too lonely to have in the dining room all by himself. Margaret immediately rang for toast, eggs and sausages for him. Since then, breakfast in bed and a pleasant morning tête-à-tête became a ritual that started their day before John went to work at the mill.

The routine Margaret followed varied from day to day and depended partly on how bothersome her morning sickness was. She devoted nearly half the day to the numerous tasks of running the household smoothly although it ran well enough without much direction from her: Dixon had fallen back into the role she first assumed with Mrs. Hale of being head housekeeper, making many little decisions on her own and not bothering her mistress about them. For the most part, her decisions were the same Margaret would have made so Margaret thought it only natural for Dixon to take over most minute responsibilities Mrs. Thornton had discharged herself.

Margaret felt relieved: She spent more time than she cared on household chores. Yet, once freed up from many of them, she worried about Mrs. Thornton's disapproval. While Mrs. Thornton was away, she did not dwell too long on these worries. Dixon was efficient and the house was maintained in an orderly fashion.

Margaret resumed her daily walk the day after her fainting spell. The doctor assured her that not only was it safe, it was good for her and might actually facilitate childbirth. These days, in her condition, John tried to take time from his often solitary work at the mill to accompany her on her walk, usually in late afternoon. When he could not, he insisted on having someone go with her. At first, Dixon went but Margaret found her too slow and unable to go the distance she usually walked. She tried to convince John that she could go on her own but he was too anxious, concerned that she could faint again or be stricken some other way while she was out alone.

One afternoon, seated in his office for a short break from contacting and rehiring workers from a list Nicholas Higgins had given him when the mill closed, John happened upon a solution. When they reconvened, he asked Nicholas: "Would Mary be interested in assisting Dixon at our house? Dixon has taken over the management of the kitchen and needs assistance with meal preparation and attending to Margaret's personal needs."

Nicholas replied with some amusement. "I will talk to Mary. But from what Mary told me of her previous time working for the Hales, I didn't think Mrs. Margaret needed any kind of assistance."

John smiled and it seemed to Nicholas that his eyes, which lighted up every time they talked about Margaret, had an added glitter. "We're expecting a baby and I want someone to go with her on her walks. You know my wife, Higgins. Those walks are nearly a necessity to her."

Nicholas grinned. "A child! A Thornton heir or heiress, maybe. What good news! I will tell Mary to go and see Mrs. Margaret tomorrow. I am sure she will prefer working for her than cooking in the hall. Actually, it seems an ideal set-up for Mary."

Margaret thought it was likewise an ideal set-up for her because she already knew Mary's character and what she was capable of. Two days after John talked to Nicholas, Mary Higgins started working in the Thornton household. She became Margaret's companion on her walk, an arrangement which proved satisfactory to Dixon.

After her daily walk, Margaret often devoted some time to reading, anticipating the end of the day when John came home. She had purchased some books in Paris—many of them literary works in French by the well-known writers Honoré de Balzac and George Sand. She had been devouring them since their return to Milton.

To her delight, she found John particularly keen to hear about them. While he refreshed himself with some tea, he spent long minutes listening and asking detailed questions about what she had read that day. She suspected that, not having much time lately for reading, he depended on her recounting to keep him connected to a world apart from the making of cotton—a world chronicled in those books. He had experienced part of that world with much pleasure just a few months ago. Consequently, Margaret made her descriptions vivid and detailed. When she thought certain passages too meaningful to merely summarize, she marked them and read them. When the passages were in French, she would read them first in French before translating them.

When Margaret finished the first of those books, one by Balzac, John said: "Merci beaucoup. What a wonderful story and your retelling transported me to the time and place where it happened."

"I am glad you liked it. I didn't think that you were at all interested in fiction. It seemed you and Papa always read and talked about the great classical thinkers."

"True but they're all grappling with universal truths about the human condition. Only, Balzac couches it in fiction. In my mind, that makes it no less true."

Margaret smiled with satisfaction. "Well, then, what do you want me to read next?"

"Would you mind alternating one of the books on Spain that we brought home from Cadiz for every French book you read?"

Frederick had recommended books on places, cultural traditions and art in Spain.

"Not at all. I would be happy to," Margaret happily agreed, then added: "Did you know that I have much experience being a reader and storyteller? I spent many months reading to my father when he was inconsolable and listless after Mama died."

He smiled sympathetically and gathered her into his arms.

Listening to Margaret talk about the books she had read was not enough for John. If he could not be with her to share her day, he wanted to go through it vicariously. Margaret was equally curious to know how his day went. So, they talked about many other things—mundane matters, news from London and Cadiz, their thoughts as they went about their day, their impressions of people they saw. They always found something to talk about.

And yet, the substance of what passed between them in the evening—what they said to each other at tea, through dinner, in their time alone in the sanctuary of their bedroom—was not what mattered most. Rather, it was everything else that did not need words, that was merely sensed or felt—the little caresses, kisses lavishly bestowed during conversations, the brief gestures of tenderness, the sheer delight they had in each other's immediate presence, the enchantment of moments together after long hours of being apart.

Mrs. Thornton returned at the end of August as summer began to wane. She was relieved to be home. But almost from her first day back, she began to feel the unease of living in a house she felt was no longer fully her own, where she must submit to someone else's decisions over matters in which her word used to be law. On the surface, nothing in the house had physically changed; the furniture and decorations and their placement were as they had been when she left. All the household rituals—meals, shopping, cleaning and washing—were done according to the schedule and the manner she had set up. Margaret, only too conscious of having some adjusting to do in a household with established efficient routines, was reluctant to interfere, much less make major changes. But changes were inevitable and on her first morning back, Mrs. Thornton had to deal with one of them. John came down for breakfast later than usual before his marriage and only had a cup of tea.

"Is that all you will have? Won't you need more if you are working at the mill?"

"I had breakfast in our room with Margaret. In fact, she won't be coming down for a while."

"Why? Is she ill?" In a slightly mocking tone she did not bother to hide, she added: "Does she have low spirits like her mother?"

Her remark irritated John. "No, mother, she is not ill and her spirits are fine. Dr. Donaldson advised breakfast in bed to manage nausea. She's pregnant."

Mrs. Thornton was dumbfounded. "So soon? Fanny has been married more than a year and is not yet pregnant."

Somewhat surprised at his mother's reaction, John replied with an amused laugh. "Cheer up, Mother, I am preserving the lineage. Is that not every mother's dream for her sons? Besides, I am not getting any younger and I most certainly want to be around to see my children grow. Fanny will have hers in due time."

"Well, anyway, I never had nausea when I was pregnant."

"Everyone is different, mother. Dr. Donaldson says Margaret should be able to resume her regular activities once those spells are over. In any case, she has them only in the morning, goes through her household routine, and usually goes out for a walk later in the day."

He rose to leave, picked up his hat but stopped short of the door. "I will be back for luncheon."

Mrs. Thornton was left staring thoughtfully at her unfinished cup of tea. John had always waited for her to finish breakfast before leaving for work. She sighed and went to talk to the servants about lunch and what needed to be done for the day. But she halted in her steps. With a feeling of dread, she gritted her teeth and walked briskly into the drawing room. She looked around, saw her sewing basket and, without much enthusiasm, picked up her embroidery. She understood clearer than ever before, that she, too, had a great deal of adjustment to do. She wished mightily that the mill were open. There, at least, she could be useful. There, she had important work to do that Margaret could not take away from her.

Margaret descended from the bedroom late morning while Mrs. Thornton was absorbed in embroidering a kerchief. "Good Morning, Mrs. Thornton. I am sorry not to see you at breakfast. I am sure John explained the situation to you."

"That he certainly did. I must say I am happy for both of you so early in your marriage."

Margaret sat down opposite Mrs. Thornton. "T hank you. It is true we did not expect a child so soon."

Margaret had caught the sarcasm in Mrs. Thornton's voice and she sat for some minutes without speaking. At length, she felt compelled to speak. "I wanted to tell you that Dixon has taken over management of the kitchen. Jane seemed to prefer this arrangement as well."

Mrs. Thornton did not look up from her work. "That she would. She never liked meal planning and could only cook a few dishes but we did not mind. We have simple tastes in meals."

"Dixon enjoys cooking and she does get inventive but you can tell her what dishes you prefer."

"Shouldn't you be the one who tells her what to do? You are now mistress of this house."

Margaret could not suppress a smile until she saw Mrs. Thornton looking annoyed at her. She hastened to explain: "Ever since I can remember, Dixon managed all my mother's affairs and when we moved to Milton, she ran our household smoothly without much direction from anyone. Dixon is quite resourceful and alert to the needs of those she serves."

"You might not have had many servants to deal with."

"No, we did not. Besides Dixon, we only had two in Helstone who cooked, washed and cleaned."

"This is a big house. It requires at least two people to clean since it gets dirtier faster from cotton dust. A well-respected manufacturer also has social obligations. John invites business colleagues for small dinners and we have annual dinner parties for them and other people from the community. John must maintain his standing in business so this household takes much more to manage than a parsonage in a small hamlet."

"Yes, of course. I am quite aware of my inexperience. I have neither organized dinners nor managed a large staff of servants." She smiled engagingly at Mrs. Thornton. "Perhaps, you can teach me."

Margaret had been deliberately ingratiating and Mrs. Thornton knew it but she was pleased that Margaret was making an effort to be agreeable. Mrs. Thornton was ready to reciprocate. "I don't think I can really teach you but I can show you how I do it."

"That would suit me fine. In many ways, this household runs itself smoothly, no doubt because you have managed it very well and you have been clear about what you expect of the staff. Perhaps, I could observe when you meet with them."

"That may be difficult if you cannot come down early in the morning in your condition. I usually meet with the staff right after breakfast before eight in the morning."

"Yes, that would be a problem for now. Would you mind very much if we started doing this, maybe in a couple of months? Dr. Donaldson assured me, my morning indisposition should stop then but, in the meantime, could we go on as before? That is, could you continue for a while longer to do as you have done running this household all these years?"

"No, I would not mind." Almost immediately, Mrs. Thornton worried that she might have agreed a little too hastily. "But wouldn't John object? It is your responsibility, after all."

"I will talk to him about it. It is only for a short time. I am quite sure he will not mind." Margaret stood up. "I have some letters to write but I will come down for lunch. John will be back an hour and a half after noon as I am sure he must have told you."

As she walked away, Margaret was struck by how easily she stirred Mrs. Thornton into agreeing to resume her role managing the house, if only temporarily. But she was also aware that this short conversation, the first she had alone with Mrs. Thornton since her return, had not been any easier than earlier ones. It was obvious they both tried to be agreeable and, yet, the strain started from the moment that Margaret came into the room. Margaret sighed helplessly as she ascended the stairs to the bedroom.

That night, Margaret told John about the talk with his mother. "You do not mind, do you? It will give us more time to adjust and, perhaps, become more companionable with each other, for the next two months at least."

"No, it is quite all right. I am glad, actually. She'll have her usual chores to occupy her until the mill reopens."

"I realized as we talked this morning that she, too, had much adjusting to do and that it may be harder for her."

"Yes, I know. I rushed out before she finished her breakfast and caught a glimpse of her looking a bit let down. I had always waited for her to finish. So much has changed and I suppose my mind was elsewhere."

"What would she do if she did not have this household to run? Embroider all day? I just cannot see her doing that. All these changes around her—the mill, the house—it must seem as if she has been uprooted from much that is familiar to her! I know only too well how difficult that is."

John put his arms around his wife. "Come, my love. Don't upset yourself. My mother is used to adversity worse than this and she will ride this one as well. In any case, when the mill reopens, that will occupy her. Sometimes, I think that is where she is happiest, anyway."

Margaret laid her head on his shoulder and allowed herself to be comforted. "I merely put myself in her shoes but you are right, I am sure." But she remained dubious. This was, somehow, a more complicated matter.

Mrs. Thornton was relieved to resume her daily chores but found that changes went beyond Dixon assuming more responsibilities in the kitchen and preparing meals fancier than she cared for. The chatter of servants had intensified, encouraged by Margaret who engaged them in conversations about themselves and who went for walks with Mary, the new maid. Most of the servants liked Mrs. Margaret's lively spirits, her extremely pleasing looks, and the sincere interest she took in them. With their unabashed fascination with the lives of the more privileged, they watched this newcomer closely.

They noted early on that when Mrs. Margaret arrived, the master looked less serious and stern, his scowl nearly disappeared, and he was much less absentminded. They thought he actually smiled more and looked younger. With work on reopening the mill going at full speed, he still found time to come home as often as he could to have lunch with his wife. He took her out for walks and left for work later than he used to. The baby, expected, probably in the spring, also stirred much talk particularly among the maids who looked forward to a livelier house.

When Mrs. Thornton resumed her responsibilities, the servants were more than a little disappointed despite Dixon's reassurance that it was only going to be for a few weeks—until Mrs. Margaret's dizzy spells stopped. Barely a week after Mrs. Thornton returned to her usual routine, the chatter of the servants began to diminish, at least, in her presence. Mrs. Thornton regained much of the comfort she used to have in her daily chores. She did find dealing with Dixon a little more difficult. Used to making decisions on her own and loyal to Margaret, Dixon balked and grumbled when taking directions from the older Mrs. Thornton. But she invariably did what she was told.

With Dixon managing the kitchen, Mrs. Thornton found herself with more time to spare than she used to. She missed even more the responsibility she took upon herself when Marlborough Mills first opened It had been a truly worthy use of her time, allowing her to continue to play a significant role in her son's life. She became more impatient than ever for the mill to reopen.

John spent his days at the mill. Reopening it consumed his time and energy and for a few weeks, he could not accompany his wife on her daily walk. He often knew when she and Mary went. Whenever he was in his office, he watched them as they came out of the house.

One afternoon, after an intense schedule of meetings and inspections, he sat in front of his desk, exhausted, staring out his window at the gray day, and wishing he was at a colorful pulsating café in Paris with Margaret. He laughed wryly at himself. Then, he heard Margaret's voice. Looking out his window, he saw her and Mary nearly out the gate. He bounded up and nearly ran out of his office.

"Mary, I will take my wife out on her walk," he cried out after them

The two women stopped and waited. He grasped Margaret's hand and hooked it around his arm. She smiled delightedly and said: "It has been awhile! I missed having you on these walks."

"I take great pleasure in them particularly when I am with you but so much needs to be done at the mill and it has kept me rather busy."

"I know. I am glad you could come today."

With a nod from her, Mary returned to the house. John and Margaret walked towards the gate, gazing at each other happily, unaware of the dark figure watching them with compressed lips from her perch by the window. They headed for the park on the edge of town.

XIII. RESTORATION

They walked along the city streets in silence and had almost reached the park when Margaret spoke. "I am curious about what you have to do to reopen the mill. Would you tell me?"

"I am glad you're curious. I expected you to be. The process itself is not complicated and in some ways, it is quite straightforward—bank transactions, facility and machinery inspections, repair or retooling if needed, hiring workers, contacting clients. The complicated part is dealing with people every step of the way—when hiring workers, talking with the bank and potential clients."

"What about customers? Can you get them back?"

"Persuading former clients to place orders again after they had already switched to another manufacturer can be rather tough. I am timing the reopening for when the demand is usually more than what is readily available so I am certain to get some orders. Also, quite a number of clients eventually come back if they see your product is superior, your prices are reasonable, your factory is reliable and they like the way you do business."

She scowled a little in dismay. "That sounds somewhat daunting!"

"Yes, but those are matters you can do something about as a manufacturer."

"I see. Are you far along in what you need to do?"

"We're hiring workers right now. I have also been working on putting in place some ideas I have. It's a good time to begin those as we start over."

"Are these ideas that you hoped would reduce strikes?"

"They may. I hope they do but nothing is ever certain and we will have to wait and see. Regardless, it makes sense to me to initiate these practices."

"Were these the practices you had been hesitant to talk about earlier?"

147

"I can tell you about one or two I'm working on. You will know soon enough, anyway, since you must have noticed some reconstruction at the mill. I want to get workers, supervisors, and masters talking to one another."

A smile crept up to Margaret's eyes but barely broke on her lips. Their first encounters clearly brought out their opposing views on masters and hands. He believed workers were inferior and were always at cross-purposes with masters. She tried to tell him once that dialogue was possible and, in fact, necessary when people worked together. He had cut her off imperiously, assuming her ignorant of his business, about which he, of course, had thorough knowledge. But later, he took steps to become acquainted with his workers, going as far as to befriend them and actually take an interest in their lives, as he did with Nicholas Higgins. That was quite some time ago.

Margaret also went through some change in her thinking, after her last visit to Helstone. She witnessed some villagers arguing and was appalled that they clung so tenaciously to their prejudices and ignorance that they failed to resolve their differences. So, although Margaret still believed in goodwill, she also realized that bringing people together, especially those on opposite sides, might sometimes be nearly impossible, even futile. The uncertainties and complexities of the task John was taking on now seemed daunting to her.

She smiled and very simply said: "I'm glad."

"I can believe it. You showed me what was possible when you coaxed Higgins to talk to me. "

"Well, I am vain enough to flatter myself that I helped by challenging what you believed in but, in fact, you have a natural compassion in you that I think I merely helped awaken."

"You are too generous. I was hard on my workers and did not care about their lives outside of the mill. My main concern had been to run the business profitably and efficiently." He grasped her hand and squeezed it tenderly. "The truth is I fell deeply, irrevocably in love with you and wanted to make you think well of me."

Margaret paused briefly in her step to kiss him. "You succeeded rather well." They resumed their walk and a little later, she added: "No matter how it happened, I believe what you are doing now comes from your inherent kindhearted nature and I sincerely wish you well."

John lifted her hand and pressed it to his lips. "I encourage you to think that way but, in fact, if what I do prevents or postpones strikes, that is good business sense."

The early signs of fall had begun to touch everything that was alive on the park. Margaret, with eyes alert to color and changes in nature, saw it first in the brown curling petals on rare, usually bright-hued meadow flowers that could still thrive in the smoky gloom. It was late summer, still warm but humid, and trees had started shedding their leaves, now turning golden or a deep red orange, many already strewn on the path they had chosen to take. Palpable moisture hung in the air, cooling their skin with every gust of the late afternoon breeze that was steadily gathering strength. The days had grown shorter and after some time of ambling along the top of the hill, they were surprised to see that evening was descending on them. Margaret gathered her shawl closer around her and they turned back for home.

As they walked down the hill, she said: "I hope I did not take you away from some pressing work at the mill."

"No. I needed a break from this morning's hectic schedule."

"How soon do you anticipate reopening?"

"In a few weeks if everything proceeds as planned."

After a short thoughtful pause, she asked: "You said you want masters, hands, and overseers talking to each other. What does the reconstruction have to do with that?"

"Some of the men have actually started working on a building behind the mill. A couple of months before you left for London, we had turned it into a dining hall where workers could get a cheap hot meal. Mary worked there for some time as one of the cooks. We're expanding the place and when the men are done, some of the women will come to make the place more convivial. I want to make it inviting for everyone—workers, supervisors, and masters. In those Parisian cafés, I saw how a place for eating and drinking could bring people together and encourage lively conversations even when they disagreed. Perhaps, the dining hall could do something similar and become a meeting place. It will serve lunch and an early dinner but it will also be open and have big pot of tea on the hearth all day to which the workers can help themselves."

"What a wonderful idea! Our trip to Paris has been helpful,"

"Largely that, yes; but our whole vacation made me think. The informality at Frederick's house in Cadiz helped him and me quickly become at ease. I hope we can have some of that informal atmosphere in the dining hall."

"But the whole atmosphere in Cadiz is so open, airy, and encourages such informality, not at all somber like here and, of course, the Spanish temperament is so different."

"You're not trying to dissuade me now, are you?" He teased before replying in a more serious vein. "I did think about all that and realized it could be a great deal harder for the men here to open up to each other but I must try, anyway. The dining hall will easily sustain itself and if it does not become the social place I was hoping for, it is there to nourish bodies at least."

"I suppose the hall can be made as inviting as possible to encourage the men to go there outside of mealtimes." She was thoughtful, for some moments. "Can I help the women spruce the place up?"

"Are you up to it? Maybe, we should ask Dr. Donaldson before you do anything of the sort."

"He did tell me I was free to do anything I want so long as it does not cause any physical discomfort."

"I'll tell you when the women start decorating. They will first come and clean. You can come after that."

"Not until then? Did you know I can wash and iron linen?"

She was teasing him but it bothered him somehow and he scowled at her. "Not my wife!" He was immediately sorry and added, apologetically: "Not in your condition, anyway."

"It's not so bad although it is exhausting work. I did it when I first came to Milton. Dixon could not find help willing to take the wages my father could pay. Why, I remember my first big job! It was washing and ironing curtains so that your first dinner at our house would be as pleasant as possible."

"I'm sorry. I did not mean to ridicule that type of work. But you do not have to do that and I would rather that you only help with decorating the dining hall."

"Yes, of course. I was only teasing about the cleaning. You have been looking so serious in our walk and I wanted to lighten your mood a little."

He smiled at her engagingly. "Is that better?" He waited for a reaction and she obliged him with a bright smile, a nod and a peck on his cheek.

As they were approaching the mill, he asked: "Did you really wash and iron all those curtains for me?"

Margaret's morning spells had lessened considerably by the time John told her that the mill's dining hall was finally finished, cleaned, and ready to be arranged and decorated. He would take her the next morning to meet with the women workers who were arranging the tables and chairs that had been stacked up on one side of the hall. She woke up earlier than usual, had her tea and toast, dressed, and came down with John to the dining room. Mrs. Thornton heard them talking before they came into the room and was therefore not surprised when Margaret appeared and greeted her.

"You must be feeling better from those spells," she remarked. She had enjoyed the short time alone with her son at breakfast and had not minded Margaret's absence. Secretly, she hoped for this morning routine to continue. "Are you ready to come and talk to the servants with me this morning?"

Smiling apologetically, Margaret answered: "I am sorry. May I prevail on your indulgence a while longer?"

"Of course. I don't mind," she answered hesitatingly. She looked at her son who calmly drank his tea, his expression noncommittal, his eyes roaming between his wife and his mother and resting, finally, on his wife. Mrs. Thornton was dismayed, unable to comprehend how he could calmly allow his wife so much freedom in deciding when to assume her responsibility in his household.

"I am going with John this morning to help some women workers set up the dining hall to be ready for use when the mill reopens."

Mrs. Thornton stared at Margaret, appalled, incredulous, and contemptuous all at the same time. She had openly questioned the usefulness of the dining hall when it first opened. When she heard from John about his plans to expand it to accommodate everyone, she had been very skeptical. She had said nothing, however, convincing herself, with some difficulty, to trust that her son knew what he was doing. She watched the rebuilding and knew it had just been completed. Now, she was vexed, almost angry that Margaret chose to direct her energy on a futile effort instead of on her proper responsibilities at home.

"Do they need your help?" She asked, hardly able to conceal a note of sarcasm in her voice.

"Probably not," Margaret said truthfully.

"Then, why do you bother?"

Margaret, in fact, was not certain why. She had offered to help in the enthusiasm of the moment but now she felt compelled to come up with a plausible reason and justify herself to Mrs. Thornton. "Well, I would like to learn about the mill and getting acquainted with the workers while helping them decorate the dining hall seems to me as good a way as any to start. I thought they would also get to know me a little that way."

It was not the answer to convince Mrs. Thornton; instead, it grated at her, unleashing her frustration at the son who was slipping away from her. "I cannot see how any of that would help. What could you gain from keeping company with workers who will always color the truth? If you want to learn about the mill, watch the work when it is running."

John, who had been quietly sipping his tea, was growing more exasperated with his mother, and he turned abruptly towards her. He saw her staring with narrowed eyes and compressed lips at Margaret who, though disconcerted for a moment, stared back with eyes that began to gather fire. John could not remain silent. "Mother, I agree with my wife. Besides, I believe she has some very good ideas to make the hall a pleasant place."

Not having actually spoken to him about her ideas, Margaret—eyes still flashing and a retort at the tip of her tongue— looked quickly at John who, with a slight shake of his head, appealed with his eyes for her to say nothing. The exchange took but an instant or two but she understood and nodded almost imperceptibly, lowering her eyes contritely.

"I never understood the need for that dining hall," Mrs. Thornton insisted, frowning at her son and shaking her head vehemently.

"I admit it is an experiment but I hope it will eventually lessen strikes. Nothing is ever guaranteed but we must try new ideas." He spoke calmly but evaded his mother's eyes.

He turned to Margaret. "We must go. I have a lot of work waiting for me."

Margaret had wanted more breakfast than her habitual tea and toast and hesitated a little but, catching the impatience on John's face, she got up. She glanced at Mrs. Thornton, who stared sullenly at her. Margaret shrugged and followed John to the door.

He paused before going out the door. "Mother, we can talk a little more this evening."

John hurried out of the house, a scowl developing and deepening in his brow. Just outside the house, Margaret tugged at his arm. "Slow down, please, I cannot walk as fast as you do."

He slowed his pace and grasped her hand. "I'm sorry."

John said nothing more as he led Margaret to the dining hall. She glanced up at him and saw his eyes dark and thoughtful beneath his furrowed brow. He was clearly upset and Margaret opened her mouth to ask him about it but decided it was an inopportune time. He was in no mood to talk and they had almost reached the dining hall. It would have to wait. Still, she could not help suspecting that John's changing attitudes towards workers had become a source of tension between Mrs. Thornton and her son. Margaret knew that the opposing views she and Mrs. Thornton had about workers was a sore point between them and, to Mrs. Thornton, the expansion of the dining hall meant that John was more inclined to side with Margaret.

Three women were unstacking chairs when they arrived. The inside of the hall had been scrubbed clean and smelled of soap. Windows all around brought in as much natural light as the smoky northern haze could dispense.

The women stopped what they were doing to greet John and Margaret: "Good morning master, ma'am."

"Good morning," they replied in unison.

He continued: "I would like you to meet my wife. She would like to help with decorating."

The three women were a little wary, each one murmuring almost inaudibly: "How do you do, Mrs. Thornton?" Their experience with the older Mrs. Thornton had not been exactly pleasant; to them, she was a stern taskmaster who they hardly ever saw smiling. They did not know what to expect of Margaret and they wondered if she would be as critical. And yet, the young Mrs. Thornton with her pleasing open face seemed as if she could break out into a smile at any moment. They had also heard that she had been a friend of the Higgins family, especially the hapless Bessy Higgins, and that she had been sympathetic and kind to workers when she first came to Milton. But she did marry one of the mill owners and the women were not certain what to make of her.

Margaret sensed their hesitation and smiled engagingly. "I don't believe I know much more about making this hall more pleasant than you possibly could but I can provide materials you would need—curtains, for example—from the mill and at its expense, of course."

With that charming smile, that sincere tone, and those words, the three women were drawn in, at least for the moment, by the handsome young wife of their master. The oldest of them replied: "That would be kind, ma'am."

"You might also think of whitewashing the walls. That would bring more light in here." She turned to John. "We should be able to get some white paint for a light wash, don't you think?"

"Yes, easily. I could ask one of the men to do the whitewashing."

The youngest of the three women, about Margaret's age, volunteered enthusiastically: "I can help whitewash. I have done it before."

One of the older women chimed in: "We should all be able to help." She glanced surreptitiously at Margaret's waist. "All three of us, not young Mrs. Thornton, of course. We could finish the job in a day."

"Thank you. I wouldn't be up to doing that just now but, if you want those curtains, I could help hem them."

John, seeing his workers warm up to Margaret, took his leave. "I have work to do as well." He turned to his wife, placed his arm around her shoulders, and walked to the door with her.

Margaret peered at his face: He appeared more relaxed but she wanted to be sure. "Is anything the matter?"

"Probably not. I found the conversation with my mother at breakfast a bit frustrating, that's all."

She nodded at him sympathetically.

He pressed her hand to his lips. "I'll see you this evening and we can talk then."

That evening, nobody brought up the subject of the morning's conversation. With everyone determined to be agreeable by talking only about the changing weather and the dishes they were being served, dinner proceeded pleasantly enough.

In their bedroom, John looked up from reading the newspaper by the fireplace and addressed Margaret across the room as she brushed her hair in front of the vanity: "I was uncertain how the meeting with those women was going to turn out."

"Oh? How so?"

"When I first told them you were offering to help with decorating the hall, they all seemed suspicious and not happy at all."

"I think I can understand that. Who would want the master's wife coming to tell them what to do?"

"It is certainly not something any of the wives of my business associates would do."

"But your mother went to the mill to keep an eye on the work so your workers should be accustomed to having Thornton women "interfere"," she replied lightheartedly, laughing at her use of the last word.

Her laugh brought on a faint frown from John. "It was different with my mother, as you probably know. Her focus had been, like mine, the efficient running of the mill."

She stopped brushing her hair and turned towards him. "Well, perhaps, mine is, too, except I approach it differently," she asserted equally irritably.

Detecting the annoyance in her voice, he put his paper down and walked towards her as she turned her back to him to face the mirror. "That is surely true. If I can charm them and get them to acquiesce as easily as you seem to have done with those women, I might prevent some problems I have had with workers in the past."

"Deciding about curtains and paint is a great deal simpler than dealing with workers problems." She put her brush down and got up.

He stood in front of her and studied her face briefly. He was getting used to that defiant expression. It had disconcerted him the first time he had contended with the conviction that was behind it, firm opinions that she had no qualms asserting, opinions opposed to his. His own convictions were so strong that he was hopeless, initially, that they could ever agree, especially when she had turned away looking just as hopeless. This time, conciliatory, he replied with a warm smile meant to coax her out of her vexation: "Maybe so but you did effortlessly overcome the distrust of those women."

She gave him her half-smile, somewhat pacified, and walked past him towards the bed. "I learned to deal with different people in my father's vicarage. I think it helps to listen and talk to people in terms they can grasp and, if you meet in pleasant circumstances, perhaps, you are more likely to talk and get to know each other."

He caught her in his arms from behind before she could reach the bed. "That, I think, goes a long way towards relieving distrust and maybe even bitterness."

She answered in a softer voice as he nuzzled the nape of her neck: "I think so, too. That is why I think your dining hall is a very good idea."

His voice was muffled: "I'm glad you think so."

She turned around in his arms. "You know I do." She stood on tiptoe to kiss him. "It's late and I am tired."

He did not let her go and, clasping her closer, he pressed his lips against her neck, drinking in a mixture of subtle fragrance and a light characteristic odor he had now associated with her. Then, he swept her up in his arms and carried her towards the bed. "Why, you are getting heavier!"

"I am getting bigger." She retorted, laughing, as he lowered her on the bed.

She took his hand and placed it on her belly. "I think I felt it kick today."

He caressed her belly and chuckled. "Your stomach is decidedly bigger."

"Yes, I'll need some new clothes."

"Can I still make love to you?

She did not answer. Instead, she pulled him closer.

Margaret, with a sewing basket, rejoined the women at the dining hall a couple of days later after they had applied whitewash. Williams came with her carrying yards of fabric. The women workers had talked among themselves about whether Margaret would come back. The older women were skeptical but the youngest one, Annie, who had liked Margaret from the beginning, could not be dissuaded from her belief that she would.

They watched through a window as Margaret approached with William.

"Did I not tell you?" Annie said triumphantly. "She would not have been a friend to Bessy if she was proud. She looks too sweet and beautiful to be mean."

"Oh Annie!" One of the older women answered as both of them laughed: "Looks have nothing to do with it. There are so many young rich and fancy women, like the master's sister, who turn their noses at us."

The other older woman continued to stare at Margaret, sizing her up. "I wonder what she wants from us. What does she get from coming?"

Annie replied: "She is a parson's daughter. Maybe, she grew up being kind and she is not at all fancy."

"Hush, they're almost here." They walked away from the window and busied themselves cleaning table tops and arranging chairs but they all turned towards the door as Margaret walked in ahead of Williams.

"Good morning ma'am."

"Good morning to you all. I have the material I promised. I brought a green fabric, a little on the dark side so dirt should not easily show on it. It would provide a cheery contrast to the white walls."

Annie came forward as Williams deposited the fabric on one of the tables. "It's beautiful, ma'am," she said as she ran a hand lightly on the material. One of the older women shook her head at her.

"I am glad you like it," Margaret smiled at Annie, touching the material as she had done. She then addressed Williams: "Thank you, Williams, you may go."

She turned her attention back towards the women and asked: "How do you suppose we should proceed with this?"

"Well, ma'am, we can begin measuring right away," Annie seemed the only one willing or bold enough to answer.

"That seems to be a good place to start. I brought measuring tape and some paper and pencil."

Annie was embarrassed and hesitant but Margaret, with an encouraging smile, waited for her to say more. Annie forced herself to disclose in a low voice: "None of us can read or write, ma'am, but we know well enough how to measure and fit the fabric."

"Well, then, we shall do it your way," Margaret declared in a lively voice.

For the next few days, the women measured, cut, and hemmed curtains for the dining hall. As they worked, Margaret tried to draw the women out, discreetly asking questions of each. The older women, as she had predicted, were reluctant to share any information about themselves, revealing only enough for Margaret to learn that the oldest woman was Marian who never married and lived alone while the second one, Mary, had grown children who worked in the other mills. Margaret was most interested in Annie who was working with her at the same table. Annie was lively and showed some native intelligence that Margaret suspected was rendered dormant by a lack of schooling and the necessity to work in the mills as a child. She was a little shy but, when prompted with questions, she talked enthusiastically about herself and her two brothers and three sisters, ranging in age from 17- to 8-years old.

"Would you like to learn to read and write, Annie?"

"Yes, ma'am, but I have no time and even if I did, there is no one to teach me."

"But would you take the time after work if there is someone who can teach you?"

"After work, I have to make dinner and clean up. I am the oldest and my mother is too sick to take care of my brothers and sisters. My younger sisters help but they are too young yet. They tire easily after working in the mills."

"I see."

A little later, Margaret continued: "How about your brothers and sisters? Would any of them like to learn?"

"I don't know, ma'am. The youngest one is curious like me. She may want to, if someone can teach her."

Margaret nodded her head and said no more.

The dining hall was finished a few days later and Margaret could no longer delay making good on her promise to Mrs. Thornton. She accompanied the older woman as she discharged her daily chores. For the most part, Margaret observed, nodded, and said little. After a week, she took over Mrs. Thornton's former duties, now properly hers forever. It was a fairly uncomplicated routine. The staff knew what they needed to do and Dixon, as before, made decisions in most unanticipated matters without bothering her mistress.

XIV. REOPENING

Marlborough Mills reopened for full operation on a dry but dreary day in October a little earlier than John had anticipated. He had originally set a date that was timed to take advantage of the coming holidays when orders were certain to increase but he had accepted an order that needed to be completed by a certain date. After estimating what needed to be done to fill the order, he thought it best to give the mill a few days leeway before it came due.

Weeks before, various workers came to prepare the mill for this day—sweeping it of dust and cobwebs, cleaning, oiling, testing, and, when necessary, repairing machines. A couple of days before, a small crew led by Nicholas Higgins retested and readjusted the machinery to ensure that, for at least the early weeks of operation, production would be efficient and uneventful. Another crew came just the day before to bring out bales of cotton from the warehouse that they piled on the platform, ready for the spinning and weaving machines.

Not all hands had been hired but John was confident that it would not take long before they were. He hoped gossip passed among workers that the mill had made changes to improve working conditions would help attract more workers. Most of those already hired were former mill hands who had signed a petition with Nicholas Higgins declaring their desire to return to the mill when Mr. Thornton brought it back into operation. Talk had circulated among cotton mill workers that Mr. Thornton was continuing to make changes in how he ran the mill and that he was open to ideas from workers, a radical step that most workers were skeptical of.

Despite assurances from Nicholas Higgins that the master was sincere in his intent, distrust of the masters was of such long standing that workers were usually not persuaded by mere intent. They waited until it was translated into reality, something that only time could show them, even in the case of this particular master who had already instituted more modern machines and better working conditions than most mill owners. Still, if it came down to choosing to work for this mill or another, Marlborough Mills was an easy choice for many for its better working conditions. A few who might have wavered were swayed by the new white dining hall where they heard good cheap hot mills could be had.

By the time John placed an announcement in the newspaper three days before the mill reopened, he had already notified all his business colleagues and contacted all his former customers, visiting them personally whenever he could. A good number of these customers placed orders. John hoped more of them would give him back their business once they saw the mill filling orders as promised. He expected some to return since seasonal high demand meant merchant orders for Christmas exceeded combined levels of production at existing mills.

On the day the mill opened, John woke up much earlier than he had done of late and bounded out of bed so abruptly that he woke Margaret up. He turned to give her a perfunctory kiss and announced: "This is the day!"

Without waiting for an answer, he hurried to change. He returned to the bedroom to see if Margaret was ready to go down to breakfast but he was surprised to find a tray of tea, toast, sausages and fruit waiting for him. "I asked Dixon to prepare breakfast early for you."

He smiled his thanks and sat down. But he was too restless for his usual breakfast, distractedly sipping the tea she handed him, nibbling on the toast she had buttered for him, and consuming in a few quick bites the sausages that he, at first, refused but which she insisted he must eat. Attuned to all her husband's moods and expressions of the past months, Margaret now contended with that side of him she had known when they first met but that had hardly been in evidence in their few months of marriage. She knew he was anxious that the day should pass without a hitch and he was clearly energized for it. His eyes shone fiercely with purpose and anticipation as if he was poised for a fight, his lips were compressed, the muscles in his cheeks taut and tense, and his brow wore a frown of intense concentration. So focused was he on his work for that day that Margaret doubted he heard anything she said while he ate breakfast.

He got up as soon as he finished his tea and gave her a hasty buss on the forehead. "I have to go."

"I know. I will come down with you."

He nodded absentmindedly and she followed him as he walked briskly out the door, down the steps, and out to the vestibule that served as entrance to the house. She moved just as briskly behind him but John seemed to have forgotten she was there. He was about to bolt down the steps when he felt a restraining hand on his arm. He stopped and turned towards his wife. Before he could even blink, she enclosed him in a tight embrace, gave him a long loving kiss, and murmured a solemn "Good luck, my love."

He gazed at her for a long minute, silent, his mind already rehearsing his first tasks of the day. But his bright eyes had softened with gratitude and he walked down the steps more calmly. He turned around at the foot of the stairs, paused and smiled at her. Then, he headed towards the mill in quick, determined strides. She muttered a prayer as she watched him disappear into the mill.

With some trepidation, Margaret walked slowly and thoughtfully back into the house. She caught sight of Mrs. Thornton standing by the large window in the drawing room and went to join her there. Mrs. Thornton glanced briefly at her and turned her attention back to the courtyard. "Well, this is the day! I did not see John at breakfast. I know he is too excited to eat but you should have insisted on him having something. He will need it."

"Dixon brought him a full breakfast in the bedroom." Margaret replied simply.

"I see." Mrs. Thornton regarded her for an instant or two and turned back towards the window. "The workers have started to trickle in." She seemed as agitated as John but more subdued and more apprehensive.

Margaret looked down at the mill yard, its bustle increasing steadily. It had been empty when John walked across it a few minutes earlier but since then, Williams had arrived and opened the gate fully. Workers poured through the gate, talking, sometimes laughing, reaching their hands out to people they had worked with in the past. The mill yard, forlorn for the last six months, soon took on the air of a country fair without the hawkers and street entertainers, its festive ambiance supplied by a mood of easy camaraderie among those who had previously worked at the mill and were returning, thankfully, if not gladly, to a familiar place. Eventually, everyone seemed infected by it, chatting easily with those standing next to them as they waited for the doors to open.

Mrs. Thornton was exhilarated by the scene on the ground and she felt as if the desolation that gripped the mill—when it had to close for want of funds—never happened. She stole a glance at Margaret whom she fancied equally absorbed by all that was going on. Mrs. Thornton turned towards the window once again. Although it seemed her eyes neither blinked nor strayed away from the activity in the courtyard, her senses were focused on listening intently and impatiently for the sounds that would announce, for certain, that the mill was indeed running. She did not have to wait long.

As the workers disappeared into the mill, one machine began to hum and, like a fugue, another followed right on top of it—then another and still another—until all the machines seemed to drown everything else out with their deep resonant humming, metallic clapping and clanging, and low steady whirring. This was all music to Mrs. Thornton's ears, surrounding her completely, penetrating her flesh the way music took hold of a musician completely absorbed in his instrument. She listened, exulting in the familiar sounds that used to announce the beginning of a good day for her son and that now assured her everything was back to the way it should be. She was thus absorbed for nearly half an hour until the whirring and clanging became regular and repetitive. Only then did she remember that Margaret stood next to her.

Margaret had, in fact, left for a while and had just rejoined her to see whether anything new had happened. For the first time since their acquaintance, Mrs. Thornton was overcome with heartfelt gratitude towards the woman her son had married. She was acutely aware that the bustle in the mill would not have taken place so soon without Margaret. It was not entirely inconceivable that struggling all over again could have subdued his spirit or, at least, seen him too old to fully triumph in succeeding once again.

Margaret spared him all that and now, Mrs. Thornton rejoiced that, finally, John had what he deserved, what he worked for single-mindedly and tenaciously in his youth. She murmured a prayer of thankfulness.

Margaret was no less exhilarated than Mrs. Thornton was when she heard the machines start up. She was happy for John, for all the people who found work when the mill reopened and, yes, she was happy for Mrs. Thornton whose life had revolved around one mill or another but particularly this one. This mill meant the most to Mrs. Thornton. She could claim, rightly, that John's success was hers as well, having invested much sweat, energy, even heartache as she endured humiliating economies to bring success and prosperity to her son. Margaret glanced at Mrs. Thornton who seemed lost to everything but the activity and the sounds that, once more, took over the mill.

Margaret quietly left a second time to talk to Dixon about the day's tasks. When she came back, Mrs. Thornton turned towards her. Margaret was struck by how her eyes glistened the way John's did, her lips in a tremulous smile. Was it gratitude that suffused her countenance? Margaret had never seen Mrs. Thornton regard her with such warmth and while it bewildered her at first, her naturally affectionate heart could not remain immune. She smiled back at Mrs. Thornton warmly, sincerely, gratefully. The two women were conscious that, for the first time, they shared the same sentiments and views of the events playing out in the huge stone building in front of them. Finally, it seemed they found something to agree on and they both wanted to relish those moments. Back of their minds, they both feared that, between the two of them, such moments could be rare and fleeting.

They went back to the window at various times during the day, alone or together, to look down at the bustle. Nothing much was said between them and nothing new or extraordinary actually happened in the courtyard. Most of the work was being done inside the mill. But the lively activity, in all its boring repetitiveness, was utter happiness to Mrs. Thornton: It signified life, in contrast to the deathly nothingness and silence of the nonfunctioning mill. She inevitably took more pleasure than Margaret in all the sights and sounds of the bustling mill.

Margaret eventually felt the need to flee from the noise. John had told her not to expect him back until the evening and after a light lunch with Mrs. Thornton, she went out for a walk with Mary. When they returned more than an hour later, Margaret looked up from the yard below and sure enough, Mrs. Thornton stood by the window, as she had done all those past years—an austere dark figure, inexorable and hawk-like, ready to defend all that belonged to her. What a formidable woman, Margaret thought with a mixture of admiration and uneasiness, fiercer even than her son in her fervor for the mill.

Mrs. Thornton soon resumed her former routine of seeing that work at the mill proceeded efficiently. One morning as she prepared to leave, Margaret walked in, dressed to go out. "You're going to the mill, aren't you? Would you mind if I came with you today?"

Uncertain at first what to make of this request Mrs. Thornton eyed her briefly. "Of course, you can come. You married into this family. You should know something about the business John spends a great part of his day on."

They walked together wordlessly towards the mill. The door banged shut as they both stepped inside. What little chatter could be heard over the din of the machines slowly diminished as workers began to be aware that the mother and the wife of the master just came in.

Margaret was incredulous to realize this was only her second time inside the mill while it was running, her first being that fateful day in Milton years ago when she first saw John in an unfortunate incident with a worker. That time, she was a newly-arrived stranger—a foreigner as Higgins once spat out at her—and she had opened a door to a world she never knew existed, one that filled her with a sense of both wonder and bewilderment. This time as John's wife and co-owner, the wonder and bewilderment were no less intense.

She scanned the atmosphere swirling around her, virtually white from countless specks of floating cotton. This must be what it was like to drift among the clouds, she thought. Strange. Ethereal. And yet, she reminded herself, they were still only bits of cotton spewing out of machines. She strove to comprehend what it meant to her. She knew what it meant to John, to Mrs. Thornton, and to all these people stepping back and forth in rhythmic unison and appearing, in the process, as if they were extensions of the spinning and weaving machines. This world was now a part of hers as well, not only because it was John's work. It inundated her daily life with noise, smoke, cotton fuzz, and the never-ending frenzy of people busy with creating it.

She looked up at the perch where she had first seen John. He was not there and in his place, stood Williams. John had not known they were coming. Margaret could not suppress her disappointment at not seeing him up where she imagined him casually sweeping his eyes across the mill floor, calmer than that first time, even smiling with pleasure at their visit.

The workers were used to having Mrs. Thornton come but they could not often predict the day and time she would be there. They were never really happy to see her: With her sharp perception, she easily spotted and called to task anyone who she thought was slacking off. Her mere presence reminded them of their tenuous hold on their work and they assumed an earnest concentration in their work whenever she was around. With a wary eye on Mrs. Thornton, they nevertheless stole frequent glances at the young Mrs. Thornton, walking behind the older woman.

The young Mrs. Thornton had a half-smile on her lips and her large blue eyes, profoundly curious, looked directly at whoever she caught staring at her before she nodded almost imperceptibly and smiled, her lips barely curved up at the corners. They stole glances as discreetly as they could, acutely conscious that the older woman would pounce on them if their attention strayed away from their work. Many of them knew Margaret by sight, knew about the work she did decorating the dining hall. But they dared not make obvious their curiosity, not with Mrs. Thornton around. Some who did briefly catch Margaret's attention were gratified to see her respond with encouragement in her expressive bright eyes.

After walking through the whole mill without talking to anyone, Margaret wearied of the exertion. It did not tire her body so much as it did her mind and spirit which could not endure for too long the noise and the stale air, thick with what she guessed must be the smell of cotton. Like that first time, she found the mill oppressive but for a different reason. This was now her life, one that she had willingly chosen—and yet—walking around among these live, loud machines so closely that she could almost feel the vibrations they made—she felt trapped. She could never do what Mrs. Thornton did and she knew clearly then that, if she was ever involved in the mill, it was not what she wanted to do.

She hurried to catch up with Mrs. Thornton and said: "I think I will go back to the house. You are staying for a while, I suppose."

Mrs. Thornton nodded her head, raised her hand briefly, and motioned her away. She had forgotten Margaret was there. Margaret turned back, controlling her urge to run. At the door, she found Williams, ready to open the door for her.

"Would you like me to take you back to the house, ma'am?"

"No, Williams, it is such a short distance." She answered and, despite the disquiet in her breast, she was amused that he would offer to help her go across the yard. "Do you know where my husband is?"

"I believe he is at the dining hall, ma'am, meeting with a union representative."

Margaret nodded, gratified in the midst of her own confusing ambiguous feelings about the mill, that John was making an effort to communicate with the workers' union. "Thank you and you should probably return to your post in case Mrs. Thornton needs your help."

Back at the house, she sat pensively in the armchair by the fireplace. It had been six months since she left London to live in this house. Mostly, it had been a happy time and she could think of nowhere else she would rather be. But at the moment, she found herself confronting her ambivalence about the industry into which he had chosen to devote his time and energy, his life.

By most indications, his manufacturing business was approaching former levels of production and he had hopes of actually making it grow. She hardly saw him at lunch anymore and he no longer had time to accompany her on her walks. But he was always home an hour before dinner, eager for the smiles and caresses she lavished on him. For a few minutes, her apprehensions did not seem to matter—she was back in Milton, not for the mill, but for John.

On the first night the mill opened, John had come home, tired but exhilarated. She and Mrs. Thornton had been waiting for him and talking in the drawing room about the events of the day. He smiled broadly at both of them. "It has been a good day. Everything went smoothly, as if we never closed."

"I was confident it would," Mrs. Thornton declared with pride and self-assurance.

Margaret said nothing and merely gave him her half-smile, her eyes bright and moist. John walked towards her, peered closely at her face, and said tenderly: "You are not about to cry, are you?"

She shook her head but she could not look at him and answer. Her tears were indeed very close to the surface. He put an arm around her waist and turned to his mother. "I am taking my wife away for a while, mother. I know you two were talking but I need her right now."

He did not wait for an answer and led Margaret out of the room. Neither was aware that Mrs. Thornton glared after them, gripped by a quick succession of emotions.

In their room, John led Margaret to the fireplace, sat in an armchair and pulled her onto his lap. "Did you miss me much today?" He murmured, enclosing her in an embrace, kissing her.

She laid her head on his shoulder and wound her arms around his neck. "I did see you a few times as we watched from the window."

"I know. I looked up the house a couple of times and saw you. You cannot imagine how much it gratified me to see you up here. It was exhilarating reopening the mill but, I realized your presence here made it much more so and more completely satisfying. I knew I had to work towards getting my own mill again but there was not much joy for me in that prospect before you came back to me."

She raised her head, pressing her cheek against his. "I am so happy that everything went well. You were so excited and triumphant when you came in, you nearly brought tears to my eyes."

He kissed her once more and remarked, smiling: "My wife cries when she's sad and she cries when she's happy and proud." Then, nuzzling his face against her neck as if he was trying to find some solace there, he continued wearily: "Yes, it has been a happy event although at this moment, I am merely exhausted and in need of your soothing embrace."

She held him closer, stroking his cheeks and his hair. She whispered: "I could ring for tea."

She felt his head shake lightly against her neck and settle more snugly against it. They held each other for some time, wordless and nearly still until his fast, shallow breathing gradually slowed down and deepened. Much later, he muttered against her neck. "Will you promise to wait for me here in this room every night?"

She nodded, kissed him, and laid her cheek on his.

Since then, Margaret waited for John in their bedroom, with a fire in the hearth and tea ready for him. Almost always after taking off his coat, he plopped himself into an armchair, stripped himself of his vest and tie and pulled her onto his lap to cuddle up by the fireplace before she served him tea. They treasured this time together. For John, to hold Margaret in his arms and submit to her tender ministrations and caresses was the sweetest way anyone could ever have of decompressing from the noisy and often intense activities at the mill. She soothed his nerves, high-strung in the days during and right after the resumption of mill operations, and she massaged his tense muscles when he complained of being particularly tired. By the time they descended to the dining room, he was reenergized for the rest of the evening.

Margaret waited impatiently for this time at dusk when the machines had stopped churning, all was tranquil and she could finally claim her husband for herself after a day when he seemed to belong to another world. She understood its draw for him, this world of machines and more modern ways of working, of intriguing new possibilities, of a type of commerce that spurred but was also changed by new inventions, of new industries that benefited many more than those engaged in actively pursuing them. Still, she could not help feeling that a world outside that of machinery—the one she had been brought up in, of books and ideas, music and art—was now even more important to hold on to.

Margaret walked towards the window to look down on the mill yard. When she entered it for the very first time, she could not believe that anyone would live next to the incessant flurry of a mill. But fate, ironic and obedient to no laws, played its trick again, thrusting her, probably for life, into the midst of that flurry. It never even occurred to her that day at the train station that, in coming home with John, it was this place she was returning to. It had not mattered to her then. Now that she had lived in it for some time and particularly after the sensation of being trapped inside the mill only half an hour ago, she found herself having trouble getting accustomed to it.

The mill seemed all-encompassing in its reach, claiming body and mind of those involved in it. Those men and women, moving in rhythm with the machines, had blank unseeing expressions on their faces, as mechanical as all other parts of machines. For the first time, she saw more fully its hold on Mrs. Thornton who seemed to have forgotten her presence.

Margaret made a resolve that day. Persuaded early on that they did not need to live next to the mill, she could and would escape its confines. Within the yard, there would not be other children to play with, no open spaces to run on, no new and strange little nooks or objects to explore. She thought the courtyard dangerous for little children. With a child coming and, probably more in the future, she knew without a doubt that she wanted them alive to all the possibilities that awaited, a life larger than what passed within the walls and gates of Marlborough Mills.

She, herself, could not escape nor did she want to, the fact that she chose to belong to a life tied not only to Milton but also to the mill. Indeed, she had learned to value the making of cotton as an occupation as worthy as any other. But she could not see herself actively involved in its operation. Not the way her mother-in-law was. Still, she could not remain detached from matters concerning the mill. Her interest, however, was in people. To her, Marlborough Mills was not merely machines and cotton but people—workers who seemed, to her, extensions of machines inside the mill, did have lives outside of it. So, if she were to be useful in Milton, it might as well be among mill workers.

Margaret turned away from the window, more at ease with her ambivalence. It was time to go down to the kitchen to see Dixon. Perhaps, when he felt more confident about the mill, John would come home occasionally for lunch, just as he did before the mill reopened.

XV. TRANSITIONS

Winter descended upon Milton as heavily as summer. For the first few weeks, it dumped snow and hail that once again forced people indoors. Confined throughout the day within the cold, gray rooms of the house and unable to go for her daily walks, Margaret was restless, impatient for the day to end and for John to come home. Her books were not enough to provide her the escape she sought and she could only spend a limited time a day on needlework before it bored her. But Margaret's restive mind often found some way to regain its equilibrium.

One afternoon, she decided it was time to rummage through the rest of her possessions that had been brought over from London. Stored in trunks still untouched since she and John returned from Cadiz, they were items she could not part with although she did not have much use for most of them. Some articles belonged to her parents. The rest were mementos of her life in Helstone which she had been loath to throw out. She was now glad she had not. Among these was a covered basket packed with pieces of rag paper and linen, pencils, charcoal sticks, colored chalks, sketchbooks, cakes of watercolors, and brushes—precisely the items she wanted. She also unpacked a few tubes of oil paint purchased in Paris, nearly forgotten after being shoved in a drawer on their return to Milton.

She took the basket and the oil paints, placed these all on the floor by the window, walked around the room, and collected a few objects that were interesting to her, either for their form or color. They included a vase, a bowl of fruit, some bottles from her dresser, a colorful book, and a candlestick, all of which she deposited on the table by the window. She started doing sketches of each of these objects, sometimes more than once, filling several pages of one sketchbook fairly quickly. So absorbed was she that when Dixon came to light the oil lamps, she hardly took notice of her.

A little later, John opened the door slowly so as not to disturb her if she was resting. He saw her silhouetted by the window, bent over a sketchbook, with pencils, chalks and many other objects scattered on the table. Margaret did not hear him come in. John approached noiselessly but she looked up at the very moment he stopped and stood next to her. She looked surprise to see him.

She turned towards the window and at the darkness outside. "My goodness! Is it that time already?"

He smiled indulgently at her. "Yes, it is nearly eight and time for dinner. Barely enough for you to take those smudges off your face and hands and dress up."

She got up slowly, wiped her cheeks with the back of her hand, shook her skirt of colored dust, and laughed. "I have made a mess in here." She regarded him thoughtfully. "And you are late today so the tea must be cold."

John tilted her face and kissed her lightly on the lips. "I know. I'm sorry. I went to meet with some new customers today. In any case, you seem to have been too busy to miss me this afternoon. I see you found your pencils and crayons."

She picked up a colored stick and said: "In fact, this is a chalk and not a crayon since there is no oil in it, mostly pigment. I have nearly forgotten what a pleasure it is to color with these chalks. Just look at those vibrant colors." She handed him the sketch she just finished as she walked towards the bathroom to wash her hands.

"This is beautiful. The colors do make the apples and grapes so alive that you are tempted to reach into the bowl and eat them. We should frame this and hang it."

She came back into the room wiping her face and hands with a towel. "That is really just a study and I did not mean for it to be framed. But I am glad you like it because I intend to do more. Those Paris art shows have inspired me and since this weather is not good for walking, I will have uninterrupted time to draw and even paint." She added, pouting a little: "But I do not have an easel. Do you know where I can get one?"

He hardly heard her question as he casually leafed through a few more drawings and smiled warmly at her. "I am happy to see your enthusiasm for drawing and painting. I am not an expert but what you have here look uncommonly good."

She wrinkled her nose at him, gratified. Then, forgetting about the easel, she turned around for his inspection. "This dress will have to do since I have no time to change. What do you think?"

"It seems fine to me. Let's go. I am starved," he answered and grasped her hand, pulling her behind him as he headed for the door.

Margaret's pregnancy had become obvious by her first Christmas with John and Mrs. Thornton told her it was time to begin her confinement. She could only attend family get-togethers and not be seen in public. Margaret was disappointed and thought it a quaint nonsensical practice.

"Why should a woman hide the fact that she is with child?" She asked John irritably.

"No reason, my love."

"Do you think me ugly now that my stomach comes out to here?" She held her hands out in front of her.

"Not at all. Just as beautiful as ever. Sometimes, more so."

"Will it embarrass you if your friends and business associates see me like this in public?"

"No, not me. It may embarrass them but that is their problem."

Margaret had organized a small celebration at the Dining Hall for Marlborough Mills children, those who worked there or had parents who did. It exasperated her that her condition apparently precluded her from going. At first, she thought of defying convention and Mrs. Thornton. But she reconsidered and decided it was probably best to acquiesce and remain within Mrs. Thornton's good graces, this early in her marriage. She believed somebody from the family had to go, however, to hand out the packages, already wrapped and labeled with children's names.

She asked John if he would go in her place. "Mary could go and help you."

He appeared to hesitate but before he could reply, she said: "Perhaps, Hannah could do it."

"You know she would not," John replied, scowling. Then he grumbled. "Not exactly my job but I will do it.

Margaret expected precisely such an arrangement.

One Sunday morning a few weeks after Christmas, John and Margaret lay lazily in bed, enjoying the luxury of getting up as late as they wanted. He was on his side facing his wife, stroking her pregnant belly when Margaret brought up a subject she had been mulling over for weeks. She had rehearsed many times in her mind what she would say to John but had put off talking about it until work at the mill had reached some degree of stability. Seeing him relaxed and refreshed from a good night's sleep, she decided it was time to tell him what had been bothering her since shortly after the mill reopened.

"Our child is coming in a couple of months," she began, smiling, as she covered the hand he had on her stomach with hers. "Some things will change."

John, still stroking her belly, looked at her expectantly and waited for her to say more. She lifted his hand and sat up. For a few moments, uneasiness written in her eyes, she stared at him and said nothing.

"Something is bothering you," he remarked as he turned on his back, crossed his arms under his head and gave her his full attention.

She regarded him for another long moment. "I have been thinking that a home next to the mill is not really the best place to bring up children."

"Yes?"

"I know that the mill means so much to you. But........."

"But........?"

"I want my children to see that life has more to offer besides making cotton, that there is a great big world out there for them to discover. If they choose to do something different, they should know that they are free to do so."

"So?"

"So, I want us to find a house outside of this compound, away from the mill."

"Is that the only reason you want to live away from the mill?"

"Is that not enough? But, truthfully, no. The noise and the continuous bustle do bother me most days."

He sat up next to her. "It took you longer than I predicted to bring this matter up."

"What do you mean? You're not angry with me, are you, for telling you frankly what I think?"

"Angry? No! I have been waiting for you to say something about this."

She stared at him, surprised. "You have? Well, I must admit I have thought and agonized about it a long time, uncertain how I should tell you. I did not want you to think I was unhappy here in a place and a way of life which you have spent so much time and effort building."

He placed a hand under her chin, lifting her face as he gazed into her eyes. "I have a couple of houses I want you to look at. You might like one of them." He wanted to relish the way her large blue eyes widened and brightened when he made this revelation.

"Do you mean to tell me that you have gone to find another house for us to live in?"

"I suspected that was what you wanted when we married but you said nothing. Then, when you became pregnant, I was certain we needed to live somewhere else because I knew this is not exactly the sort of place you would want to raise children in. But still, you said nothing. So I took the initiative to inquire about houses in other neighborhoods."

"Oh, John!" She threw her arms around his neck and buried her face on his shoulders. It was harder for her now to cuddle up close to him but John pulled her up sideways from the bed onto his lap and held her close. He felt warm tears on his neck.

"I can take you anytime soon to see these houses." He murmured against her forehead.

She rubbed her eyes with the back of her hand. "In my condition?"

"Why, yes. I was getting ready to tell you about them because the owners can only hold the houses for us for so long and we must decide soon."

"I must confess that this was something I never expected. You are too good to me." Her voice was muffled against his neck.

"Self-interest, that is all. I thought that if I kept you happy, you would keep me happy, too." He replied, teasing, as more happy tears came.

Finally she lifted her face and dried her face on the sleeve of her nightgown. Then with her hand, she wiped off the moisture her tears had left on his neck. "The mill has been your life and I was afraid that it would seem inconceivable to you to live away from it."

"True. It had been my life but now I have you and another little creature in here." He bent down to kiss her belly. "My world has opened up to so many things beyond this mill."

"But you have given me at least as much, if not more!" She exclaimed, snuggling back into his embrace."

"You came back to Milton with me and I know it is not where you would have chosen to live."

"No, not on my own. But returning with you is the best decision I ever made." She raised her head to face him. "Can we go and see the houses today?"

"Yes, of course, although we need to make an appointment with the owners to go in."

"But what about your mother? We should talk to her about this."

"Well, her needs will certainly figure strongly in our choice of a house but this decision to move and where is mine and yours, not hers. Anyway, I believe I owe us a house of our own, one that you can arrange to your tastes."

"But it won't look like this house," she said.

"If you arrange it like your house in Crampton, it will be cozy and inviting. That is all I need."

That evening, Mrs. Thornton began the conversation at dinner with a remark directed at her son: "You should not be taking Margaret out in her condition. It's rather cold out and, besides, it's just not done during a woman's confinement."

Margaret was somewhat annoyed that Mrs. Thornton did not address her about a matter concerning herself. But she held her tongue and concentrated on slathering butter on a piece of bread.

"Mother, Dr. Donaldson said that is a decision Margaret makes. She can do whatever she feels capable doing." Then looking at Margaret with an impish grin, he added: "I'm rather proud showing off my pot-bellied wife."

Margaret grinned back at him. Mrs. Thornton glanced at Margaret and scowled. "What was so important out there anyway that you would brave nearly freezing temperatures to go out?"

Margaret answered in as jaunty a tone as she could manage: "It was sunny all day so I was warm enough and actually enjoyed being out."

"But in your condition?"

Margaret chose to ignore her implication. "Dr. Donaldson advised exercise as long as I am capable."

Certain that Margaret was dissimulating, Mrs. Thornton merely nodded and compressed her lips. Margaret was less attentive to convention than any other young woman she knew and resistant to advice about proper decorum. But apart from her disapproval of Margaret gallivanting while in confinement, Mrs. Thornton had an inkling something else of consequence was afoot that would explain why Margaret and John were out in the dead of winter. She had to find out somehow what it was.

John had, in fact, anticipated his mother's suspicions and decided it was the right time to bring up the subject of moving. "If you must know, Mother, we were out looking at homes. With a growing family and children, we decided that we must find a house in another neighborhood."

As he expected, his mother was taken aback. "And what is going to happen to this house? Isn't it big enough? With Fanny married, we now have three unused bedrooms and an extra sitting room."

"The mill yard has no room where children can safely play and we prefer a neighborhood where there are other children. We will sell this house or put it up for lease."

Mrs. Thornton wanted to protest further and insist that she would rather remain in the house but this news perturbed her into silence. For an instant, she wondered whether she could still persuade her son to reconsider. But she told herself sadly, her hold on him had diminished. She glanced surreptitiously, resentfully, at Margaret who had lapsed into silence, her attention shifting between her dinner and what John was saying. Mrs. Thornton was convinced it was Margaret who had wanted to move.

Underneath her attempts at civility, Mrs. Thornton occasionally felt more incensed than glad that Margaret came back. She had reasons enough to do so since the day the mill reopened. Barely home from the mill that day, John left with Margaret for something pertaining to his wife. At first, Mrs. Thornton was confused and did not comprehend why they were leaving. Then, she was dismayed to find herself alone; hurt that she had been deprived of rejoicing with her son on a triumph she felt was as much hers as his. Did such moments not belong to her as well for all that she had done? All she could think of then, as now, was Margaret was the reason for her unhappiness. Forgotten was the gratitude she owed Margaret for having spared John long years of hard work to regain his fortune and the joy she and Margaret shared watching the mill reopen.

All that mattered now to Mrs. Thornton was the mill. It had become the focus of her life since John acquired a wife who took over all the hundred little things she used to do for him.

A home next to the mill had been her idea to which John had acquiesced and she had taken for granted that she would always live there. Since its reopening, her visits to the mill became more frequent and regular and she considered them as the most satisfying and productive part of her day. Living next door was certainly convenient. She did not waste time getting to it and she could also observe what was going on from her window.

John had changed. He rarely asked her now for her advice and opinion. Mrs. Thornton clenched her jaw and scowled unhappily, no longer certain that the mill meant to John what it did to her. Her mind and heart revolted against the move but she felt powerless. A profound gloominess took hold of her. She seemed to have aged suddenly, a feeble old woman, cast aside and helpless.

John and Margaret finally settled on a house in a neighborhood where some of John's business associates with young families lived. While somewhat larger to accommodate a growing family, it was not as imposing as the one they were leaving. Its ceilings were lower and windows all around the enclosing walls made its rooms airier and sunnier. Each of two suites of rooms on the two upper floors overlooking the backyard included a large bedroom, a bathroom and a sitting room—all flanking hallways that could be closed off for greater privacy. The suite on the lower floor was to be taken by Mrs. Thornton, the upper one by John and Margaret. A fairly large backyard with a garden would be redone to include a small playground for children. The purchase of the house was finalized but repairs and renovations postponed the move until they were completed.

On a spring day a couple of weeks after they bought their new house, John saw Dr. Donaldson from the window of his office rushing through the mill yard, followed close behind by Mary. Somewhat alarmed and irritated that he had not been called earlier, he hurried out of the office and ran towards the house. He saw his mother calmly working on her needlework in the drawing room.

"I just saw Dr. Donaldson go into the house. Is it Margaret? Why was I not sent for right away?"

"It was your headstrong wife who insisted on not bothering you until it was certain that she was about to deliver. She has been having pains since you left this morning but agreed to have the doctor come only when I said I was quite anxious about her."

"You should have sent someone to fetch me when you called for Dr. Donaldson," he snarled at his mother as he ran up the stairs.

Mrs. Thornton was left with an angry retort that never found words as John disappeared up the stairs.

John heard Dr. Donaldson's muffled voice from outside the bedroom door as he opened it. Margaret was propped up on the bed, her mouth open as she breathed through it, her attention concentrated on Dr. Donaldson whose hypnotic voice directed her over and over: "In, out, in, out, in, out........."

Dixon was there, too, occasionally wiping Margaret's face with a folded towel. No one heard him come in and he stood rooted in place, somewhat bewildered, feeling like a spectator watching a tableau from which he had been deliberately excluded.

"It's over," Margaret panted as she slowly relaxed her shoulders, her breathing becoming more regular. Both Dr. Donaldson and Dixon seemed to relax as well. Margaret saw John standing just in front of the door and she reached her hands out to him. This gesture jolted John out of his trance-like state.

"Margaret, my love," he cried, hurrying to her. He took her hand and pressed it to his lips. He sat down on the side of the bed, leaned over, and gathered her in his arms.

"The contractions are coming between 5 to 10 minutes so it should not be long now," he heard Dr. Donaldson say.

John turned to him and asked: "Can I stay with her?"

"For now, yes, but I will have to ask you to leave when she is ready. But are you sure you can stand seeing her when she's in pain?"

John was uncertain, confused and he directed questioning, apologetic eyes at Margaret. She smiled wanly at him and he thought she looked as young and vulnerable as she did on their first night together but, now, she was pale, her large eyes a little frightened, her face glistening with sweat. "Oh, my love, I did not mean to put you through all this," he cried remorsefully.

She gripped his hand and pleaded: "Stay with me a little longer."

"For as long as you need me." He pressed her hand to his lips once again and addressed Dr. Donaldson: "Is there nothing you can do for her pain?"

"She will be all right. Believe it or not, it is best that I do not sedate her. Your wife is quite young and healthy, Thornton, and this is a process many women like her go through without any problem."

John wiped the perspiration off his wife's moist face with his hand. Dixon handed him a towel. Unmindful of everyone else, he whispered words of love to her as he dabbed her face with it. For a while, this calmed Margaret who now seemed under the spell of his voice; but soon she began to grimace in pain.

"Tell her to breathe calmly in, out," Dr. Donaldson commanded John softly.

"In, out, in, out........."

Margaret delivered a blonde blue-eyed girl not long after and when John went back into the room, she was sitting up, holding the baby. She was sweaty and exhausted, strands of hair matted on her forehead but she beamed brightly at him. "We have a daughter."

He smiled broadly and, in a few quick strides, was by her side. He sat next to her, kissed her salty lips, and put his arm around her as they looked down at their daughter.

"How tiny she is!" John touched a curly golden lock with his finger. "And she is blonde!"

"Your sister Fanny is blonde. I was a blonde baby, wasn't I, Dixon?" She asked Dixon who just came back into the room.

"Yes, mistress and your baby looks like you when you were a baby."

"I am not so certain about that. I think she has John's chin and mouth." Margaret looked at her husband. "Don't you think so?"

He smiled at her indulgently. "Of course, she does."

"You must rest now, mistress. Dr. Donaldson said I must make sure you do soon. You need to have enough strength if you decide to nurse her."

"I will nurse her," Margaret asserted, handing the baby to Dixon.

"I will put her in her crib in the room we prepared for her. Mary and I will take turns watching her while you rest." Dixon left the room cradling the baby in her arms.

"Are you sure about nursing, my love?" John asked as she lay back on the bed. "Dr. Donaldson says he knows a couple of good wet nurses."

"Do you have any objections to my doing so?"

"No, not at all. He did also say that nursing her yourself is probably healthier for her and good for you."

After two days of sleeping, from which she awoke only to eat, nurse her child, and attend to her hygiene, Margaret regained her color, her appetite and the usual animation in her manner. When he came home that evening John found her sitting in bed nursing the baby. Except for a few stray wisps, her hair was neatly gathered up in a simple chignon and the pale rosiness in her translucent skin was evident again on her face and her exposed breast. The crib had been brought into the room. He kissed his wife before he sat down next to her.

"You look quite well, my love." He gazed at her, silently and tenderly, as their baby suckled at her breast. It was, to him, a glorious sight that, a year ago, he never imagined he would see.

"Margaret glanced at him briefly, blushing at his fascination. "We have to give her a name."

"Yes. How about Maria, after your mother?"

"How about Hannah, after yours? She came in to see us this morning and she appeared pleased enough. I can't help thinking she would have preferred a boy."

"Doesn't everyone? But as far as a name is concerned, our daughter looks rather delicate and fair and so unlike my mother. More like yours, actually."

"True. But perhaps, if we called her Hannah, she will grow up as strong and resilient."

"Would you like that?"

"Yes. She will need to be, in a society that favors men and boys. A good mind will help greatly, too."

John stared at Margaret, somewhat startled and yet, he could not dispute the truth of what she said. Although it was not the first time she said something that gave him pause, this time he frowned and looked away.

"Are you shocked? But you know it's true."

"It is startling nonetheless. It just never occurred to me to think of it in that way."

She had finished nursing and she held the baby out to him. "Here, take her while I button my shirt." She saw him hesitate. "It's easy. Fold your arms, palms up, and I'll put her on top. Don't worry. You will not drop her."

He complied awkwardly but when the baby was cuddled in his arms, he remarked in amazement: "How light she is and how nice she smells."

"Yes, she is our little angel. Maybe, things will be better for her when she is twenty." In a more lighthearted tone, she added: "Meanwhile, she needs a name."

He nodded. "Perhaps, Maria Hannah or Hannah Maria but........ "—gazing at his sleeping daughter and then smiling at his wife—"Margaret seems more appropriate for the young woman you described."

She shook her head at him, a half-smile on her lips. "You're teasing me."

"Not at all. She would be a formidable charmer if she grows up like my Margaret."

Eventually, when John could not be budged on the name Margaret, they compromised on Elise Margaret. They would call her Elise.

The arrival of the first child delighted the servants who had begun to dread serving a home that grew increasingly somber and gloomy after Miss Fanny married and left. They chatted about the baby endlessly for days, about why she was blonde, who she looked like, why Mrs. Margaret would not employ a wet nurse, what she should be named. Dixon and Mary, who knew childbirth could threaten a mother's life, had been deeply concerned about Margaret. Mary's mother died delivering a son while Dixon witnessed Frederick's difficult birth. Mrs. Hale lost so much blood that it had taken her several months to recover. The following day, Mary and Dixon greeted Margaret with a large bouquet of flowers that Mary and the younger servants picked in the countryside. When Margaret felt well enough to come down to dinner one week later, Dixon celebrated by preparing Margaret's favorite dishes and baking a special cake for everyone to partake of.

XVI. REENCHANTMENT

John stood by his daughter's crib looking down at her as she slept, her eyes tightly closed, her long dark lashes resting prettily on plump ivory cheeks—a tiny helpless creature, only three weeks old, who he had helped bring into the world and was now completely dependent on him and Margaret. The thought was both awe-inspiring and humbling, the responsibility and challenge it implied exceeding anything he had ever been faced with. He watched her for some time, amused at how she occasionally pursed her pink tiny lips and twitched her limbs.

"How peacefully she sleeps. Do you think she's dreaming?" John asked Mary. He had come home early from work and found Mary in their bedroom seated by the crib, rocking Elise to sleep.

Mary merely smiled and nodded.

"Where is my wife, Mary?"

"She's at her bath, master. Would you like me to tell her you're home?"

John smiled, raising a hand to stop her from getting up. "No need to, Mary. I'll go. Little Elise needs you more."

John closed the door noiselessly after him as he entered the bathroom. Margaret, with her back to the door, was lying in the tub. Her eyes were closed and her wet hair, piled up in a bun, cushioned the back of her head. She heard him come in but she neither budged nor opened her eyes and assumed it was Mary. "I am not ready to get out yet Mary. This warm water is just too wonderful to leave."

John walked towards the chair next to the tub, picked up the robe draped on it along with the towel folded on the seat, and sat down quietly.

Margaret raised her eyelids reluctantly and lazily as she sensed a presence next to her. "Oh, it is you! You are early today." She extended a wet shining arm to him.

"Yes. We completed a huge order early today, ahead of schedule. I decided to dismiss the workers right after. They have been working very hard the past few weeks, some of them staying beyond closing time." He grasped her hand and bent over to kiss her lips, warmer than usual and soft and wet from the vapor rising out of the tub.

She closed her eyes as his kiss lingered. Her lips tasted like ripe peach and he wanted to savor their lusciousness again but as tempted as he was, he merely gazed at her until she opened her eyes slowly.

She smiled placidly at him and leaned back again. "The mill appears to be doing quite well." She closed her eyes and allowed herself to go slack once more in the enveloping warmth of the rose-scented water. Still, she was conscious that he was feasting his eyes on her.

"I expected it to. There is growing demand for cotton and we will be getting new contracts soon."

"Hmm," the sound barely escaped her throat as she nodded, hardly moving her head.

John sat watching Margaret luxuriate in sensuous content in her bath, fascinated at the sight of her figure undulating ever so gently under the water with every breath she took. How different it was in that room from the noise and chaos he left not even a quarter of an hour ago! He sat for many minutes, amused at himself that he could sit there, unperturbed, relaxing and nearly hypnotized by the stillness that surrounded them—a stillness that nothing intruded into it but their breathing and the occasional tinkling of water when Margaret adjusted her position.

At length, Margaret slithered up the tub and broke into his reverie. "The water is getting cold. Time to get out, in any case. Help me up, please, John."

"I will do better than that," he replied in a playful tone.

He reached for her hands and pulled her up. She turned her back to him as he wrapped her robe around her. Then he lifted her up from the tub and unto the rug. He turned her around to face him so he could dab her face and her arms with the towel. He proceeded to dry her hair and her scalp vigorously until her head tingled. Throwing the towel back on the chair, he rubbed his palms together to warm them up and then lightly patted her cheeks and her arms until her skin took on a rosier tint.

"Does our service meet with your approval, madam?" He asked in a servile tone.

"Excellent, monsieur!" She answered in French, going along with his playful mood, flashing him a bewitching smile. "I'm extremely pleased you have not forgotten that I like to get my blood going with vigorous drying."

"Yes although it has been awhile," he said, clasping her close, kissing her. "Ah, how good you smell," he whispered between kisses. "How warm and soft."

She murmured against his mouth: "Come back to bed tonight. It cannot be too pleasant sleeping in your study."

"No! It's lonely sleeping by myself in that cold narrow bed. But what about Elise? Don't you need to nurse her in bed at night?"

"That was only for a little while so I could go on sleeping when she cried out to be nourished in the middle of the night. Now, she sleeps almost all the way through and I have caught up on my sleep. We will place her crib closer by the fireplace and I'll put her back in it." She laid her head on his shoulder, snuggling in his embrace. "I miss the warmth of you at night. Don't you miss me?"

"How could you even ask me that?" He untied her robe and placed his arms inside and around her waist.

A couple of weeks later, as he was about to go to bed, John noticed that the crib had been moved out of the room. "Where is Elise?"

"She's back in the room we prepared for her. Mary will be staying with her at night from now on."

He threw his robe on a chair and climbed into bed. Margaret lay with the sheet up to her neck. He thought it odd on a warm late spring night; he himself was without his night shirt. "Are you ill?"

"No," she answered hesitantly, throwing him a quick glance, biting her lower lip as she looked away as if she had just been caught at some transgression and was hiding her face, fearful of what he might see in it.

He was perplexed, even somewhat concerned. "What is the matter my love?"

She turned towards him but did not answer. She quickly averted her glistening eyes and sucked her breath in through tremulous parted lips. She kicked the sheet with one swift movement, baring naked shoulders, arms and a breast. Pleasantly surprised, he cradled her face between his palms to force her to look at him; then he smiled, his eyes shining under his dark brow.

As he bent over to kiss her, she placed her arms around his neck and pulled him closer, his face only inches from hers. She gazed deeply into his eyes. "You have been back with me for some time. You kiss me and caress me but you have not......" Her voice trailed and she lowered her eyes.

He kissed her face all over. "Oh, Margaret, you don't know how much I have wanted to!"

"Then why?"

He hesitated a moment, studying her face. "Because......well, I saw you suffer giving birth to Elise. I loathe for you to go through that again. At least, not so soon after."

She regarded him thoughtfully for a long moment as if she did not grasp what he meant and was struggling to do so. Then in a low sultry voice, she urged: "Make love to me." She pulled his face closer, paused, and whispered, her voice both tremulous and enticing. "I want you to."

With a sweep of her arm, Margaret pushed the sheet off herself completely. John raised his head and gazed at her—eyes closed, lips slightly parted, and head thrown back a little so her ivory throat was arched, waiting for him to bury his face in it as he had done many times before. Her shoulders were pressed against the bed and the lamp on his night table cast its golden glow on her breasts, rounder and fuller from nursing. He groaned at the mixture of apprehension and guilt that still inhibited him.

Every night that he had been back in bed with her, he had wanted to make love to her. But he always restrained himself, haunted by images of her panting continuously, her shadowed eyes frightened, and her sweaty face grimacing in pain. That image invaded his dreams for a few nights after she gave birth to Elise. How could he do that to her again? Yet, he had not expected her to ask him so directly. The directness of her plea—or was it more akin to a command?—amazed and thrilled him at the same time.

Margaret, opened her eyes briefly and caught his hesitation right away. She clasped him close and kissed him. She ran her warm trembling hands down his neck and shoulders, across his back and his buttocks, kneading them with the palms of her hands.

"Margaret, my love," John groaned once more. This time, it was a groan of surrender, of yielding his defenses to the passion that swept them together into delicious moments, fusing their whole being, allowing their bodies and their senses, not their minds, to be in control.

Later, they lay in silence with his arms around her. She ran delicate warm fingers very slowly up and down his arm, delighting in its roughness. Occasionally, she lifted the back of his hand to her lips or against her cheek. He found those moments infinitely tender, yet sensuous and enthralling, the sort he could vividly relive when, in his office, his mind wandered from his work at the mill.

Since that night, it seemed to him their lovemaking assumed a different character. He had believed that while Margaret had always responded eagerly to him, she did so out of her love for him. Now, he confronted the idea that a woman like Margaret—with a mind of her own and feelings she neither denied nor allowed society to dictate—could have desires in the same way as men. It scared him a little but it fascinated him as well and he was in awe once more of the woman he married. Usually soft, warm, and yielding in his arms, Margaret could love with more abandon. She stroked and took little nibbles of his bare skin, initiated passionate kisses and caresses, and obviously relished every bit of their lovemaking.

A week later, John came home with a big bouquet of roses in one arm and a gift-wrapped box in the other. He went directly to their bedroom where he knew Margaret would be nursing Elise before she was put to bed for the night. With the needs of a baby of primary concern for the present, he and Margaret had to modify their evening rituals. He still came home an hour before dinner and Margaret often tried to finish nursing and dressing Elise for bed shortly before he came home.

Margaret sat where she could see the door as he came in from the mill. This evening, she was humming in a low voice, rocking Elise to sleep.

She smiled, extremely pleased and her eyes twinkled as she whispered: "For me?"

"You know why, don't you?"

"How could I forget the day you promised to cherish me all my life?" She answered playfully.

"I was certain you would not let me forget," he teased back. He placed the flowers in a vase and the package on the low table in front of her. "And it is for me to remind you that you made the same promise." He bent over and kissed her tenderly, lingering a while on her lips.

He looked deep into her eyes. "You are the best thing that ever happened to me. Love me always?"

"Deeply, irrevocably. How could I resist you? I did try but look where I am." Her gaze went from him to the baby sleeping in her arms.

After putting Elise to bed, they sat on armchairs, silhouetted together by the glow from the fireplace, as John watched Margaret open the pretty package carefully. In it was a silky light green fabric wrapped in tissue, on top of which was an elegant little box. Margaret picked up the little box and placed it on the table. Then, she lifted the fabric delicately and saw there were two pieces.

"A peignoir! How lovely and how sumptuous." Her eyes half-closed, she rubbed the silk against her cheek, delighting in its sensuous feel against her skin.

"Do you remember our first night together?" He murmured with a small quiver in his voice.

She blushed a little and did not answer; instead, she put her arms around his neck and pressed her lips ardently to his. He clasped her in his arms, kissing her back.

At length, he whispered: "Open the small box."

She nodded with a smile and opened the box. In it was a bracelet of white gold and diamonds. "How exquisite!"

"You were wearing such a bracelet when I first realized I was falling for you that night I was at your house. When you refused to shake my hand." His eyes twinkled, mischievously.

"That was the night I fell asleep on my chair because I was so tired ironing curtains for you so you would feel at ease in our small home." She retorted, flashing him a saucy smile. She reached into a small compartment under the tabletop. "I have nothing as spectacular as all these to give you. I do have this for you."

The box was carefully gift-wrapped and tied with a large ribbon. Under the ribbon was a small folded card on which she had painted a yellow rose. He opened the card which read: "For all that you have been to me and done for me this past year, my deepest love and gratitude. Loving you always will be the easiest thing I do."

He held the card in his hand, fondling it for a few moments. Then, he put the card to his lips and slipped it into his vest pocket. The box contained a pen with a metal nib attached, not to a quill, but to beautifully polished wood trimmed with bronze.

"I saw one of these at the international exposition in London a few years ago."

"Yes, I first learned about them there. People are inventing new things all the time."

"But how did you get this? Nobody I know has one"

"With Edith's help. At the exposition, they exhibited one that the French patented a couple of decades ago. It held ink but it never caught on because it leaked so much."

"The handle on this is so much larger and should be easier for me to hold."

"It has a receptacle for ink so it does not need an inkwell. You can carry it around and use it for a long time before it needs refilling."

"Now, that is a great convenience!"

"Yes, I thought it would be. I have seen you struggle with thin quills that are just too small for your hand. I hope this new type of pen helps to make doing all that paperwork for the mill less tiring and less staining on your fingers. It is not supposed to leak." She reached over, took his right hand, and pressed it closely to her lips.

He grasped both her hands and pulled her over on his lap. She wound her arms around his neck as he nuzzled his face against her cheek, then against her neck, breathing in her subtle fragrance. She laid her head on his and they sat in their quiet intimacy until the darkness engulfed much of the space around them and reminded them that his mother might be waiting in the dining room for dinner.

He sighed and said: "I would have preferred to have dinner alone with you tonight. Can we not have it served here in our room?"

"You know the answer to that as well as I do."

They descended to the dining room but Mrs. Thornton was not there. Instead, Dixon waited with a couple of servants ready to attend to them. The table was laid out with a full set of silver and dinner ware, a Hale heirloom tablecloth, candelabra used mostly on special occasions, and a centerpiece of red and yellow roses brimming out of a large low vase. Before John could inquire about his mother, Dixon explained that Mrs. Thornton had pleaded fatigue and asked for soup and bread to be brought to her room.

Dixon had not forgotten what that day meant for John and Margaret. She prepared a special full-course dinner, served formally by two servants, coached to be especially attentive— offering dishes and filling wine glasses just at the right moment, taking dirty plates and silver away and replacing them promptly, even taking an elaborate bow as they retreated. The dinner was sumptuous and delicious, and John and Margaret were grateful for the care and effort Dixon had taken. But they found the formality of the whole dinner somewhat diverting and they smiled at each other every time the servants, enthusiastic but awkward at their tasks, stepped back with a bow.

Later, on Margaret's inquiry, Dixon confirmed that Mrs. Thornton had indeed come to the dining room at her usual time. She had forgotten the couple's wedding anniversary but, seeing the special table settings and the large vase of roses, she remembered. She left immediately after asking for her meal to be sent up to her. Margaret could not but be touched by the thought and generosity of this gesture. She was, once more, perplexed by how to reconcile such a considerate side of Mrs. Thornton to the sterner almost harsh face she often assumed with Margaret.

Elise was baptized when she was three months old. Edith was godmother and Fanny's husband Watson volunteered to be godfather. Both John and Margaret were hesitant about Watson with whom they always felt some unease but they did not have much choice. Mrs. Thornton insisted that the baptismal sponsors come from both sides of the family. Margaret had already chosen and asked Edith soon after Elise was born. Mrs. Shaw came with her daughter for the affair, a small one that included only family from both sides. John and Margaret had hoped to have a larger joint celebration of the christening and the blessing of their new house. Unfortunately, renovations were taking longer than estimated and their move was postponed for another three months.

Edith, escorted by Watson, carried the baby out of the church after the ceremony. John followed with Margaret and his sister. Mrs. Thornton and Mrs. Shaw trailed behind. Outside, Watson rejoined Fanny and John went to fetch the carriages. Edith pulled Margaret some distance apart from the others as they waited for the first cab. She handed Elise back to her mother and whispered conspiratorially, as they had done as children. "I have news that will surprise you, perhaps, delight you at the same time."

Margaret arched a questioning eyebrow and fixed expectant eyes on her.

"Henry is engaged." Edith announced momentously in a voice she struggled to keep low.

"Who to? One of the three Harding sisters? They have all been after him for years." Margaret asked, her voice just as low but without the drama.

"No, I doubt he even entertained that idea for a moment. No, Henry is marrying into big money." She was relishing Margaret's look of surprise and anticipation.

"Well, tell me," Margaret laughed, aware of Edith's penchant for surprises which Margaret had obligingly indulged across the years by assuming an air of impatience.

"You'll never guess. Someone from Milton who you must be acquainted with—some rich banker's daughter by the name of Ann Latimer!"

"No! How? They did not meet at my wedding. The Latimers politely declined our invitation, saying they were going abroad at the time."

"Apparently, he met her father when Henry came to Milton on business regarding your property, shortly after your wedding. Mr. Latimer was impressed with Henry's cleverness and financial knowledge and asked him over for dinner. It seems the attraction was immediate and mutual. They reached an understanding within three months but Mr. Latimer requested they wait a year."

"I am happy for Henry. Ann Latimer went to finishing school and has the fashion and polish he admires, which would be an asset to him in his career."

"I am glad to hear that if she is to be my sister-in-law. I was afraid she would be some spoiled daughter of a nouveau riche who puts on airs. Still, I would have greatly preferred to have you for a sister. Do you know her well?"

"Not really. Our paths have not crossed that often." She leaned over to whisper. "I will tell you this: She and John were seen together a few times before we were married and people from around here probably expected them to marry. I am certain Mrs. Thornton would have been much happier if John had married her, instead."

"No!" It was Edith's turn to be surprised. She relished this bit of gossip, which she knew Captain Lennox would find as entertaining as she did and she wanted to know more. "Is she a beauty?"

"I think she is very pretty."

Edith's interest was piqued even more but the arrival of carriages taking them back to the Thornton house forced her to keep her curiosity in check until they were alone in a carriage. As the party gathered to board the cabs, Edith said to her mother: "Mama, could you possibly exchange places with Margaret and ride back with Mrs. Thornton? She and I have much to catch up on."

Mrs. Shaw, momentarily confused, did not reply right away but before she could assent, John approached them and declared: "I would like to escort my wife and child back home. So, I will ride with Edith and Margaret." With a briskness of movement that Edith could not hope to match, he helped Mrs. Shaw and his mother into the first carriage. Watson and Fanny claimed the second one.

Edith really wanted some time alone with Margaret so they could talk in confidence. It irritated her that John maneuvered effortlessly to arrange the return home as he wished. She sat a little sullenly across John and Margaret who, seeing her cousin sulk, said brightly to John: "Edith has some good news for us about Henry Lennox."

Edith was taken aback. She intended the news to be relatively private since no formal announcement had as yet been made. But John, eager to hear what she had to say, directed his dark intent eyes at her. Something in them compelled a truthful answer and Edith thought: "Why not?" She and the Captain enjoyed sharing stories and, obviously, so did Margaret and Mr. Thornton. She warmed up to what was asked of her, a little hesitantly at first but as she proceeded, she infused her recounting to John with no less enthusiasm nor drama as she did with Margaret.

John who, at first, was as surprised as Margaret had been, grinned widely, glancing at his wife with a twinkle in his eye that Edith did not catch. "A happy ending then for our clever sophisticated lawyer."

Margaret countered archly: "And a very pretty lady found the man she would make happy."

Edith was delighted that John found the news as diverting as Margaret did. He proceeded to ask questions which Edith answered with great relish. But she could not help ending with a provocative question by which she meant to learn how tempted he was to propose to Ann Latimer—and, thereby, share with Captain Lennox a juicier story. "Do you think she is a beauty?"

"She is very pretty but as Shakespeare says: "Beauty is bought by judgment of the eye."

Edith thought his tone disinterested and liked his way of saying he was indifferent to Miss Latimer's looks with a quote from Shakespeare. It was a more gentlemanly approach that spoke well of him, enough to convince Edith of Mr. Thornton's lack of amorous intentions. Her romantic soul would not have desired, could not have conceived him in love with anyone else but Margaret.

Later, as they were piling into the dining room, Edith whispered to Margaret: "I like your husband, I think, even more than Henry. He has a sincerity and gallantry more appealing than Henry's cleverness and sophistication."

"But, Edith, my husband is a tradesman."

"He is a well-respected manufacturer."

XVII. DISCORD

"Well, mother, what do you think?" John asked Mrs. Thornton after he and Margaret took her around the new house for a quick look.

John and Margaret had visited the house a few times—sometimes together and, twice, Margaret went alone to make final decisions on colors, wall paper, and trim. Mrs. Thornton was seeing it for the first time. She had her misgivings but she was determined to be agreeable. After all, she could do nothing more and she was there merely to look through her suite of rooms and tell them how she wanted her furniture arranged.

Mrs. Thornton did not answer right away. John and Margaret stood together, like mimes in synchronized suspended motion, holding their breath, waiting for a cue. They were both rather anxious about what Mrs. Thornton would say. Both wanted very much to appease her—John, out of his lifelong habit of heeding his mother, often going along with her wishes, and—Margaret, out of hopes her mother-in-law would eventually accept her. Mrs. Thornton continued to believe the move unnecessary, and they feared confirming suspicions that she was profoundly unhappy.

Mrs. Thornton was not happy. She was powerless to prevent the inevitable move so she tried to resign herself to it the past six months with the thought that it was largely John's decision as well as Margaret's, not hers. She resolved to be fair in her judgment.

"The house is bright and airy. All these windows and light walls! The neighborhood seems quite wholesome. "

Margaret smiled. The comment was neutral and as such, favorable. "I hope you found your rooms pleasing."

"They are away from street noises and it's good you had them painted darker than the rest of the house. I find the lighter colors a little blinding for my poor old eyes."

The first sign of discontent, obliquely conveyed, was evident enough. "We want you to be as comfortable as possible, mother, so you must tell the movers what to do with your furniture."

But Mrs. Thornton was unaccustomed to restraining her true feelings and opinions for too long and she frowned. "It will be almost too quiet back there."

"It will be quite restful and private," Margaret answered as evenly as she could. "We have a similar suite of rooms on the floor above yours."

Mrs. Thornton turned to her son, expecting him to understand what she could not explicitly say but he was then smiling agreeably at his wife. Defeated and feeling neglected, she turned her back abruptly to them and headed for the stairs. She struggled to sound nonchalant and composed but she could not mask the dejection in her voice. "Well, then, I shall go up again so I will know what to tell you to do with my furniture."

"Take all the time you need," Margaret said lamely. She watched Mrs. Thornton walk up the stairs and disappear around the landing. Margaret stood rooted in place for a long moment before she hooked her arm around John's and said in a subdued tone: "Let's wait in the garden. Right now, that is the only place where we can sit."

As they strolled into the garden, an awkward silence crept up between them, brought on by a shared sense of guilt for imposing their own opposite wishes on Mrs. Thornton. She was clearly miserable particularly now that the move was imminent. They sat on a stone bench under a shady tree, hesitant to talk about a matter of potential contention. Margaret, restless with her unease, surveyed the garden distractedly. She observed a few things she would ordinarily have remarked upon but she could not force herself to break her silence.

John could not stay as restrained. His mother's doleful countenance weighed on him heavily. "It is quiet back here! My mother has been so used to all those sounds from the mill. This will be very different for her."

"Yes. But as you once told me, Hannah is quite resilient. She will survive this well enough and she might even grow to like the tranquil atmosphere."

"You are right about her resilience." He agreed but he could not shake off his trepidation. After a long pause, he asked irritably: "Why have you never called her mother?"

The question so startled Margaret that she could not answer right away. When she did, she was clearly trying to steady her voice which had an edge to it that she could not control. She caught the reproach in his question and it grated on her. "Is that what she would prefer? I am afraid she does not think of herself in that way where I am concerned. Your mother will never totally accept me. I have reconciled myself to that fact."

"You might make more of an effort."

"Tell me how because I do not truly know what more to do. You have lived with her all your life and must have a trick or two you could share with me." The edge had grown into distress tinged with annoyance and sarcasm.

He did not answer, only looked away. He smarted at her sarcasm but he was also sorry that he distressed her by what he said. After a few minutes, he turned to her and was mortified to see the gloom that clouded her face. She sat very still, hands clasped tightly on her lap. With her head and her eyes cast down, the afternoon sunlight against which she was silhouetted deepened the shadows under her eyes and her lower lip, curled tightly under the upper one.

He reached over to stroke her hand. "I'm sorry. That was uncalled for. I was upset that mother was so unhappy."

She nodded ever so slightly but said nothing, her eyes fixed abstractedly on the ground.

He inched closer to her, put an arm around her shoulders, and kissed her temple. "Forgive me?"

She looked up, lifted the corners of her mouth for a smile that faded with her sad eyes, and leaned back against him.

Immediately after dinner, Margaret pled fatigue and headed directly for the bedroom, leaving John and his mother on their way to the drawing room for after-dinner drinks and coffee. Conversation at dinner had often been strained between Margaret and Mrs. Thornton but his evening, she was unusually withdrawn and spoke very little. She had, in fact, been listless since their return from the new house.

John entered their bedroom nearly an hour later and found her reading by the fireplace. She did not raise her head at his entrance and barely reacted to his remark that he had expected her to be in bed. He went into his dressing room to change into a robe and night shirt.

When he returned, he discreetly selected a book and joined her. She sat, rigid, seemingly immersed in her book but her countenance—which usually registered her reactions to what she was reading—was expressionless, impassive. He walked behind her chair, briefly caressing the nape of her neck as he passed by. She acknowledged his gesture with an almost imperceptible nod.

John settled on the chair across from her, opened his book, and stared at the words on the page he had picked at random. Comprehension was nearly impossible. At dinner, he thought Margaret was indeed merely tired, as she claimed, but now in the privacy of their bedroom, she was still uncharacteristically reticent. He cast her stealthy glances from time to time, gauging her mood, wondering if he should ask how she was.

She seemed to have slipped into a silence so private that it excluded everything and everyone around her. There was, about her, an aura of remoteness that John had never seen since she came back to him. He felt reluctant to violate it. After some time, she closed her book and fixed her eyes pensively, but unseeingly, at the gas lamp on the table that separated them. John watched her preoccupation from behind his book for a few minutes.

"I am sorry about your mother." She muttered after many more moments of silence, her eyes transfixed by the flickering lamp.

He assumed that she was referring to the events at the new house that afternoon. "It was not your fault and I was callous in my remark to you."

"No. I do not mean because of something I did today." She raised her head and fixed her eyes on him.

He returned her gaze and detected a wistful melancholy in her eyes that he had not seen since the time she talked about her brother's plight. She seemed so far away from him, her eyes veiled, focused inward, trying to grasp something within that was elusive. Her mood bewildered him. He said nothing and turned his attention back to his book, pretending interest in it. He wished that he could go to her, hold her and kiss her sadness away but her self-absorption had erected an invisible but palpable barrier between them. She seemed neither to need nor want his loving reassurance just then.

Margaret spoke again, her voice tremulous. "Your mother and I are like polite strangers living in the same house. When, I join her in the drawing room, she leaves shortly after. I know she likes to spend her afternoons there so I have taken to spending mine in our room so as not to drive her out of the drawing room. I have never lived with anyone who found my presence that uncomfortable." She could not conceal the hurt in her voice.

This time, he closed his book and looked at her intently. "Has it been that unpleasant?"

"She makes more of an effort when you're around but drops most pretense when we are alone. I doubt she will ever learn to like me." Her voice did not have the annoyance nor sarcasm of that afternoon, only sadness verging on anguish. "How am I supposed to warm up to her?"

"I am sorry," he muttered sincerely. "I never meant to imply that you were not doing enough."

"No, that is not it, either. It is just that we are so different, your mother and I. Maybe she would have resented any woman you married but knowing that still does not make the situation easier."

He was sympathetic but he felt helpless, unable to contradict the truth of her statement. Yet, he doubted that there was anything that he nor anyone else could do to change his mother.

"It is hard but I can actually live with her indifference, even her avoidance of me, maybe, even learn to ignore it, in time. I realize that it must be hard for her, too, living with the woman who took from her the person around which her world had revolved."

"I am sorry I was not aware of all this." He answered lamely.

"You are busy with your work at the mill. How could you be?" The edge had returned to her voice, wrought by the perception that the situation with Mrs. Thornton was hopeless and that John could never fully understand her despair over it.

She abruptly got up from her chair and picked up her book. "I know and accept that the mill is important to you. I also realize that it is unpleasant and quite vexing to be caught in between your wife and your mother."

She walked towards the writing table and nearly slammed her book on the pile on top of it. She turned, her eyes flashing. "What upsets me most is how your mother seems so detached towards my daughter, who is of her flesh and blood."

"What do you mean?"

"She did not come to see Elise until a few days after she was born. I cannot remember if she has touched my child at all. It worries me that she might treat Elise the way she does me."

"Give my mother time. It has been a long time since she has seen, much less held a baby, and she is not very demonstrative, as you know."

"No, except to you." Her voice faltered. She sat down on the chair in front of the writing table, covered her face with her hands, and struggled to keep from crying.

"Margaret, my love!"

He could not bear to see her cry and it no longer mattered to him then that she might repel his efforts at comforting her. All he wanted to do was hold her, tell her that he would do almost anything to make her happy. He came towards her, knelt on one knee, and disengaging her hands off her face, kissed and caressed it lovingly. She had shed no tears but her eyes were moist, red, and clouded with such mournfulness as he had not seen in her before.

"Has it been that hard living in this house with my mother?"

She covered her face with her hands once again. "I miss Mama. I miss Papa and Frederick. My parents never even saw my daughter, never knew I would have one."

He gathered her close. "Oh my love."

She buried her face on his shoulder and, immovable, reticent, impenetrable, she clung to him. Then, her body began to quiver against his, gripped by a disconsolate sorrow about which he felt helpless. All he could do was hold her until she calmed down again. Happy as the two of them had been, it had not occurred to him that she would continue to grieve and miss her family that much, especially now that she had her own. Then, he reminded himself that, as strong as his wife seemed to be, she was quite young and probably needed someone for occasional counsel and implicit support, such as that her mother or father or even Mr. Bell had given her. Had she hoped that his mother could have become that trusted confidante?

Margaret raised her head and although her face was not wet with tears, her eyes were nearly bloodshot and her lips swollen as if she had bitten them hard. He peered earnestly at her face, his eyes deep with concern.

She tried to smile. "I will be all right." Then, aware for the first time that he was kneeling on the floor, she exclaimed: "But you must get up!"

"I will but will you come to bed? You look exhausted." He offered her his hands as he stood up.

She nodded, rose from her chair, and found herself suddenly lifted and being carried to the bed. He whispered against her hair: "Remember that, however trying things become, I love you more than anything in this world and I am here when you need me."

He laid her on the bed and sat next to her, looking deeply, tenderly, into her eyes. "Remember also that we will be seeing Frederick and Dolores in Paris, probably as early as next summer."

"We will take Elise along?"

"Of course. Dixon, too, to help you take care of her. Dixon would be happy to see your brother again, I'm sure."

That night, he held her in his arms where she fell asleep and remained until she awakened the following morning.

The Thorntons and their household moved to the new house as summer began to wane. In Mrs. Thornton's new rooms, her beloved furniture and ornaments from the old house had been arranged to her specifications. She had to admit that Margaret showed sensitivity to her needs in designing her rooms to suit her preferences in color and austere trimming. Her only complaint was that too much light streamed into her sitting room in the morning but she solved that problem by keeping her drapes closed. When the clutter was cleared from unpacking boxes and the frenzy of moving and settling in had ceased, Mrs. Thornton felt sad and sorry for herself—alone with all her familiar possessions, remnants from a life of content she doubted she would ever have again.

She had a good view of the backyard garden with its trees, flower beds, a large expanse of lawn, and the small vegetable and herb bed enclosed in a low fence just outside the kitchen. In the morning, she woke to the chirping of birds and in the tranquility of her new surroundings, she slept past her usual time for awakening during the first few days. Her days were generally calm and peaceful, occupied by hours of needlework in the afternoon.

The casual elegance of the house—its light moss green wallpaper, vases of flowers, Chinese vessels and pewter candelabras—was too fanciful for her tastes and she spent most of her afternoons in her large sitting room. With her spacious suite to while away her hours in, the tension between her and Margaret eased somewhat.

But Mrs. Thornton missed all the big and little things that used to help her structure her day at the old house. She longed to hear the humming, whirring, and clanging of the mill machines, to watch the bustle of workers, to be surrounded by the white cloud of cotton fluff that floated from the mill into the courtyard, and to see John stride purposefully across the courtyard—everything that reassured her all was well with her world. Restless in the interminable silences of the house, she found it irritating that she could not readily walk out and, in a couple of minutes, enter the large door into the mill. Not long after, she insisted on going with John to the mill.

The mill was a good four kilometers from the house and it usually took John half an hour to walk to it. Mrs. Thornton, although sprightly, could not keep up with his pace so he had to slow down for her and nearly an hour later, they arrived at the mill.

They had walked without speaking so as not to impede their progress but within sight of the mill, John could not hide his irritation at being delayed. "I have a meeting this morning, mother, and I am already late. They're probably waiting for me in my office right now."

He hurried towards his office and left his mother to walk to the mill by herself.

At around noon, he met her inside the mill as she walked around, moving slowly, her shoulders drooping. She did not appear to have her usual vigilance.

"You are tired, mother. You should go home. I will tell Williams to fetch you a cab."

"I can walk home with you when you finish this evening. I will wait in your office and rest there."

"No, mother. You have never stayed this long and the walk here this morning has probably tired you out even more. Go home and rest, please."

Mrs. Thornton said no more and nodded her head, unable to protest, as she had often done, the wasted expense on a cab. She was, in fact, too tired to walk home, too exhausted in spirit by her disappointing morning. The walk to the mill was too long and although acutely conscious of her son's impatience with her pace, she had been incapable of going faster. By the time she had entered the mill, she had lost the enthusiasm with which she began her morning. Worse than that, with her flagging energy and guilt at delaying John from his tasks, the walk around the mill was not the antidote she had expected against the ennui of her quiet uneventful days at the new house.

John returned home that evening to find Margaret in the conservatory, humming a lullaby and rocking Elise to sleep. She sat facing the garden, absorbed for the moment in a world peacefully centered on her child, inattentive to the sounds and stirrings that were the usual signs of life within a home. John paused at the door to watch his wife and daughter. Coming home continued to be the reward he dangled in his mind's eye that awaited him at the end of each day. He had thought at first that having a child would limit the precious sweet moments he had with Margaret. They did not have as much time alone together before dinner as they used to but not much else had changed.

John had not anticipated either that he would dote on his daughter, now as lively as any baby could be, but as individual as any adult in the house in expressing her needs, delights and frustrations. Every morning, Mary brought her in to nurse and on weekends, he and Margaret played with Elise in bed before all three of them went down to breakfast. In the dining room, the greater variety of voices and sounds and the larger, brighter surroundings entertained Elise. She usually lay in her baby carriage, her eyes alert, adding her babbling to the usual ambient noise of breakfast, and playing with colorful objects hanging on a string tied between the carriage handle and cover.

John approached noiselessly and bent down to press his lips against the nape of his wife's neck. Happily surprised by the warm soft sensation, she extended her arm behind her and around his head as she turned to kiss him.

"Good evening, love." He smiled at his wife, then, bent over the crib to kiss his sleeping child. He stood watching her for a few moments. "It would be wonderful if we could all sleep as peacefully as she does."

Margaret, standing by his side, smiled. "Wouldn't it? But having no care in the world would bore you, I think."

He chuckled a little and placed an arm around her shoulders as he led her away from the crib. "Did you see mother when she came back from the mill this afternoon?"

They sat on chairs farther away from the crib and talked in hushed tones. "Yes, she seemed very tired and went straight to her room. She asked Jane to serve her lunch there. First time I have known her do that."

"I think the walk to the mill was too much for her. That, going around the mill, making sure workers were not slacking off, exhausted her by noon. She was probably hungry, too, but she would have starved rather than come with me to lunch at the dining hall."

"Next time, you could take a cab. Or we might think of buying a barouche for our use. It would be useful to you when autumn and winter come."

He looked at her distractedly, scowling a little. "Possibly but we'll talk about that another time."

She peered closer at him. "Is anything the matter?"

"I met with worker representatives this morning—another one of my attempts to understand where my men are coming from. I figure if we resolve problems and disputes before they pester, we can go longer without having to deal with strikes."

"How marvelous! Could you prevent them that way?"

"Not really. Something always comes up to make one inevitable. We cannot control market forces. Strikes are about wages and working conditions requiring complicated and difficult resolutions that are sometimes impossible."

"Did something particularly difficult come up in your meeting?

"Something quite sensitive." He paused, frowning. "It is about my mother."

"Hannah! What has she to do with it?"

"Workers object to her coming to the mill. They had hoped that with our move to a house away from the mill, she would stop coming but when they saw her with me this morning, it was the very first topic they brought up."

He hesitated and Margaret prompted: "And?"

He recalled vividly what was said and repeated it almost verbatim. "Higgins says most of the workers claimed she disrupts work. Not intentionally, of course, but she watches them so closely that they become nervous. The children are terrified when she comes near and one woman said she nearly smashed her fingers once."

"Do you know if any of these is true?"

"Higgins has no reason to lie. He gave an argument hard to dispute—that how much and how well they work are obvious in the product and the time it took to produce."

"Meaning?"

"Meaning that they do not need someone scrutinizing them so closely. Their work should be judged from the amount and quality of cotton from the mill, produced in time to fill orders."

"That does make a lot of sense. But there must be good reasons to have overseers."

"Of course. Actually, workers do not object to having an overseer who knows and has had experience with mill operations and can give them specific instructions and guidance on doing the work. They also must trust him enough that they can report problems to him."

"They mean someone who used to be one of them?"

"Not one of us "masters," surely, although my mother is technically not one."

"And she is a woman."

He scowled. "True. Women are expected to leave such matters to men. But there is something more to the point here. She does not and cannot do what overseers do. She does not know the machinery nor modern methods of cotton manufacturing."

"I see. You do think that her being there is good."

He frowned. "She sees things I may not and has made helpful suggestions based on them. And workers do work harder when she is around."

"This is a very difficult situation for you." Margaret shook her head helplessly and hesitated for an instant. "But my guess is the workers would not think so."

"What do you mean?"

"Well, the workers may think the solution is simple and obvious. You ask your mother to stop going to the mill. But if you did, you will break your mother's heart."

"What would you do in my place?"

"I don't know. I do know that the mill has been her life as much as yours. To her, it is everything, especially now." She stopped, uncertain if she should say anymore.

He looked at her expectantly. "There is something more you have to say."

Before she could answer, Mrs. Thornton came into the dining room. The two of them paused uneasily and smiled ruefully at her.

Mrs. Thornton stared back at them suspiciously. "You two are early for dinner. What have you been up to?"

Margaret got up. "I have to take Elise to her room. John, could you ask the men to carry the crib upstairs?"

"I can take it up for you."

She picked up her sleeping daughter from the crib. "It's not heavy but it is bulky and needs two people. Anyway, you should keep your mother company."

After the crib was removed, Mrs. Thornton sat on the chair vacated by Margaret and motioned for John to sit down. "You two looked so conspiratorial when I came in. Is there something you should be telling me?"

"No, mother," he answered evasively. "We were talking about going to Paris possibly next summer."

"Again? What is so special about Paris that you must go again? And so soon after?"

"It's not just Paris, mother. Margaret's brother Frederick will meet us there with his wife. Margaret misses him and wants him to see Elise."

"I see." She nodded and said no more.

They sat quietly for some time, uncertain what to say to each other. "You look rested. I am sorry about your visit today at the mill. We should have gone in a cab."

Mrs. Thornton shrugged. "Next time."

XVIII. DISSONANCE

John had been distracted throughout dinner and Margaret struggled to keep some steady chatter going so Mrs. Thornton would not notice. As soon as he closed the door to their bedroom, he resumed the conversation he and Margaret had at the conservatory. "What were you going to say before dinner when my mother walked in on us?"

"Perhaps, we should wait until tomorrow to talk about this. You need to rest."

"I cannot sleep because this problem will keep bothering me until I have some idea of what to do. What you intended to say could help."

"All right. Let us at least prepare for bed."

Not long after, John found her sitting by the fireplace in their sitting room, staring at the low flames. He sat on the chair across from her. "Well?"

"I am not certain this will help you. In fact, it might make what you have to do a bit more difficult."

"Say it anyway. You never know." She still seemed hesitant and he leaned forward, took her hand in both of his and stroked it gently. He smiled encouragingly and waited.

She threw him a glance, then stared again at the fire. "Before you married me, your mother did everything for you at home and did all that very well. It kept her focused on something that meant a lot to her. But she relinquished those responsibilities to me when we married."

"She was right to do that." He interjected. "Those belong to you as my wife."

"I know, but don't you see?" Margaret looked directly into his eyes. "Her life revolved around you, providing you a home life that did not distract from your work. She lost that focus when you acquired a wife."

He straightened and sat back against the chair, frowning. "What does that have to do with worker complaints?"

"I am not sure exactly except that the mill is now the most important thing for her. By shifting her efforts to it, she could continue to help you be the success in business she worked so hard for, much of her life."

He nodded. "After we married, she did come to the mill at least twice as often. The unfortunate consequence is her presence became more unbearable to the workers."

"That is it, you see. Asking her to stop going to the mill would mean taking away from her what matters most to her now. Is there anything else she could do, in your office, for instance?"

"No, not really. Much of it is paperwork, more than half having to do with accounting, from supply orders to wages to profits. She would not have the skills to do those. Besides, I think they will bore her."

"Well, I don't know what more to say. Can you bide your time about making a decision? Talk to Nicholas, tell him it is a complicated matter. Ask if he can explain to the workers that it will take time; your mother needs time to disengage from the mill that she helped build."

John was skeptical, uncertain if he had the courage to tell his mother that she could no longer come to the mill. He himself never thought about whether he really wanted her to stop since she had been an asset to him in the past. How could he tell her now that she could be hurting the mill by her presence in it? He was not even certain that was true. He nodded, smiled but did not answer and Margaret did not press him. They sat silently for some time, staring at the fire, its yellow flame burning itself slowly to ashes. It was later in the night than John supposed and he was tired. He glanced at his wife, her eyes downcast, sadly pensive. She had obviously given matters that concerned his mother much thought.

Margaret, in fact, needed to make sense of Mrs. Thornton's persistent dislike of her, if only to satisfy a need of her own to know why. It perplexed her how the older woman could keep up her animosity—she who was now a mother to her, if only by marriage. Margaret doubted that any change in her demeanor could influence Mrs. Thornton's sentiments. But having made her choice about her future, she thought it was now up to her to try to reconcile herself to living with all that came with that choice.

Resigning herself to something she could not change—which she could achieve by understanding the reason for Mrs. Thornton's resentment—was much easier than changing the older woman's attitude.

Still, it took long hours of struggle with her own distress and chagrin for Margaret to accept what she had suspected: That in relinquishing duties to her son's wife, Mrs. Thornton lost her raison d'être, the concerns that gave her life purpose. They were ordinary tasks, but in their entirety, they defined Mrs. Thornton's daily existence. When Margaret understood, she also saw how profoundly depressing it would be for someone, as fierce as Mrs. Thornton was about her interests, to lose her focus. She felt sad and sorry for Mrs. Thornton and resolved to overlook the irritations brought on by their daily interactions.

Margaret kept an eye on John closely but discreetly, regretting having revealed so much of her own thoughts. After her last outburst when she lamented Mrs. Thornton's indifference towards Elise, Margaret decided she would not bother John anymore about problems between herself and Mrs. Thornton. He needed to focus on the mill. Some of those problems were uniquely hers and nobody else's, the recent ones, for instance, when she had to confront the reality that she occasionally still mourned for her parents and lamented the chance that could never be of their knowing her daughter and of Elise never basking in the warmth of their caring.

At length, Margaret said: "I am sorry if what I said makes what you have to do more complicated."

He glanced at her and smiled distractedly. Margaret got up. She would leave him undisturbed to mull over this new dilemma. With a gentle brush of the back of her hand against his cheek, she walked past him to the bedroom.

Margaret went to bed feeling sad: For Mrs. Thornton, because she would surely be devastated by being cut off from the mill; and for John, because what he had to do would cause him heartbreak. She felt remorseful that her own happiness had meant someone else's sorrow. Margaret lay still, biting her lips, unable to hold back her tears. It perturbed her that John was not there, lying calmly next to her. But she was also exhausted, no less from the tension of the last few hours than from the hectic pace of her daily routine. Exhaustion took over, coaxing her tense muscles into immobility and her mind into quiescence.

It was a fitful shallow slumber she fell into, disturbed by dreams of an unseen child, sobbing inconsolably. She searched for the child but in vain and she started to cry in anguish at her futile attempts while the child continued to sob. Disturbed by the dream, she struggled to wake herself. She bolted upright, panting for breath, shivering at the darkness around her, ominous in its stillness and silence. She looked through the door to the sitting room, wondering if John was still sitting by the fireplace. The lamps there had been extinguished and the fire had died down. She reached out her hand to his side of the bed and felt him grasp it as he pulled her gently into his arms.

He kissed her face and held her close. "You are shivering. Were you having a nightmare my love?"

"Just hold me." She implored, her face against his neck.

In the morning, John awoke to find Margaret already nursing Elise. He had decided, the past night, to try Margaret's suggestion to talk to Nicholas Higgins frankly and tell him that talking to his mother was more complicated than it might appear on the surface. It would buy him the time he needed to reflect, figure out his own wishes, and arrive at the right decision. He also conjured up some excuse the night before to keep his mother at home. But Margaret prevented any need for him to use it. At breakfast, she brought up the topic of a dinner party that they had intended to give to meet their new neighbors. She asked Mrs. Thornton for her help and the two agreed to discuss it further in the drawing room later that morning.

When he gave his wife his usual parting kiss before he left for the mill, John drew her close and whispered: "Thank, you my love. You are a treasure. Wait for me in our sitting room this evening?"

During lunch break at the mill dining hall, John sought Nicholas Higgins and asked him to come to the office one hour before closing time.

Nicholas was prompt. "Good evening, master. You wanted to talk about something worrying you."

"Was it that obvious?"

Nicholas smiled and then became serious. "Is it the matter regarding Mrs. Thornton? Your mother, I mean. Everyone around here calls your wife Mrs. Margaret. It shows they like her. That is what I think, anyway."

"Yes, about my mother, Mrs. Thornton. Please take a seat." He leaned back against his chair, scowling. "It is a rather delicate matter, if you must know."

"I do know and I understand your problem more than you think. I'm sorry to force you into a hard decision but I take the men's concerns seriously and get them resolved in their favor as well as I could."

"Of course. But realize that, as master, my position with respect to those concerns may often be opposite to yours. My mother helped me start this mill and it works as well as it does partly because of her efforts. This has been her life as much as mine."

"Everyone knows that and I have explained to the men the problems it poses but the truth is it is not their concern."

"No. But it is mine and I cannot ignore it."

"I have looked into the claims closely. The children are afraid of her and most of the workers are nervous when she is around. Her presence reminds them they could lose their jobs on the spot if she thought they were not always hard at work. You know the danger in these machines. You need a steady hand with them."

John nodded thoughtfully. "How about you? Does my mother intimidate you?"

Nicholas smiled and shrugged. "I admit that she does, in general. Your mother has a presence that cannot be ignored but she doesn't affect my work. But I admit that I prefer she does not come."

"Yes?"

"Let me put it this way. Some workers are clever enough to see that she is not a master or an overseer and has no business being around, telling them what to do, even if she knew what she was doing."

John nodded and Nicholas pushed his argument further. "What we're asking will not cost you money. No new machinery. No higher wages. But your decision in our favor means goodwill and will earn you the workers' trust. They're more likely to stay in the mill longer, work harder. You understand very well the consequence of working even a few minutes beyond time to finish a job."

John regarded Nicholas for a long moment. A scowl slowly etching his brow, he turned to stare thoughtfully out the window. Nicholas sat, quietly waiting. After a few minutes, John said: "You have argued your position well but I do need time to decide. Could you tell the workers that? They will probably see my mother back but until I make an announcement, nothing is settled."

"I'll tell them to be patient. I know that you know that if you did nothing at all, we can't and won't retaliate. All we can hope for is a favorable decision."

"I am indeed aware of that and I want to do what is right but I need time to think things through. For now, I do need to go because my wife is waiting for me." John rose from his chair.

The expression on Nicholas face changed from serious to smiling. "How is Mrs. Margaret? I don't see Mary much anymore, now that she helps care for your daughter. She used to tell me about the goings-on in your house."

John smiled brightly. "Why don't you come by sometime? Elise is growing up fast."

The two of them walked out of the office talking animatedly, settling back into their friendship, leaving their master and worker personas in the office.

John, carrying a bouquet of roses, found Margaret alone on the sofa, reading a book, when he entered their sitting room. Margaret smiled broadly, closing her book. "Roses! What is the special occasion?"

He handed her the bouquet with a lingering kiss. "I do not need a special occasion to show my wife how deeply and passionately I love her."

He smiled engagingly and sat down next to her. "The little one must be in bed for the night."

"Yes. She began to crawl today and tired herself out showing off to everyone in the house."

"Another little accomplishment that I missed."

"Let me just put these flowers in a vase and I will be back in a minute. I want these roses to last as long as possible." She rose to get a vase and some water.

She set the vase on the table in front of them and sat next to him. "We have been spending most afternoons in the conservatory and we were there again today."

"That must be a pleasant place now that fall is almost here."

"Quite. We often lay a rug on the floor and sit Elise on a cushion on the rug where she is often content to play with her toys. Today as I was doing a sketch of her and Mary sitting on a chair behind her, Elise started to crawl. It seems she wanted to come towards me at the other end of the room. She fell a few times but kept trying until she reached me. When she did, I picked her up, hugged her, and showered her with kisses. She squealed so loudly with delight that it brought the servants into the conservatory. She started clapping her hands at seeing so many of us all around her at once. After a while, she squirmed to be put down. She spent most of her afternoon crawling between Mary and me, expecting to be picked up and hugged at each end. The servants watched and clapped every time she reached one end until Dixon came to remind them of the work they had to finish."

"I am sorry to have missed all the fun."

"You'll undoubtedly see her try it this weekend. Also, I did a few sketches of her attempt. I could show them to you some time, if you want."

John grinned. "Yes, this weekend would be good. I do have that to look forward to." A little more seriously, he placed a hand on her chin and lifted her face towards his. "Since that day you came home with me, you have never been far from my thoughts, when I am at the mill. Well, to be truthful, you have occupied a permanent place in my thoughts and my heart since I fell in love with you. Now, you have given me Elise, too, and I have you both to keep me company at work."

She blushed as she smiled with pleasure. "But I could not have had her without you!" Margaret leaned her head on his shoulders and wound her arms around his chest. He clasped her closer.

"Why, yes! How could I have forgotten that?" He laughed, in self-mockery, and added, playfully: "What if I told you that, in fact, I remember the exact day and time?"

She raised her head, amused, doubting, and then, uncertain. "You jest!"

He laughed louder, gave her a peck on the nose and said nothing. She examined the expression on his face but he merely stared back at her, his eyes glowing with subdued laughter. He remained silent. Finally convinced that he could not be budged, she laid her face against his neck and said no more.

Later, she asked, her voice muffled against his neck: "How did your day go?"

"I talked to Nicholas this afternoon."

"About Hannah?"

"Yes. I told him I needed time to make a decision and he said he will explain to the workers that they may yet see my mother for some time."

"Are you inclined to decide in their favor?"

"Nicholas argued their position rather convincingly. I really do not know. I was hoping that talking with you would help."

"Frankly, I do not believe I can give you advice. I can tell you what I think and, perhaps, another viewpoint might help make things clearer."

"You did advise me to talk to Nicholas. It may not have brought me closer to a decision but it helped."

"Can you talk to your mother as well?"

"But what will I say to her? He paused thoughtfully, then continued, regretfully. "My mother and I have grown apart. I used to talk with her the way I do with you now. But since I met you, I began to see many things differently and by the time you left for London, I was talking to her less and keeping my thoughts to myself. When you came back, it became clearer to me that my mother and I had lost much of the ease we used to have with each other."

Margaret was at a loss about what to say, her eyes cast down. His confession brought back the sadness, helplessness, and culpability she felt about Mrs. Thornton.

John continued solemnly: "The mill seems to be all we talk about now but even in that, we have avoided anything that has to do with new things I have done that she thinks are useless."

Margaret looked up. "You mean those that do not seem directly related to working conditions like the dining hall and the regular meetings with worker representatives?"

"Yes. So how can I tell her now that I am inclined to side with them against her?"

Margaret smiled sympathetically and then, in a hopeful voice, suggested: "What if you argued that doing so is necessary for the efficient running of the mill? I recollect my father telling me that your mother told him the mill is everything and, to him, it meant that she was ready to endure anything for its sake."

"She would appreciate that reasoning." He hesitated. "But if it comes across that her presence at the mill is bad for its efficient operation—no, I cannot hurt her that way."

"Yes, I see. You are right." They sat, silent and thoughtful, until it was time to go down to dinner.

Back in their bedroom after dinner, Margaret sat in front of her dresser, brushing her hair and mulling over the matter that had lately dominated their conversations. When John came in from his bath, she addressed his reflection on the mirror. "Perhaps, it is best to be honest. My father used to say it was the only way to deal with truth regardless of how painful it is."

"I thought so, too, at dinner, seeing my strong-willed mother sitting there. It is worth considering that approach, but not tonight." He stood behind her chair as she brushed her hair. At the end of the day, especially when he was tired, he found it relaxing to watch his wife go through these little rituals before going to bed.

"I am afraid I am too tired to make hard decisions. Besides, the bed beckons with its warm covers." He took the brush from her hand and laid it on the dresser. "Join me?"

She smiled up at him as he pulled her up. "Ah yes, the perfect cure for tiredness. Luxuriating in a soft bed."

"Much better if your wife helps warm it up with you."

XIX. CONFRONTATION

John's misgivings about being honest with his mother haunted him again in the morning and occupied his thoughts as he walked to the mill. This situation was new for him, having never had any problems in the past being honest with his mother, particularly on matters pertaining to the mill. He had never taken a position which opposed hers so blatantly nor—worse than that—made decisions that caused her incalculable pain. They had always seemed to be of one mind on important matters about the mill. And yet, what other choice did he have if he believed the workers' request to be legitimate and reasonable and that, in the long run, granting it was best for the mill?

Of Nicholas's arguments, what concerned him most was the safety of children workers. He had always tried to protect the children in his mill but now that he had his own child, he grew uncompromising in his unwillingness to take risks with their safety. It saddened him to see anyone below 14 working in a factory but if he could not change the law nor the realities of poverty that force children to work, he could at least take steps to make working conditions as good and as safe as possible for these children. If his mother's presence compromised their safety from their fear of her—regardless of whether that fear was irrational or not—he would ask his mother to stop going to the mill.

By the time he reached his office, he knew his only choice was honesty about what he believed must be done. He resolved to come home earlier that evening to talk to his mother before dinner. As heartbreaking as the task was before him, postponing it would only put off the inevitable.

His mother was alone in the drawing room with her embroidery when John came home. It gratified him to see her resume some of her old habits. Before his marriage, it comforted him to come home from work and find her relaxed, contented, working on her needlework in the drawing room. He had taken this peaceful domestic scenario for granted. He had not hurried home for it as he now did at the end of the day, impatient to be with Margaret whom he sought with the tender anticipation of gazing into her limpid eyes and submitting himself to all the little loving ministrations that she thought he needed. The sight of his mother engaged in a pleasant, satisfying task, doing whatever she wanted to meant he had repaid her, given her what she desired and certainly deserved.

John bent over to kiss her cheek. "How are you today, mother?" He was about to render her a terrible, unexpected, undeserved blow and he felt sorry, guilty that it had to be done. He clenched his jaw until it hurt and moved with heavy steps towards the chair opposite hers.

"You're home early." Mrs. Thornton smiled in the quiet way she did when she was pleased. Anticipating the question he always asked since Margaret came, she added, pursing her lips. "Margaret is out in the garden with your daughter and two or three other idle servants."

"It's a nice day to be out. When winter comes, it will be too cold for Elise." He sat down. Mrs. Thornton regarded him curiously, wondering why he did not hurry out to seek out his wife as he had always done after greeting her with a perfunctory buzz on the cheek. She was finally used to him seeking out Margaret right away when he came home instead of taking some time to talk to her.

He sat wordlessly for a while, looking through the conservatory and out into the garden as if he wanted to escape to it. He stood up, poured himself a drink and sat down again. Mrs. Thornton, puzzled, could not restrain her curiosity. "Is anything wrong? Did you have a fight with your wife?"

He shook his head. "No. No. Actually, I wanted to talk to you about the mill but I don't know quite how to."

"Just say what's on your mind."

"I wish it was that simple."

"Is there trouble at the mill?" She prompted. "Another strike? Orders you can't handle?"

"No, none of that. We're doing quite well." He hesitated, anxiety written on his face. "But there are some concerns that workers have."

"I am not surprised. All these things you have been doing for their benefit—they're taking advantage of your goodwill. Are they asking for more? That would not surprise me."

"They are asking for something but not higher wages or anything else that will cost money."

"Whatever it is, you should not give them anymore. You have done more than any other master in Milton. You do not know if what you have done will stop strikes or increase your production."

"No, we do not yet know about strikes. It will take time to see such results but I do know that workers at Marlborough Mills are more likely to stay working for me, to work harder to fulfill orders or even stay after work hours to finish a job."

"They have always preferred working for you because you have more modern machines. What could they possibly want now that worries you?"

John glanced at his mother, quickly averted his eyes but forced himself to direct them back to her face. Then, in a quivering voice he tried, without much success, to steady, he plunged into what must be said. "They have requested that I ask you to stop going to the mill." It seemed to him that the words tumbling out of his mouth were like darts he was flinging at his mother.

Mrs. Thornton was dumbfounded, mystified by the request, unable to comprehend how her presence could matter to the workers, unless they slacked off on their work. "Take care, John. They have their ways of bringing you down if you let them and this may be one of them. They do not want anyone watching to see if they are doing their work."

"That is not it exactly because they suggested more supervisors for that if I saw the need. Besides the level of production is at its peak considering how many hours they have worked so efficiency is high."

"They have no right to ask me to stop coming," she protested vehemently but she fixed her eyes anxiously on her son and felt somewhat shaken by what she saw in his demeanor. He avoided her eyes and it was obvious to her that he did not share the outrage she felt at what the workers asked of him.

"Mother," he began hesitantly as he reached out to press her hand. "This is an extremely difficult decision for me. I know only too well that I would not be where I am without you. This mill has been your life as well as mine and, to some extent, you grasp its worth more than I have."

She snorted and retorted: "You used to but Margaret has brought you farther away from it with her fancy southern notions about workers and their rights. What does she really know about them? Then, there are those distractions with classics and Parisian trips."

John clenched his jaw to suppress an instantaneous irritation at her remark. It did not surprise him but it did vex him and he replied only when he felt in better control. "This has nothing to do with Margaret."

"Well, you changed after you met her," she answered bitterly.

He decided it best to ignore this remark and he continued as if she had not said it. "Mother, please. It pains me to tell you this because the mill means so much to you."

"You told them, of course, that you won't do it?" She asked, searching his face but when he could not answer right away, she repeated: "They have no right!"

"Actually, mother, they do because, by law, you are not the mill owner. And you are not an overseer who can tell workers what to do." He answered regretfully, sadly.

"You—are you asking me to stop going to the mill?" She asked more weakly, helplessly, admitting her inevitable defeat. "I always do as you ask."

Distressed as John was to see his mother so mournful and disconsolate, he had already gone too far and had no other choice, at this point, but to speak as plainly as he could. "I have mulled agonizingly, painfully, over this and I am exceedingly sorry that, in the end, I saw no other way but to ask you to stop coming to the mill. There is a good chance that, in deciding in their favor, the workers will trust me always to be fair on questions having to do with mill operations and it is reasonable to expect them, in return, to be more loyal to the mill. Who knows whether, perhaps, they will think twice about strikes?" He could not tell her then his concerns about the young children and their fear of her. It seemed to him too cruel, unnecessary.

Mrs. Thornton listened to these words without much comprehension. It was not that she failed to literally grasp what he was saying. Rather, it was that these ideas were alien to her. Why should a master care to be perceived as fair? She thought workers were too ignorant to understand what fairness meant and had too much self-interest to be loyal. They were interested only in getting all they could from those who had succeeded, those of superior mind and work ethic.

Mrs. Thornton despaired that she no longer knew how to reach her son and talk to him in ways that proved them to be of like mind. She had never felt him as removed from her as he was then. It was, in fact, this conviction that depressed her even more than her anger at being deprived of a role in the day-to-day operation of the mill. She had assured him that she would do as he asked but she could not resist one last question, the answer to which would render finality to her belief that he was no longer within reach of her influence. She tried to sound unconcerned. "So, you believe it is in the mill's best interests that I keep away from it?"

To John, her question was laden with despair despite her attempts to mask it. It filled him with remorse and he could only nod, biting his lip as words failed him. This was the most difficult undertaking he had ever done and, in that instant, he wretchedly regretted having acceded to the request. And yet, in his heart, he felt he did the right thing.

Mrs. Thornton rose wearily and announced in a voice as steady as she could muster: "I am tired and would like to rest. If I am not down at the usual time for dinner, do not wait for me."

John watched his mother walk away, head held high.

John sat in the drawing room for some time, sorrowful and helpless, convinced that he had betrayed his mother. He sat, heavy, immovable, a lump insensible to his surroundings, to the activity going on far away from where he sat, and to the growing darkness into which he wished his darker figure would disappear. Eventually, he was roused from the black void he had sunk into by the lively sound of Margaret's voice. She had just come in from the garden, invigorated by the pleasant exertion of playing with her daughter, attended indulgently by Dixon and Mary. Margaret was talking to Elise, who seemed to be answering back in her own language.

John saw his wife and his daughter pass by the drawing room. He wanted to call her name as she walked by but no sound came out of his mouth. When they were no longer in view, Margaret's footsteps suddenly stopped. She had caught, by the side of her eyes, the fleeting image of a dark figure in the unlighted drawing room. She retraced her steps and seeing him sitting there, desolate and wretched, she knew what had happened. She continued talking to Elise as she approached him. "Look Elise, Papa's home."

Elise, mimicking her mother, smiled at her father and extended one hand out to him. John got up with a sigh and absentmindedly greeted them both with kisses, his daughter, on her belly, which made her squeal at being tickled, and his wife, on her lips.

Margaret peered at him with concern. "You talked to Hannah."

He nodded and put an arm around her to lead her out of the drawing room. They walked up the stairs in silence. Sensing his distraction, Margaret placed an arm around his waist and headed for their bedroom. She deposited Elise on the middle of the bed, and gave her the hand mirror from the dresser to play with. She sat on John's side of the bed, tagged at his arm, and motioned for him to sit down next to her.

"Do you want to tell me about it?

"What is there to tell? She is extremely unhappy and disappointed and I let her down."

"I am so sorry." She answered sympathetically: "You said yourself she has been through worse. So in time, she will come around, I am sure. She loves you and that fact will prevail."

"Yes, but many things have happened and we have both changed." He was miserable. "She would never forgive me for this."

Margaret, soaking in his sorrow, could not speak. He sat mournfully for some time and then said regretfully: "The fact is, much of what has been good for me this past year has been devastating to my mother. First you, and now, the matter about the workers and the mill. It is unfortunate but there it is."

Reminded of her part in depriving Mrs. Thornton of what was most precious to her and already sad for John, Margaret was struck with guilt once more. She bowed her head to hide eyes brimming with sadness and cheeks flushed from the strain of holding her tears back.

John raised her face and said in a clear but soft voice. "Still, as much as I have disappointed my mother, I want you to know that I would not change a thing and would always be most grateful that I have you."

Margaret was bewildered. Such words calmed her own turmoil and gave her a warm glow all over. She could listen to them endlessly but why had he thought it necessary to say them when he was the one in need of soothing words? He had spoken to her lovingly but his eyes were dark with pain and the muscles on his face were taut with the burden of his mother's misery. She regarded him earnestly and a pang of guilt hit her again, but this time, it freed her from her own anxieties so that she could set them aside to help him calm his.

But Margaret felt helpless, at a loss for words in the face of his agony. She had learned from experience that words did not always help someone freshly and totally absorbed by sorrow and remorse. But he might find solace, she thought, in the presence of someone who empathized and understood what he was going through. Margaret placed her arms around his neck and pulled his head gently down on her shoulders. She stroked the back of his head and down the nape of his neck. After some time, she whispered into his ear and he lay down on the bed, his head on her lap. She ran her fingers soothingly through his hair and, with the lightest caress, on his face, tracing its outlines. Soon, his already drooping lids closed slowly.

That night, Margaret asked Mary to put Elise to bed after Margaret had nursed her. When she and John were finally alone, she rang for a light supper to be brought to their bedroom. Mrs. Thornton had made a similar request and the household wondered and speculated about what might have happened.

John and Margaret did not see Mrs. Thornton for a few days. She stayed in her room and only Jane, who brought her meals and attended to her requests, was allowed to come to her. John tried on the third day to see her but Mrs. Thornton did not answer and later sent a message through Jane that she was not to be disturbed. She would come out when she was ready.

More than a week later, Mrs. Thornton finally descended from her room after John had left for the mill and Margaret was in the drawing room talking to Dixon. Margaret and Dixon heard the characteristic rustle of Mrs. Thornton's crinoline as she entered, her face resolute and unsmiling, her eyes blazing in the way Margaret had seen John's eyes do in profound anger.

"Leave us Dixon. I want to talk to Margaret. Close the door behind you."

Dixon glanced, first, at Mrs. Thornton, then with concern, at Margaret. She hesitated, rooted in place, until Margaret, with a slight nod, gave her leave to go.

Margaret turned towards Mrs. Thornton. "I am glad you are feeling better. Have you had breakfast?"

Mrs. Thornton ignored her question. "We need to talk."

"What about? Perhaps, we should sit." Margaret, determined to be as agreeable as she could, smiled and ignored the hostility obvious in the older woman's tone.

"I prefer to stand." Mrs. Thornton's voice was both tense and icy.

Margaret remained standing, braced herself for a contentious encounter, and resolved to remain calm, reasonable, and patient. But she was totally unprepared for what came next.

Mrs. Thornton, eyes narrowed and gritting her teeth, unleashed the resentments she had been nurturing a long time. "I never liked you with your airs and southern graces. I find them pretentious and annoying. I never understood what my son saw in you."

Margaret was too stunned to answer.

"You have changed him and he has lost his focus. I do not recognize him much anymore. A Milton girl would have known better than to interfere as you have. You......"

Margaret regained her composure and interrupted in a strong, cold voice. "Mrs. Thornton, please take heed of what you say. John is still the John you knew, doing what he believes in the best way he can. If you want to credit me for something, I would own up to nurturing his compassion but he has always had that. It is what has made him fair to his workers and conscientious about keeping the mill productive. His workers depend on it, you depend on it."

"And you do not?"

"On the mill? No, not in the way you do. It is important to me because it is a significant part of John's life. It is what you taught him and what fate threw in his path. If he was doing something else, he would still mean the whole world to me."

"Fancy words. You did not even know what he was when you rejected him. Now, you speak as if you know him better than me. You have seduced him with words like those but you cannot do that to me. The truth is he would not have turned against me but for you."

"He has not turned against you. He did only what he thought was in the best interests of the mill. It agonized him deeply that he made you very unhappy in doing so but he believed you were strong, resilient and would overcome this as you have other adversities before it. You told me yourself that you have faced setbacks, defeat, even tragedy—and he watched you ride them all."

"I have always done what was best for him at the expense of my comfort, my needs, my wishes. He would never do anything intentionally to hurt me."

"No, he would never hurt you on purpose. But you also taught him the mill is everything and he made a decision, as painful as it was, that he believed was best for it. He knows you're strong enough to take it."

"He knows! Of course, he knows! But you, what do you know? You are merely an ignorant upstart from the south with pretensions of book knowledge and aristocratic ideas and now, you think you know him better than I do."

Mrs. Thornton was desperate. Margaret countered her attacks with an equanimity and forcefulness she had not expected. All those solitary days in her room, she nursed the pain of what, to her, was the ultimate proof of her son's rejection when he sided with the workers demand for her to stop going to the mill. It was the negation of what she had given of herself, the nullifying, it seemed, of what her life meant. She saw all those in her last conversation with her son and it devastated her. The pain percolated in her breast until she feared it would burst out and destroy her unless she did something about it.

She had felt betrayed by her son but she threw the blame for that betrayal on someone else. That person was in front of her now. At first, Mrs. Thornton merely felt that Margaret, unwelcome and a foreigner could not be trusted. But what she feared most happened: Margaret not only claimed John for herself; she changed him materially. Now, the mill was lost to her, as well. Margaret had taken away the last thing that was precious to her.

Disconcerted by Margaret's composure, Mrs. Thornton had no choice but to savagely perform an exorcism. "Get out of our lives! You do not belong here. Get out of our lives! I want my son back." Her voice cracked and by the time she had flung her final insult at Margaret, her anger had drained her energy.

"Mrs. Thornton, please, do not say anything more you might regret. Like it or not, I am your son's wife and I have every intention of remaining so." Margaret's eyes were on fire and her tone grew from emphatic to challenging.

Mrs. Thornton advanced towards her and retorted scornfully but her voice was now subdued, quivering, spent. "You are only his wife. I am his mother. Blood is thicker than water."

Margaret lifted her chin high and declared, with blazing undaunted eyes: "We should end this conversation right now. You made your sentiments towards me very clear and I can say no more that will make my intentions equally clear." She turned around and sailed out of the room, her jaw clenched and her eyes welling up with tears.

When certain that she was no longer within sight of Mrs. Thornton, she ran up the stairs to her bedroom, locked the door and sat by the window. She dropped her face on her hands, trembling from a chaos of emotions. Her shoulders heaved and shook but except for a few gasps of air, no other sounds came out of her struggle. She was enraged, that much she could tell. It was always her first response to the perception of being attacked. But stronger feelings that she could not grasp had also taken hold of her, a mix of sadness, desolation, perplexity, even fear—of what, she could not identify. Mrs. Thornton declared she was not a Milton girl and she knew she was not a London girl and certainly no longer was she Margaret Hale of Helstone. What was she and did it matter where she belonged?

It was a long time before she felt calmer and her body stopped shaking. She walked into the sitting room towards the window, and stared blankly out at the garden for some time—her body motionless but far from tranquil and her mind still in turmoil. She wondered if she should say anything at all about it to John. He knew, as she did, that his mother did not like her so she reasoned that that fact did not bear repeating. And although the violence of Mrs. Thornton's declarations and accusations troubled her deeply, Margaret tried to imagine what Mrs. Thornton had gone through the last few days when the remaining focus of her life was taken away from her.

Margaret wanted to excuse the older woman's behavior but her heart rebelled. It cried out as one would at the injustice of being found guilty without a trial. She clenched her jaw to control her mounting anger. At that moment, Mary, with Elise in her arms, walked out into the garden, humming a nursery song. Mary sat on a bench and, cradling Elise on her lap, took the child's hands and guided them to clap and sway as she sang to her. Margaret watched them for some time, walked back towards the bedroom and checked herself on the mirror. She headed for the garden, resolved to make the day go as it always had and say nothing to John about what passed.

Mrs. Thornton came down for dinner that evening. She had taken extra care about her appearance, adorning her hair with a pearl comb and her front bodice with lace she wore only on friendly social visits. She walked into the room, her head held high and her manner more formal than usual. She greeted them with a faint thrust of her chin and sat down at her usual place.

"Good evening mother. You look very well this evening." John rose to assist her but she had sat down before he could reach her. He was relieved to have her finally rejoin them at dinner.

"Good evening, Mrs. Thornton," Margaret said simply, suppressing an impulse to flee.

Conversation at dinner was hushed and strained. Margaret hardly said anything except to nod and occasionally make a very brief response to John who was keenly aware that the conversation had practically turned into his performing a monologue. He persisted, however, rambling about the weather, the delicious dishes, Elise's antics and everything else that did not pertain to the mill.

For a while, a modicum of the old routines and habits returned to the household although, when John was at the mill, Mrs. Thornton kept to her room more than before. She went to breakfast earlier and always seemed to just be finishing as John entered the room. She was ready to leave by the time he started breakfast. They had barely enough time to interact beyond the usual morning greetings. Still, she made it a point to remain until she saw him. Margaret, who attended to Elise every morning only saw her at dinner, an arrangement that suited both women.

John assumed his mother was still hurt and angry with him but that, when she was ready, she would resume her old habits. Breakfast had been their time alone together since Margaret came as Mrs. Thornton was finishing her last cup of tea. John intended to wait patiently for his mother to start talking to him as she used to. But weeks passed and John could wait no longer.

"Mother, please stay and talk to me while I am having breakfast, like you used to do You seem to be always leaving when I'm coming."

"But I have finished and have things to attend to every morning."

"I am sure those things can wait a few minutes. Mother, I beg you."

"What do you want from me?" She asked with some vehemence.

"Nothing in particular, merely to talk to you. It was always a nice start to my day."

"Well, things cannot be as they had been. You have a wife now. Talk to her. I am at last free to spend my day as I choose to and I like it that way. I prefer to go back to my room right now." She stood up and hurried out of the room. John was dumbfounded and could only watch her receding back unhappily.

When Margaret came in for breakfast, he related to her what transpired, adding: "The situation is becoming unbearable. I can understand her anger at me but how long can she ignore us and act as if we did not exist."

"A long time. She has treated me as if I was just a visitor here and it did not change after we married. I am learning to ignore it. But, she is not my mother. I am sure it must be much more upsetting for you."

"Have I failed her?"

"She probably blames you much less than you think. She loves you. That will finally prevail, I am sure of it." Margaret looked away. It was more of a struggle than she had thought to forget, much less excuse or justify Mrs. Thornton's angry, bitter reproach at their last acrimonious encounter. She longed to unburden herself to someone. It was often John she shared her deepest thoughts with, but this time she knew she needed someone else to talk to. But who? Not Edith who disliked conflict. Anyway, she was too far away. This was confidence better shared face-to-face. Not Aunt Shaw, for the same reasons as Edith. She had to admit, finally, that she had no one to turn to.

"Margaret, my love, is anything the matter?" John's anxious voice jolted her out of her thoughts. Only then did she realize how long a silence she had lapsed into.

She looked at him thoughtfully and came very close to yielding to the temptation of telling him about his mother's bitter accusations. She blurted out, instead: "Perhaps, I should go for a visit to London. That may give you a better chance to mend your relationship with your mother."

As soon as she said this, Margaret regretted it. She did not know what came over her except that she had the urge to run away from wherever Mrs. Thornton was.

He shook his head vigorously. This was one of those rare instances when he did not hesitate asserting his authority as her husband. "I doubt that it will help. I need you here so I prefer that you stay."

"I am sorry. I do not know why I even suggested it."

They finished breakfast in silence. Margaret stared at the milky dark brew in her cup and sipped it slowly. It reminded her of teatime in Helstone. As a child, she used to sit silently with a cup of very milky tea, next to her mother as she entertained visitors or friends. She liked those social visits. The ladies remarked how proud her mother was to have a daughter who behaved so much like a little lady. How she longed to be back in Helstone! Back in that parish house parlor where she could look up from reading a book or drawing and see the large bush profuse with yellow roses in late May through June; back where she never had to wonder whether her parents and her brother cared for her. It was something she took for granted.

John watched her as he drank his tea. She had lapsed back into a pensive mood, oblivious of him. He drained his cup and squeezed her hand gently. "I have to go." He stood and waited for her to walk him to the door.

She arose wearily, avoiding his eyes, almost annoyed that he had broken her sweet reverie, and brought her back to the gloomy present. He put his arm around her and lifted her face. She looked up momentarily, then laid her head on his shoulder to hide her anxiety. He clasped her closer. "I love you. You are the best thing that ever happened to me. I don't know what I would do without you."

Margaret suppressed a sob and John held her for some time before leaving for the mill that morning.

John was deep in thought, a vague unease slowing his pace. Something had happened that Margaret was reluctant to tell him, something that made her to think of going to London so he and his mother could concentrate on making peace. He was, himself, too wrapped up in remorse, too worried at his mother's continuing unhappiness, too unsettled by his own concerns that he was unprepared to ask what might be troubling her. He needed her and could not imagine not having her to come home to at night, particularly when he could forget about his agonizing guilt only when he held her in his arms. "I know her," he thought. "She would tell me when she is ready."

He walked more briskly, conscious of arriving at the mill an hour later than usual with so much waiting to be done and orders coming due soon. A purposeful alertness supplanted his unease and he hurried into the mill.

Margaret ascended slowly to her bedroom. She felt tired. It was uncharacteristic of her to want to lie down in the morning but she needed rest just then. Mary could take care and amuse Elise for a while. Dixon was in the bedroom, putting it in order. "You are rather late this morning. You have usually finished doing all this by the time I return from breakfast."

"I wanted to see how you are. You have not been your usual self since that day in the drawing room with Mrs. Thornton."

"No," Margaret answered, her voice soft and forlorn.

Dixon, clearly worried, studied her face. "How about if I brush your hair? You envied your mother as a little girl when I did that for her. You are now the mistress."

Margaret did not answer, only nodded and sat in front of her dresser. Dixon carefully released Margaret's hair from clips and pins and brushed it slowly, soothingly. She went about her task in silence but she watched Margaret's face closely, anxiously, waiting for the cloud in her eyes to lighten and the tension in her cheeks and her mouth to slacken. For nearly an hour, Dixon brushed her hair, gently massaged her scalp and, finally rearranged it back into a chignon. Margaret smiled, calmly, gratefully at Dixon's kind and familiar reflection on the mirror. She got up, put her arms around Dixon and kissed her cheek.

XX. RESPITE

In the evening, John came home just as Margaret finished nursing Elise who had fallen asleep at her breast. He waited for her to button her blouse. "I would like to tuck Elise in bed tonight."

Margaret looked at him, unsure if she heard him right but he held his arms out, waiting for her to hand Elise to him. "Of course. What a marvelous thing to do!"

John held Elise upright in his arms, her warm little body draped peacefully on his chest and her head slack and drooling on his shoulder. He found it surprisingly comforting and gratifying to hold her, so small and fragile in his arms and so completely trusting. Margaret gazed with amazement at her husband cradling his child tenderly in his arms. Who would have imagined such a picture? She followed them into Elise's room and helped John lay Elise in her crib. It was the first time he had ever done this and he felt awkward and hesitant. He rocked her in her crib a few minutes and then stood with Margaret a while longer, watching her sleep.

Later, back in their sitting room, she asked: "Shall I still ring for some tea? It's almost dinner time."

"Do."

Margaret was surprised. She had expected him to decline tea less than a quarter hour before dinner. Shrugging, she rang Dixon who was always ready with the tea-laden tray, sat down on the sofa, and picked up a book of poetry lying on the coffee table. John rejoined her shortly, dressed down to his shirt, opened at the collar and with neither cravat nor vest. Momentarily surprised, she regarded him with both curiosity and amusement. "Are you coming to dinner very casually tonight?"

He smiled but did not answer as he sat next to her. Dixon arrived with the tea tray a few seconds later. She threw him a perplexed glance. "Good evening, master."

"Good evening, Dixon. Please ask Jane to tell my mother we won't be coming down for dinner tonight. I am exhausted and I need my wife here to take care of me. But do serve us dinner here. Bring everything at once. We won't need anyone to assist us through dinner."

Dixon turned to Margaret who seemed pleasantly diverted. She nodded to affirm his instructions. Dixon retreated towards the door, puzzled and scowling.

Margaret arched an inquiring eyebrow at him. John smiled mischievously, tugged at his shirt and said: "Cadiz." He pointed at the table by the window. "Dinner in our Paris hotel room." He gathered her in his arms and in between kisses, murmured: "I intend to make up for all these difficult weeks with my mother when I have taken you for granted—your patience and understanding, your caring."

Dinner that night was the most relaxed and intimate they had ever had since their honeymoon, sprinkled with playfulness, kisses, and animated conversation that drifted from the changing weather, their growing daughter, their new neighbors to the merits of leisurely pursuits. But they studiously avoided any subject related to the mill and the workers request regarding Mrs. Thornton.

Early in their meal, Margaret noticed John glancing warily at a deep green dish, unfamiliar to him, that he had absentmindedly served himself. She spooned a little of the same dish on her plate and offered it to him. "It's good, really, just spinach, egg and cream made into a custard."

He hesitated for a moment, then accepted the bite she offered. "Why, yes. Quite good actually."

"And healthy for you, as Dixon used to say. It's a dish from my childhood when Dixon asked cook to make it so we would eat our vegetables. It was a hit and became a staple at our house. Later, the same dish was prepared with other vegetables instead of spinach." She explained as she fed him more bites from her plate.

"What about you? Are you feeding me so you wouldn't have to eat your spinach?"

"You can feed me what's on your plate." She answered with a sassy smile, opening her mouth for a bite.

The rest of the meal proceeded as casually. During dessert, he undid the buttons on his sleeves and rolled up the cuffs. "The wine warms you up. We don't have to be in Cadiz, do we, to live with careless ease?"

"No, nor do we have to spend the whole day lazing around."

"We should do this more often. I rather like it and I'm heartily sorry again for all I said about life in the south."

"Small doses of it are all you need."

"Yes, but on a frequent enough basis." He asserted grinning broadly.

She laughed, leaned over and gave him a peck on the nose. "What do you think of driving to the countryside on some weekend and dining alfresco? In late spring or summer, of course."

"A picnic! That would be a first for me. We could take a carriage somewhere far from Milton for the day. It sounds like real indulgence."

"Are you uncomfortable spending your day in that manner?"

He stared at her thoughtfully. "I used to be. But some of my happiest moments have been with you and me doing what would typically be called leisurely pursuits."

"Did you never go to a fair or vacation in the country or by the sea?"

"When my father was alive. But that was so long ago. After he died, I could only remember work and sacrifice." He frowned. "That sounds pretty grim to me now. I never questioned it because of what we set ourselves out to do. The challenge was energizing and I was young and eager."

"A single-minded quest for a goal. You should not feel sorry for it. It is quite admirable, actually. Everyone should be engaged in some useful occupation. But I also believe that one needs time away to refresh body and mind in order to continue doing one's work well."

"Everyone? I thought only men have occupations," he asked, facetiously.

"Yes, everyone and yes, I am thinking particularly of women." She hesitated, then settled for saying what she thought was obvious. "Women do have paid occupations when poverty forces them to work, as you very well know—if not in mills or factories, mostly in servile positions. Most of the rest of us run your households to enable you, men, to do your work as best you can. Is that not also an occupation? Imagine what it takes to run a household—managing, budgeting, organizing, instructing. Are those not the same tasks you do to run the mill?"

"Well, there is some special knowledge required to run a mill and, some specific skills, of course."

"Managing a house requires a certain type of knowledge, too, and certain skills. It is work, though unpaid and always taken for granted. Is raising a child to be productive less valuable than producing yards of cotton just because the mother is not paid for her effort?"

He smiled. "When you put it that way, it makes me wonder why I value what I do so much."

"I do not mean to imply that what you do, what men do is less worthwhile. Besides, in privileged upper classes women are, indeed, frequently idle because some hired assistants do all the work of running a household and even raising children. As for women of noble birth, all they need to do is keep the family line going and uphold the family tradition and standing."

"That is harsh judgment of that segment of women."

"Maybe, but perhaps society is also to blame for how girls are often raised. Still, many women rise above that helpless attitude they learn to assume and, when there is adversity, you see them facing it bravely and squarely and succeeding—your mother, for instance."

"You speak as if you admire my mother."

"Yes, on account of her strong will and tenacity and her devotion to you that made you who you are now, I do admire her very much."

He smiled gently and capitulated. "I think it would be ungracious of me to argue against you on this point since I have been the fortunate beneficiary of two extraordinary women's affection and goodwill."

She arched her eyebrows at him, smiling coyly. "You are generous with your gratitude, probably more than most. I'm sure there are men—probably rare—who do what they do quite well without a woman's support. And there are women who make demands that undermine a man's work."

"I said only what is true for me. I realize how fortunate I have been having such a mother and now, an even more remarkable wife—luckier than most men, certainly—and my gratitude is commensurate to what I have been given."

She gave him her half-smile, paused for an instant or two, picked up a tart with her hand, took a bite and ate it slowly. Then, staring thoughtfully at the tart between her fingers, she declared: "Someday, I hope women can go to university and work in professions of their own choosing, even those done traditionally by men and, perhaps, we can then get what we need or want for ourselves without depending on a man. I hope that chance comes soon enough for Elise. I read about a woman who became a doctor."

John regarded her for a very long moment. Where was she getting those ideas? What had she been reading lately? This was the boldest of all the comments she had made about women and it provoked in him both some trepidation and admiration.

He turned his attention back to the tart he had starred eating with a fork but he put the fork down and, pointing at the tart in her hand, asked: "Was that something you did as well when you were a child?"

"You mean, eat tarts with my hand? Fred started it when we were children to see what he could get away with. Mama, usually conscious of decorum, was easy on him. But we were not allowed to do this at dinner." With mischievous glee, she added: "Now, I can."

He laughed, then picked up his tart. "It's tastier this way."

Later in bed, as John drifted off to sleep, Margaret lay awake gazing at him, stroking his hair. His last waking memory was of his wife kissing him good night and murmuring against his lips: "I love you."

A few weeks later, the Thorntons had their first dinner party at the house for new neighbors, John's business associates and their wives. Fanny and Watson were the first to arrive. John and Mrs. Thornton were in the drawing room. He was looking out the window, drink in hand and she was examining the table settings, askance at their mix of dinner plates and silverware.

More people were expected at dinner than the number of service in the Thornton dinner wares and Margaret had Dixon unpack those of her mother's. The latter were much older and daintier but less ostentatious and Margaret had them placed in alternate positions for the female guests. The patterns were clearly different but Margaret thought the mix rather charming. It apparently grated on Mrs. Thornton's sense of taste and propriety and she turned away with disdain from the table.

After greeting her mother and brother, Fanny plopped herself down on a couch. "How tired I am already. But I must rally for I have some news. Where is Margaret? I want her to hear it, too."

John replied: "She's getting Elise ready for bed."

"She must still be nursing," Fanny said a little contemptuously.

"Yes. It has its benefits," answered John irritably, then he looked past Fanny. "Well, here she is with Elise." He walked towards them and kissed them both. "Has my little girl come to say good night?"

Elise, her eyes alert, first looked around the room and seeing strange faces, leaned against her mother's bosom and tried to hide her face. She raised her head when her father gave her a peck on the cheek, then reached her arms out to him and said something inarticulate.

John took Elise from Margaret and kissed her face and her belly a few more times. The child gurgled and imitated her father, kissing him back on his cheeks.

Fanny remarked: "She has the color of my hair, at least when I was a child."

"Yes, she does." Mrs. Thornton said. It was the first time she spoke that evening.

"Well, now that Margaret is here, I can tell you." Fanny announced, glancing towards Watson who was pouring himself a drink. "I am expecting."

Watson turned and raised his glass to all but addressed John in particular: "I am hoping for a boy."

"That is great news," Margaret exclaimed, smiling at Fanny and Watson. Mrs. Thornton smiled, pleased but apprehensive. John shook Watson's hand vigorously.

Fanny smiled tremulously, turning fretfully to her mother. "Mother, you must come and stay with me. I need you at least during my confinement, if not before."

"Of course. At once, if you wish since I am not needed here nor at the mill." Mrs. Thornton did not attempt to hide the bitterness in her voice.

"We have leased a flat in London for six months for my lying-in and you must come then."

"London!" Mrs. Thornton was flabbergasted. "Why would anyone wish to go to London for that?"

"But mother, you cannot refuse. Watson will be back and forth from London to Milton on business and I am scared to death to be alone. I think about growing so big and getting ugly and how I will endure the pain when the baby arrives. You don't know how frightened I am." Fanny covered her face with her hands, nearly in tears.

Mrs. Thornton sighed. "All right, Fanny. I suppose I need not go anywhere once I am in London."

Margaret sat down next to Fanny and placed a sympathetic hand on her shoulder. "It can be scary but you are young and if you take good care of yourself, everything will be all right. If you want, I can ask Edith for the name of her doctor. He is the best, as my cousin tells me, and has a very reassuring manner. He will follow you closely through your pregnancy."

Fanny looked at her with grateful eyes. "Thank you, I would like that. He might be better than the one a business associate recommended to Watson. I am really scared going through this and Watson does not give me enough sympathy."

Margaret smiled and stroked her arm, trying to reassuring her. "You will get through it, you'll see, and afterwards, you might wonder why you were so scared."

Among the visitors to their first party were Mr. Latimer, his daughter Ann, and Henry Lennox who was staying with the Latimers. Although Henry Lennox often came to Milton on business or to be with his fiancée, Ann Latimer, Margaret had not seen him since her wedding. No word was exchanged between them on that day beyond the formal and awkward best wishes muttered with a hasty buzz on the cheek. The many months in between brought major changes, restoring the informality and ease of their former interactions in London. Henry was relaxed and friendly when he greeted John and Margaret and she, in turn, was happy to respond in the same way.

New to the city and attending his first social gathering was a young doctor, Dr. Hartley, who recently arrived from America. Margaret had invited him when Dr. Donaldson informed her that he intended to transfer his young patients to this new doctor, a specialist in children's diseases. Dr. Hartley was born in England but moved to America with his parents when he was a child. Curious about his heritage and the country his parents grew up in, he decided to return to England and practice his profession there.

Tall, broad-shouldered and handsome, he easily became the evening's sensation and everyone, eager to hear what he had to say about the world on the other side of the vast ocean, pumped him with questions. He clearly relished the attention. He talked freely and enjoyed satisfying everyone's curiosity. His manner, frank and casual, offended some and delighted many, particularly the young women who immediately thought him a good catch. They waited only for an introduction before giving him their card and asking him over for tea. Margaret was curious as well but, as the busy hostess, she only had time to inquire about how he found his new surroundings before other visitors claimed her attention.

Dr. Hartley was, in fact, fascinated with his young hostess. He had expected to meet someone plump, maternal and older. Instead, he was introduced to this very lovely woman, a few years younger than he. He first noticed her expressive eyes: Were they blue or green or both? They were so clear he could see deep into them. He watched her move among the guests with poise and a simple natural elegance he seldom saw among young women he knew in America. Eavesdropping on her conversations with others, he discovered that she was also intelligent and had well-considered opinions she did not hesitate to share.

The young doctor was smitten. He could not help remarking to Dr. Donaldson: "Mrs. Margaret Thornton is easily the most enchanting woman in this room."

"Careful, Hartley," Dr. Donaldson replied with amusement. "John Thornton can be a formidable adversary and he is very much in love with his wife."

"I don't doubt it,"

Dr. Donaldson's caution proved to have no effect on Dr. Hartley. Before the night was over, Dr. Hartley fancied himself infatuated with the mother of his little patient.

Henry, who dutifully stayed by Ann Latimer's side most of the evening, came up to Margaret when Ann's attention was sought by her father. He remarked in the teasing tone he used when she seemed distant and he wanted to provoke her into making a response. "I think you have a new conquest tonight."

She looked at him, puzzled, and he gestured with his head towards Dr. Hartley. "He could hardly take his eyes off you. He banters and flirts with the pretty women but his gaze is always darting in your direction."

Diverted but somewhat embarrassed; she laughed, her eyes twinkling but hardly any sound issued from her slightly-open mouth. "I probably remind him of someone from home. I imagine he must be homesick." She changed the subject and remarked with more liveliness: "So, are we going to be neighbors or will you two settle in London?"

"Both, I imagine. We will have a townhouse in London. My practice is mostly there and Ann has embraced London fully but we will also keep house here with Mr. Latimer. Ann is quite attached to her father and I will be a legal consultant in his bank."

"You look happy and content. I am glad."

"Yes. We suit each other quite well, Ann and I. My future father-in-law has also convinced me to limit my practice to business law so we will spend a great deal of time here."

"Mr. Latimer must be grooming you for a top post in his bank."

"Yes," he answered simply. Then, he smiled broadly. "Oh, here's Ann."

Miss Latimer had left her father talking with another guest and was then approaching them. "Ann, you have met Mrs. Margaret Thornton," Henry said, gesturing towards Margaret.

"Yes. Good Evening, Mrs. Thornton." Miss Latimer glanced at her and turned towards Henry, hooking her hand around his arm in the same possessive gesture Margaret had seen her assume with John so long ago.

"Good Evening, Miss Latimer. Thank you for coming tonight. Miss Latimer and I met a few times when I first lived in Milton but we never really had the chance to get acquainted. I believe we saw each other last at Fanny's wedding, did we not, Miss Latimer?"

"Yes." The answer was curt, spoken in a cold manner not lost on either Margaret, who was somewhat amused, or Henry, who was perplexed. This demeanor was so unlike Miss Latimer who was always gracious, even ingratiating, when potential clients were involved.

"I told Ann I have known you many years and we were thrown a lot into each other's company in London. She also knows Mr. Thornton kept me on as your legal adviser in financial matters."

Margaret knew Henry was addressing Miss Latimer, trying to reassure her. "Yes, Edith is quite fond of Henry and he was a fixture at Harley Street, coming unannounced, but always welcome, for breakfast or dinner. If we happen to all be in London at the same time, I am sure we will see a lot of each other there. Edith likes to gather friends for dinner parties. Perhaps, we will become better acquainted."

"I hope we need not wait to go to London for that. We intend to have our own dinner parties here for friends, business associates and clients. Ann is a perfect hostess." With anxious eyes, Henry regarded Miss Latimer who was tenaciously watching her father across the room.

"I am in awe of perfect hostesses since I have neither talent nor experience for it as you and Edith have." Margaret gave Miss Latimer a sweet disarming smile.

"Thank you." It was all Miss Latimer wanted to say but Margaret, smiling engagingly, held her gaze. "Perhaps, we will be better acquainted."

"I would like that very much." Margaret replied warmly, sincerely.

John had also noticed Dr. Hartley's interest in Margaret when the doctor was introduced to them, in the instantaneous look of surprise followed by an intent gaze of undisguised admiration. He knew that look; he had it when Mr. Hale first presented his daughter to him. After dinner, when Margaret ushered the ladies to the drawing room—leaving the men behind to talk about business and other serious topics of no interest to the women— John arose with an apologetic smile. "Excuse me. I must talk to my wife but please continue. I will only be a moment."

He called out to Mrs. Thornton. "Mother, please show the ladies to the drawing room. I want to talk to Margaret."

Margaret paused in her steps, lifting questioning eyebrows at him. He drew her aside and whispered, his lips brushing her temple: "The American could hardly take his eyes off you through dinner and seemed too distracted to fully attend to those around him."

She smiled her sweetest as she answered saucily: "Is that all you wanted to tell me? If that is true, then he should have noticed how often I gazed at you adoringly."

He laughed and drew her closer, caressing the nape of her neck, aware that Dr. Hartley was watching when he gave his wife a long deep kiss. She laid her head on his shoulder and murmured with some amusement: "Was there a message in that little show we just put on?"

He grinned impishly and answered, his lips delicately nibbling at her cheek. "Of course. I am not above making sure every earnest young or old man realizes you are off limits. There is something of the ape in us men. We send out signals that we protect our territory when challenged."

"And there is something of the vamp in us women." With that remark, she clasped his face with both hands and kissed him passionately. Then, she turned around abruptly and walked away, leaving him behind, his mouth slightly open as his bemused gaze followed her receding figure.

XXI. UNCERTAIN RAPPROCHEMENT

Mrs. Thornton decided to join Fanny and Watson in London as soon as she could. The afternoon before she left, she descended from her bedroom to talk to Margaret and attempt some semblance of a reconciliation. She told herself that proper decorum compelled her to do so since she was going away for some time. She agonized for many days over when and how to do it and chose a time when Margaret was in the room adjacent to the kitchen which, Jane told her, Margaret had turned into a painting studio. Mrs. Thornton was curious to see it and could not imagine why anyone bothered to have a separate room to paint in.

Most afternoons after Elise started her nap, Margaret spent a few hours sketching or painting in the studio, emerging from it usually by late afternoon. On warm sunny days, she often came out earlier to take Elise, by then up from her nap, to play in the garden or to promenade out in a pram with Mary.

Margaret relished her solitary afternoons, usually also a time she had alone with her thoughts. The act of creating—her mind and hands thoroughly engaged in committing observations and imagination on a blank canvas—helped her think more clearly and reassess incidents or matters she might not initially comprehend. She often reached a point, through this means, when matters eventually fell into some perspective, if not resolution. When she was particularly distressed, the confusion of thoughts and emotions poured out of her through the motions and energy of applying pencil or brush to paper or canvas and she produced colors and lines that did not often take on recognizable shapes. She made them anyway. Somehow, those spontaneous gestures released tensions she had bottled up.

More often than not, she passed her days in relative ease and commonplace concerns and the marks she made were more controlled and purposeful. She could, thus, focus better on painting specific forms and colors, paying more attention to technique and envisioning the finished painting clearly. On the day Mrs. Thornton came, Margaret was painting a portrait of John and Elise together.

When Mrs. Thornton knocked on her door, Margaret was transferring one of her many sketches of the portrait on a canvas, in preparation for painting it. Her sketches were all strewn on a long, old kitchen table discarded from the renovation. She did not get up to open the door at the knock, expecting either Dixon—who might need to see her about some household decision that could not be made without her—or Mary, who might want instructions on Elise's care. Apart from them, only John ventured into the room when Margaret painted but he hardly ever knocked. He walked in quietly, touched her gently, or kissed her softly on the nape of her neck if she was painting or sketching, careful not to startle her out of her concentration.

"The door is unlocked. Come in please."

Margaret was in the midst of sketching in some details and did not look up when the door opened. "I will be with you in a minute." But she stopped and turned her head when she heard the rustle of stiff crinoline. "Mrs. Thornton, what a pleasant surprise."

Margaret was surprised to see the person she least expected but she convinced neither herself nor Mrs. Thornton that she actually found the interruption pleasant. After their last acrimonious encounter, conversations of any real substance were nearly nonexistent and they studiously kept out of each other's way until dinner when John's presence eased tensions somewhat. Margaret surmised that she owed this unusual visit to Mrs. Thornton's acute sense of propriety which dictated that she must part with her daughter-in-law as amicably as she could.

Mrs. Thornton, with an almost imperceptible smile, nodded her head but said nothing; her direct and frank manner made her incapable of casual pleasantries. She surveyed the room quickly until her attention was arrested by the sketches on the table. She examined what she could see without picking up any of them for a closer scrutiny.

With unalloyed but restrained admiration, she remarked: "You have captured a good likeness in most of these, particularly the expression in John's eyes."

Margaret smiled, amused by the observation but gratified by the implied compliment. "I do see those eyes every day."

The older woman did not answer but looked around again, her manner unhurried, reverting to its cold formality. She pointed at a divan by the window. "May I sit down?"

"Of course. Please come around this way."

She led Mrs. Thornton around the long table of sketches that stood between her and the divan. With her request to take a seat, Margaret suspected that Mrs. Thornton came for a weightier reason than merely to say goodbye. But wary of encouraging anything beyond a superficial exchange, she did not inquire into the reason for the visit. She stood awkwardly by, picked up a towel off the table, busied herself with wiping the charcoal off her hands, and waited for her mother-in-law to say something.

Mrs. Thornton sat quietly and frowned, watching Margaret with some annoyance. She wanted to tell her to sit down but she held her tongue.

After some minutes, Mrs. Thornton said in as steady a voice as she could muster: "I will be away for a few months and I did not want to leave with"—she paused, groping for the right word— "misunderstandings between us."

Margaret stopped wiping her hands and turned her head to stare at Mrs. Thornton who, for an instant, averted her eyes downward, her composure unsettled by the directness in Margaret's gaze. Margaret could not believe that this proud, aloof woman was actually going to apologize. And yet, Mrs. Thornton's grave manner and the anxiety in her eyes indicated she intended to do so and what she was about to say caused her much discomfort, if not outright pain. Margaret pulled the chair from in front of her easel and sat down, a few paces away from the divan. She gripped the soiled towel in her hand, rested her hands on her lap and waited.

Mrs. Thornton spoke deliberately and clearly, anxious to be understood. "All the things I said to you when we last talked in the drawing room were uncalled for. They were hurtful and unfair. I am well aware that my son has been happy with you. I am grateful for that and for the fact that he was spared from the struggle and humiliation of starting over. It is as if his financial collapse never happened."

"I did not marry John to rescue him from his financial troubles." Margaret could not help retorting. She had listened, the calm, casual expression she had put on to mask her uneasiness gradually giving way to astonishment

Mrs. Thornton shook her head, annoyed at being interrupted. "I did not mean it that way. I saw his despair when the mill closed. It seemed no man could be anymore despondent than he was and it broke my heart. I was angry at a world that was so unjust to one who had toiled earnestly and honestly."

She gritted her teeth, oppressed by a turmoil of emotions. She flashed narrowed eyes at Margaret that were averted just as swiftly. "Then he brought you home with him, you who once rejected him and hurt him so deeply. He was different,—I saw that right away—happy, changed from the last time he confided in me."

She paused again and looked away for a long moment. "I should have been thankful."

Mrs. Thornton glared at Margaret. "But somehow, it did not seem fair. I could not do anything about his despair, I who had stood by him all his life, made him who he is. And you—you change your mind about him, come back, profess your love for him—suddenly, everything is right once again for him."

Her voice broke when she finished and, though she kept her chin thrust upward, her eyelids dropped and she took a long deep breath, relieved, exhausted, angry, defeated. Mrs. Thornton had already gone through an intense struggle in her room. Her proud unyielding nature revolted against having to admit her mistakes to someone she still hated. But she thought she needed to be fair and admit the unjustness and hurtfulness of her accusations; in fact, she also feared alienating her son completely if she persisted in openly antagonizing his wife.

Margaret's reaction to this confrontation was no less complex, stirring painful emotions that she would rather have kept dormant. She felt some remorse on being reminded of having hurt John with her rejection; sad and sorry about Mrs. Thornton's profound suffering at losing her self-imposed role in the mill; and hurt by insinuations—implied in what she thought Mrs. Thornton left unsaid—that she was, a part of a world that had been unjust to her son and to Mrs. Thornton herself. But what most astounded Margaret was Mrs. Thornton's confession. She could not fully comprehend it.

Mrs. Thornton admitted having wrongly uttered hurtful words and, more amazing to Margaret, she acknowledged her resentment. And yet, she did not actually apologize, never said she was sorry. Margaret was not surprised; she doubted that proud, unbending Mrs. Thornton ever repented anything she did. Did she ever let go of her resentment and if she did, how long could she sustain it? Still, Mrs. Thornton did admit she had been wrong, a gesture extremely difficult for her. Margaret could only imagine the agony it took for her to go through with it.

Margaret glanced surreptitiously at Mrs. Thornton who sat very still and had turned her head towards the window. Margaret fidgeted in her seat, wondering what to do next but could not think of how to reply; indeed, Mrs. Thornton did not seem to need nor expect a reply. She glanced furtively once again at the older woman who sat as if she had hardly moved a muscle. In fact, she was now scowling at something outside the window. They stayed rooted in their seats, for a long while.

A sudden urge seized Margaret to get up and run out into the garden for some fresh air. It would have been very easy to do— only a few paces separated her from the garden through the door she always left open to air out her studio. But she kept to her seat, reluctant to disturb Mrs. Thornton's restless repose. And yet, she must say something; perhaps, Mrs. Thornton was waiting for her to do so before she felt she could leave. Margaret gripped the towel tighter in her hand, still at a loss about what to say but conscious that every minute that passed while she sat, saying nothing, became increasingly oppressive.

She forced herself to open her mouth, to form some words. What came out was polite but impersonal. "Thank you, Mrs. Thornton, for being very frank with me."

Mrs. Thornton turned towards her, forced a smile, and nodded. Indeed, in her mind, nothing more needed to be said and she could get up, leave the room, and go back to the sanctuary of her bedroom. But she could not shake off a heaviness in her bosom that she could not define and she remained in her seat.

Margaret waited. It seemed Mrs. Thornton had clammed up. Margaret started to walk towards the door to the garden. She cast a swift glance at Mrs. Thornton and something in her expression made Margaret stop. She initially intended to bid her a polite "good afternoon" as she walked by but, passing that close, she saw melancholy and weariness in Mrs. Thornton's eyes that softened the usually stern expression of her compressed lips and resolute jaw. Margaret had seen her worried and angry before but a deep, weary sadness had seemed alien to her.

Margaret felt a pang of remorse. "Please be assured that you have my good wishes and that you always have this home to come back to."

She smiled tremulously, gave Mrs. Thornton a slight bow and strode out to the garden where her pace quickened. She stopped at the gate and took several deep breaths. Encounters with Mrs. Thornton always threw Margaret into a conflict of emotions and while she thought she was learning to care less about the older woman's good opinion, every new meeting involving only the two of them disturbed her calm and sense of balance. She sat on the nearest bench and, finding that she still had the towel, busied herself again with wiping the charcoal off her hands. After sitting for nearly half an hour, she walked slowly back to the house. She could see through the window of the studio that Mrs. Thornton had gone. She proceeded through the conservatory and up to her daughter's room.

Elise was awake from her nap and playing on Mary's lap. The sight of her daughter had never yet failed to lighten Margaret's spirit and she took her from Mary. "Let's go down to the conservatory, shall we, ma puce?" She smiled at Mary. "Shall we go?"

Usually, that was all Margaret said to Mary but this day, she wanted to be alone with her thoughts as she played with Elise. "Come with us if you have nothing pressing to attend to, Mary. Dixon can use your help in the kitchen for that special dinner she is preparing for Mrs. Thornton."

Uncomplicated, unassuming Mary understood what was expected of her. She was loyal to Margaret and, though not as protective as Dixon, just as affectionate and acutely attuned to her mistress' moods and demeanor. "Yes, Mrs. Margaret. I will be back before dinnertime."

It had turned dark enough that some gas lights were already lighted in the hallways. In the conservatory, the waning sun still bathed the interior space with a faint orange cast, imparting a residual warmth Margaret found soothing. She was glad to escape the coolness in the rest of the house. She sat on an armchair with her daughter on her lap, picked up a couple of toys from a basket of objects, and handed one to Elise. The child smiled, took the object in both hands, examined it for a few moments and then placed it in her mouth.

"No, no. Dirty." Margaret shook her head and carefully pulled the toy from Elise's mouth but the child only bit at it again as soon as her mother let go of it. They went through the same routine a few times until, finally, Margaret took the toy away and gave Elise a hard biscuit before she could start crying.

Margaret watched her daughter chew on the biscuit, her mind still preoccupied with the recent encounter with Mrs. Thornton. She continued to believe she should attempt a deeper reconciliation with Mrs. Thornton, reminding herself often of the mother and son's shared history, a history that she could never fully appreciate, much less share. The truth, however, was Margaret had yet to find a way to woo her strong-minded mother-in-law. Certainly, not the way she did Aunt Shaw who was susceptible to appeals to her affection and her feminine vanity. Frank and sincere intercourse would go nowhere either. Mrs. Thornton was not in the habit of looking intimately into her feelings and her beliefs and, even if she were so inclined, she would not choose to speak to Margaret about anything revealing of herself.

Margaret had faith in the passage of time, however. She could easily recall those seemingly endless days of grieving, right after her return to London on her father's death, when she felt so numb and drained that she thought she would never recover. But time—precious reliable time—brought perspective, a lessening of pain, new challenges that must be faced, and, finally, a renewal of the spirit. So, Margaret convinced herself to trust once again that time could eventually bring with it some resolution.

"Perhaps, when Mrs. Thornton returned after a few months away with Fanny, things would be different. After all, she did admit that what she said to me was hurtful and unfair."

Elise turned her head towards her mother at the sound of her voice and only then did Margaret realize she had muttered audibly to herself. "No, I was not talking to you. In any case, it is a start, don't you think?"

She nudged her daughter's cheek playfully, raised her on her feet, and tickled her stomach with her chin until the Elise started giggling.

John heard laughter, punctuated by Elise squealing with delight, as soon as he entered the house. He went straight to the conservatory.

Margaret looked up, still smiling broadly. "You're home very early today. It is probably not even five yet."

"About a quarter before. I am leaving for a few days tomorrow so I thought I'd come home early. Was I interrupting something?" He asked, teasing.

John had insisted on accompanying his mother to London partly to assuage her apprehensions about traveling anywhere outside Milton and partly to reestablish at least some of their former understanding.

Margaret greeted him with a kiss and laid her head on his shoulder. John pulled her close with one arm, taking his daughter with the other.

He kissed Elise on the cheek and his wife on her forehead. "Are you going to miss me when I leave for London?"

"Well, it will only be a couple of days. But do you realize we have never been apart even for a day since we married?"

"I was thinking precisely that as I was sitting at my desk, doing some accounting. In the middle of all that, I felt the urge to come home right away. I took a cab, can you imagine?"

She raised her head and kissed him again. "Let's go up to our room."

"Perhaps we can dine alone in our room tonight?"

"I would have liked that very much but Dixon fancied doing something festive tonight. She is preparing your mother's favorite dishes."

"Ahh!" He replied, amused. "I was not aware that Dixon liked my mother that much."

"You know Dixon and how much pleasure she gets from seeing everyone enjoy her meals."

"Yes. Lucky for me I have a much longer walk to the mill."

Some late afternoon light streamed into their sitting room, but a gas lamp on the wall had already been lighted. Margaret took Elise from John, sat her in her playpen, and gave her a rattle, teething beads and rag dolls.

"She will play undisturbed until nursing time. Well, at least, I hope she does. She gets more restless when she is tired and wants attention."

"Leave her for now and come over here." John took her hand and pulled her gently towards him as he sat on the couch opposite the crib. He clasped her waist so she landed on his lap. "This time, I take care of you and you take care of me,"

He nibbled playfully at her throat, then slowly up her chin and her mouth. Margaret placed her arms on his shoulders and laid her forehead against his. She asked, her voice almost muffled: "How was your day?"

"Just the usual bustle; otherwise as uneventful as it could possibly be."

"That is good, isn't it?"

"Yes, of course. We will get a bit more hectic when some orders come due in a few weeks just as new ones arrive. I will have to hire a few more hands and I may also need a little help in the office."

She planted a kiss on his lips and got up off his lap but he held on to her hand. "Where are you going?"

"I was going to ring for tea."

"Not just yet. Sit with me awhile. I am leaving early tomorrow before you're up and I will not see you for two days."

"It will only be one night away." Margaret sat down on the couch and nestled herself contentedly in John's embrace. They quietly watched their daughter play for nearly half an hour, laughing or remarking about her little antics.

Margaret did not tell John about her encounter with Mrs. Thornton in the studio. She thought it did not serve a purpose and would have required telling him of the previous painful meeting in the drawing room.

Mrs. Thornton left for London with John just as Margaret awoke. Settled in their private compartment a few minutes before the train was scheduled to leave, John saw the anxiety in Mrs. Thornton's eyes and tried to reassure her. "It is not a long trip, mother. These trains are safe and fast. We will be in London before noon."

Mrs. Thornton nodded but did not answer. She kept her eyes focused on what was passing outside her window—people rushing everywhere on the platform as the train slowly rolled out the station; the densest part of the city that went by too quickly as the train picked up speed; the landscape that increasingly evolved from gray to green. Mrs. Thornton grew more anxious.

She broke her silence with a brief remark. "Why London for her lying-in?"

John, engrossed in reading the Milton daily, looked up briefly. "You will have to ask Fanny that." He was about to resume reading his paper but he put it down when he saw his mother's still apprehensive countenance. "Try to relax, mother. You may find London quite diverting and I am sure Fanny will be all right."

"I have no desire to see London. I cannot imagine anything there of interest to me. I am going only because Fanny needs me."

"Can I do something to make this trip more comfortable for you?"

"No. It will have to end at some point. Go back to your paper. I will survive."

John nodded, smiled calmly and returned to his paper. He looked up from time to time, smiling in the same way whenever he caught her attention. The train ride to London was relatively uneventful but Mrs. Thornton remained uneasy. She sat opposite her son, worried and silent, through most of the trip.

They arrived at Watson and Fanny's apartment in time for a long leisurely luncheon, after which Fanny showed Mrs. Thornton to her room. There, pleading fatigue, she stayed to rest. Shortly thereafter, John left the Watsons for Harley Street. He was staying with Edith and Captain Lennox until his return to Milton Sunday afternoon.

Watson and Fanny had initially planned to put him up in a hotel. With only four bedrooms and Mrs. Thornton staying with them, Fanny told him there was not enough room in the apartment. But a short letter from Margaret to Edith produced an immediate reply. Edith, in her usual effusive style, declared they were always welcome and she would be offended if either or both of them came to London and did not stay at Harley Street. Captain Lennox could not wait to renew his acquaintance with the fascinating Mr. Thornton, and she was keen to hear first-hand accounts of her cousin and her goddaughter.

John did not return home until way past dinner time on Sunday. Margaret had waited to have dinner with him in the sitting room where he found her curled up on the couch, sleeping, her fingers entwined on top of an open book. For a long moment, he stood gazing lovingly at her before he took the book gently from under her hands and laid it on the table. He kissed her lightly, trying not to wake her up. When he bent down to pick her up and carry her to bed, Margaret opened her eyes and greeted him with a smile, her eyes half-closed and glazed from sleep.

"What time is it? Have you had dinner?"

"It is way past eleven. I am sorry to be so late. I missed my train and came in on the last trip back to Milton. Did you wait to have dinner with me?"

"Yes but don't worry about it. I am too sleepy for dinner anyway. I can ring for a glass of milk."

"Let me go and fetch you some. No need to wake any of the servants up. I could use a glass myself."

When John returned from the kitchen with two glasses of milk on a tray, the lights in the sitting room had been turned off and Margaret was in her dressing room changing. He went into the bedroom and deposited the tray on the table in front of the fireplace. He had had a long day and he was exhausted. Plopping himself on the nearest armchair, he took off his vest and jacket, peeled off his cravat and unbuttoned the top of his shirt.

Before long, Margaret entered the room in her robe and nightgown and sat on the opposite chair. She smiled at him and picked up a glass of milk. They each sipped milk, quietly and slowly, listening to the crackle of the fireplace, sometimes exchanging glances across the table. They did not talk and took care not to make any noise that would disturb the silence around them. When they finished and still without a word, they went to bed. John turned off the lamp by his bedside, kissed Margaret good night, and gathered her close in his arms as they both sank into deep slumber.

Margaret never asked John how the trip to London was with his mother. Not that night nor the subsequent ones. She thought he would tell her when he was ready. The night following his return, he came home with flowers and was particularly solicitous and charming to her. She naturally attributed all this to their first brief time being away from each other. She had missed him, as well, the night he was gone. Several times that night, she reached out in the dark for his reassuring presence and the first time she did so, his absence jolted her into full awakening.

At dinner in their sitting room, John gave her an account of his stay at Harley Street, describing in detail his evening with Edith and Captain Lennox. Margaret listened until he finished his stories and, then, remarked, greatly amused. "You surprise me. I would never have guessed that vases of flowers, table settings, and roast trimmings would interest you enough to notice, much less describe them. And, in such detail, too!"

He laughed. "Normally, they are a haze to me but how else could I convince you where I was the night I was away? Besides, I'm sure Edith would have wanted me to let you know she went out of her way to please me."

"Yes, my dear cousin likes you very much. Frankly, I was uncertain how she would regard you because she was as snobbish as they come in London about people in the trades. But she does have an affectionate heart that serves her well."

Dinner came to an end a couple of hours later but John hardly said anything about his mother or Fanny except to say that Fanny was, as usual, getting everyone to fuss over her and his mother fell into her indulgent maternal role almost as soon as they arrived.

John did not tell Margaret that he missed his train because an emotional parting with his mother had detained him longer than he had intended. He was getting ready to leave on an earlier train and had gone in to bid his mother farewell in her bedroom. She was almost like her old self with him, touching his face affectionately and rearranging his cravat. But she seemed to be avoiding his eyes and John could not help saying: "I hope you have forgiven me for deciding in favor of the workers."

She glanced at him and turned around to sit on the only armchair in the room. "You decided what you thought was best for the mill."

"But you are still unhappy. Is there anything else I can do to make it up you."

She clenched her teeth and answered, her eyes somewhat defiant. "I want you to tell me that you can see why I said all those hurtful things to Margaret."

"What hurtful things?" He was perplexed and his voice could not hide the reflexive anger her answer elicited. "What do you mean, mother?"

Mrs. Thornton realized then that Margaret never said anything to John about their encounters but it was too late to take back what she said. He stared at her demanding an explanation. "Mother, what did you say to my wife?"

"I did talk to her the day before we left and told her I did not mean those hurtful words."

"Mother, what hurtful words?"

"I forget exactly. I was frustrated and angry. I told her that she did not understand us and did not belong in Milton. I'm sorry but I believe those to be true. For me, she will always be from the south. But I said something I should not have. I told her to get out of our lives. That was wrong. She is your wife after all." She avoided his eyes.

John glared at his mother with narrowed eyes as she explained. He did not, could not, speak for a moment or two. Then, in a voice he struggled to keep under control, he snarled under his breath. "Mother, you had no right."

He rushed out of the room. Just outside the door, he spun around to face her and, in a low voice still quivering from suppressed anger, he said: "You must see that I love Margaret with all my heart. I do not care what she knows or not about Milton and cotton. What I care about and find amazing is that she loves me for who I am and what I am. So, you see, she belongs nowhere else but with me, in Milton. I can no longer be happy without Margaret, mother." He turned around and left, ignoring her pleas and her obvious distress at what she had wrought in him.

"John!" Mrs. Thornton cried: "Please do not leave like this. John!" She started to rise from her chair to stop him but he had moved too fast and was running down the stairs in what seemed like a flash. She sat down again and compressed her quivering lips to steady them. Her hands clutched tightly at the handkerchief in her hand. She had not anticipated the violence of his anger. The few times in the past that she had witnessed it, it was directed at someone else and never at her. She sat very still but her body ached from tension. What was she to do?

Her despair did not last long, however. Fanny came in to ask what had happened and as she reassured her daughter that it was but a misunderstanding that should sort itself out, she also convinced herself that her son would come back. He had to. She knew in her heart that he would and could never disregard what was due to her as his mother.

John hurried past the drawing room, ignoring Watson and Fanny who gawked at him, startled. He bolted out the door and, in hasty angry strides, headed for the train station, unconcerned that it was too far to walk. After some distance, he slowed down but kept walking until he came upon a park. He stopped under a shady tree and leaned against it, trying to calm himself further. He stood there a long time His anger began to swell once more as he recalled Margaret, sad and even despondent, clinging to him. Once she talked about leaving for London and staying there a while. Was that, perhaps, after his mother's harsh, unfair tirade?

He clenched his jaw and compressed his mouth to suppress an urge to shout, hit something, or run away. But he knew only too well he could not. He had never been this angry with his mother, never parted with her in acrimony. His rage tore him up. He felt guilty—and angry at himself—for being angry. What right had he to be angry at his mother—he who had hurt her deeply when he decided against her in favor of workers? As Margaret told him once, his mother had already been through frustration and despair over changes she had to endure after he married.

Mrs. Thornton hated disruptions in her life and John suspected that it would have suited her if he never married. She had taken pride in the fact that women thought him a good catch but because he never showed any serious interest in any of these women, it had not bothered her. But Margaret changed all that.

John thought his mother might have learned to live with his marriage were it not that Margaret's influence extended to the way he saw important matters related to running the mill. Consistent with Margaret's views and perceptions, he had made changes at the mill which his mother considered wasteful, at the least. Worse, she probably thought these changes emboldened workers to ask him to tell her to stop coming to the mill. In his mother's reckoning, Margaret was to blame for the workers' request. After taking her son away, Margaret then deprived her of the mill, everything she lived for.

John thought he finally saw what Margaret already knew. She had seen into his mother's heart before he did, had been alive to the desperation Mrs. Thornton felt over all the changes resulting from his marriage. John took in a long deep breath, his eyes sad and thoughtful. Understanding his mother's despair and her animosity towards Margaret did not easily come with acceptance, did not mollify his anger at his mother or at himself for not having seen right away. If Margaret had loved him less or had not been strong, she might have escaped to London by now, away from his mother, away from him. That possibility perturbed him deeply and he wished with all his heart that he was home with her, prostrate at her feet, telling her how sorry he was for what she had to endure.

And yet, distressed as John was at what Margaret had been through, he could not reproach his mother for too long. He and she were alike in many ways: Easily provoked to anger when threatened, they jealously guarded what they thought they could rightly lay claim to. That was precisely what she had done, ill-advised though it was.

His mother's incontrovertible beliefs, sometimes inappropriate and even destructive, also led to much good. What he was, he owed to his mother. In return, he owed her not only the comfort he could now give her but also the generosity and respect that allowed her to make mistakes. As hurt as Margaret must have been, she understood what his mother was going through. Mollified, John knew he should do no less and as a son, he needed to do more: He must forgive.

John felt his chaotic emotions gradually getting spent. He walked to a bench nearby and sat for a long time. It was growing dark by the time he retraced his steps slowly to the Watson apartment where his mother waited. He would have to take the last train to go home to Margaret.

XXII. PASSAGE

In early December, Margaret began to plan for the holidays that were coming. She was going to have her hands full with preparations this year. They would be celebrating their first Christmas in the new house and Elise's very first one but her efforts were going to be directed at the mill. It was doing much better than had been expected the past year and she thought it appropriate, as a gesture of gratitude and goodwill, to have a bigger celebration at Marlborough Mills.

Her intent was to put together gift baskets for the workers and their families and celebrate Christmas Eve with a dinner at the Dining Hall for everyone involved in the mill including masters, overseers, workers, and their families. When she was pregnant the year before, she had not been able to do more than supervise the purchase and wrapping of gifts for the children. She realized her current plans were rather ambitious, probably unheard of in the other mills but were in keeping with John's desire to encourage communication between masters and hands. She hoped John would go along with them.

On a pleasant weekend afternoon, John and Margaret sat reading in the conservatory, trying to concentrate on their respective books with relative success. They were often interrupted by the continuous babble and occasional screams from Elise who was playing with Mary on a thick rug on the floor. Accustomed to her daughter's utterings, Margaret sometimes glanced curiously at the two figures on the floor but generally she ignored them and went on reading. John was not quite as successful and found his daughter's utterances inevitably more distracting. He looked up so frequently to see what was going on that, eventually, he decided to put his book down and watch his daughter play.

"Is she saying something you can understand?"

"She is saying something. I am not sure exactly what it is, though." She barely looked up from her book.

"But how do you know?" He persisted.

Margaret turned towards him. "Well, if you listen for a while, you'll notice there are sounds she would utter repeatedly and they have a rhythm unique to those sounds. So, I think they must mean something, to her at least."

"Fascinating! Like what?"

"I don't know, really. They bear no resemblance to real words." Margaret put the book, open face down, on the table next to her and asked jauntily: "Does all this really interest you or do you just want my attention?"

"It does interest me more than you might think but, I would not object to taking a turn in the garden." He grinned, grasped her hands and pulled her up from her chair. Margaret grabbed a shawl she had flung on the back of her chair, draped it around her shoulders and strolled into the garden with him.

"It is cooler than I thought. Are you warm enough in that shawl?"

"Not really. But if we walk briskly, we should warm up.

After several energetic turns around the garden, John slowed down a little. "You are in good shape. You had no trouble keeping up with me."

She smiled broadly at him. "I take care of a frisky little girl who weighs more than 15 pounds and I carry her up and down the stairs several times a day. I have to be in good shape."

He smiled, placed his arm around her waist, and drew her close. "Yes, of course. She is growing fast and more active every day." Invigorated by their brisk pace and the fresh cool air, they took a few more turns, slowing gradually to an easy pace. Halfway around the garden, John paused. "I wanted to talk to you about something I have been thinking about since I came back from London."

"I had something to tell you as well but it probably is not as weighty a matter as yours." She detected the gravity his voice had just taken on and the scowl that had crept back on his brow.

"Perhaps, you should tell me first what you had in mind and we shall see."

She eyed him closely. He seemed determined to hear her out first. "Well, it is about what we should do for the mill this Christmas."

"Do you think we need to do more than last year?"

"As a matter of fact, I do. The mill seems to be doing better than you expected and you said it will probably do even better at least through next year."

"Yes, orders are increasing and new clients are planning to give us their orders next year. I, too, thought we might do more for Christmas. Do you have something specific in mind?"

"I do have some ideas I wrote down with costs attached to them. They are merely estimates, of course, particularly the number of children Nicholas gave me."

"I am impressed. Figures do not intimidate you?"

"You can thank Henry Lennox for that. When I came into Mr. Bell's inheritance, he told me that, although I might have a lawyer and financial advisers, I should have some understanding of finances and learn to handle my own. He spent many hours teaching me about money, earnings, and investments."

John knitted his eyebrows at the image this little revelation conjured up of Henry Lennox and Margaret huddled together over a sheaf of papers in the Harley Street study. The idea of his wife spending hours with a man who had shown a long-standing interest in her irritated him. He tried to suppress it but, for some reason, it rankled him now more than ever.

"I already knew basic budgeting, of course, when I had to assume my mother's responsibilities after she became ill." Seeing the frown on his face, she paused, hesitated, and then when he said nothing, resumed what she had started to say. "But I never before had to deal with large figures and the greater complexity of interests and earnings. Expenses for gifts and a dinner at the mill dining hall are easier to figure out, in comparison."

She saw the lingering frown on his face and wondered if he was reacting to the manner in which she just spoke. She was proud of what she learned about the intricacies of money and its management. Numbers were never supposed to interest girls and, growing up, it suited her that she only had to learn basic arithmetic operations. But Henry was quite persuasive about the need for her to know how her inheritance was being managed. Women, he said, were much more likely to be victims of someone who was tempted to deceive and cheat. It surprised Margaret to find the subject fascinating and not that difficult to grasp and she became an eager, inquisitive student. So, yes, she might come across as proud, even self-congratulatory about understanding figures on balance sheets.

She searched John's face, trying to read what was on his mind but he seemed to be staring at her blankly, his mind somewhere else. "You are not ready to hear any details, are you? Perhaps, we should talk about what is on your mind, instead?"

"I'm sorry. My mind did wander into something unrelated. If you have those figures, I can look at them this evening. I am sure your plans will be doable."

"I shall give them to you before dinner." She looked away, feeling a little let down at the detached formality in his voice. "Something is bothering you. I have seen you staring into space often since your return from London."

She led them back to the house and he followed, walking slower and a few paces behind. She turned her head briefly back at him. "Do you want to talk about it? Our sitting room, perhaps, if you need privacy. Or is your study a more appropriate place?"

He threw her a glance, wondering how it occurred to her to mention his study which he used mostly to work on matters associated with the mill. Although their books especially those of her father's, were stored in the shelves there, they took the books they wanted and read elsewhere, usually in their sitting room and lately, in the conservatory on nice days.

"That is a good idea, actually. Let's go to my study."

She nodded wordlessly and hurried back into the conservatory without waiting for him. Elise turned when Margaret entered the room and raised her arms up to her mother, uttering something unintelligible but vaguely familiar. Margaret picked her up. "Are you tired, ma puce?" She held her daughter close to her bosom, kissed her on both cheeks and then nuzzled her belly playfully.

John came in but did not approach. He watched his wife and daughter from a few paces away. Though he still seemed absentminded, the somber undertone to his manner had been replaced by a warm smile that reached his eyes. Margaret gazed at him, his eyes, now soft and loving, and that brief earnest look dissolved the distance recently wrought between them.

She handed Elise over to Mary but her daughter clung to her and started whining. "You have to go with Mary right now, my angel. Mama and Papa have something they need to do." She addressed Mary. "She probably needs a nap. I'll come as soon as I can."

She turned around, hooked her arm around John's and nudged him to walk on but on seeing Elise cry, he hesitated. "Don't worry, she will be all right. She's just tired. Mary knows what to do."

Margaret seldom went into John's study, regarding it to be a private space to which she usually needed an invitation to enter. It was not that John gave some indication that she had to but she knew how her father used such a space for contemplation and peaceful moments alone.

John's study was about half the size of their sitting room, lined with bookshelves that nearly reached the ceiling and equipped with a large secretary with deep drawers for files. The room had a stove instead of a fireplace and next to it, a side table and an armchair, the only other seat in the room except for the chair in front of the secretary. At the mill house, John had a larger study that also served as his bedroom before he married but here, he wanted a relatively spare space devoted to work and contemplation.

He offered the armchair to Margaret, took the desk chair and pulled it closer so he sat facing her. For a long moment, he looked at her without saying anything. She gazed back at him, waiting.

"Why did you suggest my study?"

"I don't know. You seemed so detached and preoccupied. I might have thought a neutral environment appropriate. Besides, we are talking about matters pertaining to the mill."

"I have been preoccupied lately and, yes, I suppose my mind has sometimes been elsewhere." He paused as if he was searching for the right words. "You have never asked me even once since I returned from London how the trip with my mother went."

Margaret started to open her mouth as if to protest at what sounded to her like an accusation but John gently placed his fingers on her lips.

"No, you need not answer that. I think I do know why and I am grateful. Actually, it is the old house at the mill I wanted to talk to you about. So far, no one seems interested in buying or leasing it for business purposes and I doubt that anyone who wants a house and can afford it would want to live next to a noisy, dusty mill. Perhaps, we should reconsider its sale."

"What did you have in mind?"

"The mill is continuing to grow and I will soon need to move into a larger office that can accommodate another person to help with bookkeeping and correspondence."

"You want to use the mill house as an office?"

"Well, part of it, yes. And I thought of turning over my old office to the workers as a meeting place where they could discuss work-related matters."

"That is a radical idea, is it not—giving workers a place at the mill to congregate for that purpose? And exceedingly generous."

"I hesitate to take full credit for being generous. The thing is I do need more space and in moving, my old office will be empty. Why not put it to some good use?"

"I think it is wonderful but I think there will be objections from other mill owners."

"Of course, they will object but this is our mill, to do with as we see fit. I will confess to having apprehensions. This decision to involve workers in creating better conditions at the mill might not really pay off in the end but I must try, anyway."

"What if they use the office to plan a strike?"

"That poses a dilemma. Strike is arguably a work-related matter but it is against the interests of owners or managers. I sincerely do not know. I'll have to think about that one."

"Perhaps, they will have enough scruples to meet elsewhere if it is a strike they are considering."

He nodded but a frown had begun once more to crease his brow. "Margaret, I really must talk to you about something pressing on my mind."

"I am listening."

"About the mill house—I will only need the ground floor for my office. But I have also been thinking about mother. You and I both know that she does not seem too happy living here and would have preferred to stay at the old house. We could turn the top floor into a flat for her. She will need only one maid to live with her and perhaps two others to come during the day to cook, clean and wash and another person, on occasion, to run errands."

Margaret could not hide her surprise and stared at him for some moments, at a loss about what to say. The possibility of Mrs. Thornton returning to the old house never occurred to her although she could not deny it might be an arrangement that would suit everyone. But the suddenness of the suggestion bothered her and she needed time to comprehend it. She was reluctant agreeing too readily to a decision in which the reason remained vague.

"Have you said anything to Hannah about it?"

"I did mention it to her just before I left London and she seemed to think it a good idea."

Margaret, upon hearing this, could not fail to be curious about whether something significant did happen in London. "I'm afraid I am not always as patient as you might think. My curiosity does get the better of me, as in this case. Did something happen in London between you and your mother?"

"We did talk in the afternoon before my return about the mill and the workers' request. You are quite right. She did not admit to it directly but she did not need to. I could tell from the deep anguish in her voice that she feels the loss of her involvement in the mill probably as she might the loss of someone she cared deeply about. Once I saw that, arriving at the decision for her to move back to the mill house was easy. There she could still feel she is a part of the mill, hearing the drone and clanging of machines and observing the activity from the drawing room."

"It does seem like a logical step to take. Your mother has not been happy here and yet, we have only been in this house a few months."

"True, but after only a week of being home from London, I saw that you were more relaxed and that everyone else seemed to be, too. The house is cheerier. I had to admit, sadly, that living apart from mother was best for everyone."

"I regret very much that your mother and I could not get along well and it probably affected everyone. Well, the mill house is available and we can afford to put Hannah up in her own household. What else is there to say? It is not really my decision but yours and your mother's." She felt suddenly exhausted and inexplicably sad. "Now, I must attend to Elise so, if you don't mind, I would like to go."

"Margaret."

"We can talk again later but I do have to go."

As soon as she was out of the study, she bit her lip to hold back tears. She was confused by her reaction. John's decision made much sense and life after Mrs. Thornton left for London had been undeniably more at ease for everyone. On the face of it, the decision was simple and logical, probably satisfactory to everyone involved and it had always been there waiting for someone to seize upon it. This thought did not lessen Margaret's unease.

That evening, Margaret ordered dinner in the dining room as if she wanted to preserve some distance and a level of formality with her husband. She smiled and kept her end of the conversation going but John sensed that a certain reserve had taken hold of her and her mind was far away. Dinner ended early and they walked silently up to their bedroom. As he closed the door behind them, he caught her in his arms and held her so she could not wriggle out of his embrace. He nuzzled her neck and her shoulders.

"I don't know anymore how I could live without you."

She choked down a sob, grasped his hand and pressed it to her lips. He turned her around in his arms and kissed her all over her face. "What is wrong, love?"

"I don't know. I am confused. Hannah is not happy here with us and your decision seems like the perfect solution to appease everyone and yet I feel sad. And let down."

"Oh, my love! I might as well tell you that I made this decision more for your sake than my mother's."

"What do you mean?"

He led her towards the bed where they both sat down. "I had been so busy at the mill that I never had much chance to pay attention to what goes on in this household but I did have time for some reflection on the trip back from London. My mother's ill regard of you has not been lost on me and it saddens me deeply. I felt helpless that I could not change her attitude and manner towards you but, the more I thought about it, the more I realized I could make things much better for you if my mother were to live elsewhere and you did not have to deal with each other from day-to-day. The old house seemed the perfect answer. It is available and she would be back where she wanted to be."

She looked at him with sorrowful eyes. "I am so sorry. You should not have to be burdened with problems between your mother and me. You have so much to worry about at the mill as it is."

"I do not deny that the mill is important to me but if I had to make a choice between it and my loved ones, I would abandon it in a heartbeat. So, you see, I cannot help but be bothered."

"I was hopeful that when Hannah came back, we could start over again."

"I expected that she would have grown to like you by now." He paused, looked into her eyes and gave her a tender impish smile. "I assumed that she would have seen all that I love about you and would have been captivated like I have been."

She matched his tone with a lighthearted answer. "It is only natural that she should see something quite different. Love is blind and you cannot see my little follies."

He smiled, in mock ridicule. "But I can. Your Shakespeare is a bit rusty, for one."

She wrinkled her nose up at him and laid her head on his shoulders. Some minutes later, he grew pensive and said, somewhat regretfully. "Mother might have learned to like you if I did not ask her to stop going to the mill."

"Or if we did not move." She looked up, finishing the thought for him. "We both did things that she was either not happy about or which hurt her. But what are we to do? What do people do when what they desire clashes with each other? We make decisions but we cannot always have control over their consequences."

"My mother is a wonderful woman in so many ways, and her strong convictions have often served her well—but, not always."

A lingering uneasiness persisted in her mind that he still had something he was loath to tell her. "I have not caused a rift between you and Hannah, have I?"

"No, do not ever think that. Is that what you have been worried about? We're inevitably on a different footing, mother and I, but it would have happened some way or another whether I married you or not. I had already begun to change before I married you. Well, you did start me thinking, as did your father but, as you just said, we do not always have control over what happens. That is just the way it is."

"It is true, in any case, that your mother and I are both bull-headed. Neither of us would give in to the other—precisely what we need to live peaceably together."

"Perhaps. But maybe you should just accept that you can never live with each other."

"Come, come. Don't worry about it." He lifted her face, kissed her and added playfully. "Remember that in marrying me, your vows only obligated you to live with me, not with my mother. Anyway, I can only do battle with one strong woman at a time."

She laughed softly and pretended to slap him on his buttocks. He exclaimed playfully: "Ouch! Remember, you also promised to love me."

She laughed once more, rested her head on his shoulders and wound her arms around his chest. I love you so much that sometimes it hurts."

That night, Margaret lay awake in bed trying to make sense of her lingering apprehensions. Why should the fact of Mrs. Thornton living separately continue to pester when she should be relieved that life would be more naturally at ease? She knew people would talk and speculation would never stop about why, after moving to a larger house in a good neighborhood, Mrs. Thornton set up her own household. But that did not bother Margaret. She chafed somewhat at the nagging notion that she failed to develop at least a tolerant if not a companionable relationship with her mother-in-law. But again, something more than that oppressed her.

Events, encounters or emotions that unduly disturbed Margaret always induced introspection and scrutiny until she, at least, understood them or, better still, accepted them pacifically. She learned much about herself from hours of reflecting over bothersome things—what was important to her and what made her happy; what hurt her or made her sad, what she could do to cope or prevent them from happening again. This self-awareness gave her the confidence to confront new, unexpected or trying situations and eventually find some way to live with them calmly enough. Still, her confidence was also nurtured by older, more mature, and affectionate adults who she could rely on. Her mother had always been there to provide her solace when she needed it and her father could always be relied upon to explain matters too complex for her limited experience.

While at least one of her parents lived, Margaret felt someone was there she could turn to for wisdom or reassurance and who accepted whoever she was without questions or reservations. Had she hoped that, with them gone, she could turn to Mrs. Thornton? Margaret found a flaw in this reasoning—she did not trust Mrs. Thornton's judgment about many things of importance to her; their beliefs and attitudes clashed too much for that.

Feeling oppressed by thoughts that could not be reconciled and emotions that remained in some turmoil, Margaret wrapped herself in her robe and tiptoed into the sitting room, closing the door to the bedroom quietly. She sat on an armchair by the fireplace where only glowing embers were left of the fire that had burned there. They were barely enough to keep her warm and she folded her feet up onto the chair and under her robe.

She stared into the darkness for some time until, without a warning, tears flowed freely but soundlessly down her cheeks. Her shoulders and chest heaved upwards but the only audible sounds she emitted were occasional inward gasps of air induced by the incessant flood of tears. This was so unlike her, she thought detachedly, she who prided herself on her self-control. Even when she succumbed to the sorrow of her parents' death, she had not allowed her tears to overwhelm her.

The few instances she let her tears flow freely had been for happy reasons when John held her in his arms and comforted her. With John, the certainty of kisses and embraces rewarded her tears. In the present instance, she was crying for nebulous and confusing reasons.

Margaret began to form a growing sense that in crying, she was cleansing herself, purging herself. Of what, however, she was not too certain. Of the sorrow of loss or the shame of defeat? Of the passing of a period, sometimes innocent and even sweet? She did not restrain her tears and they drenched not only her face but also the top of her robe. They were soon exhausted and after a short period of calm, she dried her face with the sleeves of her robe.

She sat in the dark for some minutes, her mind blank, drawn into the rhythm of her breathing. Her body grew slack, her limbs so limp that, had she wanted to, she could not have lifted them. She submitted to the stillness for some time until she began to feel the cold seep through her robe. The embers had nearly dissolved into dirty white ash.

Her feet searched her slippers but were met with only the cold floor. She hopped towards the bedroom, and opened the door noiselessly. She climbed into bed and slid closer to John where the bed was warm. John, halfway between sleep and wakefulness, murmured something unintelligible, placed an arm around her waist, nudged his face against her cheek, and fell back to sleep.

Deep dreamless sleep claimed her consciousness shortly thereafter. She greeted the following morning, refreshed, feeling lighthearted and impatient to begin preparations for the holidays.

XXIII. CELEBRATION

The day before Christmas was very busy at the Marlborough Mills dining hall. Deliveries of meats and produce started earlier that week and in the morning, several women workers joined the cooks in preparing a Christmas Eve meal to be served mid-afternoon. Under Margaret's supervision, the hall was made ready for the celebration by workers including Annie, Marian, and Mary, the three who had originally painted and decorated the dining hall with Margaret's help.

The men secured a tall Christmas tree at one corner of the room that easily became the centerpiece of the simple room decoration. Gifts for the children were either hung on its branches or arranged underneath its trunk. The women tied the green curtains in red ribbons and, on the middle of the tables, placed wreaths of candles encircled with pine branches and holly berries, gathered earlier by children of the mill. A huge wreath that the women strung together of laurel leaves, rosemary, thyme, pine boughs, pine cones, and more holly berries were hung on top of the fireplace imparting aromas released by the heat and blending with both savory and sweet smells from the pots on the hearth.

Workers and their families started trickling into the mill courtyard before noon and were milling by the dining hall entrance, their younger children playing nearby. Shortly thereafter, Williams opened the mill gates to a carriage bearing the Thorntons who came to start the festivities and join the workers for the Christmas Eve meal.

The carriage stopped in front of a crowd who, though curious, tried to look elsewhere when the door opened. Mr. Thornton descended and turned around, offering his hand to Mary. The driver alighted from his perch, walked to the back of the carriage and unloaded a perambulator, assisted by Williams. The crowd began to take more interest in what was happening in front of them.

Nobody had yet seen the new daughter and nothing had been said about her being brought to the mill that day. So when Margaret poked her head out with Elise in her arms, all eyes were on them. She handed over her daughter to Mary, took her husband's hand and descended from the carriage. Some workers had never seen Margaret but they had heard stories, mostly from Annie and Nicholas Higgins, that Mr. Thornton had an uncommonly handsome young wife with a generous heart. The workers all knew that it was through her kindness and enthusiastic exertions that they were all there to enjoy a dinner together and they were consequently predisposed to like her.

Margaret addressed Williams: "There are three huge boxes on the seat that must be unloaded very carefully. Dixon insisted they remain upright. Please take them in and place them on a table."

She took Elise back from Mary and walked into the dining hall, greeting everyone immediately around her with an engaging smile, sometimes a slight nod, and a "Good afternoon." Elise gawked at the crowd, bright eyed and curious. John walked alongside his wife, a protective arm on the back of her waist, occasionally nodding at someone in the crowd but was content to let his wife do much of the greeting and smiling. Mary followed, pushing the perambulator.

To the crowd, it was a spectacle that most of them did not often see. They were accustomed to only catching glimpses of the mill owners' families peeking out of their carriages or seeing them from some distance. It was a distance rarely crossed and was social rather than physical.

The Christmas Eve festivity was generosity unheard of for mill owners and, for the master's family to join their workers in the celebration was quite inconceivable. How extraordinary, many of them thought, to stand so near to the master's wife that one could extend one's hand and not expect the young Mrs. Thornton to recoil from it. From what they had heard, she would probably grasp the offered hand and shake it. But no one tried.

For masters and hands to mix in social situations was entirely unimaginable but, in paying for a holiday dinner and gifts for all workers and their families, Marlborough Mills was breaking taboos. John's colleagues thought, as the older Mrs. Thornton did, that it was a concession to workers that would surely be followed by more impossible demands and, consequently, by strikes if demands were not met. Their families looked down with disdain at any form of interaction with hands outside the mills and were, thus, contemptuous of the Thorntons for breaking class barriers.

Acutely alert to how British society of landed gentry and noble classes looked down on manufacturers and tradesmen, most in this nouveau riche group found Margaret Thornton perplexing. She was clearly a young woman who bore all the graces of a gentleman's daughter, apparent in the proud turn to her head when she moved, in how she spoke or chose her words and in the refined manners that could seem haughty on first acquaintance. They knew she had rich connections with whom she had lived in London and it was rumored that her mother, a former Miss Beresford, had some noble ancestry.

Milton's rich manufacturing families had expected Margaret to thumb her nose on the working class but they were appalled when she, instead, demonstrated a vexing independence of mind and did quite the opposite. That was more than three years ago. Much had happened since then, including one that surprised nearly everyone and inevitably caused consternation in many young women. John Thornton married the very woman who had defied what he believed in and openly challenged the reasoning for his beliefs. Even so, this unexpected marriage was merely fodder for malicious gossip among the manufacturers' families and something Mr. Thornton's colleagues could ridicule him about behind his back.

What worried manufacturers the most were changes that had been instituted at Marlborough Mills since its reopening. It proved to many of his business colleagues that John Thornton had been influenced by his wife's revolutionary views. In this belief, they did not differ much from Mrs. Thornton and like her, they blamed Margaret, a foreigner from the south for the Christmas celebration, a blame they dared not voice to John Thornton.

The arrival of the Thorntons enlivened a crowd eagerly awaiting the beginning of this first attempt at bringing together, for a holiday celebration, two classes often at odds with each other. Most came for the free dinner and gifts but among these, many were also prepared to enjoy the camaraderie they anticipated from sharing a holiday dinner with people they often met only at work. Festivities began as soon as the Thorntons had settled themselves on chairs by the laden Christmas tree. For about a half hour gifts were distributed to the children first by Margaret with John's help and, later, by young Thomas Boucher who Margaret spotted in the crowd, beckoned over, and asked to read out names while she and John handed out the brightly-wrapped packages.

Before long, the concatenation of children's voices drowned out the hum of adult conversations as the children played or showed off gifts to their parents and friends. Two little girls, however, were more curious about Elise than about their gifts and they approached her shyly, keeping a safe distance. By then, wide-eyed and babbling incessantly, Elise sat on her mother's lap, watching all the activity around her. Margaret smiled at the two girls. That was all one of them needed to induce her to come nearer.

"What are you saying?" She asked Elise who gaped at the children all around the room.

Margaret answered. "She is too young and cannot yet talk like you but she has her own way of saying what she wants to say."

"Will she learn to talk like me?"

"Yes, she will. She is listening to us all the time and soon she will learn to talk like we do."

The child's mother came and tugged at her child's hand. "Susan, do not bother the mistress. I am sorry Mrs. Thornton."

"It is all right. Susan was not bothering us. I like talking to her and Elise seems to enjoy having her around. How old are you Susan?"

Susan raised her five fingers far apart. Then she asked: "Your little girl's name is Elise?"

"Yes." Margaret beamed at her. "You are a smart little girl to pick up on that."

The second little girl, who had stood back, took a few steps towards them, glancing up at Margaret with every step, shy but alert to signs of disapproval. Margaret smiled at her encouragingly and the little girl continued to approach. Before long, a few more curious children joined them, gradually drawn into talking to the lady who brought them gifts and asking questions about her pretty blonde baby. The lively chatter of young children inevitably drew the older children and soon a minor commotion developed around Elise who babbled and squealed in delight at the flurry of activity around her.

The adults, at first concerned about bothering and offending their master's young family, attempted to restrain their children. But, they saw that Margaret not only did not seem to mind, she beckoned the children over with smiles and kind looks. She asked them questions, answered theirs simply and frankly, and encouraged them to talk to one another. So, the parents left their children alone. Later, after handing Elise over to Mary, she read to them from the picture books that some of the children received as gifts. She stopped after one page and, once again, motioned for Thomas to sit next to her and read the rest of the story.

Nicholas Higgins, who was engaged in lively conversation with John and a few other workers, watched Thomas with pride and said: "It was Mrs. Margaret who taught Thomas and the other children to read but Thomas is a bright one and caught on quickly. Now, he is teaching his brothers and sisters."

The lively informality of the gathering continued until Marian, who supervised the preparation of dinner, announced that it was ready to be served and everyone claimed a place at one of the tables. When all were seated, conversations were momentarily hushed as Marian opened the boxes Margaret brought. Propped up on trivets placed on the middle of each table, they served as the centerpiece. Each contained a large Christmas cake covered with creamy white frosting and adorned with green and red candied cherries. As the cakes were lifted out of the well-secured boxes, they filled the room with aromas of citrus, cloves, and brandy. Remarks about the cakes restored the vibrant buzz of conversations and enjoyment of the other festive dishes animated the entire dinner.

The first festive dinner at Marlborough Mills lasted nearly three hours. The Thorntons thought the expense and effort it took had all been worthwhile, judging from the camaraderie evident at every table, the smiles and the mumbled "thank yous" they received from workers who ordinarily shied away from talking to John, the short speeches Nicholas Higgins and the overseers gave when the cake was served, and the continuing conversation among workers who lingered around the Dining Hall long after the celebration was over. It would not be realistic to assume that everyone came away from the festivities with goodwill towards the Thorntons. A good number had come for the dinner and the gifts for the children but had remained skeptical of the Thorntons' intent. They feared that the celebration was a clever but underhanded ploy to blunt the motives for, or increase the workers' qualms about, going on strike in the future.

Later that night, John and Margaret retired into the solace of their sitting room. They had put Elise to bed together, finished a light supper in the dining room and dismissed the household help early to enjoy their own Christmas Eve dinner. Dixon protested that her master and mistress ate too little of the Christmas repast she had lovingly prepared. Margaret had to convince her that they sampled a little from every dish and found each one excellent but that they were truly full from the dinner earlier at the mill where they had partaken of the Christmas cake that Dixon baked for the occasion. Margaret firmly ended any further discussion with an order that the rest of the household should all sit down together and enjoy a Christmas dinner of very special dishes. Then, to assuage Dixon's hurt feelings further, she said more mildly: "This dinner is a wonderful gift you have given the whole household: Not only to us but to all of you who serve us."

Dixon grumbled but ordered a servant to set the long wooden table in the kitchen, cover it with a fresh white tablecloth, dress it with candle lights and a big crystal bowl of apples and oranges and gather the household for a festive meal. If a Christmas dinner was indeed her gift, she was determined to offer it in the most elegant way she could.

John and Margaret ascended their chambers after asking for after-dinner drinks to be served in their sitting room. Margaret was tired and burdened more than usual by the various layers of street dress that she had worn all day. She headed straight to her dressing room, changed into a nightgown and robe, released her luxuriant hair from restraining clips and pins, draped a shawl over her robe for extra warmth and returned to the sitting room.

A tray with cups, a carafe of mulled wine, and a plate of decorated biscuits were laid on the table, waiting to be served.

John sat on an armchair by the fireplace, reading a newspaper. Margaret took the armchair opposite, the same one where weeks ago she had shed copious tears. She felt at peace this Christmas night. The events of the day lifted her spirits and seemed to her the rewarding conclusion of the cleansing process that started with her tears.

Her face was aglow from the fire burning in the hearth and her eyes were lighted from within as she gazed at her husband. She waited for a few moments until he looked up from the paper. He regarded her for a long moment, captivated by her beauty once again. She looked at him with eyes large and brilliant from barely subdued agitation and sensuous lips parted tremulously from anticipation—he wanted to believe—of his kisses. He laid his paper aside beside the tray and smiled one of those smiles that brightened his eyes.

"I can see you are ready for a drink." She smiled back at him, but her voice quivered a little. She poured mulled wine into a cup, conscious that he watched her closely. A wave of warmth coursed through her bosom and down her whole body, infusing her cheeks with a rosy blush. She averted her eyes when they met his as she handed him a cup. She was momentarily confused, then amused at her confusion. They had been married nearly two years and he still had the power to make her blush deeply when he looked at her like that.

She was about to turn around to return to her seat when she felt his hand gently clasp her wrist. He had taken the cup she offered him with his other hand and set it back on the coffee table. Then, he kissed the inside of her wrist. Margaret gasped at the burning sensation his lips left on her skin but before she could take another deep breath, she found herself cradled on his lap while his lips pressed against hers, first lightly and then more deeply. He muttered against her cheek: "It has been a while since we have had a quiet moment like this together."

Margaret thought that it was hardly a quiet moment when she felt herself trembling deliciously inside. She wound her arms around his neck and with her face against his, she answered in a low voice, talking a little too rapidly and, she thought, a little too much. "Not since before our first party here. It seems so much has been going on with preparations for the party and, not too long after, for Christmas at the mill. This was the first big celebration I have ever organized almost single-handedly. I helped my parents a little during festive occasions at my father's parish but there were not half so many people there and different families helped with preparations and brought in dishes to share. Then there was Edith's elaborate wedding but that was all about dainty and pretty feminine touches and all I had to do was faithfully follow Edith's directions."

"I would say from the looks of it that your first attempts at organizing a big affair met with much success and left many with good memories and, I hope, some goodwill for the mill as well."

John's relatively neutral tone took the edge off of her agitation and she asked with almost naive enthusiasm: "Do you think so? The goodwill part, especially?"

"We cannot really know. But I hope so. When we masters talk about what to do to prevent strikes, none of us ever considers the value of developing good relations with workers. Not friendly necessarily but at least one that allows for and even encourages talking among masters and workers. I do think that what you did tonight made that more possible."

Margaret smiled broadly and kissed the tip of his nose lightheartedly. "I am glad I can help. Strikes are quite unfortunate, miserable for workers and a big headache for masters."

"I am afraid they are inevitable. We cannot control markets appreciably and workers are becoming more enlightened about their rights. Still, I think that we can prevent acrimonious strikes before they happen or, at least, make them less bitter when they do happen if we can get masters and hands talking to each other even about matters outside of those that concern the mill."

"If this Christmas celebration made it more likely that masters and hands talk seriously and calmly about work at the mill, do you think other things we do for workers and their families might help too?"

"Do you have something else in mind?" He smiled at her enthusiasm.

"I might but I need to think about it more. It might cost some money to do but we have hardly used profits from Mr. Bell's investment in Watson's speculation."

"Ah!"

"Is that acceptable to you? I am still not certain how you feel about money earned from risky ventures."

"I have moral objections to investing in such ventures if the capital is not my own or it rightly belongs to others who could be hurt by failed schemes."

"Mr. Bell had more wealth than he could use and he invested some into Watson's schemes. Surely if we used such profits to help others, that would be a good thing, would it not?"

"It would seem so." He answered warily. "But I cannot shake off the thought that I have no right to the money and therefore have no right to spend it even for charitable purposes."

Margaret nodded and picked up his cup. "It is getting cold. Do you still want it?"

He took the cup from her and took a sip of the wine, now lukewarm but still infused with enough spirit that it tingled as he swallowed it. "Still good."

She poured herself a cup, replenished his and returned to her chair. They sat for some minutes, sipping their wine. She broke the silence. "You have told me at least once before that you were uneasy about using the money I inherited although, legally, it is yours now, as well. I thought I understood why but there must be some other reason."

He looked at her a long moment. "Yes. Mr. Bell."

"Mr. Bell! I don't understand." Then, a suspicion percolated in her mind. "Well, maybe I do. But I think he had always known, maybe even before I admitted it to myself, that I was in love with you."

"I believe he did what he could to drive a wedge between us. He was subtle and underhanded about it. So, yes, I resented him and I wanted to punch his face more than once." He smiled in a self-mocking way before adding: "But, of course, I could not. He was my landlord."

"I thought you liked him."

"I did. In many ways, I liked him. He was one of the cleverest men I knew and it was a delight talking to him. I had no quarrel with him before you came. After that, he lost no chance to provoke me in your presence."

"You mean such as that incident at your mother's last annual dinner? He did succeed in provoking you then. You studiously avoided talking to me for the rest of the evening."

"Yes! Just when you began to think better of me."

They were both silent, sipping their wine thoughtfully. At length, he said: "My sense of pride will allow me to take money from your inheritance only as a loan to be paid back with interest. I do mean what I said about the challenge of rising on my own resources. But I am also a practical businessman so I know that if one does not have capital to do business with, he borrows it. You—on the other hand—were given this inheritance. I have no qualms about you using it for your projects. I trust your judgment."

"Are you saying that I can go ahead with whatever plans I might come up with and use profits from the speculation?"

"I suppose I am saying that. Go ahead and use it any way you wish and show me your plans and cost calculations only if you want my opinion or advice."

"Well, I must say the challenge of doing all that is exciting but scary as well. And, of course I cannot do without your opinion or your advice and I do need you to go over any cost estimates I make."

"I can teach you a thing or two about handling money that I am sure Henry Lennox did not." He was teasing but she did not reply, merely nodded and smiled.

They sat for some time, sipping more wine, nibbling on Christmas biscuits, occasionally gazing at each other. Soon, however, John remarked in a matter-of-fact tone with a hint of wistful sadness, "This is the first Christmas I am spending without both my mother and sister."

She replied casually: "It is my third without my parents."

He looked at her, a mixture of surprise and solicitude on his countenance. "I am sorry. It was thoughtless of me to forget."

"I am a little more used to my family's absence than you are to yours although I admit it sometimes makes me quite sad on holidays like this. My mother was a great believer in Christmas and always insisted on baskets tied with large gay ribbons and filled with staples for those in my father's parish who were less fortunate. I used to go around with her a week or two before

Christmas, gathering together contributions from families able and willing to share. It was the one time in the year when our home became truly colorful. We had traditional dinners that seemed more elaborate when she and my father were going through trying times." Her voice trailed to a melancholic softness and she stared pensively into space.

That was all the incentive John needed to resume the loving advances he had started earlier before talk about strikes interrupted him. He kneeled on the floor by her feet, and clasped her in his arms. She entwined her arms around his neck and laid her head on his shoulder. He whispered: "I suppose I did not think about your parents because I thought your daughter and me are now your family. We will always be here with you."

She rubbed her cheek against his then murmured against his neck, "And Elise and I, with you."

After a long moment, she slid down on the floor and sat down next to him. He had not anticipated her action but he was quick to adapt to it and he dropped effortlessly to the floor next to her, placed an arm around her shoulders, and leaned against the chair. She turned to gaze at him and caressed his cheeks with the back of her fingers. Then, she kissed him, took off his cravat, flung it on the chair, and slowly unbuttoned, first his vest, then the top part of his shirt. He sat immobile, charmed, fascinated, excited, wondering what she was going to do next. She nestled her cool cheeks against his bare neck, warm, pulsing with the steady beat of his heart, and exuding a faint agreeable smell of soap, sweat and, probably cotton dust. She wound her arms around his chest and he held her closer to him.

She thought that these were some of her favorite moments— neither of them needing words and luxuriating in the warmth and feel of their bodies close together, keenly conscious of each other's presence. He relaxed and laid his head lightly on her hair, as content as she was to stay in this attitude. He held her for a long time, occasionally pressing his lips against her hair or her cheeks. Neither of them spoke nor noticed and minded the hard floor underneath the rug they sat on and it was not until the clock struck midnight that they budged.

"Merry Christmas, my love."

She lifted her face up for his kiss before answering, her lips brushing his: "Merry Christmas, my darling. It has been a long, frenzied, wonderful day, has it not?"

"Yes and you must be tired." He said softly as he pressed his lips to hers again.

"Quite. And so, to bed?" She rose on her feet in one lithe movement, belying her claim to tiredness. "We'll have a quiet cozy Christmas day to ourselves."

He raised an amused eyebrow at her and sharing the same thought, they chuckled in unison. "Well, as peaceful as unintelligible chatter and occasional crying allow."

They descended to the drawing room late Christmas morning, with John carrying Elise and Margaret walking behind them. The large Christmas tree towered over everything in the room and the candles adorning it were already lighted. Those of the household who had not gone home for the holidays were gathered around the tree ushered there by Dixon when she heard the Thorntons coming down the stairs. A new piano stood on one corner of the room. A large sheet, thrown over it was unsuccessful in its attempt to hide or disguise it. It had not been there the day before and Margaret, guessing it was to be a surprise, said nothing.

She had bought gifts for the servants and she gave them out after Elise, with much help from her mother, tore open the ones she had received. John said nothing about the piano until everyone began to pile into the kitchen for a late Christmas breakfast, laid out on the large kitchen table. Margaret, suspecting the servants would be uncomfortable in the dining room, told Dixon to serve everyone there including the master and mistress of the house.

"That piano is too big to hide," he said wryly.

"Yes. I'm deeply touched. Thank you." She hesitated. "But I have never been good at playing."

"Perhaps. But I had more pleasure listening to you than I did to Edith despite her superior skills and since that evening, I have imagined having that pleasure repeated. Besides, Elise will have to learn when she is old enough."

That was all that was said about the new piano. Margaret returned to it that afternoon when Elise napped, the household bustle had died down, and John was in the conservatory, reading a newspaper. She took off the sheet and folded it neatly, laying it on a table nearby. She sat on the bench, opened the cover noiselessly and placed her fingers gingerly on the keys—not to play them, only to reacquaint her fingers with their springy smoothness.

Music, beautifully played, gave her great pleasure and for that reason she did not deign to play. She never thought she was good enough and was content to listen to those, like her cousin Edith, who had real mastery of the instrument. Perhaps, Elise would learn to play better than she did but that was not for a few years yet. Meantime, she could not neglect the new piano. She would have to try it out, if only in gratitude at her husband's generous gift. She did not think she could ever play as well as Edith but she was certain she could do much better with practice. If her playing gave John pleasure, that was incentive enough to spend some time learning to play better. Besides, she thought, music did give her pleasure and calmed her spirit when she was alone playing the piano. Above all, she wanted her children to grow up learning to love music. For that, she needed to bring music into her home and until Elise was able to play, she would have to be its main source.

XXIV. GROWTH

Snow fell profusely for weeks after Christmas and the Thorntons spent much of January indoors. Margaret had anticipated the need for something green and vibrant in the bleakness of a northern winter and, in late October, ordered a few pots of plants and flowers brought in from the garden. She had them placed all around the edge of the vast space of the conservatory. Dixon, taking her cue from Margaret, cultivated new pots with herbs and salad greens. Soon after, Margaret planted more pots of colorful pansies, poppies and tulips and scattered them among the greenery. By December, the conservatory was a lush indoor garden that became—with the addition of a couple of stoves at each end—the coziest and most inviting common space in the house where the family preferred to spend an afternoon. To accommodate preoccupations other than reading and conversations, Margaret replaced two large armchairs and a settee from the old house, with two new sets of four ample wicker chairs and a table. A large trunk at one corner was filled with woolen blankets and shawls that could be brought out when extra warmth was needed.

On weekends, John sometimes took home business correspondence and accounting books from the mill and worked on them at one table while Margaret wrote letters or dealt with household expenses at the other. On sunny Sundays, they had long, leisurely breakfasts there while Elise played. Except on particularly cold winter days when doors to it had to be closed, the conservatory substituted for the garden. A small space between the groupings of chairs was laid with thick rugs and secured with a small fence so that Elise would have a place in which to play. There, her tearful and happy struggles and her little antics frequently provided distraction to her parents while they rested, had breakfast or tea, or went about their work.

Elise was learning new skills and had attempted to walk by pulling herself up to a standing position and taking steps. On her first attempt, she fell and cried. Mary ran to help her but Margaret, watching from the table where she worked, told Mary to leave her alone unless she fell on any other part of her body but her buttocks.

Now that Elise was growing more independent, impatient to do things on her own, Margaret was thankful that she could summon up her experience helping Edith take care of her son, Sholto. It had taught Margaret enough about young children that she could take Elise's failed attempts in stride. She watched Elise closely but left her alone, allowing her to fail without much of a fuss, confident that Elise would try again once she was ready.

Margaret, listless at her cousin's frequent dinner parties and other indulgences of social life in London, now settled into a full busy life in Milton. She devoted her day to taking care of Elise, managing the household, and painting in her studio. Although the main task of caring for Elise fell on Mary, Margaret spent some playtime with her daughter everyday, attending to her needs in the morning and at bedtime.

By the time Elise was at her early afternoon nap, Margaret was eager for solitude in her studio, painting or sketching or, every once in a while, just thumbing through some books she brought back from Paris. She continued to work on the portrait of John and Elise, still unfinished since Christmas, when the frenzied pace leading to it claimed her attention for many weeks. The portrait was her first work on a relatively large mounted canvas. Although she had made countless sketches, including some in oils, it was taking her longer than she had thought. She had erased sections of it and corrected others a few times.

One day, in frustration, she decided to put the unfinished picture aside and start all over again. With a fresh canvas on her easel, she laid a wash of pthalo blue but she could not begin to make any mark on it. She regarded the canvas a long time, her arms leaden, unable to make the first stroke with the charcoal in her hand. In exasperation at herself, she put the charcoal back in its box, wiped her hands of stains, and walked out of her studio.

Momentarily aimless from frustration, she went into the drawing room, walked around, opened a couple of books lying on a table, and closed them without reading either. She walked around again, occasionally glancing at the gleaming mahogany expanse of the piano. Although pushed to a relatively dark corner of the room, it could not escape her attention and after passing near it a few times, she stopped and stared at it for some minutes. She had neither touched it nor even come close to it since Christmas and she approached it slowly, hesitantly. She sat down on the bench, lifted the cover carefully, ran her fingers slowly over all the keys twice and hit a few at random.

Margaret started playing the rondo she had performed with Edith the night before her wedding. Her fingers felt stiff and she made many mistakes. She repeated the first bars several times until, frustrated again, she stopped—this time because she could not remember the rest of the piece. But she was surprised to discover that, alone, with no one around to judge her, she found pleasure in playing. She loved the silky smoothness of the keys and delighted at the sounds they produced despite her certainty that, because she was playing from memory, her notes were frequently off. So, she blundered through a few more pieces she could recollect. By the time she exhausted her very limited repertoire, she resolved to devote at least an hour practicing at around the same time on days when John was at work. That evening, she wrote to Edith to select and send her some music sheets. Perhaps, she might surprise John one leisurely afternoon with an air or two.

In February, the incessant snow that came with January began to ease up but still occasionally descended upon the city. It did so in the middle of the month, agitated into renewed fury by bitterly cold wind—forcing the closing of the doors to the conservatory and the shuttering of windows all over the house. John was home since the storm forced the mill to close. In the afternoon, he and Margaret retired to read by gas lamps in their sitting room where the fire crackled—radiating heat, casting a golden glow, and suffusing the whole room in comforting warmth. It might have been a cozy calm evening but for the howling wind and the pounding snow on the roof.

It was that part of the day when the bustle of the house was at its ebb and Margaret was alone. She regarded it as her quiet hours, to spend on herself as she pleased. Often, she painted in her studio after practicing on the piano. Sometimes, she read or even did some needlework. But since the end of the holidays, she had been preoccupied, instead, with ideas brewing in her head, some of which she had begun to work on. But she was at an impasse and, on this stormy afternoon, she paced the room restlessly, unread book in hand, keeping company with her thoughts. John sat nearby, pleasantly absorbed in his journal.

At the Christmas festivities at the mill, Margaret realized—as she talked and read to the children—that if she were to do something for workers, she could start with the children. At home, while watching her daughter play, she thought about how differently her child would be brought up. Elise would have all the privileges that came with money and informed solicitous parents, particularly a mother determined to give her daughter the best education available to girls. She knew of at least one recently established school for women that provided an education nearly comparable to that of men. She knew as well that, while still rare, a few women had become doctors, scientists, painters, and writers. If her daughter desired a profession, Margaret would make sure that Elise acquired the education she needed.

Opportunities open to Elise were sadly unimaginable to the children at the mill. While Margaret knew she could not offer them the same, she could help improve their chances at a better life. But she was uncertain how much she could commit herself to, with responsibilities to her husband and her daughter. She thought of young Thomas. Perhaps, she could start there. The expense of sending Thomas to a boarding school for boys would hardly put a dent on their investment earnings but would be one of its most worthwhile uses. Nicholas could be convinced to spare Thomas from having to work at the mill if a much brighter future awaited him.

But Margaret was not satisfied: She had to do more for the children. Amidst the jumble of her ideas, she remembered Bessy Higgins who probably died from want of care for a malady contracted as a child working at a mill. In lamenting Bessy's plight, Margaret began to believe it to be the master's moral obligation to make care available for free to workers with maladies stemming from mill work. The more she thought about it, the more convinced she was that medical care was what the mill needed most.

She asked Dr. Donaldson to tea one afternoon. The doctor, always happy to fit the young Mrs. Thornton's invitations into his busy schedule, freely shared his opinions and endorsed her enthusiasm. He gave her useful information about doctor's fees, medicines, equipment and other supplies that she needed to calculate the costs of holding a clinic within mill premises.

Margaret had what she needed to lay some plans. She wanted them ready before talking to John. Some decisions remained to be made—where and how to set up a clinic, what hours to open, and how to find a doctor willing to provide care at the mill. Considering the scarcity of doctors, Margaret thought the last task the most daunting.

The medical clinic was Margaret's priority but she could not give up the idea that children should be taught to read and write. But she suspected that very few parents would bother to take their children to lessons—even those forbidden by law to work. Free medical care, she knew, would be welcomed. But illiterate parents, confronted with more immediate needs compelling children to work, would be hard to convince that reading and writing were essential. Work in mills or other factories did not require them.

That stormy afternoon, Margaret decided to talk to John only about her plans for the medical clinic. Before she could say anything, John looked up from his journal and asked: "Is this dreary day making you restless?"

He had never seen her this way and it distracted him from his reading. She was often content to read, write letters, or plan and review household expenses while he read his journals or did some mill-related work.

"Yes, this weather is getting to me. I have not gone beyond the walls of this house for more than a month."

"We are having a spell of bad weather and if this keeps up, I may have to close the mill again tomorrow."

"Are you behind in completing orders?" She asked as she walked by him.

"A little. We can handle it. I am probably now seeing some results from all the changes we have made. More and more workers are willing to stay and catch up."

She stopped pacing and sat down on the sofa. "Wonderful!" Her tone was lively but distracted.

"Yes. I told the workers that we might need to open two or three Sundays to fully catch up. Higgins canvassed how many would come, with pay, of course. Practically everyone said they would. That says a lot because Sundays are sacred, the one day they have for rest and recreation. Most would not give those up, even with pay." His voice was animated, his eyes glowed from within.

Margaret caught her breath, swept into the wave of pride and gratification that seized him as he talked. He paused and she waited.

"I realized when Higgins told me the results of his canvassing that the mill is not just a factory that produces cotton. The mill is really more the people who work there and that without them, we could not make cotton. The mill would just be a lot of machines sitting idle."

"That was what I saw on the day I came back to Milton, a sad, desolate place with big silent machines." She smiled, pleased at his insight.

"That desolate atmosphere was already there right after the workers left on the day we closed." He said sadly and was thoughtful again for a minute or two.

"I told you early in our acquaintance that my responsibility was the efficient running of the mill and anything outside of that was not my concern. That is still true when it comes to how workers spend their money or what they do outside the mill. But I am now persuaded that I must take some interest in their general well-being since it affects how well they work. You showed me that."

She exclaimed: "Me? But how?"

"Williams told me that since Christmas, efficiency is up. It has helped keep us from being too far behind schedule despite mill closings caused by severe weather. It must be what you did for the mill on Christmas."

"Well, I would like to think I helped but I believe the decision you made in their favor was not lost on them. They appreciate how you agonized about asking your mother to stop coming to the mill. I am sure Nicholas made them fully aware of that."

He nodded with a satisfied smile. "Yes, he has been an ally—the terrific firebrand all the other masters are leery of has been a helpful bridge between me and the workers."

He put his journal on the side table and sat next to her on the sofa. "Listen and do not distract me from what I wanted to do—tell you how grateful I am for the many different ways you have helped." He took the book she was still holding and placed it on the tea table. He clasped her hands and pressed each one to his lips.

"Thank you," he murmured simply, gazing at her with soft smiling eyes.

Calmer now, she leaned against him and laid her head on his shoulder. He held her close.

At length, she looked up at him. "I must take advantage of your good mood and ask you something I have been mulling over for weeks now."

"Go on." Then, teasing her a little, he added: "I am ready to acquiesce to anything you ask."

She straightened and said: "I want to start a medical clinic, mainly for the sake of mill children but it will serve every worker who comes to it."

He smiled broadly. "You have been mulling! That would be a big step, a very big one. But I think it the best possible way to help workers. Even Mr. Bell might agree it is a worthwhile use of profits from his investments."

She smiled, pleased that he approved. "Well, you knew Dr. Donaldson was here twice for tea about a week ago. We talked about my plans. Dr. Hartley came, too, the second time."

A scowl flitted across John's forehead and he listened, warily. Margaret continued, choosing her words carefully. "Dr. Donaldson thought I had a good idea and knew, from our first meeting, that I was worried about finding a doctor for the clinic. Dr. Hartley came to offer his services for half his usual fees two afternoons a week. That may not be enough but it is a start. Now, I have to talk to you about where we can hold the clinic and finding someone who could assist him and, perhaps, provide nursing care even on days the doctor is not around."

"The smitten Dr. Hartley could not say no to you. I heard that he is rather busy, much sought after and not only for his medical skills. Yet, he finds the time to help here." John sounded irritated.

"You are not going to be jealous, are you? You know I would never do anything to encourage him."

"No, you would not." He scowled again. "The problem is the good doctor does not need your encouragement. Your idea about the clinic was probably all he needed to cement his ardor. Blast these Americans with their pioneering spirit and enthusiasm for equal treatment for all."

"John, you do not mean that."

"No. In fact, I admire them; they embrace modernity more than many of our noble parliamentarians." He paused, then grinned mischievously. "You gave me just the right incentive to help you. I suspect the doctor hopes you would volunteer to assist him, if only temporarily. I will help you find him an assistant. As for space, what about my old office or the dining hall? They are usually free most afternoons."

He paused again and smiled wickedly, another idea hatching in his mind. "I have a better idea. We will clear and close off an area for him next to my new office. We have a large space there. That way, he does not have to worry about his instruments and medicines and he can choose any time and any day to work."

"That is a better choice, I think. We can open all day with a doctor's assistant and even expand services later." She reached over, pulled his face next to hers and kissed him. "Now it is my turn. Thank you, my love, for you," she whispered, grateful for his open-mindedness and his good humor, flattered by his jealousy, and wonderfully surprised by the influence she had over him.

Mrs. Thornton returned in the spring with Watson. He took her directly from the train station to a renovated flat on the top floor of the mill house. The large bedroom that John and Margaret had occupied was divided into her bedroom and sitting room. The flat also had a drawing room, an extra bedroom, kitchen, dining room and a bedroom for Jane. It was repainted or re-papered, hung with new curtains in Mrs. Thornton's preferred colors, and furnished and decorated as before.

Margaret and John, Elise in his arms, were in the drawing room, waiting with tea, tiny cakes and sandwiches that Dixon had especially prepared. Margaret approached first, giving her mother-in-law a brief welcoming hug. To Margaret's surprise, Mrs. Thornton hugged her back and whispered a sincere "Thank you."

John and Elise followed right behind Margaret. He kissed his mother on the cheek and said: "Give grandmama a kiss, Elise." The child looked at her grandmother and turned away, hiding her face on her father's shoulder.

Mrs. Thornton, surprised at being addressed "grandmama," remarked wryly: "She has probably forgotten me. I have been away six months, half her life."

Elise raised her head, looked towards her mother and extended her arms out. "Mama."

Mrs. Thornton said: "Oh, she is talking already, is she? But she cannot be one year old yet!"

"Just a few words," John replied as he handed his daughter back to his wife. "The usual. Mama and Papa, of course. No, yes. Clap. She learned that because she likes to clap. Her first birthday is early next week so you're home in time for it."

In her mother's arms, the child grew bolder, looked at her grandmother again, smiled and putting her hands together, said: "Clap!"

Mrs. Thornton returned the smile and clapped. Margaret, pleasantly astonished once again, smiled warmly at her mother-in-law and then at her husband.

Mrs. Thornton was glad to be back to the familiar smells, sounds, and places in Milton. In London, she hardly ever went out. Fanny required her attention constantly and during much of winter, the weather kept everyone within. Mrs. Thornton had time then to think. Her last talk with John convinced her that if he had to make a choice, he would choose his wife over his mother. It was a crushing realization she struggled to accept.

The Watson household was different from the one she left in Milton. It ran fairly smoothly despite Fanny who was inept and clumsy, falling apart at the smallest problems. The servants were properly trained and Watson employed a middle-aged, competent personal maid who was at Fanny's disposal all day, advising her on what to do when problems arose in the household.

Mrs. Thornton thought Watson a good match for her daughter. He had been proud of snatching a "price" in the young, pretty, and vivacious Miss Thornton, nearly half his age. She did not have as much settled on her as other women he might have chosen but he was himself very rich, a fact that he knew greatly favored his acceptance. Once married, he was good-humored, patient, and gentle, indulging Fanny's whims and expressed desires, and even encouraging her feminine frailties.

Still, Mrs. Thornton could not help wondering if, underneath Watson's affection for his wife, lay some underlying contempt that he might not admit to himself. She had, on occasion, seen an expression in his eyes very near that sentiment, often accompanied by a fleeting scowl and a clenching of his jaw when Fanny could not grasp what he was saying or asking her to do.

By contrast, Mrs. Thornton remembered the great mutual attachment between Margaret and John, the sort one had for someone outside of oneself and which she doubted her daughter was capable of. Margaret and John had an ease and openness which, to Mrs. Thornton, meant that they would rarely hesitate to let each other know what they felt and thought. Above all, what they uniquely had was passion. She could see it in how they looked at each other, how they touched, how they talked, and she was certain, how they quarreled and made love. She never saw anything akin to it between Watson and Fanny nor, in fact, among other couples in her acquaintance. She herself had it for the first few months of her marriage but it quickly wore out. Why, she could no longer recall but she did have memories—vague now—of those months being the closest to heaven she had been on earth.

Eventually, Mrs. Thornton understood that marriage did not interest John before Margaret because he had not met anyone who could match his capacity for loving and living. With this understanding, Mrs. Thornton thought she finally saw in Margaret what John had seen in her. She was now more determined to try to like Margaret, however uncertain she was that she would ever understand her. Such was Mrs. Thornton's frame of mind when she returned.

April started with a happy celebration of Elise's first birthday to which the Thorntons had invited a few children from the neighborhood and from among the families of John's colleagues. The large conservatory was decorated for a tea party and a table prominently graced with a birthday cake was set in one corner. In the adjacent dining room, refreshments for adults were laid out.

Mrs. Thornton sat in one corner of the room watching the celebration. She had luncheon with John and Margaret as well as Edith and Captain Lennox who arrived by train a few days earlier with their son Sholto and his nanny. Edith came to help Margaret prepare and celebrate. Watson, Elise's godfather, scheduled a meeting in Milton around the day of the party. Fanny, wary of traveling a couple of months after delivery and anxious to make the most of her residence in London, sent her excuses. John had also expressly asked Nicholas Higgins to bring the Boucher children to the party but Higgins very gratefully, yet firmly and politely, declined the invitation.

Dr. Hartley came when the party was nearly over. After greeting his young patient and handing her a gift, he was whisked by his host to the dining room to partake of the spread there. After coaxing the doctor to try some hors d'ouevres, John started some small talk that lasted while the doctor ate. When Dr. Hartley finished, John poured more drinks for the two of them and led Dr. Hartley to the relative quiet of the drawing room.

"I wanted to talk to you about the medical clinic. I think it is wonderful and noble of you to agree to serve in this clinic at half your usual fee. I hear from everyone that you are quite busy, much sought after."

Dr. Hartley replied with a slight frown at the meaning implied in John's remark. "Not that busy. I do have the time and it is the right thing to do to offer medical care where work poses health hazards."

"My wife, as you know, is extremely grateful to you and, on her request, I have put some men to work on a clinic space for you next to my office. It will be used for nothing else."

"That is very generous considering that I will only be opening the clinic twice a week."

"Margaret—my wife, that is—hopes to be able to find more people to help. I believe she is thinking you could train someone to provide other services that would not absolutely nor immediately require a doctor."

"Mrs. Thornton is a rather remarkable woman, Mr. Thornton."

"My mother? Do you think so? In what way?"

Dr. Hartley stared at John, surprised and unable to respond right away. He suspected that his host knew exactly who he was referring to but had chosen to appear to misunderstand his meaning. He answered self-consciously and with a blush: "I meant Margaret, your wife."

"Oh, Mrs. Margaret Thornton! Yes, I have been uncommonly fortunate." John smiled broadly and looked at the doctor for a long moment, his eyes steady, inscrutable. Then, he continued: "Still, there is a thing or two my remarkable wife can learn about Milton folk."

Dr. Hartley, somewhat disconcerted, regarded him earnestly. John smiled, his eyes now twinkling with mirth. "Oh, nothing too serious. In fact, anyone not from around here, could learn from what I am about to suggest you do."

"Should we not ask Mrs. Thornton, your wife, that is, to be here to hear this?"

"We should," John said as he turned in the direction of the conservatory where the chatter of children was drowning out the voices of Margaret and Edith. "But she is quite busy at the moment, I'm afraid. I can talk to her later. I see her all the time but I may not have another chance to talk to you again for a while."

Dr. Hartley could only nod. John explained the necessity of charging a fee, even a nominal one, for medical services the doctor would provide. Milton citizens would expect to pay. Otherwise, they would question and would neither appreciate nor respect the doctor's skills and knowledge. It was a peculiarity of the local character that needed to be observed. Dr. Hartley did not question John's suggestion—in any case, it sounded more like a command—and the two proceeded to discuss what constituted a nominal fee and when the clinic should start.

John ended their discussion with a parting comment. "Of course, all that we've talked about is tentative. The final decisions on this rest with my wife. After all, this is her project although it is essentially a service to Marlborough Mills. I expect she will talk to you about final plans."

Dr. Hartley left the party feeling discontented. He had expected the pleasure of talking to Margaret again. But he did not see her after her initial welcome, thanking him for coming and bringing a gift. It was clear what John Thornton had communicated without actually saying a word about it. If he had any hope at all that Margaret might cast an interested eye at him, Mr. Thornton would be there, vigilant, dashing any hopes he might have had. He could not help wondering if she had some inkling of how he felt about her. If John Thornton could see it, she probably could, too. More than anything, it was this thought that depressed him. Margaret, though gracious, had always been decorous, even formal, in her manner with him and she clearly adored her husband and child. With a sigh, Dr. Hartley resigned himself to admiring the young Mrs. Thornton in silence.

That night, Margaret remarked as she and John were getting into bed. "I am exhausted from attending to all those children. Two or three I can manage but more than a dozen with half of them below five is quite a lot of work."

"Would you do it again?"

She laughed. "Why, of course. It does not follow that if it is exhausting, it is not enjoyable. I cannot do what teachers do daily with a roomful of them but an occasional party for children has its rewards."

"My remarkable wife!" He chuckled, kissing her forehead, drawing her close as she snuggled in his arms.

"What is so remarkable about exhausting myself, trying to make 20 children happy?"

"Dr. Hartley thinks so although he did say it on account of the medical clinic."

"You took up all of the good doctor's time. I looked in on you briefly and you two looked quite absorbed in serious conversation."

"Why did you not come in and join us?"

"I could not leave Edith alone with so many children and, anyway I only had a moment to spare. Actually, a few of the young mothers complained that you had taken him away and you made a few of them unhappy. They wanted to talk with him as well. It seems Dr. Hartley is quite the ladies' man. What could you two have been talking about?"

"The medical clinic, of course. I told him about the rooms we were preparing for the clinic." John went on to recount nearly all that he and Dr. Hartley talked about except for their brief repartée about her.

"I think a nominal fee is a good idea. It shows responsibility over the care of their health." Margaret agreed when he finished. "But what if someone who needs a doctor's care cannot pay?"

"I thought about that." John answered thoughtfully. "Perhaps, we can set up a way for that person to pay gradually. I imagine we will pay the doctor's fees no matter what. The nominal fees can go into a reserve fund from which they can borrow. I should talk to Henry Lennox. He is getting quite a reputation in financial circles and now spends half his time here since his marriage. We could have him look through your plans for the clinic."

"A reserve fund seems a good idea and talking to Henry would probably help. When do you suppose we can start the clinic?"

"I imagine in about a couple of months. The workers are putting up a wall for the doctor's examining room. Then, there is clean-up and after that medical equipment can be brought in."

"I have a list of medical furniture and supplies but I have to ask Dr. Donaldson where to order them."

"Well, then, it seems you are about to have your medical clinic."

Margaret wound her arms around him and laid her head on his shoulder. "You are a treasure and I should thank Hannah for raising you the way she did."

Not long after, Margaret found someone eager to train as a nurse under Dr. Hartley. Catherine, younger sister of the governess to a neighbor's children, was seeking employment. She had initially sought work as a governess but jumped at the opportunity of learning some new skills and helping the handsome young American doctor. In fact, Margaret discovered that many a young daughter of John's colleagues would have seized an opportunity to work side by side with the universally admired doctor if they did not think it beyond their dignity to work.

Catherine was sturdily built, plainly dressed, and quite lady-like in bearing and manner. Her pretty features were not easily evident, masked by freckles on an otherwise clear skin and by the way she pulled her straight reddish hair back in a tight bun. It did not help her looks that her intelligent eyes focused, hawk-like, on the person she was talking to. Margaret thought it gave her an air of being purposeful and efficient. Margaret interviewed her one afternoon in John's office, liked her immediately, and, after a half-hour, knew she was right for the job. Although the final decision rested on Dr. Hartley, Margaret—by now acknowledging her influence on the doctor—did not doubt that Catherine was as good as hired.

Curious about Catherine's origins, Margaret engaged her in casual conversation when she finished with questions pertaining to the job. She learned that Catherine was Irish and her father, finding a better-paying job, moved his family to England when she was a child. Her father had an older brother who inherited the family farm that he tended with his own family and two energetic spinster sisters who Catherine talked about with both pride and indulgence. Catherine liked talking to Mr. Thornton's wife, barely two years older than she. She knew that Margaret Thornton had already gained some notoriety within the gossiping families of manufacturers for her southern ways and origins and her exertions on behalf of workers. The young Mrs. Thornton, she also knew, received the greater part of the blame for what they saw as the change in Mr. Thornton. The two women both parted from their meeting with a desire to further their acquaintance.

XXV. COMFORT

Something quite significant happened in the third year of John and Margaret's married life, at least in Margaret's reckoning. It started out full of pleasant little surprises when they decided to celebrate the end of their two years together with a short trip to Helstone and the Southampton coast as spring was giving way to summer. They could not agree, at first, about whether to leave Elise at home in the care of Mary and Dixon or take Elise and Dixon with them.

"It will be all right to leave her here. It is only a week, after all. What harm could happen?" John asserted.

"I don't know but I cannot help feeling uneasy about it." Margaret looked hesitant.

"Did you not tell me that you rely on Dixon's general good judgment and that she helped your mother care for you and Frederick?"

"I have no doubt Dixon will be solicitous, as will Mary so I am not certain exactly why I am apprehensive. I just am." Margaret lapsed into thoughtful silence, recalling the misery of being taken away from everything she was attached to and was familiar with when she first went to live with Edith and Aunt Shaw. She was arguably older then and understood the reasons she was sent away. Still, those reasons were never enough to console her those first few weeks of crying and feeling abandoned. More upsetting in her experience, however, was watching the Boucher children, at least three of whom were below five years of age, after their mother just died.

"Perhaps, I am still haunted by the Boucher children. They cried for days when their mother died. They were too young to know what death was, but seemed to realize that she was not coming back. But they asked for her, anyway. Nothing I could do, that anyone tried to do, could console them. It was heartrending."

"But, my love, those were different circumstances. One week will go by so fast that neither you nor Elise would even notice."

"Elise will know I am not there. She is too young yet, too dependent on me. We have never been separated and I can easily imagine her crying or fretting the whole time we are away."

John was growing exasperated and decided to say no more. Margaret sensed his irritation. She conceded, in her mind, that he was probably right and that, perhaps, she just did not trust the care of her infant daughter to servants. Dixon was solicitous enough and did help her mother considerably in caring for her and Frederick but she had an impatient streak not entirely suited to the continuous care of a helpless infant. Mary was conscientious but inexperienced and needed much direction.

"Perhaps, Dixon might like returning to Helstone for a visit." Margaret ended their argument with a shrug of the shoulders. "I am going to my studio to paint."

Mrs. Thornton resolved their disagreement in a manner neither John nor Margaret ever anticipated. Shortly after Mrs. Thornton moved to the old mill house, John insisted on her having dinner at their house on Friday evenings. On the first such Friday, he and Margaret asked her to stay the night and through Saturday. Mrs. Thornton, making good on her resolve to be nicer to Margaret, allowed herself to be persuaded.

The suite of rooms that had been hers when she lived in the house had not been converted for any other use. The drapery and wall coverings had been left as they were and the bedroom and sitting room furniture had been replaced only with the barest minimum. The bedroom had a bed, a night table, a dressing table and its matching chair while the sitting room was furnished with only a divan, a coffee table and a writing table and chair placed perpendicular to a window looking out onto the garden. The spare furnishings would appear to have mitigated against comfort. But the bed had been covered in rose-colored, sumptuous linens of silk and down that belonged to Mrs. Hale and when Mrs. Thornton lay down on them, they felt like a warm caress on her skin. When she awoke the following morning, she realized she slept more soundly than she had ever done while living in the house.

After breakfast, instead of ascending straight to her sitting room as she used to do, she joined the young family in the conservatory. She sat on a wicker chair by one of the tables, watching Margaret and John play with Elise. Not long after, Mary took over the care of Elise and her parents proceeded to work on individual tasks at separate tables. John joined his mother at her table. Not inclined to read and devoid of her needlework, Mrs. Thornton continued to watch Elise at play. Elise soon tired of the toys that she had been offered and, curious about a relatively unfamiliar person in the room, she approached Mrs. Thornton in her slow childish waddle, stood next to her, and raised her arms to be picked up. Mary, just behind a few steps, was about to take Elise away but Mrs. Thornton raised her hand to stop Mary and told her to lift Elise up to her lap. Uncertain what to do next, Mrs. Thornton asked Mary for a book to read to the child. Later, all three of them went for a walk in the garden, leaving John and Margaret in the conservatory.

By the third week, everyone assumed, Mrs. Thornton was going to stay the weekend. From then on, spending such Saturdays with her son's family became a habit for Mrs. Thornton. She began to nurture a real affection for Elise who was bright and alert and whose round blue eyes, very much like her mother's, were expressive and curious. They were beautiful eyes, Mrs. Thornton thought one day, this child's and Margaret's. The thought startled her and made her look in the direction of her daughter-in-law who was then reading an apparently humorous book to John who was laughing as he went through some mill accounts. Once again, she saw the two wrapped up in each other, seemingly oblivious of their surroundings.

Mrs. Thornton was struck by how much John had changed. He was actually busier and more involved in the mill now but, at home, he was relaxed, gentle, funny, and openly affectionate towards his wife. Somewhere and sometime during the two years or so that he had been married, he had let go of that reserve Mrs. Thornton thought was natural to the Thorntons and even the women they married, at least until Margaret. She also saw, as if for the first time, that Margaret was indeed quite beautiful especially when she looked at John with radiant eyes and a tender smile on her lips. In those moments, she was utterly bewitching and Mrs. Thornton thought that if this was how John saw Margaret, then it was no wonder he seemed so smitten with his wife.

Mrs. Thornton felt a pang of remorse for her past resentment towards Margaret. She did not deny that Margaret continued, at least occasionally, to make her feel left out, alone and totally supplanted but now, she allowed that her daughter-in-law never deliberately did anything to do so, that it was not her fault John was sometimes so completely absorbed in her that he was oblivious of his mother. It was thus that the transformation of Mrs. Thornton's attitude towards Margaret actually began. By the time John told his mother he and Margaret intended to visit Helstone and the adjoining coast on their second anniversary, Mrs. Thornton was more agreeably predisposed towards Margaret.

At dinner on a Friday evening, two weeks before the projected trip, John started the usual conversation by informing his mother of the trip.

"Are you taking Elise with you?"

John looked at his wife. "Margaret is apprehensive about leaving her alone with Dixon and Mary but I am insisting on having my wife to myself for one week. What harm could happen in such a short period?"

Margaret smiled and shrugged. "We have not decided with certainty about what to do."

"I understand how Margaret feels. She has strong maternal instincts with which I am familiar and which you, being a man, can never know about."

John and Margaret, both pleasantly surprised, simultaneously stared at her. Mrs. Thornton smiled at them mildly, amused at their reaction. Then, she said to Margaret: "I can stay and supervise her care while you're gone. Will you be more at ease with that?"

"Yes, why, yes!" Margaret, even more startled at this offer, broke into a broad smile, her eyes suddenly moist. She was too overcome, her maternal anxieties quelled by the unexpected kindness and generosity of her mother-in-law. She did not pause then to consider that this arrangement did not change the possibility that her daughter might fret and cry over her mother's absence. Despite their differences, Margaret did not doubt that Mrs. Thornton's gifts and skills at mothering were at least equal to, if not better, than her own. In any case, it had not been lost on her that Elise and her grandmother were steadily growing fond of each other.

"I cannot take care of her the way you do. She is too heavy for me to lift and carry but I have led her by the hand as we walked in the garden and if Mary puts her on my lap, I can read to her. I would certainly be happy to stay here while you are away and with Mary and Dixon, we can make sure she is content and properly cared for."

John looked at his mother with grateful smiling eyes. "It seems mother just put an end to our argument."

"Yes," was all Margaret could utter in a slightly quivering voice. She turned towards Mrs. Thornton with eyes moister than before. "Thank you!"

Mrs. Thornton nodded, embarrassed by the couple's expression of sincere gratitude. She was touched, ready to express the kindlier regard towards Margaret that she finally gave herself permission to cultivate. It surprised her how tranquil and easy she was to have at least some regard supplant hatred and jealousy. That night, she went to sleep, at peace, in her old room, pleased with herself for finally seeing Margaret as she really was.

That same night, as soon as they gained the privacy of their room, Margaret buried her face on John's shoulders. He clasped her close, caressing her back as little convulsions shook her upper body and her tears wet his shirt. He had watched her when his mother offered to stay with Elise and knew it took Margaret all her self-control to prevent her tears from coming. Across the two years they had been married, he learned that his wife had the strange habit of crying when she was both grateful and happy. Yet, she could also hold her tears back tenaciously when she was hurt and angry—emotions betrayed by her eyes which either flashed fiercely or was clouded with sorrow.

John stayed silent through her tearful happy outburst, kissing her wet face occasionally. Eventually, she calmed down, raised her head, gave him her half-smile, and without a word, walked slowly to her dressing room to prepare for bed. She looked back at him and the words "I love you" broke from her lips without a sound. Then, she disappeared into her dressing room.

When John went to bed, Margaret was already there, peacefully asleep. He gazed at her for a moment before he climbed in, snuggled close, and went to sleep.

John and Margaret did not talk about that Friday night conversation with Mrs. Thornton until they had been on their trip for a few days and had left Helstone. On a leisurely walk along the coast, Margaret brought the matter up. "I had always hoped Hannah would learn to accept me, if not actually like me, as your wife. I did not expect that she would ever show me any affection. My only hope when she came back from London was that we could tolerate each other well enough. When she sided with me that night and smiled at me with such gentleness, I was incredulous. Incredulous and grateful."

John smiled warmly but did not reply. They walked for some distance before Margaret spoke again. "Do you suppose she will consent to coming back to live with us? She and Elise seem to have developed a special closeness."

John smiled indulgently and with some amusement at his wife's childlike trust. "Did it not occur to you, my sweet little wife that, perhaps, she can be more generous with her affection because she lives in her own house where she can once again rule? I think tension will return at home if she returns."

"You are probably right but I am still in awe of how events have turned out. I thought that when she returned from London, she might be more favorably disposed towards me but her attitude has changed beyond anything I ever hoped for. I have often wondered whether something happened in London."

He looked at her thoughtfully but did not answer until after they had walked some distance. "If you must know, mother and I did have some sort of confrontation on the afternoon I left London."

Margaret glanced curiously at him and looked away. She had, in fact, suspected as much.

"She wanted me to understand why she said so many harsh hurtful things to you. She assumed you had told me about them."

Margaret was silent. She stared resolutely at the footsteps left by those who had strolled along the same path, still intact in the sand, resistant to the waves that swept over them.

He recounted in detail what transpired between him and his mother, concluding: "I told her I did understand how she felt and why she might have said those things to you but I also told her very emphatically that she would be taking my happiness, my main reason for living away from me if her words caused you to leave me. I am sure that made her think hard."

Margaret stayed silent and they continued their walk at a slower pace. Memories of the confrontation with Mrs. Thornton still pained her, and for some moments, it marred the regard she had started to feel for her mother-in-law. Then, she reminded herself that nothing but distress, unhappiness, and confusion attended such recollections and, anyway, was it not pleasanter to dwell instead on what she meant to John?

Farther into their walk, Margaret said: "It is not going to be that easy to make me leave you."

"You did consider going to London to ease the tension with my mother. That bothered me immensely. Was that shortly after that unfortunate encounter?"

Margaret paused in her steps and reached up to caress his cheeks. "How long do you suppose can I stay away from you? The night you were in London, I slept fitfully and kept reaching out to where you usually lie."

John grasped her hand, pressed it to his lips, and in a tone hoarse and contrite, said: "Words are not enough to express how sorry I am about my mother's cruel words to you."

She smiled tremulously and kissed the hand that grasped hers. They stood, gazing at each other. "Let's not dwell on it. The day is too beautiful and we only have a day left to enjoy the coast."

He nodded, placed his arm around her shoulders, and they resumed their walk.

The trip to Helstone meant much to Margaret. Her last visit three years ago with Mr. Bell had not been entirely pleasant. It reminded her too painfully of people who had been most dear to her but who she had lost. She was convinced, at the time, that she would never want to return and would have to content herself with her memories of Helstone. Later, on looking back, she realized that wounds from the loss of people she cared for and the love she was too inexperienced and too proud to reciprocate still pestered, affecting her perceptions of the village. But time once more wrought changes, happy ones which gave her hope that visiting Helstone with John would bring back at least some of the old pleasures the place gave her. Margaret wanted to show John where she grew up but, in her heart, she knew this journey was for herself, too—her attempt to rekindle deep sentiments that had strayed.

She took him through the many paths she used to walk; the stumps of trees and grassy mounds she had sat on as she did sketches of the scenery; the secret nooks that she and Frederick used to hide in; the spots where hedgerows of roses used to grow; and even neighborhoods she had visited with her mother on parish business.

She wanted him to see and feel what growing up in Helstone was like for her—to step on a thick carpet of grass, so rare in Milton, and have it release an herbal fragrance that lingered on her shoes and the hem of her skirt; to catch her breath as bright red poppies swayed gracefully with the breeze that also cooled her cheeks; to listen to the music the wind made with the grass, the trees, and everything else in its path; to keep discovering pieces of nature in all its varied beauty. On one of their walks, a well-trodden path parishioners took to the church and the parson's house, they happened upon the hedgerow of roses John found on his first visit to Helstone and from which he plucked the rose he offered her. She had missed those bushes on the walk with Mr. Bell.

The parson's house was the only social visit they planned in Helstone. John recollected having walked by it before. It was the largest house in the village on the south edge of town. Margaret had written the parson, informing him she was coming with her husband. When they arrived, tea was waiting and the parson's wife received them with more than the usual courtesy accorded to relative strangers.

Margaret was curious to see how the parson and his wife would react when she introduced John as someone born and bred in an industrial city in the north where he was now a manufacturer of cotton. Recalling the remark the parson's wife made about the wild north, Margaret felt a perverse delight in presenting her husband, looking tranquil and nobler in his countenance and bearing than the parson ever could. It amused her that the couple and even their children treated John with deference often accorded to landed gentry. As they were having tea, the parson offered them a room in the house during their stay, apologizing for the modesty of the accommodations. John and Margaret politely and graciously declined. They had already checked into an inn in town.

After tea, Margaret requested the parson's wife for a look around the house. Although the house had been extensively renovated to accommodate the present parson's much larger family, Margaret thought he could still get a general idea of where the Hales gathered for daily activities and where there had been a piano that she reluctantly practiced on. She was grateful to see her old room still intact and she could show him where she read her books and did her lessons as well as where she cried her heart out at night when she had been chastised. After taking him on walks to experience the idyllic landscapes of Helstone, the Parsonage visit was intended to give him a glimpse into country living.

When they were walking back to town, John asked: "Why was there that wicked twinkle of in your eyes while we were having tea?"

She smiled broadly as she recalled the mixture of surprise, embarrassment, and eagerness to please on the countenance of both the parson and his wife when she introduced John. "On my last visit here three years ago, I nearly lost my temper when the parson's wife insinuated that I had become wild in my ideas because I had lived in the north where life was "more wild.""

"I see. I was the specimen from the north to prove them wrong."

"Well, yes, I wanted to show them how ignorant they were of Northerners. That was all incidental, of course. Primarily, I wanted you to see where I grew up. You have always told me you wanted to know all you could about my life here. The house is much altered but enough was left of what it had been to give you a glimpse into my childhood."

"I had a rather pleasant, illuminating visit and I thought it generous of the parson to welcome us to his house for that purpose." He turned towards her, his eyes teasing. "How did I do as a specimen?"

"Admirably, of course," she replied, her lips in a slight pout as she felt somewhat chastised. "You are mocking me a little for laughing at their ignorance and you think it insolent of me to do so after their kind reception."

"No, you were not at all insolent. One can easily see how sincere your gratitude was to them when we parted but I do not often condone laughing at ignorance."

Margaret was silent for a couple of minutes before she answered with some defiance in her voice. "You were not here three years ago when the parson criticized my father's questioning of church policies and declared ignorance better than all that "book learning"—those were his very words and the very idea his wife called wild."

John was taken aback but did not answer until they were near the inn. He stopped and turned to face her. "I am sorry. I do not agree with that type of ignorance. We cannot know everything but I believe we must learn all we can in matters of conscience and faith."

Margaret nodded but said nothing. He gazed at her with contrition in his eyes. She looked even more beautiful in the clear and mellow southern light. Her ivory skin had a bright velvety cast and her eyes were an even deeper blue. There were so many times in the past when he disagreed with and even disapproved of her ideas but later realized she had a good reason for them. He had wanted to apologize afterwards, admit she was right, and take her in his arms to kiss away her hurt look or her displeasure. Before that fateful day at the train station, he did not have the right to do so. He did all those now as they stood on the street. There were but a few people passing them by but he did not doubt that they watched, particularly because he was kissing the old parson's daughter, one of their own. He found, upon arrival in Helstone, that many townspeople still remembered the Hales, even after so many years absence, and were glad to see Miss Hale come for a visit.

He wondered if his spontaneous gesture of affection offended southern sensibilities but he did not care. People were not so different. In a northern city like Milton, people might not openly express either offense or shock but they would gossip and, if the kissing couple was not married, the gossip could be the ruin of the lady's reputation. John placed an arm around Margaret's shoulders and led her towards the inn in silence.

They stopped outside the inn. "Will they think us wild for kissing in the open?"

"Yes!" She answered with an impish smile. "But we are from the north. We have an excuse."

When they sat down to dinner at the inn on their last evening in Helstone, Margaret seemed both pensive and wistful. "I thought I would never come back here. My previous visit was too sad because many of my illusions were destroyed and the associations of this place with my parents were too vivid and too painful."

"So, why did you come back?"

"I have faith that time heals wounds. Besides, that time, I also despaired that I had sunk in your opinion. I thought if I came with you, I would have new and pleasant memories."

His face lighted up into a smile of serene happiness at her admission of his influence on her. "Did my opinion matter that much to you?"

She did not answer but wrinkled her nose up at him. His regarded her with a mischievous twinkle in his eyes.

"I suppose it was only fair that you were suffering the same way I was. Did you ever imagine the agony I went through thinking that you could never be mine? That would have been about the same time."

Their dinner of perfectly roasted chicken and boiled, buttered vegetables arrived, claiming their full attention, eliciting praises about how fresh and colorful the vegetables looked and how much tastier everything was. A dessert of freshly-picked berries and cream followed and dinner came to an end with tea.

"I rather like it here. Perhaps, we can get a country house here. It is not far from Milton, only four hours by train."

"You do intend to enjoy the fruits of your labor!"

"Where have you been all this time?" He feigned incredulity. "Have you not noticed that my life has largely been one of pleasure and enjoyment since I married a beauty from this village? Of course, I cannot be idle like your typical landed gentry. I must work, but I find even that more satisfying since she came into my life." He paused before adding: "Well, I do have to keep her happy with visits to Paris and Helstone. But, I enjoy those anyway."

She smirked. "Paris? What a snob! But are you sure? I will wager, if she is a woman from these parts that her needs are simple and being with you is enough."

"You do not know this lady. She is insatiable. But I would like to get her a house here if she wants it."

Turning somewhat more serious, Margaret said: "Edith suggested buying a house with us where we can all be happy together at certain times of the year but she wants a townhouse in a coastal town south of here. Some place my aunt used to lease for the summer."

"It sounds almost like being in Cadiz but much cooler and rainier. I prefer a country home here in Helstone because of what it means to you. I will seldom have long spells I can spend away from the mill but I can come for weekends and for a week every now and then."

"Well, we shall see!"

XXVI. REALIZATION

argaret went with John to the mill on the Monday after their return from Helstone. She wanted to see the progress of the renovation on the rooms for the medical clinic after he told her that he expected it to be completed in less than three weeks. She could not quite believe that the medical clinic was about to become a reality, ready to see patients possibly on the first week of July. It had immersed her in months of planning, coordinating, and working on tasks, both small and big, that she had never done before and she found it hard to imagine that it was actually going to come to fruition.

Margaret was both amazed and grateful at how smooth the process had been of making the clinic happen. Everyone she approached had been more than receptive and willingly complying with requests for information or help. Drs. Donaldson and Hartley were the most obliging, professing belief in the necessity of the clinic and enthusiastically donating their expertise in its planning. Not long after Catherine was hired, Dr. Hartley started training her at their clinic and, three months later, he was certain that Catherine, an enthusiastic and apt learner, would be prepared to assist by the time the clinic opened. Meantime, Dr. Donaldson facilitated the ordering of equipment and medicines which arrived promptly and were, at the moment, temporarily stored in a locked area in the warehouse. Even Henry Lennox gave generous legal and financial advice gratis when John sought him out for his opinion on appropriate but nominal fees for the doctor's services— fees subsequently set jointly with Dr. Hartley.

At a meeting with overseers and work representatives several weeks earlier, John announced the pending availability of medical services two afternoons a week and nursing care every workday at a clinic, then under construction in the mill premises. Shortly thereafter, Margaret painted a colorful sign that was posted at the entrance to the mill: It included projected opening date, doctor's fees, free nursing care, and hours when the doctor and the nurse would be at the clinic.

Margaret stood in front of the clinic, clutching in her arm a second sign she had painted and which she intended to place directly on the door to the clinic. It listed the doctor's name, his fees, the nurse's name, and hours of operation. She was in no hurry to put it up since she had all morning to ask one of the carpenters to do so. In any case, none of them was in sight. They were all inside the clinic where much of the renovation remained to be done. For the moment, she preferred the silence in the new hallway to the clinic, where everything looked fresh and new.

John had taken the drawing room as his office and the library as an office for an assistant he intended to hire. The clinic occupied what had been the dining and breakfast rooms and the kitchen. Margaret contemplated the door to the clinic for some minutes, initially, with much satisfaction—she relished the idea of its being there and felt proud that its existence was largely her doing. But her satisfaction was soon tempered by apprehension as she wondered if workers would really come to use the clinic. Despite the success of the Christmas Eve celebration, she knew there was still much skepticism, if not distrust, among mill workers that could make them reluctant to seek services at a clinic provided by a mill owner.

By noon, Margaret had surveyed the renovation, talked to the carpenters and put up the sign. John told her he was going to be too busy to see her so she had arranged for a cab to pick her up shortly after noon to take her back home.

Before she left the mill, Margaret went up to Mrs. Thornton's apartment to pay her respects, more out of duty than of anticipation at a pleasurable visit. Although they no longer suffered discomfort in each other's presence and the affection between Elise and Mrs. Thornton brought them together in an unspoken bond, a cozy companionability seemed to elude them. Margaret knew her mother-in-law had seen her come in with John and suspected she had been looking at the renovation being done on the floor below her apartment. Margaret thought it time to talk to her about it and confirm the opening of a medical clinic.

After the usual greetings, Mrs. Thornton invited her to stay for lunch. "It would be nice to have company for lunch. John rarely comes to have it with me. He schedules meetings with workers during lunch in the dining hall." She could barely hide the disappointment in her voice.

The unexpected invitation surprised Margaret. It was extended casually and, she surmised, out of proper decorum because of the hour, but there was an earnestness in Mrs. Thornton's manner that she could not help reciprocating. "I would like to stay for lunch but the cab I ordered will probably be here in about ten minutes. Perhaps, next time."

"Oh? Were you intending to come back soon?"

"Actually, yes. I would like to spend more time here in the next few weeks to watch and provide some guidance to the renovation going on below. I know you know what it is for."

Mrs. Thornton was momentarily disconcerted at Margaret's frankness. She did know from snippets of conversation between John and Margaret that she had heard in the conservatory. "Yes, I do. Is there still much work to be done?"

"For the renovation of the rooms, I suppose there are only finishing touches. But equipment would have to be brought in and properly placed, medical supplies stored safely, things of that sort. I would like to oversee some of that work, make sure that everything is done right and the opening of the clinic occurs without any major hitches."

Although Mrs. Thornton had been curious when she asked her question, the answer she received was more than she wanted to hear. It tempted her to break her resolve not to interfere or even share her opinions on mill business. She nodded, looked away and when she turned towards Margaret again, she said simply: "Well, then, if you are not too busy, do come and have that lunch with me."

Margaret hesitated. "I do want to but I am uneasy leaving Elise for too long and I may not be able to come as often as I would want nor stay as much as I need to. Her needs come first."

Mrs. Thornton smiled gently and, once again, proposed a solution. "Why not just bring her and Mary along? You can leave them here with me. My apartment would be a cozy place for Elise to play and rest while you are doing what you have to do at the mill."

By now, the attachment between Elise and her grandmother was obvious and still growing so Margaret was no longer as surprised at the offer as when Mrs. Thornton first proposed to help care for Elise the week she and John visited Helstone. But she continued to be in awe of what the offer signified and was, therefore, no less grateful. She smiled warmly. "That would certainly ease my mind considerably because I can come and see her here anytime I have a break in my tasks. I would not have to rush home right away. Thank you so much. I will bring her and Mary starting tomorrow. Is that all right?"

"Of course. In fact, come and have lunch with me then. Maybe, you can persuade John to come along."

Mrs. Thornton was actually quite satisfied at this arrangement. She desired, discreetly, to have a hand in molding Elise, possibly into the kind of daughter she would have wanted, one who knew and cared about her father's business as much as she did. When Elise was old enough she meant to teach her all she knew about it. Mrs. Thornton was grateful to have Elise at that time for another reason: Caring for the child provided a pleasant distraction from the work that had been going on since her return from London. She was relieved it was nearing completion but the impending opening bothered her.

Mrs. Thornton continued to believe that anything done for workers outside of directly improving working conditions were misguided favors to them. But she no longer voiced her opinions about the mill to either John or Margaret and they never asked her. In any case, Mrs. Thornton told herself that what went on below her apartment and inside the mill was no longer her concern.

She was certain the money to pay for the clinic came from Margaret's inheritance and she believed Margaret could use it so freely because she came by it without having to sweat blood and tears the way she, herself, did to help John. At such moments, Mrs. Thornton's resentment towards her daughter-in-law returned. But watching Elise at play, Mrs. Thornton would relent again, struck by how like her mother this trusting affectionate little girl was, not only in looks but also in her many gestures and expressions. She thought then that there must be a lot of Elise in Margaret. Besides, why blame Margaret solely when John most probably decided the clinic was a worthwhile effort or he would not have gone along with it?

The clinic opened as scheduled, without fanfare, and marked only by signs posted on the gate to the courtyard and the doors to the mill and the dining hall. Initially, very few people came. On the first day, two women sought Catherine out with complaints about a headache for which she dispensed some medicines for free. Word of the free medicine was probably passed around. The following day, a few more women came with the same complaints.

On the third day Dr. Hartley arrived in the afternoon to see his first patients. When he heard from Catherine what had been happening, he asked her to send in the first patient who came in with a headache. He wanted to be certain the rash of headaches was not a sign of some common illness, either spreading all around Milton or locally. The first such patient balked—seeing the doctor meant paying some fee she did not have. When Catherine told the doctor, he directed her to tell the patient that the first visit to the doctor was free. While this arrangement was not agreed upon between him and the Thorntons, Dr. Hartley was certain they would not object. After all, the initial plans were to provide totally free medical services. Word of the free first visit to the doctor was spread around and, on the second week, so many workers and their families asked to see him that Catherine began scheduling patients.

The medical clinic was well underway and, to Margaret's relief, apparently bringing in patients. For a few weeks after it opened, she stayed away from the mill and spent the quiet hours she had for herself painting. When John talked about what was happening in the clinic including Dr. Hartley's declaration of free first visits, she merely nodded with a smile. Margaret was happy her first major endeavor for the mill proceeded without a hitch but now, it was no longer in her hands and she preferred it that way. The responsibility for keeping it going rested on Dr. Hartley and Catherine.

Getting the clinic started had consumed her so much in mind and spirit that she was, for the moment, exhausted and unable to concentrate on anything but her usual daily tasks and her painting. It was obviously a different sort of exhaustion from that she suffered mourning all the losses of loved ones when she first lived in Milton. But it had similar effects. She needed time to take stock, to reflect, to regain some state not so much of tranquility but of being back on an even keel. This time, she had Elise to distract her, her painting to pour her feelings on to, and John to comfort her and hold her in his arms as she fell asleep.

John knew something was going on with Margaret because the nervous energy he had seen in her during the last few weeks of work on the clinic had been replaced by a calmness in her manner, her countenance, and in her conversations. She did not talk as much and she clung to him more. He did not ask her questions but, at night, he held her close and, when he made love to her, he was more gentle and even playful.

Margaret regained her usual spirit and energy in due time and her thoughts inevitably turned to her plans of a school for the children of the mill. She did not plunge into them, however, as she had done with the clinic. The school was going to be a more difficult task to realize. As it was, she had not yet found a way of persuading parents to allow children to take time out from work and come regularly to a place where they could learn to read and write.

Her mother had managed the parochial school in Helstone, where inhabitants had greater faith in their pastor and in the authority of the parish. Mrs. Hale had an easier task telling parents to send their children to school. It helped, as well, that work in the farms was seasonal and younger children could easily walk to school upon finishing their lighter chores in the farm. With only her experience in Helstone to draw upon, it was inevitable that Margaret's first step was to visit the nearby parish, talk to the pastor and possibly seek his opinion on how to approach parents in Milton about schooling.

The pastor was not hopeful. "It is a struggle. First of all, it is hard to make parents see the need for children to learn to read and write. The few that do have no time or are too exhausted to be bothered to bring their children in."

"I see. The parish is too far for most young children to walk to by themselves."

"Yes, so you would not be surprised to learn that those, who do come, live not too far from here. But even so, many do not come regularly. I suspect that sometimes they are too weak from hunger to make that walk or muster the enthusiasm to come. In any case, how can you teach children who only come sporadically? And as you very well know, the older children have to work at the mill so, as far as literacy is concerned, they are a lost cause."

"How frustrating it must be. But, yet, you do keep it going."

"Yes, for the very few who genuinely like to learn or who believe they need those skills to rise out of their present situations. After a while, you begin to satisfy yourself with reaching that small handful." The parson paused, looked at Margaret intently and asked: "Was your father not a parson somewhere in the south? He probably did not have to deal with this problem."

"No, his congregation was small and not quite so scattered. And he was probably one of the very few figures of authority in the village so he or my mother could meet with each family and gently cajole them to do what was right. But even in a small hamlet like Helstone, there are problems, although they are different from those in a large modern city like Milton." Margaret started to rise from her seat. "I must not take any more of your time. Thank you for talking so frankly with me."

The pastor nodded, rose from his seat and extended a hand. "I am sorry I could not give you the answers you need but I will pray that you find a way to interest these parents on schooling. My advice is do not be discouraged. If you can help one or two children, then you would be doing them a world of good and that may be enough."

The conversation with the parson persuaded Margaret that, for the moment at least, she should focus on the one thing she was certain she could accomplish: sending Thomas Boucher to a boarding school. She returned to the mill one afternoon a couple of months after the clinic opened, finally prepared to look at what she had created there. She also intended to catch Nicholas Higgins during a break in his work to talk to him about Thomas.

Nicholas needed no convincing that Thomas was better off going to school than working in the mill but he was reluctant to have someone in his family singled out for special favors by the Thorntons. Margaret assured him that Thomas was not likely to be the last child she and John were helping. They meant to seek other children with potential and offer as many of them as they could the same opportunity. Thomas was going to set an example for other parents and children of what was possible to attain with further education. So long as Thomas continued to be diligent and to advance in his studies, the Thorntons intended to pay for his education until he chose some profession with which to earn his living.

Earlier that evening, Margaret sat in John's office, waiting for him to finish his work so they could go home in a cab with Elise and Mary. She sat, relaxing for a while, enjoying her solitude, her mind wandering through the three years she had been married and how full it had been. She had given birth not only to a daughter but to a medical clinic and now she was contemplating on doing more. She thought about her parents who she knew would have been proud of what she was doing, her father, in particular. It gratified her to find John very enthusiastic about sending Thomas to a good boarding school. He apparently had always been interested in the boy's welfare and, a few times in the past, had helped him along in his reading. She sensed in her husband a particular fondness for Thomas.

Margaret's thoughts were interrupted when she heard John come in. He smiled brightly and gave her a peck on the lips. "I knew you were coming today but I did not see you at all today. Until now. Did you talk to Nicholas?"

"Yes, briefly; it did not take much to convince him but he was anxious not to have his family singled out."

"That is so like Nicholas."

"Yes. Now, I have to select a boarding school and make all the preparations for sending him off."

"I am glad. Thomas has a much better future ahead of him than all these other children here."

"You think something is special about him, don't you?"

John replied, smiling as he reminisced. "As a matter of fact, I do. I first saw him sitting outside my office, reading and waiting for Nicholas one evening after work. Higgins told me later you had been teaching Thomas to read. In my mind, at the time, he was the son you and I would never have so I suppose I wanted him to have the opportunities my own son would have."

She laughed at his revelation. John looked at her, puzzled, and had her laugh not been so spontaneous, it would have irritated him. "You find humor in that?"

"Well, yes. You know Edith's son Sholto. When I moved to London, I was the only one who could subdue his temperamental outbursts. I used to take him into his nursery, close the door, and he and I would have a battle of wills that always ended with him hugging me with tearful, puffy eyes, quite exhausted. I developed an attachment to him and he, to me."

"I fail to see what that has to do with my fondness for Thomas."

"I will tell you. Sholto was very sweet and trusting in his affection but I confess mine sprang partly from a sad awareness that it was the closest I would ever come to being a mother. So, you see, I played pretend as well."

Mollified by her explanation, he smiled broadly and asked, teasing: "But Henry Lennox?"

She arched an eyebrow at him and considered whether she should answer a question to which he already knew the response. Then, in a moment of insight, she realized her husband never tired of hearing her reassurances of love and he likewise took pleasure in giving her the same in both words and actions. They gazed at each other for a long minute during which he waited in anticipation and she softened into tenderness.

Margaret, matching his tone, replied jauntily in French with an elaborate shrug: "*Aucune chance!*" She added with a twinkle in her eyes: "My mind and my heart were too full of this tall dark charmer from a dirty bustling city in the north. How could a bland Londoner, clever and sophisticated he may be, compete with that?"

They sat smiling at each other across his desk.

At length, he returned to the matter of schooling. "Now that I am better acquainted with my workers and have my own daughter, I understand why you are trying to bring schooling to these children. We take it for granted Elise will receive instruction, the parents of these children take it for granted they will not; yet many know that some education is essential to rise out of doing factory work."

"Well, it may be like breaking an ingrained habit. If you grew up in a family in which no one went to school, you might never think of it as a choice you could make. But I am a hopeful person and I believe there may be a few parents among the workers who could be convinced to send their children to school if they see what Thomas can do."

"But how do we come across another Thomas? Should I look out for another child sitting and reading just outside my office?" He teased again.

Margaret smiled indulgently but opted to reply seriously. "I actually taught all the Boucher children to read but only Thomas showed an eagerness to learn and was the only one who really persevered. If we had classes, we might discover another child like him."

"Why, yes, of course. So, why can we not start those classes?"

"For many reasons—where to hold them, for one. The bigger problem is how to induce children to come. Those two things are, of course, related. I talked to the rector of the church closest to the mill, hoping to get his advice on how to convince parents but also prepared to just offer the parochial school financial help to pay more teachers to take more children. But his school is having trouble with attendance. Parents see no need for school. For the few who see some value in it, their small children find the school too far to walk."

"If the classes were held in my old office, parents can just drop off their children before going into the mill. Is the office too small?"

"It can only hold 10 to 12 children. I cannot estimate the number who would actually come but I suspect, not many. We also need to hire teachers. I can do some teaching, at least in the beginning, but I do not have time to teach everyday and, I must confess, neither do I want to. I am not the most patient person with a roomful of children."

John and Margaret did not arrive at solutions that day. The cab had come to take them all home.

Eventually, Margaret decided to start some basic reading and writing classes when Catherine offered to help her teach. On her first visit to the clinic, she mentioned her wish to start a school for children at the mill and Catherine apparently gave the idea much thought. She sought John out to tell him she might be able to help. The offshoot was her first invitation to tea, set on a Sunday afternoon.

Catherine arrived promptly, eager but also intimidated into shyness by the unexpected invitation from her employers. But she found her apprehensions allayed by the informality with which they received her. Tea was served in the garden-like atmosphere of the conservatory and the Thorntons' daughter was there, sitting on a rug on the floor among her toys, nibbling on a biscuit. Mary Higgins was taking care of her and Margaret had poured her a cup of tea as well. The conversation meandered into many topics and both Thorntons made some effort to ask her opinion on every one of them. When tea was over, Margaret led Catherine into the privacy of the drawing room, leaving John and Elise in the conservatory.

"John told me of your interest in my plans for the children's school."

"Well, yes. I told you during the interview that I trained as a governess. I think I could help with teaching."

"What about the clinic?"

"Afternoons at the clinic are not as busy as mornings except when Dr. Hartley is in. Sometimes, no one comes at all. I thought, perhaps, my time would be better used at the school on the Wednesdays and Fridays the doctor is not in. If there is an emergency, I will be around." Catherine paused, disconcerted by Margaret's intent gaze. "I am merely making a suggestion if you would not mind closing the clinic for nursing care on those afternoons."

Margaret smiled engagingly. "Your suggestion makes a lot of sense to me if, as you say, the clinic is not busy some afternoons. How long has it been that way?"

"Actually, since we opened. When they have a complaint, the workers come in the morning. Mondays are usually busy all day probably because of ailments that start on the weekend."

"Let me think about it. Frankly, your suggestion came as a surprise. Your offer to teach has made it more likely for the classes to happen but it is also making me ask myself how committed I really am. If I go ahead, the classes will take me away from home those afternoons I take over teaching."

Catherine's offer of her services did clinch Margaret's decision to go ahead. After a few more afternoon teas, she and Catherine agreed on what to offer, where, and when. Classes would be open to both children and adults, and were to take place Monday through Thursday afternoons in the master's old office. Margaret would teach two days and Catherine, the other two. The space was small but Margaret had not expected too many children to come. She subsequently went to a workers' meeting to talk about the availability of free reading and writing lessons. Except for her impulsive outburst during the strikers' riot, she had never addressed a big group of workers and she was apprehensive at the prospect of doing so. She had expected John to make the announcement as he had done for the clinic but he insisted that this was something she must do.

The realization of Margaret's wish of a school for workers children was off to a modest start. She thought scaling down her ambitions proved to be the right decision when, on the first week, only six children and no adult came. The following weeks did not bring in too many more children and for a long time, the classes often only had ten or fewer pupils.

XXVII. FRIENDSHIP

Sharing the task of teaching threw Margaret and Catherine into company often and a true friendship blossomed between them. Margaret knew early on that she and Catherine shared more interests and had more similar dispositions than the other two young women her age who had been her friends and companion. Certainly more than she did with Bessy who had neither the education nor exposure to ideas that Margaret acquired from her father. Edith, of course, was like a sister to her and she would always be dearer than any other young woman could ever be but Margaret thought she and Catherine could never be what Edith was.

Fortunate to have had a father rich enough to indulge all that she desired, Edith grew into a great many young men's ideal of a woman—lovely, feminine, graceful, and preoccupied with all the affairs of a lady. Margaret would always be grateful to her and her aunt for their solicitous care and patience when she needed those most. But, once recovered from her sorrows and deep malaise, Margaret thought the life she shared in London with Edith and her husband too languid and too dull. She preferred to devote her time to the sort of exertions she had taken on as a parson's daughter and which now absorbed her time in Milton.

Catherine understood such preoccupations, not only from a necessity to earn a living but also from a belief—borne out of her Catholic upbringing—that she should work for something of use to others. Much acquainted with Margaret's superior attributes, Catherine could not help feeling some envy. But, she was grateful, too. Margaret had not only given her a job but treated her as a friend, an equal whose skills Margaret respected. Believing her to have had proper training and more experience, Margaret deferred to her judgment on many matters concerning the reading and writing classes. She invited her to dinners she gave for small parties of friends, exposing her to a society that would otherwise have been indifferent to her. She lent her books and told her stories of people she and Mr. Thornton met and places they visited.

Even Dr. Hartley, who talked to her only about matters pertaining to work, began to show more curiosity about her, inquiring minutely about her interests and her family. It seemed he enjoyed their conversations as much as she did and, indeed, he expressed admiration for the breadth of topics she could talk intelligently about. Catherine wondered, then, whether she could nurture his curiosity into a genuine interest in her.

She had been infatuated with him from the time he was pointed out to her as the young doctor from America. But she never imagined, much less hoped, that he would pay her any attention, especially when young women of beauty and means were vying for his favors. Resigned to admiring him from a distance, she seized the chance, when it came, to work with him. She told herself she could pretend he was hers for those few hours they worked together.

When Dr. Hartley paid her more attention, Catherine was elated. Then, he began to ask in detail about Catherine's friendship with the young Mrs. Thornton, what they talked about, the books they read together, what kind of a friend she was, and how frequently they met. At first, Catherine thought his questions sprang from natural curiosity. Margaret, after all, attracted much talk because of who she was and what she did. Later, however, his inquiries became much more about Margaret than about her and her opinions. Catherine knew then that Dr. Hartley's interest in Mr. Thornton's wife transcended mere curiosity.

She resolved to observe him closely when all three of them were together and she contrived an excuse to have Margaret come to the clinic on a day when Dr. Hartley was doing consultations. Her suspicions were confirmed. The doctor could not take his eyes off Margaret and he hung on every word she uttered. But it was also plain to Catherine that Margaret was easy but business-like in her manner towards him. Even so, Catherine was depressed to learn the doctor was captivated by someone she could not hope to compete with, someone who was her friend. Used to disappointments, Catherine had learned to be philosophical. She talked herself into believing she never expected Dr. Hartley to reciprocate. She was privileged to have seen into his heart whereas all those other women pined in vain for his attention and did not know his heart was taken.

All her equivocations did not satisfy Catherine, however, and one Saturday afternoon while she and Margaret were in Mr. Thornton's study talking about reading lessons, she asked: "May I tell you something that may sound impertinent to you?"

Margaret smiled, amused at such a request. "Perhaps, you had better not. In such a case, I might prefer to be ignorant."

Catherine took Margaret's blithe reply seriously and her eyelids drooped in disappointment. "Of course, I am sorry."

"Come, come, it must be important or you would not risk asking me, if it were indeed impertinent. We are friends, after all, in addition to being colleagues so we can be frank without fearing to be misunderstood. Do tell."

Catherine looked at her for a long moment, hesitant, wondering if she could lose a valued friend. In the end, she trusted in Margaret's good sense and reasoned that if the latter did not care for Dr. Hartley, she would not take offense. Catherine boldly proceeded: "Were you aware that Dr. Hartley has deep feelings for you?"

Margaret was caught off guard by the question but she recovered quickly and stared at Catherine, studying the expression on her face. "Yes, I am and, if I had failed to notice, at least two people made sure I knew it."

"Mr. Thornton?"

"Yes, and I doubt that anybody else noticed except those with some interest in the matter." Margaret answered irritably. In fact, she had been at least a little offended by the question although she was not certain exactly why. Perhaps, she did feel that Catherine was too intrusive and that the matter was too private for someone she had only known a few months to pry into.

Catherine blushed deeply and lowered her eyes. They lapsed into an uncomfortable silence, Catherine with her eyes cast down and Margaret, trying to concentrate on a book in order to give Catherine time to compose herself.

After a few minutes, Margaret looked up from her book, saw both misery and regret on her friend's face and, somewhat contrite, said more mildly. "I have no interest in Dr. Hartley except in his capacity as a doctor in a clinic I am invested in and as my daughter's physician. I love my husband very much, everyone can see that."

Catherine stayed silent, studying her hands, unable to look at Margaret who, seeing Catherine too overcome to talk, attempted some levity in her next remark. "We must make the good doctor notice the pretty face behind those freckles. Perhaps, he would then see the good mind behind the face and the warm heart that beats within that chest."

Dropping her face on her hands, Catherine began to sob and her body quivered, although hardly any sound came out of her. Margaret, flabbergasted at what she had wrought in her friend, sat and watched for a few moments. Then, unable to bear her suffering, she pulled her chair next to Catherine's and placed an arm around her shoulders. "I think that Dr. Hartley has not been tempted by any of those pretty young women who invite him into their parlors, rich though they are, because he requires a good mind and an energetic spirit—precisely what you have and what most of those other women do not. He is himself heir to a fortune in America so he is very likely indifferent to wealth."

Margaret was uneasy speculating in this manner but what else could she say? She had suspected, for some time, that Catherine harbored tender sentiments for the doctor but she did not realize, until now, how strongly Catherine felt. She understood, at that moment, why Catherine was compelled to probe into how she regarded Dr. Hartley. Having known hopelessness, herself—even for the relatively short period that she believed John no longer cared for her—she could empathize with Catherine's misery. She wished she could lift her out of it but she could not summon other words that would help. All she could do was wait for Catherine to regain her composure.

Catherine soon calmed down and dried her face thoroughly with a handkerchief she pulled out of a pocket in her skirt. She turned to Margaret. "I am sorry. Now you have seen my heart which I did not really mean to reveal to you. You will not tell anyone about this?"

"No, of course not. You may not believe it just now but I do understand how you feel and I think the doctor is blind if he does not see your wonderful qualities."

Catherine looked as if she would cry again. Instead with a long deep sigh, she replied wryly: "He sees no other woman but you."

"That is regrettable but an end has to come to unrequited feelings." Margaret retorted haughtily, feeling some irritation again. But just as quickly as she replied, she stopped abruptly, regretting her remark, realizing as soon as she said it that it applied to Catherine as well. What had been meant to reassure a friend that she was not a rival might, instead, have sounded callous.

They were silent again for some minutes. Catherine struggled to hold back more tears and Margaret bit her lip, stared at her book and tried to read; but comprehension was nearly impossible. How could she be so unfeeling?

Margaret was relieved when Catherine broke the uneasy silence. "Would you help me if I asked you?"

"But how? I cannot and will not intercede on your behalf, you must see that." Margaret was wary and hesitant.

"No, no," Catherine protested. "I only want your help with how to improve my looks, how to style my hair and choose my dress, for instance."

Margaret's face lighted up, grateful for the chance to take action and, in the process, atone for her insensitivity to a friend. "I will do what I can, certainly, although I am hardly an authority on such things. My cousin Edith, whose tastes are generally deemed impeccable, used to select my dresses until I developed my own tastes. I can write her for some advice. I will describe you and, perhaps, even do a sketch of you. Meantime, Dixon knows something about styling hair. We can start there."

"Perhaps, Dr. Hartley will take serious notice of me, then. If not, somebody else might."

A few weeks later, somebody else did notice. John came up to Margaret as she went through her ritual of brushing her hair before going to bed. He nudged the nape of her neck with a few kisses and then said: "I talked to Miss Rea this morning. One of the workers injured a hand and we had to take him to the clinic."

"Was he seriously hurt?"

"No, fortunately. She fixed him up well enough that he felt able to return to his machine." He took the brush from her hand and pulled her up from the chair towards the bed. "Something has changed about your friend, her lips are redder, her cheeks rosier and clearer, and she has done something to her hair. I was surprised to find that she is actually quite pretty."

"You may only admire her from afar," she declared saucily.

"I have resisted prettier women before; except one, and she is the loveliest, most precious pearl I could ever hope to find." He dropped down on the bed, pulling her on top of him.

The following day was Saturday and, for Margaret and John, it meant an intimate, leisurely morning. Since Mrs. Thornton had been visiting regularly, Saturday mornings had become a time together for her and Elise who did not see her parents until late morning or even noon. Her parents did all they could to promote the affection between Elise and her grandmother. For Margaret, forming such a bond with someone other than her parents meant that her daughter was becoming more independent.

On one previous Saturday, Margaret watched from their bedroom window as Mrs. Thornton led Elise by the hand around the garden. John came up to her, curious about what interested her so intently. "I think Hannah will be as devoted to Elise as she was to you and Fanny."

"Of course, she will. But I wonder if mother realizes how much like you Elise is, in looks and manner."

"Oh, please say nothing about that to her. Hannah has, at times, been almost affectionate to me but her manner is still often guarded—gracious but guarded. I do not want that to happen between her and Elise."

Margaret saw John wince at what she said but he only smiled and placed his arm around her waist. "It won't. To me, what matters most is that you two are more at ease with each other and she has finally accepted that I need you and want you and you are in Milton to stay."

John and Margaret were grateful for mornings they could have alone together, wallowing deliciously under the sheets and delighting in each other's touch; she, running her fingers in a delicate caress over his skin; and he, holding her close, sometimes nibbling at whatever part of her he could reach, always playfully at first and often culminating into passionate lovemaking. They relished such moments—precious hours affirming what each meant to the other, treasured hours cut out of busy schedules—and sought them whenever they could since that first time they made love again after Elise was born.

Such mornings ended with breakfast in bed and a lively tête-à-tête, often about some topic started at an earlier time. This particular Saturday morning, John observed: "You and Miss Rea are up to something."

"Whatever do you mean?"

"Why, the change I noticed only lately in Miss Rea's appearance and in her demeanor! I also saw you opening a package with Dixon a week ago with lady's things from Edith and yesterday, I saw them on Miss Rea."

"You do surprise me sometimes. I did not realize you paid any mind to these things."

"Well, I do not, ordinarily, except when they involve my wife."

"I promised not to say but you are my husband and I can probably tell you. Catherine....." Margaret hesitated, looking at him with pleading eyes. "But I feel bad betraying a confidence."

John smiled sympathetically. "Yes, I can see that. Anyway, I think I know what this is all about. I have seen how Miss Rea looks at Dr. Hartley. He may not pay attention to how she feels but I cannot see how he could fail to notice the change in her looks. It is quite striking."

"Yes, one can rely on Edith to know how to bring out a woman's physical beauty. I always thought Catherine's features rather pretty but men, as usual, did not notice them behind the plain and austere exterior she presented. I am thankful Edith enjoys being of use in such matters. She wrote us a rather long letter of instructions on styling, potions, feminine accessories and ladylike demeanor. The package contained many things she talked about in her letter and were her gift to Catherine."

John chuckled. "Good. I wish Miss Rea well and all of you success for your efforts. Me? I look forward to being freed up from paying Dr. Hartley more attention than he deserves."

Dr. Hartley, as John surmised, did see and, after some time, even guessed Catherine's true sentiments for him. Convinced since

Elise's birthday party that the young Mrs. Thornton was immune to his feelings and Mr. Thornton was indeed the formidable rival Dr. Donaldson warned him of, Dr. Hartley finally opened himself to the charms of other women. But to the chagrin of both Catherine and Margaret, he ignored Catherine and escorted around many pretty heiresses of manufacturing fortunes. To Margaret's relief, Catherine had gained more confidence in her looks and was learning to be more philosophical about her unrequited feelings. Although Dr. Hartley made her unhappy once again despite her efforts at making herself more attractive, Catherine reassured Margaret she was finally beginning to accept the doctor's indifference.

At her cousin's request, Margaret kept Edith informed of Catherine's little adventures. After the most recent events, Edith decided to play matchmaker, albeit a discrete one. As soon as the Thornton household had settled in their new house, Edith became a more regular visitor there in late spring and at Christmastime when the two families came together to celebrate holidays in Milton or London. In the autumn of the Thorntons return from Paris, Edith came to visit to hear a first-hand account of the reunion with Frederick. She and the captain brought along a friend who had resigned his commission to become a barrister.

Charles Bennett was an earnest, sensitive young man of 29 who was not cut out for the military but joined it to placate his father. When his father died, he decided to do what he always wanted—set up a law office in one of the industrializing northern cities which he saw as being on the forefront of change. Edith heard of his intent and invited him to come with her and the captain to be introduced to the Thorntons, "prominent people" in Milton.

Her plan was to have him meet Catherine in the relaxed ambiance of a small dinner party of close friends. She asked Margaret to invite Catherine to dinner on their second night there. Edith had met Catherine on one of her previous visits. With additional coaching from her on enhancing feminine charms, she declared Catherine as attractive as any in her London circle, nearly as clever as Margaret, but more desirous to please and less prone to speak her mind. More appealing, therefore, to a lot of men in her acquaintance and perfect for drawing out shy Captain Bennett who liked clever but soft-spoken women.

The night before the London party arrived, Margaret spoke to John about Edith's matchmaking. He surprised her by getting into the spirit of it. "I will ask Dr. Hartley over for that evening. He has never refused an invitation to dine here and his presence will double the intrigue."

"You astonish me. When I first knew you, you were grave in manner, serious in purpose, and not given to laughter. Only by a glint of merriment in your eye could I tell you were amused. Now, you take part in our devious, frivolous feminine machinations."

He laughed. "Frivolous? No! Devious? Yes. I know now that finding a wife or husband is serious business so why should I not help? If that paragon of masculinity, the Captain, gets involved, why not I?"

"It seems out of character for you somehow." She frowned a little, eyed him closely, and then smiled merrily. "But I like it when you laugh so spontaneously."

"I did not have much to laugh about before. Now, I do. My world has grown, burst out of a cotton pod, freed from breathing, living only for cotton."

Margaret turned her attention back to her dinner, staring at the almost uneaten dish on her plate. John glanced at her quizzically, her eyes had taken on that faraway look when she was absorbed in some reverie. This time, he knew it was pleasant since a half-smile lingered on her lips. He resumed his dinner and ate in silence, watching her for some minutes as she ate very slowly. She looked as if she found the food difficult to swallow.

He could not help asking: "Are you not feeling well?"

She did not answer right away but continued to slowly fork the food into her mouth. Without looking up from her plate, she said: "What if your world were to grow more?"

John was uncertain, at first, about what she meant. He put his fork down, frowned, and tried to comprehend her question; then a happy suspicion lighted up his eyes. "You mean another child?"

She looked up at him and nodded, a smile slowly lighting up her face. "It is not too soon for you, is it, to have a second one? Elise will be three years old by the time this one is born."

"No, oh no!" He reached out, squeezed her hand, and raised it to his lips. Then, flippant again, he said: "Paris, isn't it? That is what I would like to think, anyway."

Edith's expectations were met in so far as Captain Bennett and Catherine did find each other agreeable. They stumbled upon much to talk about and, seated next to each other at dinner as Edith planned, they spent most of the evening in conversation. Dr. Hartley was placed across the table between Mrs. Thornton—who mostly listened or talked to her son—and Captain Lennox, who claimed Margaret's attention. He could not miss what went on in front of him.

But the hoped-for romantic alliance did not come to pass as Edith envisioned. Captain Bennett was of an inherently wary frame of mind to trust first encounters and Catherine's hopes that Dr. Hartley might return her affection were revived when she noticed how often he looked at her at dinner. Dr. Hartley did pay her more attention after that dinner but while sensible of her charms, he seemed immune to them. A month later, his attention to Catherine waned and he resumed escorting other women.

It took a year before Catherine gave up on the doctor. Captain Bennett had decided by then to open a law office with the intention of settling in Milton if his practice grew. Edith—suspecting he was too shy to renew acquaintances formed on his first visit—wrote Margaret about his move to Milton, with entreaties to invite him for tea or dinner to which she must, of course, also invite Catherine. By such machinations, Edith continued her matchmaking which Margaret, for the sake of her friend, assisted.

In time, Captain Bennett and Catherine realized how suitable their dispositions were to each other. He proposed and she accepted. Edith was triumphant although it bothered her romantic notions that the attachment was not based on the sweet passion that she believed swept her off her feet upon meeting her captain or the intense ardor wordlessly exchanged between Margaret and John. Still, her success gratified her and she allowed that mutual respect and affection were enough to unite two people in matrimony.

Eventually, Dr. Hartley married a vacuous beauty, the heiress of a very rich manufacturer, a Miss Lambert who came back from finishing school and immediately became the belle of the society the Thorntons moved in. John, who had a high opinion of Dr. Hartley's good sense, thought the choice imprudent. "He was dazzled by her beauty but he will tire of her soon enough. I feel sorry for Dr. Hartley. I think this is an impulsive choice he will regret."

"Miss Lambert does dazzle and Catherine would definitely have been a better match for the doctor, in mind and temperament. I would have wagered for a more lasting and true conjugal felicity between her and the doctor. Still, I do not think, for an instant, that Charles Bennett is less capable of making Catherine happy."

"Well, he is steady, calm, almost phlegmatic in disposition and, therefore, less riveting than the exuberant, impulsive, virile American. Perhaps, reliable, loyal, and true do suit Mrs. Catherine Bennett better."

"Life with Captain Bennett, from what I gather, has been tranquil and Catherine is serenely happy. Dr. Hartley might have brought her more adventure and perhaps, periods of intense joy but, probably also more heartache."

A scowl flitted through John's brow as he tried to suppress the irritation he felt at this remark. He was confident of Margaret's love, so why should it matter if she thought Dr. Hartley a more exciting match? Did he not think so, himself?

John realized then that he continued to be vexed by suspicions that Dr. Hartley never overcame his attachment to Margaret. When he first met Miss Lambert, he was struck by how she had nearly the same coloring and build as Margaret. Miss Lambert was arguably more stunning and—conscious of her beauty—vain enough to flaunt it. But the more he looked at her, the more John saw that the brightness in Miss Lambert's ivory skin was enhanced by careful choice of colors in her dress and her blue eyes were enlarged by subtly applied shadows. They had neither the depth nor lively expressiveness he saw all the time in his wife's eyes.

Despite his vexation, John felt sorry for Dr. Hartley and he remembered his own agony, nearly forgotten now. And yet, had his own story not had a happy ending, he was certain he would not have settled for a shallow substitute, one who could not live up to the attributes of the original.

XXVIII. EPILOGUE

The much awaited first reunion of the Thorntons and the Hales took place three years after John and Margaret visited Frederick and Dolores in Cadiz. The two couples decided to rendezvous in Paris in the month of September when the weather was turning temperate, not as hot and humid as in the height of summer but not yet as wet as late fall or winter. They were all desirous to meet to cement sincere and happy alliances curtailed by the short time they spent together in Spain. This reunion of brother and sister was not nearly as tearful or poignant as the one in Cadiz—the pain of their shared losses having slowly receded. On their first meeting at the apartment they rented in Paris, the generally happy years immediately preceding prevailed, expressed in warm, exuberant embraces between each of the couple and the other.

This visit was rendered particularly meaningful by their having become parents for the first time and they were anxious for Elise and little Frederick, born only two months apart, to know and be known by the other family. Acquainting their children with relatives on the opposite end of the continent was akin to an initiation ritual, a poignant one for Frederick but more so for Margaret whose sense of being all alone and rudderless after her father died had been acute, a sense that still occasionally haunted her. Although no longer disconsolate with grief at losing her parents, she often recalled—with a quiet melancholy—that they would never see her so happily settled and her daughter would never know her grandparents. Margaret was determined Elise should know she had family she could claim proudly on her mother's side, an uncle she could turn to, if it became necessary. She did not doubt that Elise could rely on her grandmother for support. But grandmama was not likely to be around all her life.

Dixon accompanied the Thorntons. She had initially hesitated to come, fearful of traveling to a foreign country with strange customs and an even stranger language. Margaret had asserted they needed someone to help take care of Elise but Dixon continued to vacillate. When Margaret told her they would have to take Mary if she did not want to go, she was taken aback. Not long after, she received a letter from Dolores, profuse with hopes of meeting her. Dixon finally consented to go, admitting that she was, indeed, eager to see Frederick again, curious about Dolores, and not immune to boasting that she had seen Paris. Besides, there was no better place than Paris to spend money accumulated from her years of service.

The party was gathered for the month in a large furnished apartment next to the Jardin du Luxembourg on the Rive Gauche. Frederick, who traveled to Paris once or twice a year on business, had arranged to lease it on his last trip. It had four bedrooms—two large ones for the two couples, a third for the children and a fourth for Dixon and Juana, the maid who took care of little Frederick.

Dixon was inevitably apprehensive of sharing a bedroom with someone who spoke no English. But within a week of arrival, the two women were communicating with a combination of gestures, the few words of English Juana learned from Dolores and the three or four words of Spanish Dixon could recall that Juana taught her. Thrown into each other's company all day, in a society new and strange to both, and similarly entrusted with their masters' children, they formed a casual alliance that needed few words. Towards the end of their stay, each admitted that the other actually helped her enjoy the stay in Paris.

The apartment had a drawing room, a dining room and a well-equipped kitchen that turned out to be more useful than anyone had expected. In need of breakfast on their first morning, the whole party went out searching for food. A block from the apartment, they happened upon a store, through the glass doors of which they could see the interior, already packed with people, although it was still quite early. Delicious aromas wafted out every time customers entered or left with their purchase.

The sign on the store said *boulangerie*. "Why, of course—a bakery! What else could smell so good?" Margaret exclaimed, smiling broadly as she stepped inside, followed close behind by Dixon with Elise in her arms.

After an instant of indecision, the rest squeezed themselves into the bakery's crowded interior. It was redolent with the delicious, irresistible aromas of baking and warm from the blazing stone hearth visible from where they stood. They looked around, in marvel at the abundance before them. Loaves of crusty bread, long and short, fat and thin, filled two large baskets on two ends of a long counter and, in between, buns and flaky rolls of all kinds almost crowded out sweet and savory pies filled—according to the lady at the counter—with cheese, ham, or a combination of both, all freshly baked.

Margaret, in the interest of efficient ordering at the busy bakery, made choices for the whole group. After asking a few questions, she chose a warm country bread, a selection of both sweet and savory pastries and small soft golden buns rich in egg yolks called brioche, which—the friendly baker's wife serving her claimed—"*Les petits aiment beaucoup.*" With the makings for a hearty breakfast beautifully packaged in a box and directions to an *épicerie*, the party headed towards the store, bought tea and milk, and returned to the apartment for a morning feast. For about a week, Margaret and Dixon returned to the bakery on subsequent mornings until the baker's wife became familiar with *les femmes anglaises* and Dixon was confident that, if Juana went with her, she could order what was needed simply by pointing to them.

On the second morning, when, Margaret and Dixon returned to the *épicerie* for more tea, some coffee, fruit preserves, milk, and cream, they noticed a number of other food stores in the vicinity, some still closed. Margaret dragged Dixon back in late morning to see what the stores offered. They returned to the apartment laden with a selection of both familiar and new food items. At a nearby charcuterie, they found hams, sausages, and other cured meats; at a cheese shop, a wide selection of cheeses unknown in England; and at a small market with open stalls, fresh fruits and vegetables.

Dixon, born with sensitive taste buds and a sharp sense of smell, enjoyed good food and, across the years, had learned to be creative with ingredients to make the most of the limited larder the Hales kept. Her natural gift for concocting delicious dishes was unleashed when she took over the Thornton kitchen, for which she could purchase the best ingredients that could be found in Milton. The bounty in Paris delighted her beyond words and on the first Sunday, she offered to make dinner, which everyone gratefully accepted.

Recognizing the excellence of her ingredients, she prepared them simply and presented a dinner of very fresh raw oysters from the Brittany coast, roast lamb with small potatoes and creamed wild mushrooms, and fresh figs and berries served with orange-infused liqueur. It was a delectable unexpected feast, an indulgence after the typical fare in cafés and brasseries the two couples consumed during a day of sampling the city's cultural offerings. They requested it again and looked forward to a similar feast on subsequent Sundays.

Frederick had selected the apartment for its proximity to the beautiful, large garden next to the Luxembourg palace and it turned out the wise and happy choice he thought it would be. The garden became Dixon and Juana's preferred place to take the children when their parents were out somewhere in the city. They went nearly everyday, joining the many families who promenaded or played in vast spaces shaded with trees and equipped with chairs, benches and grassy areas. By the second week, the couples needed a break from the continuous stimulation of art and shopping galleries, museums, theaters, and cafés in a city still in the middle of its massive reconstruction. The whole party went to the garden and whiled away that weekend and remaining ones pleasantly relaxing, chatting, exchanging stories, and watching others around them do the same. Just as Dixon and Juana had seen other families do, they packed a picnic basket of bread, cheese, fruit, cured meats, wine for the adults, and milk for the children.

Margaret went back to the garden with John or Frederick for long leisurely walks, usually in the evening, the summer light still lingering on the horizon. She brought along a sketchbook and pastels, bought at a Paris art store, and stopped many times to sketch views of the garden. Except for memories, she had no record—not even entries in a diary—of her first glorious, wonderful visit to Paris on her honeymoon. This time, she wanted more vivid images than she could summon from flawed slowly-fading memories so, whenever she had time, she made sketches of Paris scenes, of landscapes, of everyone in her party and of Parisians going about their day-to-day business.

As in Cadiz, the Thorntons and the Hales effortlessly fell into talking and sharing their experiences. In conversations they had in cafes or after dinner at the apartment, they recounted in much detail both small and big events of their lives, often talking into the night. When they had exhausted what they needed to say about their separate lives, they found many other topics of interest—things they had seen and done that day, their hopes for the future, their views on what was happening around them. The ease and genuine affection that began to develop in Cadiz between the two couples deepened in those long, intimate conversations, anxiously nurtured by Frederick and Margaret who were constantly reminded of how little time and how infrequently they had a chance to be together.

Margaret was particularly gratified to see John and Frederick often engaged in endless conversations that began when they started talking about their work. John, who had been in business much longer than Frederick and had struggled through more complex problems, talked freely about them and Frederick listened intently, convinced that he could learn from someone as wizened by experience as John obviously was.

Their conversations inevitably evolved into more intimate topics. One day, John mentioned his close friendship with Mr. Hale and how they spent hours talking about the classics and philosophy. Frederick's interest was particularly piqued. He had listened to his father talk of those things but, while they interested him, he had been more eager for adventure. He chose to go into the military instead of Oxford. Older and settled in his own home, he thought about devoting some time to reading a few of the books his father had talked about, partly for his own enlightenment and partly to pay homage to a father he had admired. He quietly listened to John, his usually glinting eyes gradually shrouding with sadness. Noticing the change in Frederick—who had turned introspective in the way John saw Margaret do—John lapsed into silence, uneasily but patiently waiting for him to speak.

"I have made it a point not to regret what I have done across the years, not even what the British naval authorities called a 'mutiny'. But not having been there for my parents and my little sister, when father was forced out of his living, has never ceased to bother me."

John did not answer, merely nodded in sympathy.

"I particularly regret not being there during my father's darkest hours. I admired my father very much and, yet, as a young man, I tried to be different from him. Now, I listen to you, I envy you those hours of study you had with him, the trust he had that allowed him to confide in you."

John did not know what to say, dumbfounded by the remorse and sincerity, tinged with bitterness, evident in Frederick's voice. He was struck by how much like his father Frederick was in those moments of sadness and regret. There was about him the same poignancy in baring his soul to someone who was a relative stranger. John had believed that the father, in the midst of grief and despair, could not help himself. Talking to Frederick then, John saw that Mr. Hale—assuming an implicit unspoken compact that John would be compassionate, not apathetic nor judgmental—had given him his trust in a moment of great vulnerability and pain. With the son trusting him in the same way, John recognized the courage it took to do so and he felt some humility in the face of it. If he had been in Frederick's shoes, he would have withdrawn into a shell instead of laying himself open—to what, he could not exactly define—to pain, hurt, ridicule, perhaps? They were strangely intimate moments for John, more so now than they had been with Mr. Hale with whom age and the relationship of teacher to pupil induced some distance. That night drew John and Frederick closer.

The month was over sooner than it suited everyone except John. He was as engaged as anyone in all they set out to do and agreed with Margaret that this reunion in Paris with Frederick and Dolores was as happy, fresh, and heartwarming as they had hoped for. But after only a week of being away from the mill, he could not help thinking and worrying about it when he retired to bed. He now had a trusted assistant who ordered supplies, tracked the progress of orders, worked on the accounting books, and when called to do so, could competently handle all the responsibilities of running the mill. Still, John could not shake off the uneasiness of not tending to the mill himself for a whole month. For a few nights, he lay awake wondering how it was doing and whether he was shirking his responsibilities in being away so long. His mother certainly thought so.

John visited his mother at her apartment the week before they left for Paris to tell her they were going to be away the following month. He knew her concerns about the mill running unsupervised for that duration. As he had expected, she listened, refrained from voicing displeasure, compressed her lips, averted her eyes, and resumed her work after a noncommittal nod. Since her return from London, she had been careful not to say anything likely to offend, hurt, or be construed as disapproval. Even so, John was constantly aware of what she actually felt and thought.

Alone in their room in the Paris apartment, Margaret noticed his unease and suspected the reason for it. She was sitting on the bed and had just put aside the book she was reading when John came to bed, gave her a perfunctory kiss and turned on his side to go to sleep. This was unusual for him who almost always tenderly cajoled her into joining him under the sheets. He lay awake, restless and unable to find a position he could settle into, turning one way, then the other, then on his back. Margaret slid down and lay silently watching him toss and turn for a few minutes. When he turned to face her again, she came closer and placed a hand on his arms to stop him from turning over. She gazed into his eyes, as if she was probing into his thoughts but he merely stared at her with glazed eyes. With a touch soft and soothing, she stroked his cheeks and his hair, clasped his face with both hands and kissed it all over with the same deliberate tenderness. His eyes slowly regained their depth, his concerns arrested for the moment, swept away by her caresses. He gave her his full attention then, made passionate love to her, and, soon descended into peaceful sleep, the mill forgotten for a while.

John's disquiet about being away from the mill for a whole month did not cease. At night, at least, with Margaret in his arms, sweetly soothing his worries away, he gradually began to let go. By the end of their stay in Paris, he could agree, with only a fleeting apprehension, to the next reunion three years hence. Still, he was relieved to be returning to Milton.

The reunions became a regular family affair John and Margaret planned for, every two or three years. Twice, they had to reschedule when the threat of a strike troubled John too much. Otherwise, nothing catastrophic ever happened when they were away and he began to look forward to their month-long sojourns almost as much as Margaret did. Perhaps, because of the relative infrequency of their meetings as well as the deep affections nurtured across the years, the two families were always sincerely happy to see each other, usually tolerant of minor irritations often inevitable among relations, and forgiving of rare transgression that caused someone pain.

The character of their get-togethers inevitably changed with time. The size of the apartment the couples rented grew as more children arrived. Margaret bore John a son in their fourth year of marriage and a second two years later; a daughter arrived, unexpected, after many years. Frederick and Dolores, about every two years, had two more sons. At some point, it became necessary for the Thorntons to rent one apartment and the Hales, another. The gatherings often took place in Paris and, later, elsewhere in France until Edith suggested Italy to Margaret. That year, Captain Lennox, Edith and their children joined the two families before going to Greece. After that, the Captain and Edith timed some of their lengthy trips to the continent to coincide with the reunion of the Thorntons and the Hales.

The Thorntons kept frequent company with Edith and Captain Lennox and were regular visitors a week at a time every summer at the big country house on the south coast of England that the Lennoxes purchased. Practically all the time they spent there, Edith and the Captain hosted friends and relatives including, occasionally, Henry and Ann Lennox as well as Captain Bennett and Catherine.

John had never anticipated being thrown into company with individuals who had nothing to do with cotton and manufacturing. He was inevitably drawn into the various circles that formed around Margaret towards whom people gravitated because of the projects she took on and the openness and sincere interest she took in certain people. He met friends of the Lennoxes at their dinner parties in London and the coast—generally well-educated young men, sometimes struggling financially and grateful for her sumptuous dinners. Members of smart London society, their conversations ran the gamut from theater to politics to the latest modern inventions. Not that Edith was remotely interested in such subjects; in fact, she hardly listened to them. But she cultivated these friends for the lively intercourse they kept up at her frequent parties.

These friends of the Lennoxes fascinated John and, indeed, they were insurance for a diverting evening. However, he found that most of them lacked real experience to back up their words— these clever, garrulous, sophisticated men who always had ready opinions to offer. He could not help comparing them to Frederick, who could have been one of them and with whom he had forged the closest of friendships. None could boast of having gone through similar adventures or having had their mettle tested the way Frederick's had been.

The Thorntons and the Lennoxes also began a tradition of spending alternate Christmases between Milton and the coast. By then, the Christmas Eve festivities at the mill had become a yearly happening that ran smoothly without the Thorntons' presence.

The first year they spent Christmas on the coast with the Lennoxes, Catherine volunteered to stand in for them, dragging Captain Bennett with her. She was married by then and kept her job teaching at the mill school two days a week, more out of a sense of purpose than of necessity. She had stopped working at the busy clinic which had expanded to two nurses and a full-time doctor. Captain Bennett, who had been reluctant to go to the Christmas dinner at the mill, told John later that he found the social exchange with the workers interesting and, in some cases, even stimulating. He and Catherine continued to attend the festivities in subsequent years, even after John's assistant and his wife took over managing and presiding over the festivities. The Thorntons continued to go to the Christmas Eve dinner at the mill with their children whenever they were in Milton for the holidays.

Margaret gave up teaching classes at the mill when she became pregnant with her second child. Through Catherine's sister, she met and hired two women, former governesses who wanted to augment their pensions and were willing to teach at the mill. They not only took over Margaret's classes, they also offered others that included arithmetic and some rudimentary study of history and nature for those who had advanced in reading. School hours were stretched.

With school running from morning until mid-afternoon, Margaret decided to offer pupils a free hot lunch, prepared at the Dining Hall. The decision had an unanticipated consequence. More parents began to bring their younger children to school and the school grew. Larger quarters were needed so an addition to the Dining Hall was built to accommodate 25 to 30 children. Margaret—who had continued for a few more years to take care of paying the teachers and buying books and other school supplies for the children—decided it was time to hire a full-time school master to whom she gladly and thankfully passed on management of the school.

John knew strikes could never be eliminated and the measures he put in place could change neither the market for cotton, with its ups and downs, nor the solidarity among workers forced to join those from other mills during a general strike. But at Marlborough Mills at least, he and worker representatives could often sit down and talk to resolve problems before they became too big to pester and he was often able to avert the threat of a local strike. The relative infrequency of strikes at his mill could not escape the notice of other manufacturers and gradually, some of them tried a few of the procedures he had installed.

After the last failure of Marlborough Mills, John reacted with trepidation to all the general strikes over which he had no control. When one threatened to erupt a year after he reopened, he took Henry Lennox's advice and invested money in banking, metals, and new chemicals. It was the best advice Henry ever gave him, greatly lessening the threat of another financial collapse. The Thorntons fortune never grew, however, as much as that of Fanny and Watson. They used a substantial part of it to expand the medical clinic and the school for children, and continued to send older children from the mill to boarding schools. Their efforts received their first reward when Thomas Boucher, with a degree in medicine, returned to Milton years later and took over the clinic full-time after Dr. Hartley returned to America with his wife and children.

A decade after the mill reopened, John added a special division to the mill, spurred on by the invention of new dyes a few years earlier. It produced high-end fabrics woven with exclusive designs. The idea for the fabrics came to him when he saw some of Margaret's paintings. He wondered how they would look on cotton the mill fabricated. Taking one of her paintings of flowers, he asked if she could simplify it and redesign it into a repetitive pattern. He did not tell her exactly what he intended to do with it. When she presented him with a design he thought would work, he took it to the mill to see if it could be woven into or imprinted on a fabric. It took several trials over a few weeks before he saw a piece he thought was good enough to put on the market. He settled for a printed design with colors that resisted fading. Only then did he take a sample home to show Margaret and to tell her of his intention to sell the fabric with her design on it. The mill, at first, produced a small amount and it sold so well that they had to produce a larger batch.

Later, he asked Margaret for more designs and after two years, he was prepared to form a new division using original designs she created. The fabrics were produced only in small batches and sold for higher prices. Profits from this division, however, were small, attenuated by the costs of special dyes and the many samples needed to come up with the right colors and fabrics that had no flaws. Still, the division became the more rewarding part of the business to John for the new directions it opened up in textile manufacturing and the creativity it inspired in his wife. Finally, Margaret found a way to become directly involved in the manufacture of cotton.

Margaret and Elise sat in the conservatory having tea in the black attire they wore to the funeral. Everyone who came to the funeral had left and the house was finally quiet. Now 19, Elise was home from school for a few days. Neither she nor her mother had appetite for food or drink but Dixon, grown slow and feeble but still directing the running of the house, insisted on serving them. She enticed them with Elise's favorite accompaniments of berries, cream, and freshly-baked scones and asserted that tea would occupy them, out of habit, and help take their minds away from the events of the last few days.

After the funeral, John took it for granted Elise would go with him to the mill house. They needed to take a quick look at it and ascertain that it was properly secured until they could go through Mrs. Thornton's possessions and dispose of them as she had instructed. But Elise, looking mournful, declined to go. "I don't think I could endure seeing the house without grandmama in it."

Johnny, the oldest son, protested: "But you know the house better than any of us. We all knew she was closest to you. You owe her."

"Johnny, let your sister be," their father admonished. He placed an arm around Elise's shoulder. "Of course, you need not come. Maybe, next time, you will be ready. I am sure any or all these three would come and help."

The three younger children did indeed prefer to be busy rather than sit mournfully in the house. They went with John, leaving Margaret and Elise at home.

After a quarter hour of silence sipping tea, nibbling at a scone and eating one tiny berry at a time, Elise, observed: "Grandmother did not really have too many friends, did she? Everyone that was there was either Papa's business colleague or your friend."

"I do not think it would have bothered her in the least if we were the only ones there. Hannah was an island unto herself and cared only about her children and grandchildren towards whom she was fiercely protective."

"I believe she lived a good long life although she never thought she would outlive her own daughter."

"No, parents always assume they will die before their children."

They lapsed into silence again, sipping tea for a few more minutes. "I think grandmama started her decline after Aunt Fanny died." Elise stopped, unwilling to complete the thought that crossed her mind. Instead, she said: "I am relieved to be going back to the university in two days. I will be too busy at school to miss her too much." Her voice broke and she bit her lips to choke down a sob. She dropped her face on her hands.

Margaret reached over and stroked her daughter's arm in sympathy. Elise, Mrs. Thornton's first grandchild turned out to be her favorite. Margaret thought that, perhaps, it was because Elise was there at the very time when—finally accepting that she was cut off from the mill—Mrs. Thornton was ready to shift her focus to a new purpose.

Little Elise, trusting and gregarious, was eager to receive and return the affection which Mrs. Thornton was ready to give. She had been captivated by Elise's large expressive eyes and impressed by her alert and curious mind. Molding Elise to her way of thinking and her ideal of a daughter became her new focus. Over the years, they formed a special bond, one similar to that Mrs. Thornton had with John and as in that case, her devotion to Elise was single-minded. To her, Elise could do no wrong. Mrs. Thornton developed a fondness for all her grandchildren, more from her belief that affection was inevitable among those who shared flesh and blood, than from an attachment nurtured through frequent and close interactions. None was as compelling as her affection for Elise.

Unhappily for Mrs. Thornton, Elise was also her mother's child and, asserting her independence of mind when she was old enough to notice and to care, she sided with her parents on matters pertaining to the mill. At 17, she was eager to leave home to study at a university for women. Mrs. Thornton had, by then, lived long enough with her son's "radical" ideas and no longer reacted with the same vehemence with which she protested them during the first two or three years. But she continued to believe that higher education was a waste of time for Milton men and particularly so for women. Still, she accepted Elise's views and ambition with equanimity, albeit with a melancholy lost on the young woman, who was confident of her grandmother's unconditional acceptance and oriented in her thoughts and desires to the promise the future held for her.

Elise, a little calmer, dabbed her eyes and smiled tremulously at her mother. "Why did you not go with Papa to grandmother's house?"

"I could not leave you all alone by yourself, could I?"

"I can take care of myself." Elise asserted, somewhat annoyed at the implication in her mother's answer.

"I know you can but grief at losing someone you care about can sneak up on you in ways you never imagine."

"Papa seemed to handle it well enough. He did not shed a single tear. I suppose he felt he should not and stood in front of the coffin as rigid as a stone, his jaw clenched the whole time. How could men do that?"

"Your father has been mourning and, believe it or not, he did cry but, alone, with me in our bedroom." Margaret could not mask the hurt she felt at her daughter's remark. "It might not have been obvious to you but your father and Hannah had a relationship as special as yours was with her, probably more so because of their shared sufferings and triumphs. The past month has been some of the saddest he has been through."

"I am sorry, Mama. I meant no disrespect. But this is so hard, so painful." Elise's voice quivered with the struggle to remain composed.

"I know," Margaret leaned forward, touched her cheek affectionately and squeezed her hand.

They sat in silence for many minutes, until Elise spoke again. "I remember grandmother telling me in the middle of reading me a book that you had cast a spell on Papa. She probably meant to be funny. I was five, enchanted but also scared by fairies and spells so I never forgot her remark. I would recall it every time she spoke of changes Papa made at the mill after he married you. I could sense she disapproved and, when I was older, I suspected she blamed the changes on the spell you cast on him."

Margaret was flabbergasted but was even more startled at what Elise said next. "She was right, you know, about Papa and you but she only saw part of it. When I was growing up, I sometimes felt excluded when I saw you and Papa so wrapped up in each other as if only the two of you were in the room. As I grew older, I wanted to shout at you whenever that happened so you would know I was there."

Elise glanced at her mother who gazed anxiously at her with brow knitted, and mouth agape, as if she just sucked in her breath. "But don't misunderstand me. I know you and Papa love me very much. You have both been wonderful to the four of us—irritating on occasion but, generally, I don't think we could have asked for better parents."

The concern in Margaret's eyes faded a little but this confession from her daughter was so unexpected that it left her speechless, uncertain what to make of it. After another long moment of silence, Elise asked: "What have you two decided to do with grandmama's belongings?"

"It seems she had written instructions after Fanny died on what to do with them and, as you know, last Christmas, she gave you the most precious possessions she had that she had not given your Aunt Fanny at her marriage."

"Yes, as if she knew that she will not see me again." Elise's voice quivered once more as she spoke.

When Mrs. Thornton fell seriously ill, John and Margaret insisted on her being cared for in their home. Jane came to attend to Mrs. Thornton and the two other servants were sent off on vacation with pay until they were called back. The mill house had remained empty since. Mrs. Thornton deteriorated fast and passed away within a month of falling ill. Elise, at school at that time, had last seen her grandmother alive the past Christmas.

"I feel guilty about some things grandmama gave me. Her tastes in jewelry and décor are not exactly mine and, yet, I feel I must use them." She looked expectantly at her mother.

Margaret nodded without answering, reluctant to tell her daughter what to do. Elise would have to consult her own conscience on such matters.

"Do you suppose I should have gone to her house with Papa? I would not be of help to him there. I know I would start crying." Elise paused, on the brink of tears. "But maybe I should have gone because I was not here when she was suffering. I should have been here when she died." Elise burst out crying, uncontrollably.

"Her condition deteriorated so fast even the doctors could not tell," Margaret replied, holding her daughter in her arms. She stroked her back tenderly, wordlessly while Elise let all the tears flow that she had choked back in the past few days. It took her a long time to calm down.

That night, John handed Margaret a package as he climbed into bed. "We found this in mother's wardrobe. It is addressed to you. She never mentioned it and we would have missed it but for your little daughter's sharp eye and fascination with mysterious boxes."

"When Elise was learning to talk, Hannah invented that game of "What is in the box?" Elise enjoyed it so much and it worked so well that grandmama used it with the other children. Cristina took to it the most." Margaret, both puzzled and curious, put her book aside and took the package. She laid it on her lap, reluctant to open it.

From the time Mrs. Thornton returned from London after Fanny's confinement, she and Margaret grew to be comfortable enough with each other that they could sit together in the drawing room, going about their tasks in tranquility, for a long time. They often did not talk and neither ever alluded to the encounters in the drawing room or the studio. Frequently on Fridays, Mrs. Thornton would arrive at their house early and join Margaret in the drawing room while she was practicing at the piano. Margaret thought Mrs. Thornton came early on purpose to listen to her. She always carried her sewing basket, walked in quietly so as not to disturb Margaret, sat on the same chair every time, and without saying a word, began to do her needlework. She remained as unobtrusive as she could, offered no polite praises nor said thank you when Margaret finished. But, she smiled warmly at her whenever their eyes met. Margaret matched Mrs. Thornton's dignified silence and usually left the room after her practice with just a sweet smile and a nod. Mrs. Thornton stayed in the drawing room until Elise awakened from her nap and grandmother and granddaughter went out with Mary into the garden.

Margaret developed some affection for Mrs. Thornton on account of those peaceful moments and her attachment to Elise but she was never certain how Mrs. Thornton regarded her. She still sometimes felt her disapproval—no longer voiced but conveyed nonetheless in familiar gestures she associated with past unpleasant encounters. Margaret ran her fingers over the package, wondering if it might contain some clue but, when she lifted it to shake it a little, it was so light and made no noise that she thought, with wry amusement, that it was empty.

John waited to read his daily journal to watch Margaret open the package. He was equally curious about what it contained and, when she stared at it, shook it and stared at it again for what seemed such an interminable minute, he almost prodded her to open it. Finally, she lifted the cover off the box slowly and carefully as if she was afraid to disturb what was inside.

Inside lay an exquisite lace collar carefully wrapped within a piece of fine muslin. The lace looked vaguely familiar to Margaret and she knew she had seen it before, no doubt adorning Mrs. Thornton's neck. She picked up the collar and found a small note tucked inside, neatly written with the same flourish as that embroidered on Mrs. Thornton's linens. It contained one short sentence: "Thank you with all my heart for all you have been to John." The note was neither signed nor dated.

John remarked: "Mother's favorite lace! It's nearly twenty years since I last saw her wear it. I thought she had given it to Fanny."

Margaret glanced up at John briefly, a half-smile on her lips, her eyes shining. She handed him the note, leaned against him and laid her head against his shoulder. He read it in one cursory glance and put it carefully back in the box before removing the package off her lap and placing it, along with his journal, on the table next to him. He smiled tenderly and gathered her in his arms.

"Have I ever told you that you are the best thing that ever happened to me?"

"Do you think as many times, at least, as my telling you that loving you is the easiest thing I do?" She muttered as his lips brushed hers.

THE AUTHOR

EJourney thinks of herself as a flaneuse, watching life unfold, then writing and illustrating what she loves about what she sees. In a past life, EJ, who has a dormant Ph.D. in the field of psychology from the University of Illinois, did mental health program research, evaluation and development. Now, she does art in various media—from oils to digital paintings—and writes when she feels she has something to say. Some of her musings on Art and Such, Travel, Tasty Morsels, and State of Being reside in cyberspace at http://www.eveonalimb.com.

EJ did the digital "paintings" (cover and all other illustrations) for *Margaret of the North*, on an iPad using SketchbookPro.

The website for this book
http://www.margaretofthenorth.wordpress.com.

Enjoy a video trailer for the book:
http://www.youtube.com/watch?v=pD-sJTRERZI&feature=player_embedded.

"Friend" or connect with the author:
http:// www.goodreads.com/author/show/5989910.E_Journey or leave a comment on any post in the book website.

Download a free book of travel essays by the author:
Mindful Journeys: Paris and Other Illusions:
http://www.goodreads.com/ebooks/download/15755424-mindful-journeys.

Printed in Great Britain
by Amazon.co.uk, Ltd.,
Marston Gate.